BROKEN ANGEL

THE LOST YEARS OF GABRIEL MARTINIERE

THE PEOPLE OF THE MARTINIERE LEGACY

JOYCE REYNOLDS-WARD

ANGELICA RAMIREZ MARTINIERE SMILED WEARILY AT THE DARK-HAIRED newborn boy in her arms. She hadn't known how she would feel about this child, considering who his biological father was, not even wanting to think about his name. But now that he was here after a long, hard labor, things were different. He looked up at her, trusting, and while he was definitely a Martiniere—there was *something* regal about this boy. A presence that, thankfully, didn't remind her of Philip. But not Saul, either. This child was very much himself.

He's going to be a handful, she thought, and swiftly freed one hand to cross herself.

Her husband Saul, the Martiniere—the title belonging to the head of the Martiniere family and the family-held conglomerate, the Martiniere Group—hovered next to them, beaming. He didn't seem to notice Angelica's signing of the cross, focusing instead on the child, crooning wordlessly at him.

"He's a beautiful little boy, Angel," Saul said, stroking the baby's cheek. "Even if he isn't biologically mine…he's still *mine*. I'll *make* him my boy, not my brother's." He smirked. "I think he's going to be darker-skinned, like you. He is such a beautiful boy—and won't that just frost Philip's ass?"

"I look forward to watching your bigot of a brother see our little angel grow up." She paused, her throat tightening. "Are you going to make any claim on Renate's boy?" It had taken several tries with in-vitro fertilization before her sister-in-law had conceived. Angelica felt sorry for Renate, tied to that arrogant ass Philip.

Saul looked up at her and pursed his lips, frowning, his pride momentarily fading. The disputes between Saul and his younger twin Philip over the leadership of the Martinieres had escalated to the degree that their mother Donna had forced them into a devil's deal of a compromise. Philip and Saul would each sire a son via in-vitro fertilization, using eggs from the other's wives. Saul would raise Philip's son and Philip would raise Saul's son. The two boys would be raised as potential Martinieres-in-waiting, given management of family divisions to prove themselves worthy of the title of the Martiniere. The boys were, essentially, hostages guaranteeing their fathers' good behavior.

"I don't think so," he said finally. The smile returned as he refocused on the child, pride returning, as if he were looking at his own biological son instead of his brother's. "I'll put my energy into raising *our* son to be great. I won't be able to overcome Philip's influence all that easily with Renate's son, but—" he shrugged. "We'll see what matters most. Heredity or environment."

"Philip will probably take credit if our little one does well," Angelica sighed and shook her head. "How can you two be so close in genetics and yet so different?"

"I have no idea, my love." Saul held out his arms. "May I hold our son?"

Angelica eased the baby into his arms. "What shall we call our little angel?"

Saul studied the boy. "Well, he's the son of an angel—"

"Saul!" Angelica laughed.

"You danced like an angel when you were still performing, my darling. Let's give him an angel's name. He'll need all the help he can get to overcome Philip."

Angelica cocked her head sideways as she thought.

"Gabriel," she said finally. "Gabriel, after my grandfather—and your middle name Marcus, not just for you but your mother's father. Gabriel Marcus Martiniere."

"Gabriel Marcus Martiniere," Saul repeated. "Welcome to the world, little Gabriel. And may you prevail over your biological father." He kissed Gabriel's forehead. "My boy. My beautiful, beautiful boy. *My son.*"

Angelica watched her husband and her son. Saul smiled at the bundle in his arms, enraptured by Gabriel's steady stare. A foreboding she couldn't explain swept over Angelica, and she crossed herself once more.

Please, Mary Mother of God, keep my son safe. Watch over him and protect him. You and all the angels, because he needs all the help he can get.

1 / TESTIMONY

JULY 2028

HIS TIE FELT TIGHT ENOUGH TO CHOKE HIM, EVEN THOUGH HE'D BEEN careful to give himself plenty of breathing and swallowing space when he'd tied it that morning with trembling hands. Gabriel Martiniere ran a finger underneath his collar to check. Lots of room, enough to accommodate the bulletproof vest underneath, which *should* be the case with his bespoke suits and shirts.

Nothing more than nerves, then. For good reason. Gabe glanced around the small room that felt claustrophobic in spite of the pale gray walls, light pine furniture, and diffused natural light. It was too damn bright. Sterile. Like he'd died and was going into the light.

"You doing all right?" asked Anne Wright, the assistant US attorney babysitting Gabe, along with a full complement of US marshals.

"Nerves." Gabe was unable to say more than that through the tension in his throat.

"You'll be all right," Anne said, patting his hand. "We'll keep you safe."

Gabe didn't respond. He wasn't as concerned about physical attack as he was about the preprogrammed Martiniere mind control responses to verbal cues that could cause him harm. Neither Anne nor any of the other Feds seemed to fully understand the implications of the Martiniere programming. They kept brushing off that level of mind control as science fictional.

The Martiniere program wasn't fictional, as Gabe knew too damn well. Just two words, and he'd be paralyzed long enough for something bad to happen. Even with a bulletproof vest and Plexiglas shielding around the witness stand.

Broken Angel.

His uncle Philip had delighted in using psychotropic meds to program those control words into Gabe at the age of twelve, after the deaths of his parents and sister in a suspicious plane crash.

Broken Angel.

Those words locked Gabe down so that he couldn't retaliate during Philip's beatings.

Broken Angel had paralyzed Gabe so that Philip could tie him down before flogging him, and Gabe couldn't fight back.

His cousin Serg Vygotsky had tried to help Gabe develop resistance to Philip's programming over the past year, once they had committed to Gabe going public about the Martiniere Group's illegal abuses of indentured workers. Counterprogramming that Serg had access to through his family's security organization, Vygotsky Security. And while the counterprogramming reduced his susceptibility to those words, Gabe still reacted. It delayed the lockdown but didn't eliminate it.

But neither Serg nor Gabe's other cousin and ally, Justine, Philip's daughter, were here. And once he was done with this testimony, the marshals would whisk Gabe off into a witness protection program.

However, Philip would be in the courtroom, sitting at the defense table. All it would take for Philip to stop Gabe's testimony were those two words.

Broken Angel.

His uncle had authorized illegal mind control and manipulation of Martiniere Group indentured workers. Until Gabe had assembled the evidence and turned it over to the Feds, no one could prove what had been only rumor. He had been assigned to implant that mind control programming into indentured Martiniere workers, without their consent. It had taken two years to get the records Gabe needed to document Philip's authorization of the indentured mind control programs, with Serg and Justine's help. A little longer to create a worm that trashed the mind control programs, set to activate when Gabe left the labs.

His cousins had been willing to stand with Gabe—but they had too much to lose by testifying.

Gabe didn't have anything or anyone to lose, unlike his cousins.

Except them.

This testimony came with a price. He'd have to walk away from being a Martiniere.

Worth it, if he could stop what Philip was doing.

Gabe inhaled shakily. The waiting was the hardest part. He'd refused lunch because he wasn't hungry. Still wasn't, and it was now almost three o'clock. Something was slowing things down in the courtroom.

"Water?" Anne poured him a glass, and sipped from it to show Gabe it was safe. His minders had *finally* learned that Gabe was cautious about contaminants in food and water, after weeks of him telling them that the Martiniere arsenal contained easily administered psychotropic and neurotoxic substances.

My ancestors include the Medicis and the Borgias.

And his uncle embraced that ancestry in more ways than one. There were some *old* Family traditions connected to that history.

"Thank you." Gabe carefully took a small swallow on the opposite side of the glass. Not too much. Just enough to ease his throat. Just in case. He and Serg couldn't code for the words in Philip's voice, and if the conditions were right—he didn't want to embarrass himself.

One of the marshals entered the room and spoke softly to Anne. She nodded.

"The judge has ruled that, based on the information you've provided, Philip will be attending your testimony virtually."

A relief. But still difficult. "And Joseph?"

"He is also attending virtually. Both will have audio cutoffs."

"Thank you." Gabe stood up, clenching and unclenching his hands to help him relax. Those precautions still didn't mean that there wouldn't be someone in the courtroom capable of saying those words in the correct tone.

But keeping Joey and Philip away from the courtroom was a start. And perhaps he wasn't risking embarrassing himself if those words got used.

The marshals crowded around Gabe as they left the small room. It opened onto a brightly white, restricted-access corridor that once again made Gabe think about death and going into the light, as they walked toward the courtroom. Doors to other small rooms lined the hallway. He supposed that both Joey and Philip were behind one—perhaps two—of those doors.

The marshals remained clustered around Gabe as they entered the courtroom that was brighter than the corridor—if possible. He was here.

So why did it feel like he was the one on the judgment seat and not his uncle?

The marshals didn't step away until he was safely behind the Plexiglas. Gabe took a deep breath before swearing in, his heart pounding in his ears. Direct examination would be easy enough, even with the objections from the Family attorneys. He'd practiced enough times with Wright and the lead prosecutor, Terrance Johnson.

Cross-examination worried him. Rolland McKenzie, the Martiniere Group's lead attorney, knew Gabe well—Rollie had been the administrator for his inheritance, before Gabe turned twenty-four. Rollie McKenzie was aware of too damn much, including those two fatal words. Had spent a lot of time drinking with Gabe.

Rollie might be the one to use the words to stop his testimony, even though it could threaten his legal license. If Philip threw enough money at him, then Rollie might just do it. Barring Rollie from the courtroom wouldn't change things. Philip could train any of his attorneys to use those words.

Gabe just had to hope that Serg's countermeasures would be sufficient protection.

The first few questions from Johnson went smoothly, with minor points of clarification from Rollie McKenzie. Gabe relaxed and kept his focus on Johnson, not on Rollie, not on the cameras, not on the screens where Philip and Joey glared at him. Maybe this testimony wouldn't be as traumatic as he feared.

And then it happened.

"Objection!" Rollie bellowed before Johnson could finish a question about an instruction to Gabe directly from Philip. "The witness's credibility is a broken an—"

"Objection!" Johnson cut off the rest of the word.

But Rollie knew the right inflection of tones, and he'd said just enough. Gabe's throat tightened and he swallowed hard, unable to move. His breath came quick and fast, and try though he could, he couldn't break free from the lock. His vision distorted into pulsating shapes and colors, the bright light of the courtroom lancing hard into his head. Voices echoed around him. He swayed in the chair and grabbed at the sides of the witness box to keep from wobbling.

They got another psychotropic to me!

This was worse than previous incidents he'd experienced. Whatever that substance was, it managed to renew his programming to circumvent what Serg had done to counter the previous version, triggered by that partial code phrase. But how? Food? Water? All food and drink had been monitored and checked.

Clothing—ah. *Clothing*. Possibly his underwear. *Clothing*, damn it.

"Mr. Martiniere. Mr. Martiniere." The judge's voice seemed to come from far away. "Are you all right?"

Gabe struggled to move, to speak without slurring and sounding drunk. Finally, he managed a faint rasp, despite the flashing colors and blaring voices around him.

"No. I'm not."

At least this demonstrated what he had been warning them about. Hopefully.

But speaking triggered more reactions. Spasms wracked Gabe's body and he fell out of the chair. He dry-heaved, grateful that he *hadn't* been eating or drinking much over the past few days. Even then, his sphincters released and he couldn't keep from wetting himself. Then soiling himself. He rolled toward the jury box, carpet rough against his cheek, gasping. At least this might be enough of a vivid illustration to convince the jurors of what mind control could look like when used to shut someone down. But oh God, it *hurt*.

His head pounded. He gagged. Agony throbbed through him. Would it ever stop?

More chaos, lots of noise, and then marshals took his arms. Helped Gabe to his feet. Guided him, staggering, swaying, and stinking, out of the courtroom, down more corridors, until they were in the basement and eased Gabe into the van they had used to bring him to the courthouse.

His body quivered with involuntary spasms. Oh God, this was a *bad* lock. Gabe had heard whispers in the labs about a new psychotropic drug before he went to the Feds—one that reduced resistance to code words. It included a feedback mechanism that augmented the effect of the code words once triggered, and caused hallucinations. But as of three months ago its existence had only been conjecture.

No, what was happening to him sure as hell wasn't a lab geek speculation. This was real.

Shit.

They finally reached the secure compound where he was being held.

"Underwear," he croaked, at last able to speak. "Psychotropic. Administered that way. Scan. Need safe clothing."

It wasn't until Gabe had stripped everything off and showered that he felt close to normal. His head pounded and he hurt all over, but noises didn't blare at him and lights didn't strobe anymore. One of the marshals provided him with a t-shirt and sweats—*"they've been scanned, Mr. Martiniere. We're scanning all your clothing right now. You were right about the underwear."*

Gabe reeled and couldn't walk in a straight line as he went into the living area, his legs barely able to keep him upright. Multiple people waited for him.

"Going to bed," he mumbled, waving them off. "My head hurts." And he was embarrassed as hell by what had happened. Best to sleep it off right now. Maybe tomorrow would be better.

He took as much acetaminophen as he dared to counter the aches.

It felt like his worst hangover times three. Once the acetaminophen kicked in, Gabe dropped into a restless sleep. He roused when someone tried to climb in bed with him.

"Go 'way!" he snapped.

Anne Wright stroked his chest under his t-shirt, her hand slowly slipping lower. "I can make you feel better, Gabriel," she crooned, fingers tracing the skin just under the top of his sweat pants.

"No." Ice clutched at his gut. She *had* been flirtatious during their interviews and he'd played along. Mistake. "I'm not interested. Go *away*. I hurt."

"I'm disappointed in you—*angel*."

Fuck. He was in a world of hurt right now. She even knew the correct tone. Thank God she was stupid enough to say the second word and not the priming word. Gabe shot up and grabbed her face firmly with both hands to keep her from saying the full code.

"You do *not* use that word around me," he said harshly. "*Lilith*." The counterword that Serg had devised for him. And now he knew how he had been betrayed. He just didn't know how Philip had gotten to Wright.

Wright froze, her face paling.

So they programmed her as well. That's a relief.

But not unexpected. Philip wouldn't give someone like Wright this knowledge without holding some sort of power over her.

At least she was sufficiently ill-prepared to think the partial code was adequate, and didn't understand the relationship between the two words. If he'd still been under the psychotropic's influence, saying part of the phrase might have worked. Now the partial just served to fuel his growing rage.

"Doesn't feel so good on the other side now, does it, *Lilith*?" Gabe whispered, his voice sharp, malign, and full of every damn compulsion he'd learned from his grandmother Donna, the Matriarch of the Martinieres, creator of the mind control foundations. Part of him reveled as Wright flinched from that code. She'd feel it for a few days. "Marshals!" he bellowed. "I've got trouble here!"

A gamble, because they might be just as twisted as Wright. God, he hoped not, because he was as good as dead otherwise.

Fortunately, they weren't. But from the glare Wright gave him as three marshals hustled her out the door, Gabe knew he'd made a potent enemy.

GABE MADE IT THROUGH THE NEXT TWO DAYS OF TESTIMONY WITHOUT further incident. Gerry Rothman replaced Anne as his babysitter. Gabe went straight from the courtroom to the plastic surgeon, and then to another secure site to recover. After that, it was back to work with weapons and fighting practice.

Part of being a Martiniere, even though he was now Daniel Garcia, independent investment analyst.

The witness protection program located him in a nondescript, furnished house on the edges of Tucson, Arizona. Most of his clients were online only, which kept life simpler. Gabe joined a gun club to keep in weapons practice, but shunned the social gatherings affiliated with the club, and stayed clear of their political activity. After several trials of martial arts studios, he settled on a gym instead to work out and keep in shape, with home practice of the forms he'd learned with Serg. Not perfect, but at least he didn't have to deal with sketchy people.

Despite his caution, Gabe couldn't shake the sensation of being watched. Tucson had a lot of indentured workers, and the red and black Martiniere trefoil logo was a common ID tattoo, both permanent on the back of people's necks, and temporary, on their hands. Perhaps that was what bothered him.

The gym and the gun club were Gabe's refuges. Even there, he felt as if his every move was under observation.

He went to ordering what little food he ate online and having it delivered, to avoid being watched in the supermarket. Testing the food for what possible adulterants could have been slipped into it before eating it. Sneaking around to find a black-market pistol that was allegedly untraceable, and rigging up his own concealed carry holster. Driving far into the desert for pre-dawn jogs, carrying his weapon, and even then spooking worse than a green horse just under saddle at the slightest reflection or movements. Fighting back an instinct to swing his pistol toward someone else on the range when he was at the club, if he felt their eyes on him. Leaving the gym if the only exercise machines open were in the center instead of next to the wall. Or if someone came along and used free weights next to him.

And he'd catch them watching. Was it really this bad, or was he imagining it? But eyes were on him at the gym—someone abruptly looking away when they realized he saw them in the mirrors. Quick turns away when they were at the club. Vehicles that matched his routes through traffic, pulling away when he turned onto secondary roads, but later drifting past his house. Never stopping, but driving by slowly, several times.

Maybe he shouldn't have relied on Federal witness protection. It might have been safer to risk Vygotsky Security and possible leaks to Philip. He could trust Serg, at least.

To distract himself, Gabe focused harder on going through the motions of life as Daniel Garcia. Daniel didn't date, didn't socialize, didn't do anything to attract attention. Daniel noted the slap-on-the-hand financial penalties doled out to the Martiniere Group in his newsletter when *US v. Martiniere Group* settled out of court. Daniel advised his clients to be careful about investing in companies that relied heavily on indentured workers supplied by the Group.

Striking back at Martiniere Group clients through investment recommendations *was* the only means Gabe had to affect the Group, since it had always been a family-owned conglomerate and not open to public investors. It was the beginning of some sort of strategy. And, surprisingly, it earned Daniel some media attention for being a maverick.

That recommendation lost him a handful of investment clients. Indentured agricultural labor supply companies were damn popular amongst investors these days.

Thanks to Philip's promotion of indenture.

Still, he gained some clients to replace the ones he lost, thanks to that media attention. Gabe deferred follow-up requests for coverage when he started feeling more eyes on him. After a couple of weeks, it seemed to fade away, Daniel Garcia appearing to be a flash-in-the-pan nobody. Letting it drop went against all of Gabe's competitive instincts, and yet—the rise in attention had attracted observers. He didn't dare encourage it any further—which pinpointed the problems with *that* strategy for attacking Philip. Too much risk, not enough gain.

Gabe needed to figure out another means of striking back besides this. But his life was on hold—and Gabe wasn't sure how to fix it. He didn't dare get back into agricultural robotics and nanobot research, even for investment purposes, because the Group and its subsidiaries were so deeply involved. One of his clients wanted to know more about investing in agricultural microbial application startups, and it was a welcome excuse to return to a familiar subject, even if it was just his minor at the University of Paris.

All the same, he was just marking time. Spinning his wheels. Not getting anywhere with stopping Philip, after that brief little flurry of media attention.

Most of all, Gabe was lonely. Growing up as a Martiniere had meant being part of a bustling, large family with very little time to himself. Even when he'd been at Northview Military Academy during his teens, there'd been other students to hang out with.

Not so in this solitary life. Loneliness was a dangerous vulnerability—and he knew it.

But he just didn't know who he could trust.

GABE FORGOT THAT IT WAS SOCIAL NIGHT AT THE GUN CLUB WHEN HE WENT to shoot on the Friday before Thanksgiving. If it hadn't been such a frustrating day, with poorly behaving internet, he would have left the moment he saw the number of cars parked in the lot. He was able to ignore the social activity and fire a few rounds at the mostly-empty indoor range. As he left, he heard a familiar voice that sent chills up his back.

"Gerry!" Anne Wright called. "Range's open now."

"Be right there," Gerry Rothman answered.

Gabe hurried out, but not before he spotted Anne. Her eyes met his. A predatory smile spread across her face.

"Hurry up, Gerry!" She moved toward Gabe.

Fuck. She knows my codes.

He forced himself to take a deep breath, then strode to his car without breaking into a run, planning to call Serg as soon as he got back to the house. Screw this damn witness protection hellhole. He should have gone with the Vygotskys to begin with.

Before he opened his car door, someone grabbed him. Gabe fought that person off, until several others joined in. He glimpsed a Martiniere red and black trefoil indenture ID tattoo on the hand of one of his attackers.

"Broken Angel," Anne hissed, the tone slightly off but still accurate enough to lock him down.

Damn it, she's learned.

A needle stabbed Gabe's arm as someone yelled a warning.

And then everything went dark. But he thought he heard Serg's voice bellowing commands.

GABE LAY STILL WHEN HE REGAINED CONSCIOUSNESS, KEEPING HIS EYES closed. No restraints on his wrists or ankles, which was a surprise. What had happened? Where was he? On a bed. Another surprise. Wearing what felt like sweats, not the jeans and polo with light jacket that he'd worn to the gun club. Bare feet, not even socks. Someone had taken the time to undress him, put him in lighter clothing. Most unusual of all.

He ached, but not as badly as he'd expect given those last memories. The sound of breathing not his own—someone was in the room with him.

Who?

Lingering, faint cat-piss stink of meth cooking. *What* the *hell*? He couldn't think of any of the Martiniere labs he'd worked in that smelled like this, much less having a bed in them. So possibly he *wasn't* secreted away in one of his damn uncle's labs. Even if this wasn't the best bed in the world, saggy and lumpy, Philip wouldn't give him this much comfort. Or have his clothes changed.

Faint sound of traffic, occasional voices from outside, clang of footsteps against metal rungs. No soundproofing, so again, not likely to be in a lab. Distant blare of a Spanish broadcast of some sort, too far away for him to easily follow the words, especially with his head pounding.

He couldn't gather much else about his surroundings without opening his eyes. Gabe blinked fuzzily, doing his best to feign confusion. Though it *was* hard to focus, objects around him unclear. He glanced toward where he'd heard the person breathing. Even blurred, Gabe caught his breath as he realized who sat there.

"About time you woke up," Piotr Vygotsky, Serg's father, growled.

Gabe inhaled deeply. What did it mean that Piotr was here and not Serg? And what had happened to his attackers?

He glanced around, worried. They were in a cheap motel room, at least from the layout of mirror, dresser, television, two double beds, window, and bathroom. Door opening to outside, not a hallway entrance. Round table canting at an angle by the window, under an ancient hanging light that put out a yellowish glow, a little bit of daylight spilling through orange curtains that didn't quite close.

Whose side is Piotr on?

Serg *had* been feuding with his father, and then there was the Martiniere indenture tat that Gabe had spotted on one of his attackers.

But this wasn't a place that Philip or his supporters would frequent.

It *was* the sort of location that Piotr favored when doing an extraction. Gabe had participated in enough practices along with Serg during the security training that all Martiniere heirs were required to undergo.

Is this an interrogation or an extraction?

Piotr preferred chemicals for interrogations, not beatings. This could easily be an interrogation. And where were they? Tucson? Somewhere else?

"Gabriel. Damn it. Say something." Piotr sounded worried. He wouldn't sound worried if this were an interrogation, would he?

Gabe tried to speak but his thick, numb tongue didn't want to cooperate. "In. Terro. Gation? Or?" He started to cough, gasping for breath.

Piotr darted over and raised Gabe to a sitting position, pounding his back until Gabe stopped coughing.

"They hit you with a worse drug than I thought, damn it. Here. Slide back." Piotr helped Gabe scoot against the headboard built into the wall. He stuffed pillows around Gabe to keep him upright and went to the big dresser under the wall-mounted television. Gabe now noticed the duffles and bottles on the dresser. Piotr poured something sparkling into a glass he pulled from one duffle and brought it to Gabe. "Drink this."

Gabe eyed the drink. Bright red. Bubbling. Safe?

Poisoning is not Piotr's usual methodology, he reminded himself. That bubbling red drink was the carrier for a number of Piotr's potions. And if Piotr were interrogating him, then Gabe was screwed anyway because Piotr would be interrogating him for Philip. In that case, there would be something to make him talk in the drink.

Damned if I do, damned if I don't.

Gabe reached for the glass with a trembling hand. Piotr helped steady the glass as Gabe drank, then set it on the built-in nightstand next to the bed.

Tingles prickled his tongue and throat, but at least Gabe could move his tongue.

Not damned.

A relief.

Piotr surveyed him again. "Better?"

Gabe nodded, not wanting to speak yet. He felt stretched thin, wobbly and weak. Worse than when the psychotropic had been triggered during his testimony.

"Now. As for your question. You tell me. Interrogation or extraction? Explain your reasoning." Piotr leaned back in his chair, crossing his arms, a gesture reminiscent of so many training sessions that Gabe blinked back wetness in his eyes.

No. He mustn't show weakness. This *could* be an interrogation, after all.

"Could be either," Gabe said, slowly because part of his tongue was still numb. "Location—cheap motel. Could be interrogation. You. Using chemicals. Me. Body condition. Suggests interrogation."

Piotr nodded. "Go on."

"Saw. Feds. Before attack. Anne Wright. Gerry Rothman. Recognized me. Saw. Martiniere tat. On attacker." Gabe swallowed hard. "Wright. Froze me. Code phrase. Before injection. Possibility. Cooperation between. Martiniere Group and Feds."

"That is one way to look at it," Piotr said. "And case for extraction?"

Gabe gestured toward his glass. Piotr filled it. This time Gabe was able to hold the glass on his own, his hands steadier. After he finished drinking more of that non-alcoholic bubbly red stuff, his tongue seemed to have shrunk back to its normal size and the numbness was fading. But it was still hard to talk for more than a few words at a time.

"More likely. Extraction. Warning yell. Before shot. One of my attackers." He closed his eyes for a moment, struggling to remember. "Think. Was person. With indenture tat. Yelling." Gabe opened his eyes again. "No restraints. Worry in. Your voice. And Feds. Would be here. If interrogation."

The pieces fit together. This explanation made more sense. Extraction, not interrogation. And Piotr had intervened just in time, because Gabe didn't think that Wright and Rothman had anything good in mind for him.

Piotr nodded curtly. "And your conclusion?"

His voice was firmer, more confident as the numbness wore off. "Extraction. But why? Betrayed?"

Another nod from Piotr as he picked up his phone and punched a button. "All clear, Sergei," he said in Russian. "Come on in." He sighed, continuing in English. "I know that look in your eyes, Gabriel. You had to convince yourself more than anything I could say to you. I was also not certain what your cognitive condition would be when you woke. I needed to do my own assessment, and this was the most effective means to fulfill both of my goals."

Bright light flooded the room as Serg entered, carrying a bag that smelled like barbecued ribs. Gabe winced away from the glare, throwing one arm up to cover his eyes. His stomach growled.

"He is still reactive!" Piotr snapped at Serg in Russian. "Use your head!"

"What did they use on me?" Gabe asked. His Russian was rusty, but he could still speak and understand it with reasonable fluency.

And thank God, his ability to talk in more than bits and pieces was returning.

"Not positive without further analysis and I do not have safe lab access at the moment. Certain enough to have an antidote, uncertain enough to worry about it being effective. That doesn't matter." Piotr switched to French. "Things are very complicated right now, Gabriel. You have been unconscious for twenty-four hours." He changed back to Russian. "Sergei had been pestering me to contact you. When I finally listened to his arguments, I realized that he was right." His lips tightened. "We have had you under observation for the last week. But we were not the only ones."

"I *thought* I was being watched." So he wasn't imagining things. His skills were still functional.

Piotr nodded. "But it was not just Sergei that convinced me that we needed to make contact. I saw that Daniel Garcia made recommendations not to invest in indentured labor, recommendations that went viral. That set a chain of events into action and forced my hand."

"Daniel was an idealist, and angry that Philip dodged significant sanctions."

"Your actions as Daniel damned near got you killed!" Piotr glowered at Gabe. "Bad enough that Philip's people infiltrated the Feds and co-opted your minders. Bad enough that he managed to slither out of that damned case with just a slap on his wrist. But for you to stick a target like that on your back, boy—Philip *ordered* your death. A very painful one, and Joseph was more than happy to carry out those orders. You were supposed to die in that attack. Fortunately, we were close and I had the antidote ready. I guessed a possible poison correctly. But it was touch and go for a few hours."

Gabe stared at Piotr. Did this mean—but Serg had been worried about Piotr's loyalties—

"I had to do it," he said finally.

Piotr shook his head slowly. "You fools. You damned romantic fools. All three of you. Justine. Sergei. And most of all, *you*, Gabriel. You are Saul's son. Unofficially the Martiniere-in-waiting. Heir to the Family leadership. The Group. How could you have been so damned reckless?"

"Joey's the Martiniere-in-waiting, since Philip is the Martiniere."

"The Board will never approve Joseph as the Martiniere-in-waiting," Piotr said. "There *is* no successor to Philip, now that you have disappeared."

"But—the implants—the devices—" Gabe fumbled for words. "It had to stop, Piotr."

"And by acting without consulting with me, you condemned your effort to failure," Piotr snarled. "Your grandmother and I have been working on a solution to this situation for five years."

"But—Donna-gran—she's so sick—"

"Have you considered the impact that the testimony of the Matriarch of the Martinieres would have had in a case like *US v Martiniere Group*? From someone that Philip cannot affect with control words? You looked like a *fool* on that witness stand when McKenzie triggered you, Gabriel, and even your later testimony didn't make up for it."

Gabe closed his eyes, then opened them again. "She's so sick," he repeated. "She couldn't have held up to that questioning."

"Not as ill as reported. She just needed time to recover from cardiac surgery, Gabriel. And if the three of you had possessed any sense, you would have come to family elders for assistance before firing off a half-assed attack that ends up leaving Philip stronger than ever!"

"How could we, when to all appearances you're supporting Philip?" His head was starting to hurt again, and thinking in Russian didn't help. Gabe switched to French—almost as easy as English, not as easy as Spanish, but if they were still in the Southwest, Spanish wasn't the right choice either. "We had no reason to believe that the elders of the family supported any contest to Philip's authority."

"Idiots." The word stung more in French than it would have in English, Spanish, or Russian.

Gabe sighed and shook his head, his gut tightening. "So. What now?"

Piotr's sigh was even heavier than Gabe's. "You must disappear. Completely. Philip has retrenched. We cannot legally go after the Group because of double jeopardy. You must bide your time, Gabriel, and wait for another opening. If that comes before Philip's death."

"I see," Gabe said, returning to English. "My fucking mistake. Damn it, damn it, damn it." He shook his head.

"You were impatient," Piotr said. "And more than a little cocky and arrogant about your ability to pull it off without help." He slapped the table. "But what's done is done. I can give you a week to build a new identity. After that Philip will become suspicious about my being out of touch. Did the Feds give you any behavioral coaching?"

"No."

"Figures. And we need to get you out of here tonight. We are still too close to Tucson, and while to all appearances Sergei and I are cooking meth, too much longer and we do not fit the profile."

Gabe tried to get up, but his legs buckled. Serg kept him from falling on the floor.

"Don't try walking yet," Piotr said. "Unless you need to use the restroom."

"That would be good," Gabe said.

Serg helped him. Gabe sat on the end of the bed after coming back out.

"Think you could eat?" Serg asked.

"Oh God yes. I'm starving." And his head ached, but he wasn't about to take any more medications. Food would help.

Piotr looked away from his computer as Serg brought Gabe a plate. "So. Gabriel. An investment analyst. *Really.*"

"It wasn't my first choice," Gabe said. "Just the one that worked with my skill set." One bite of those delicious ribs and he was ravenous.

Piotr shook his head. "You need to pick something more working class to put Philip off your track, but I have no idea what it could be."

"Ranch hand," Gabe said. He'd already been thinking this through. "I've done enough on-site work during school, and with the Group, that I could do a credible job of it. And—" a wistful realization that maybe he could make one of his childhood dreams come true. "Maybe an occasional rodeo cowboy. Saddle bronc rider." He had no desire to tangle with bulls, and he *had* been fairly decent at bronc riding during his brief stint on the Northview Military Academy rodeo team.

Serg raised his brows. "Funny. That's what Gabe Ramirez was

doing before he got sent off to that damn revolution in Brazil. He's disappeared. It'd be easy for you to pick up his mannerisms, step into his place. Without being indentured, that is."

"Really?" Gabe Ramirez had been his roommate at Northview, and not too bad a rodeo hand himself. *Gabe and Gabriel.* They had a lot of fun with the names and confusing people. "But wouldn't someone make the connection between us? Especially given my mother's maiden name?" He'd occasionally called himself Gabriel Martiniere Ramirez after he graduated from Northview, to reflect his repugnance of Philip and honor his Hispanic ancestry. The Ramirezes descended from Spanish nobility, after all.

"It is possible," Piotr said. "But really, Gabriel. Ranch hand? Rodeo? That is a waste of your talents."

Gabe finished wolfing down his section of ribs and grabbed a handful of fries.

"Do you honestly think that someone with my history of bespoke suits and fondness for the arts would deign to—" and here he imitated Philip's sneering tone. "—lower myself to something as déclassé as rodeo? Or slum around working as a ranch hand?"

Even though he'd loved every damn bit of his short time as a rodeo rider, the only ones who knew about his dream to ride broncs were Donna-gran, Justine, and Serg. Their grandmother had taught them how to ride horses, though her preference was for eventers and show jumping.

Piotr chewed his lower lip thoughtfully. "True."

"And ranch work is one of those jobs where it's easy to relocate," Serg added. "It'll be hard labor, though, Gabe."

Gabe shrugged and snagged more fries. "It will keep me in shape. And like you said, I can keep wandering. Funds will be a challenge, but at least I won't have to stay stuck in one place and feel like they're moving in on me. Like here."

"We can arrange cash drops," Piotr said. "This will not last forever. Give it five years. By then, Philip will have something else to be angry about and forgotten why he's mad at you. He will still want to make you pay, but he and Joseph will have moved on. They will want to break you to their wishes, not outright kill you, like they do now."

"Sounds good to me," Gabe said. "And with National Finals coming up soon, well, that works out just fine for me finding job connections."

"Then it is settled," Piotr said. "Time to get you dressed and out of here."

———

A COUPLE OF WEEKS LATER, GABE RAMIREZ DRIFTED BEHIND THE SCENES AT the National Finals Rodeo, looking for job leads. He kept his excitement tamped down, but the little boy inside of him was dancing with joy.

Free to be a cowboy.

Sooner or later, he'd get tired of this life. But it was sure a lot better than being locked down in that depressing little house, working at that damn depressing job.

And besides, rodeo came with buckle bunnies eager to attach themselves to any cowboy with a winning smile, a slick line, and a shiny silver belt buckle. Gabe didn't have any intentions of getting himself tied down to any woman, but that didn't mean he couldn't flirt a little. Most buckle bunnies were cute and he could chat them up, even if he knew better than to sleep with them. It beat Daniel Garcia's solitary life.

Besides, who knew? He might just run across the rodeo queen he'd always dreamed about when he was that starry-eyed little boy.

He noticed a particular redheaded Pendleton Round-Up princess, but never talked to her. She was just one amongst many at the NFR. And he didn't think about *her* very much, either.

2 / THAT REDHEADED RODEO QUEEN
AUGUST 2029

OVER ONE YEAR ON THE RUN NOW, STAYING AHEAD OF PHILIP'S BOUNTY hunters.

Gabe exhaled heavily as he waited for the next round of saddle bronc competition to see if he'd scored in the money at this little rodeo somewhere on the Oregon-Washington border. Right now, it was barrel racing time.

Gabe was barely in third place, tied with his buddy Craig Yellowhawk, who perched on the fence next to him. He couldn't dial into the moves of the buckers well enough to finish in the money consistently. But he didn't have anywhere else to be, and he still wasn't sick of hanging out at rodeos. Craig had invited Gabe to stay at his place for the night. Despite their thirty-year age difference, Gabe and Craig had become fast friends while working in a frozen food factory near Pendleton.

Gabe considered the next round of bronc riders. He and Craig might have gotten lucky. None of the top riders were here. But there were still some good riders left in that next go-round. All the same, the broncs were tough, and the riders not *that* good. He and Craig might still manage to earn something.

"Hey bitch!" Troy Ridley, one of their competitors, yelled at the woman heading out to run barrels. "Come over here when you're done, honey, and I'll give you a *good* ride!"

Gabe winced. Troy and his followers sat on the fence about ten feet away, drinking heavily. He'd been loudly rating each barrel racer on her attractiveness, potential ability in bed, and how much verbal abuse he could dish out before she'd cry. Gabe was surprised that Ridley hadn't been booted out of the rodeo yet—then again, Ridley was a local boy. That might affect things.

Craig shook his head. "Asshole's on a roll tonight."

"Sure is," Gabe said. "Awfully damn tempting to shut his mouth for him." But that would be stupid.

"You hear anything more about that girl in California?"

Gabe and Craig had been amongst a group of cowboys who'd come across Ridley beating the crap out of a girl at another small rodeo in the middle of nowhere. They'd called the cops and exacted their own vengeance before the authorities showed up.

Gabe shrugged. "District attorney called and asked if I'd testify in front of the grand jury. I said yes. She's still in pretty rough shape."

He wasn't eager to appear in court again, even for just a grand jury hearing. Not after the mess that his appearance in *US v. Martiniere Group* had been. But the DA had been desperate for grand jury witnesses, and Gabe couldn't stand abusers. Even if it risked his freedom from Philip.

"Next up, Ruby Barkley on Sunshine," the announcer said.

"Oh, this is gonna be good," Craig said. "Ruby's a hell of a good rider, but that damn palomino mare of hers is unpredictable. You never know what that Sunshine horse is gonna do—run or buck."

Gabe scowled. The name *Ruby Barkley* sounded familiar. "Have I seen her run before? I recognize the name."

"Not likely. She sticks pretty close to home when she's not at college. Lives with grandparents. But Ruby's one of the Pendleton Round-Up princesses."

"Ah." He'd seen her at National Finals last December, shortly after dumping the Feds. Back then he'd been even more skittish and cautious, slipping into his new life.

"Hope to hell you lose, you damned bitch!" Ridley bellowed.

Craig chuckled. "Ruby kicked the shit out of Ridley for getting handsy with her a few years back, when she was Thunder County

Days Queen and still in high school. I would not cross that woman. She's *tough*."

"Hmm." Gabe leaned forward as the big palomino mare with the redheaded rider burst out of the gate. Now that was interesting. A woman capable of intimidating Ridley.

The mare crowhopped around the first barrel but Ruby straightened her out. The second barrel was beautiful and fast, and Gabe got an idea of just how good the pair might be.

Then Sunshine sucked back and started bucking within two strides of the third and last barrel. Gabe whistled as the big mare bucked high and hard.

"That woman would make a pretty damn good bronc rider," he said to Craig.

Craig laughed. "What do you think she's riding right now?"

The golden mare sent the third barrel flying. Ruby got her straightened out and pointed toward the gate. Sunshine dropped to a trot.

"Hey Ruby, this isn't supposed to be saddle bronc barrels," the announcer said. "Tough luck, folks. That's Ruby Barkley, Pendleton Round-Up Princess, unfortunately disqualified. Good ride, Ruby, just in the wrong event. Folks, let's give this good cowgirl a hand."

"Well, maybe the Ice Princess won't be so high and mighty now," Ridley jeered as a scattering of applause came from the stands.

"She did a damn good job riding that buck through the third barrel!" Gabe yelled at him. "If that girl was riding saddle broncs, she would have placed better than you did, Ridley!"

"Boy, you *are* looking for a fight," Craig said.

"I think I'll wander off for a while," Gabe said, ignoring whatever it was that Ridley hollered back, his focus on the redhead and her golden mare. "Make sure no one bothers her." He slipped off the fence. From the way that mare moved, she might start bucking again. He'd give good money to see how this rodeo queen handled it.

Craig snickered. "Ridley calls her the Ice Princess for a reason, Gabe. Nobody, but nobody, gets very far with Ruby Barkley."

Gabe shrugged. "I think there's gonna be more fireworks with that mare. Gotta feeling it's gonna be well worth my time to watch."

"All right, Ramirez. But just a word of advice." Craig lowered his voice. "I know people from Thunder County, where she's from. Heard rumors. Her parents killed each other when she was six. Or her father beat her mother to death and Ruby shot him in self-defense, before he could kill her. Different stories. You watch your step with that lady, buddy. She could hurt you."

"I'll keep it in mind." Gabe adjusted his hat. "And, really, I'm just going to watch her ride that mare. I think it'll be a treat."

He trailed behind Ruby and Sunshine at a safe distance as they headed to an empty warmup pen. Everything about the golden mare suggested she was ready to break in half with more hard bucking that befit a bronc instead of a barrel racer. High head and wide eyes. Loud roller snorts through wide-flaring, red-lined nostrils. Flattened ears. Pulling against the reins, trying to get more purchase against Ruby's tight grip as she pranced and jigged. The palomino was fast, all right, but why was a Round-Up Princess bothering with a bronc like her? Didn't Ruby have better options? She should be well-mounted as a member of a prominent court like the Round-Up.

He leaned on the fence, careful not to spook the mare or distract Ruby as she opened the gate from horseback. Sunshine put up a fuss but Ruby was firm and steady. Gabe's respect for the rider grew as he watched her maneuver the mare through the gate without an explosion.

The mare's calm evaporated once Ruby spun Sunshine and sent her across the pen in a hard gallop. Three strides, and the big mare took off in a series of high, twisting bucks that would dislodge most riders.

Damn, she's good.

He'd bet on Ruby Barkley scoring better than Troy Ridley if they ever rode against each other in saddle broncs. She'd beat most men.

The palomino stopped bucking and ran hard. Halfway around, she broke into another, less-intense, series of leaps. Ruby booted her and got the mare running again. Gabe watched, entranced, as the bucks lessened until horse and rider made two clear circuits of the pen. Then Ruby eased Sunshine back to a trot and worked her in big serpentine loops. After that, she asked for a gallop in the opposite direction. But that was it for the dramatics. While the big mare was frothy with sweat, her ears pricked forward now and her head was much lower.

Show was over. He could rejoin Craig.

Except Gabe didn't feel like it. He was lonely, damn it, and it'd be nice to have someone to talk to besides Craig. Especially someone as cute as Ruby Barkley. And her reputation as the Ice Princess meant she wasn't likely to be interested in playing buckle bunny head games.

As horse and rider ambled around the pen in a big, relaxed walk on a long rein, he climbed up on the fence, cautiously watching the golden mare's reactions. He clapped softly. His grandmother Donna would be scheming to throw Ruby up on one of her show jumpers if she had seen this performance. Especially the sparky warmbloods.

Ruby looked up, startled.

"That was a damn good ride," Gabe said.

"Thank you. Got to get her cooled off before my grandfather gets here with the trailer, or else I'd talk more. Don't want to hold him up too long. He's been haying all day."

And that was another piece of the Ruby Barkley puzzle. Why wasn't she here with her own rig?

Curious, Gabe leaned forward and pushed his hat back so that she could see him more clearly. He grinned at her.

"Wouldn't want to delay your grandfather," he said. "I'll walk with you while we talk, unless you think it will set her off again. Or if you want to be left alone."

Ruby glanced over at the arena, a worried expression tightening her face. Gabe was willing to bet that she was thinking about Ridley.

"It might set her off. She reacts poorly to some men."

"Should I stay by the fence?"

That earned him a closer look. He smiled bigger and tried to look harmless. The tense lines in her face softened a little. He'd made a good impression.

"No. I want to get her past that reaction to men. See if it's just Troy or what. She doesn't react to my grandfather."

He had to admire the mare as well as the rider, then. Gabe chuckled and eased off of the fence, moving slowly and watching the mare as he walked toward her.

"Well, I don't blame her for reacting badly to that loudmouth Ridley."

"He does have quite the following."

Sunshine tensed. Gabe stopped five feet away, watching the horse and not the woman.

"Less than you think," he said to Ruby. Then he changed his tone to a soft, coaxing voice, just like Donna-gran had taught him years ago. Her vocals were integral to Martiniere mind control, so they worked with horses as well. "Hey there, pretty girl," he wheedled, watching Sunshine's facial muscles. "You need to be nicer to your human. You gonna let me come up to you, pretty thing? Pretty girl. Silly pretty girl." He advanced slowly. "Come on. I'm not going to hurt you or your human."

The golden mare snorted and shook her head and neck. Gabe froze for a moment. Then her ears flipped toward him and the tense muscles around the mare's eyes softened. Her lips were still tight, but the palomino was willing to tolerate him.

"Pretty girl. Pretty girl." He extended the back of his hand. The mare stretched out her neck as far as she could reach. Gabe stood still as she sniffed his hand, then breathed softly on it. He moved a little closer and slowly ran his hand up her head to scratch the big diamond-shaped star at the top of Sunshine's blaze. Most horses liked being scratched there, in his experience.

"You know horses," Ruby said, a surprised note in her voice. "More than being a bronc rider."

"My grandmother first put me on a horse when I was three years old. Think your pretty girl will mind me walking alongside while we talk?" he repeated. "Just wanting to make sure."

Ruby shrugged. "One way to find out."

Gabe moved to Sunshine's side, scratching her neck under the mane. The mare blew a long, relaxed, exhale and turned her head toward him. The horse had accepted him. Now he had to work on her rider. At this point he was becoming *very* interested in Round-Up Princess Ruby Barkley, more than just casual chatting. No coy high-society games from her. A straight shooter. A horsewoman.

"Nice mare, even if she does buck. Looks like she could have won tonight, if she hadn't decided to pitch that fit. She's got the speed, and that one barrel she didn't buck through looked pretty dang nice."

They started walking. Gabe rested his hand on the mare's neck. Her muscles remained relaxed.

"Yeah, bucking's her issue. I got her for cheap because of that habit."

"Oh?" So Ruby wasn't afraid to rehab difficult horses. Another point in her favor.

"She has a history of setting back when tied. Rearing and bucking, too. I've not seen the problem with tying. Rearing and bucking, yes. But I got her from a girl whose boyfriend beats up on horses, and she's not easy on them either. I think I can get Sunshine past that. I think it's a reaction to rough handling, not her nature."

Definitely a decent horsewoman, then. Not everyone would take on a mare with those problems. "That's not good. You don't get far with a sensitive mare like this by beating her around."

"No. You don't." She paused. "I'm Ruby Barkley." Her tone was a little softer, but still self-protective.

"One of the Pendleton Round-Up Princesses. I know. My name is Gabe Ramirez, and I've got to say, I'm impressed by a pretty lady who can sit a horse as well as you do. I followed you over here because this girl looked like she still had some fight in her, and didn't know if you might need some help."

"As you can see, I didn't," she countered. But the edge in her voice had shifted from tense to slightly flirty, and there was a twinkle in those blue eyes. She was *liking* his chat. Ice Princess? Didn't seem that way.

Then again, her horse had accepted him. That might be the key to the Ice Princess.

Gabe chuckled. "I also wanted a chance to admire a damn fine horsewoman working with a tough horse." Yeah, he was impressed. "And." His tone tightened a little bit as he remembered that girl in California. "I heard Ridley muttering around about coming over here to harass you with some of his buddies. He won't mess with you when I'm around."

"Oh? I appreciate the thought, but I can handle myself with him." Confident. He liked that in a woman.

"From the way he talked, it sounded like you two had a history."

He wasn't going to bring Craig into it just yet. "Figured you didn't need the hassle, especially with your horse acting like this. And it gave me the excuse to introduce myself."

"Yeah. History." A bitter tone in her voice. "He's the king of handsy-ness. And of refusing to take no for an answer."

"He does have that reputation. Not just with you."

Sunshine's neck tightened under Gabe's hand as they heard loud, drunken, male voices.

"Hey Ruby, you goddamn bitch!" Troy Ridley, in finest form. And now he had the excuse he'd been waiting for all night to shut the fucker up.

Gabe glided away from Sunshine. "Leave her the fuck alone, Ridley!"

"Or what, Ramirez?" Ridley started to climb the fence, beer bottle in hand.

Gabe allowed his lips to part in a feral grin as he approached the fence, putting on his Martiniere glower. Ridley was too drunk to notice but his companions moved back. *Good.* And oh, he was *so* going to enjoy kicking Ridley's ass. Ridley didn't have Martiniere training.

"Or I'll kick your goddamn ass *again* for harassing women." He shoved Ridley back over the fence, leaping over it, his grin widening. "Like this."

It was almost too easy as the others hung back to give them space. And it felt damned good to send Ridley staggering. A few blows, and Ridley was on hands and knees, shaking his head.

"Get him the fuck out of here," he growled to Ridley's companions. "You guys know better. He's too fucking drunk to be fighting. Lucky for him that I'm not an idiot or he'd be hurt worse." He caught a glimpse of Craig hanging back by one of the bull pens, close enough to intervene if needed, but otherwise not obvious.

"You'll pay for this, Ramirez!" Ridley snarled.

Gabe laughed, thinking about the trial awaiting Ridley. "Don't think so, Ridley. I don't pick on people smaller than me."

Still, he stood there, fists loosely clenched, until Ridley's buddies dragged him away. Then he exhaled, releasing the anger, and turned back to the fence. Ruby was schooling Sunshine in tight figure eights at a trot—the mare must have gotten agitated from the fight, maybe even her rider as well. Damn it.

He eased over the fence and approached them cautiously.

"Sorry. The mother—" he caught himself, not knowing how she felt about swearing. "Excuse me. The *fool* should know better. Sunshine okay? Not freaking out?"

"A little worried, but she's settling. And a few swear words don't hurt my fucking ears. I wasn't born yesterday."

Gabe laughed, relieved. He hadn't lost any ground with Ruby, and Sunshine pricked her ears at him, the muscles around her eyes soft once more. As he put his hand on Sunshine's neck again, both woman and mare exhaled softly. He was accepted. By both of them.

"All right. You said your grandfather's picking you up?" Maybe she was younger than he thought. But she was in college, and a rodeo princess. Shouldn't she have her own rig?

"Yeah. My truck died." She sighed. "It was probably stupid to come to this rodeo. She did so well last week in Umatilla. But Sunshine doesn't like this arena, and I figured that maybe with practice she would get better about it." A regretful tone.

"Must live close."

"Over in Thunder County—for the summer, anyway. Then it's back to school."

"College?"

"Senior year. Oregon State. Agricultural robotics."

Not stupid at all, for sure, not when she was studying *that* field at *that* university. Close enough to his own ag robotics and programming studies at the University of Paris. Beauty, brains, a horsewoman, and not afraid of being profane. And close to legal age, if not already there. God, he really *was* in danger of falling in love with this woman. Already. He should walk away because she was a huge risk. But his loneliness kept him there.

"Ag robotics. That's a big field."

"Lots of places to go with it. I keep thinking that if we can track field data down to the plant level, that would open a lot of possibilities for pinpoint treatments. Hope to apply it to Gramps's ranch."

Be still his beating heart. Crud. Very close to his own field.

"Oh yeah." He wanted to let her know he wasn't just any dumbass bronc rider, but he didn't dare talk about his own ag robotics experience. The field was too damn small. "I'm in a somewhat related field. I've got a degree in microbial ag." Close enough. After all, microbial ag *was* his minor.

"Really?" Interest rose in her voice. "Where are you working?"

And that was the catch. What could he tell her? He hadn't figured on meeting an intriguing woman while on the run. Didn't have a story ready.

"Nowhere, at the moment." He fumbled for a reason. "I'm riding the circuit for—reasons." His glib phrases seemed to have whispered away, damn it. "Not a good idea for me to settle in one place."

"Are you in trouble with the law?"

Ah. Another explanation offered itself.

"No. But I owe enough on student loans to be far too attractive to the Martiniere Group indenture bounty hawks, with the degree that I have." Aha. Perfect. That way if Joey or Philip's heavies came down on her looking for him, she'd think it was just student loan debt.

"I worry about that myself," Ruby said softly, her voice troubled. "So far, Gramps and Granma have been able to help me. It's not living well—I'm working part time and eating ramen—but I've been able to keep my head above water."

"That's good," he said, a sudden flash of what life in indenture would be like for *this* woman. No. That absolutely couldn't happen. "You don't want to see indenture as a woman." Joey and the way he abused any indentured woman—he was bad as Troy Ridley, if not worse. "Especially with your focus on ag robotics. You really don't." The Martiniere Group would gobble her up—and Joey would target an employee like Ruby for harassment, even if she wasn't indentured. Especially if she didn't have a protector.

"If I have to drop out first to avoid indenture, I will."

"Hope you don't. Does this girl go on vacation when you return to school, or are you doing remote studies this fall?"

She shook her head. "Too many hands-on labs to study remote. At least for my focus. And I'll be taking Sunshine with me. I work at one of the lesson barns near Corvallis. Pays for housing for me and one horse in return for stall mucking and feeding."

"Who are you working for?"

"Lora Smith."

He whistled in respect. Lora Smith was not just anyone. She was an Olympic eventing bronze medalist. That meant—damn. Ruby was *good.* Tonight wasn't a fluke.

"Not everyone gets to work with her. But—rodeo? I thought she was more dressage and eventing." His cousin Justine had occasionally lessoned with Lora Smith in Los Angeles. He hadn't known Smith was in Oregon.

"She is. The other job I have is helping her with rehabs and colt starting, plus riding training horses at the small shows. I like learning new things."

Yes. Ruby was *damn* good if she was doing that with Smith.

"Eh, my grandmother did low-level eventing, so I know a little bit about that world." He heard footsteps on gravel and tensed, wondering if Ridley had gotten away from his buddies, and was on his way back to hassle Ruby some more.

"Ruby?" Cautious, but older than Ridley. The man came into sight. Skinny, lanky like Ruby, face lined and dusty, head covered by a green ball cap advertising a seed company, long gray hair pulled back in a pony tail.

"Just cooling Sunshine off." Ruby's voice was tired and perhaps a little cautious herself. Gabe bent to check between Sunshine's forelegs to see if she was still hot, so Ruby wouldn't have to dismount if she needed to walk Sunshine more.

"She's still wet but cool now, Ruby. Should be fine," he said softly to her.

"Who's this with you?" Demanding, protective tone in his voice. Must be the grandfather.

"Gabe Ramirez." Gabe straightened up and spread his hands, doing his best to look unthreatening, even though he was taller than the man. "Came over to see if your granddaughter needed any help with this mare and—Troy Ridley and his buddies were talking trash when she came out of the arena. Troy won't bother her if I'm around."

That earned him a grudging but respectful look, if still somewhat suspicious. "Ron Ryder. Appreciate it. Ruby. She blew up on you again?"

"Yeah, first and third barrels," Ruby said as she reached forward to rub Sunshine's neck. "But she settled once I rode through it here in the pen. And she was calm around Gabe. No tension."

"Well, that's something," Ryder said. "She doesn't hate all men. Just certain ones."

"Mare's got good taste if she doesn't like Troy Ridley." Gabe took advantage of Sunshine's relaxation to show off for Ryder a little bit and scratch the golden mare's jaw. "I like that in a horse."

Ryder snorted. "You're not a fan of Ridley, either." Statement, not a question.

"Don't like men who talk down to women. Especially loudmouths who think that getting rough with horses and women is a good idea."

Ryder eyed him speculatively. "Heard that Troy got into a little legal trouble. You know anything about that?"

"I might," Gabe admitted while Ruby dismounted. He faced Ryder straight on. "And he tried to start something with Ruby a little while ago. I finished it."

That earned him a sharp laugh from Ryder. "Got it. All right, Ruby. Let's get this cranky mare back home."

"I'll get the gate for you." He walked next to Ruby, fighting back the itch to take her hand. Damn it, he wanted to see more of this woman. "Well, Ruby Barkley. I'm sure I'll see you and this pretty girl around some more." He closed the gate after them, tipped his hat, and walked away, fighting back an urge to look behind him as she led Sunshine away, focusing instead on Craig.

Craig handed Gabe a check. "We held on to third."

"Good." Gabe worked his shoulders to loosen them up. She *was* a Pendleton Round-Up Princess. He'd be sure to see her again *somewhere* on the circuit.

Craig chuckled and elbowed Gabe. "And yet another man falls to the lure of the Ice Princess. Looked like you were making some good time with her there."

Gabe rolled his eyes. "She didn't seem so icy to me."

"She's still dangerous as hell, Ramirez. A lot of men have tried and failed to crack that shell."

"I always appreciate a challenge."

"Mm. Well, she's gonna be at the Sweets rodeo next week. Court appearance." Craig smirked. "I suppose you're gonna want to stay over for the week instead of the night."

Gabe laughed. "Might as well see if I can lose this check on the entry fee. Think you might have some work on your place to keep my hands busy this next week, now that the frozen food rush is done?"

"Man, I can *always* use an extra hand on the place, especially at my age. Be worth it to watch you crash and burn with the Princess."

"I won't crash," Gabe said, a confidence he didn't quite feel in his voice. "Give me six months. You'll see. We'll be dating by then."

"Stake money on it?"

"One hundred bucks."

"It's a bet."

Gabe grinned to himself as they walked to Craig's truck. One way or another he'd figure out Ruby Barkley.

The question was, what would he do after that?

GABE FELT A LOT BETTER ABOUT THE SWEETS RODEO—CALLED THAT because it was part of a celebration of the local onion crop—when he saw who the stock contractor was. One of his favorite buckers was in the lineup—now, if he could just manage to draw Skydancer. That would be his best opportunity to impress Ruby.

But there were other, good horses from that contractor as well. Many of his favorites. All the same, he really hoped he drew Skydancer.

Soon enough, he and Craig were hanging out by the in gate for the Grand Entry. Ruby was back up on Sunshine, but the palomino mare was completely different from the weekend before, relaxed in the warmup before the entry started. Redheaded rider and golden mare tore around the arena at high speed, a gorgeous sight.

Craig elbowed him. "Man, she's got her hooks into you *bad*. Stop drooling."

"Can't help it. They're a nice pair when they're clicking." Gabe grinned at Craig. He was in the last batch of saddle bronc riders, and he'd pulled Skydancer. He actually had a decent chance to impress Ruby tonight…and Sweets had a dance afterward.

It was just going to be a question of when he could relieve Craig of his hundred dollars. Oh, this was going to be a good night.

Soon enough it was time to prep Skydancer for their ride. Gabe made extra certain of his equipment.

"Hey there, big fella, we're gonna win tonight," he said softly to the big chestnut and white draft-cross Paint. "You feelin' good?"

The stud raised his head high, fixing Gabe with his one blue eye. Then he snorted, clearly a challenge. Gabe laughed. He eased down on Skydancer's back, made sure he was set and ready before the gate swung wide. The stud felt *good* under him, muscles coiled tight, rump braced against the chute's corner, ready to jump high and hard.

Skydancer didn't disappoint. He bounded out of the chute with a huge, high leap. Gabe fell into the rhythm of the big stud's leaps and twists, rhythmically raking his taped spurs across the horse's shoulders and keeping his focus. The eight-second buzzer startled him as much as it did Skydancer, breaking into their flow. But then the stallion took off running. Gabe leaned forward to encourage him, a big grin splitting his face. That had been a *good* ride, and he knew it down to the bones in his little toes. Sky loved to run when he got a chance after the buzzer sounded, and Gabe didn't mind encouraging it.

The pickup men finally caught up with them, and just like the ride, it was a perfect dismount. Exhilaration filled Gabe and he threw his hands up high, laughing as the crowd cheered louder than they had all night. The two of them had put on a *good* show. Skydancer broke away from the pickup riders once they pulled his flank cinch, still into galloping big and hard, snorting with each stride. Gabe paused to watch the big stud, savoring Skydancer's enjoyment of their audience.

Skydancer charged toward him. Gabe faced him without fear, laughing hard because he felt connected to the big horse, thrilling because they shared a bit of jubilation at a good performance. The horse paused in front of Gabe and reared, tossing his head to cheers from the crowd. Gabe tossed his head in return and snorted.

"Thanks for the ride, big fella!" he shouted, saluting Skydancer, then bowing as the crowd roared even louder while Skydancer galloped to the gate. Then he dared to turn and look at the scoreboard.

GABE RAMIREZ was in first place, several points ahead of his nearest competitor. A safe lead.

Gabe whooped and pumped his fists. He picked up a run, slowing only to scoop up his hat and plop it on his head. He sure as hell hoped Ruby had seen this ride. One of his best ever.

She was at the gate in full Round-Up Princess regalia, blue eyes shining bright, freckle-sprinkled pale cheeks flushed. Yes, he'd made a good impression.

"Well, if it isn't Princess Ruby Barkley," he said. Damn, she looked good in her princess outfit. "You're looking lovely tonight."

"High scoring cowboy's full of flattery." But there was a big grin on her face as she said it.

Gabe laughed, leaning on the gate next to her, brushing elbows. Was it his imagination, or did electricity spark between them?

"Ain't that the truth. Skydancer gave me a good ride. He's one of my favorites. We usually score well together when I draw him 'cause we both love to show off and can match our rhythms. Oh, it feels great tonight. But I know damn good and well it can go the other way on me the next time with a horse I'm not in tune with. Still not good enough to make that work."

He'd made even more of a positive impression on her with that speech, from the way her smile grew, more authentic than the standard queen version. He could already tell the difference in her smiles. And another brush of elbows sent a sharper tingle through him.

Oh yeah, there was chemistry between them all right.

"So true about the flow. I know how things can change," she said. And he could tell from her momentarily distanced smile that she was thinking about that fast, hard, elegant Grand Entry gallop on Sunshine.

"I bet, with that palomino of yours. No bucking from her tonight."

"She likes this arena. So far, that's the only factor I can identify. If she likes an arena, she doesn't buck."

Time to move on before she had to go back to work opening gates. "Going to be at the dance tonight?"

She shook her head, smile fading. "No. I need to head out. Leaving early tomorrow for Corvallis."

Damn it.

"I was looking forward to a dance with a princess, especially since I had such a good ride. I didn't think Oregon State started up this soon."

She hesitated, the glow diminishing. "Uh, no. Couple of things. Lora wanted me back early, and then Dr. Green asked me to assist at a late summer seminar."

Whoa. She wasn't just shining him on. "Asa Green asked an undergrad to assist? Damn, lady. You're *good.*"

The compliment flushed her cheeks again and she grinned, showing him a dimple in her left cheek, even as she shrugged. "He's my advisor, and he recruited me for OSU over Washington State. Based on my 4H presentations and some other things I did in high school."

"Ah. I see." He had to look those up. 4H presentations weren't enough to get Green's attention. He suspected that he'd discover Ruby Barkley was a research powerhouse in her own right.

"I'll still be at the Round-Up."

He tightened his lips. Now that was too damn risky. "Too public. If there's one place the Martiniere bounty hawks are gonna be, that's it." He sighed, surprised at his disappointment. "Oh well, Ruby Barkley. Here's to hoping we see each other on the circuit next year."

Looks like I owe Craig a hundred bucks. Easy come, easy go.

Though it wasn't about the money. There was just something about this woman.

It was one of the hardest damn things he'd ever done to turn and walk away from her.

"Gabe?"

Hope flared. "Yes, princess?" He whirled to face her.

"I'll be at several shows in the Valley this fall. Might even do some barrel racing with Sunshine. Gotta see what Lora wants me to do. If you're headed in that direction...."

It *was* something, and it told him that she wanted to see him again.

"Let me give you my number. Text me with your schedule. I'll make it if I can. No promises, but I'll try."

Now what kind of temporary farm work could he find in the Willamette Valley?

"Sure," she said as she handed him her phone. "I could give you *my* number, too."

His breath caught and their eyes met. He couldn't hide the big grin or the leap of joy within him at that.

"Princess, I'd love just that." He handed her his phone.

Numbers entered; phones handed back. Their fingers brushed and he felt that jolt again. From the rising flush on her cheeks, he suspected her reaction was much the same as his.

"I'll be seeing you this fall," he said, giving her a salute like he had Skydancer.

"I'll hold you to that." Another big genuine smile, and then she turned back to her gate duties.

He went to find Craig.

"Congrats on the win," Craig said. "You get very far with the Princess?"

"Mm," Gabe said, rocking his head side to side, half-smiling. "She's gotta go back to Corvallis tomorrow so she's not gonna be at the dance."

Craig snorted. "I warned you, Ramirez. You ready to pay up?"

"Buuuut—" Gabe drawled out the word. "I *did* get her number. We're gonna meet up in the Valley this fall. You and I agreed on six months. I'll have a date with her by the end of the year."

Craig's double take was priceless. "Ruby Barkley never gives her number out. Never."

"Well, it just happened." Gabe smirked at him, waggling his phone.

Now he needed to figure out how he was going to pull this off.

OCTOBER, 2029

. . .

Dealing with Ridley's grand jury took longer than Gabe thought it would. It wasn't until October that he was back in Oregon, looking for work in the Willamette Valley. Timing worked in his favor, though. He found a slot at a Christmas tree farm and a cheap studio apartment in an old 1950s-era motel where other farmworkers lived. At least his brown skin helped him blend in.

Online research confirmed his first suspicions. Ruby *was* a powerhouse in several ways. Junior Miss Rodeo Oregon. Teen Miss Rodeo Oregon, in addition to being the Thunder County Days Queen and Pendleton Round-Up princess. Competition outfits designed by her grandmother, who was an ex-rodeo queen herself. Advisor Vickie Chandler, who'd been first runner-up for Miss Rodeo America in her day. Sunshine was probably the best barrel horse Ruby owned, judging from what he could find of her placements.

And that was just the rodeo background.

Then there were her ag robotics skills.

Ruby hadn't won bot design competitions, but she consistently placed in the top five of the ones she entered, ever since her freshman year in high school. Gabe recognized one entry that had caught the attention of his cousin Arthur, a member of the French branch of the Martinieres, back when he was interning in Artie's division. Solid work. She was better at design than he was, for certain. He might be the better programmer but she was still no slouch.

His phone crashed and it took him several weeks to safely replace it and upload his data. That required careful negotiations with Serg because Gabe wasn't about to get just any phone. He needed every bit of Martiniere and Vygotsky security that Serg was willing to smuggle to him.

And he'd missed several texts from her during that process. Damn it.

But. Even as he scowled at his phone, debating between how risky it might be to drift by Lora Smith's barn and chance Lora recognizing him, or just plain texting Ruby, another text popped up.

> Spending my birthday at a jumper schooling
> show at the Hunt Club.

Complete with date and address. Tomorrow, damn it. Not much time to prepare.

He checked his funds. If he managed things right, he could buy her dinner. Yeah. That sounded right. Now if his beater car would hold up for the hour and a half drive to the show....

———

GABE HEARD HIS COUSIN JUSTINE'S VOICE WHEN HE WENT INTO THE ARENA, so he slipped out of the bleachers and went around to the stable alleyways.

Damn it.

He'd have to be extra careful. He pulled his hat low over his eyes and walked through the stable. No sign of Lora Smith's string. Must be in the temporary stalls outside. He chose not to wonder why Justine was *here*, of all the damn places.

He found Lora's setup, with one horse in a row of four stalls, three for horses, one for tack. No sign of Ruby or Lora, so they had to be warming up. Gabe checked the outdoor arena and spotted Ruby on a big dark bay mare that reminded him of her Sunshine horse. High-headed, big-eyed, looking at everything. He suspected the mare was a greenie from the awkward way she moved, not the coordinated and conditioned grace of an upper-level jumper. The bay mare was washy, foam forming on her neck where the reins rubbed, and between her hind legs.

Green or not, the big mare was a warmblood, with a strength close to that of Skydancer's. If she chose to buck...then again, he suspected that was why Lora had hired Ruby. If Ruby could sit Sunshine's big leaps, then she'd ride through warmblood antics easily.

As Ruby rode the dark bay toward the arena, Gabe followed, hanging back. She looked even better in the form-fitting breeches, tall boots, white shirt and jacket than she did in her Western wear. Legs that went on forever, long-waisted, her red hair neatly corralled into a bun just below her helmet.

Mmm. He liked long-haired, long-legged women. Ruby fit his preferences perfectly.

When their number was called, Ruby had to circle the big mare in a big canter loop several times to get her focused and coordinated. Gabe nodded approvingly as Ruby gently twitched the rein to get the big bay's attention back as she stared pop-eyed at everything, breaking into a trot when she was distracted. Ruby balanced the need to correct the young horse with keeping the mare's confidence, not pushing.

She's a good greenie rider.

Then the big mare bolted at a double combination, clearing the fences with two feet at least to spare and going long, landing and taking off again instead of cantering a stride first. Gabe nodded again. That young horse had scope. The mare knocked down a rail at the next fence, which seemed to settle her.

He waited impatiently as Ruby and Lora talked after the round was finished.

Come on, come on.

He could *feel* the eyes of Justine's security on him. He needed to set up tonight's dinner and then get the hell out of here. Too exposed. At last, Ruby dismounted and led the big mare toward the gate. He opened it for her.

"Thanks," she said, not really noticing him. He pushed his hat back a little. But before he could speak, she stopped and took a second look. "Gabe?"

"None other, princess," he said, relief flooding through him as they walked toward Lora's stall row. "I thought I'd see if you wanted to do a birthday dinner after the show."

"I've got to get the horses settled in." She grinned. "But yes."

"Not a problem. Lora helps you?"

"No, most of the time once the horses are unloaded, I do the rest of it."

They stopped in front of one of the stalls. "I'll see you later, then. I know where the barn is, have a pretty good idea of when you'll get back. Can't hang out here too long. Too many bounty hawks around even at this little show."

He started to walk away.

"I don't even get a birthday kiss?" she called after him.

He couldn't help grinning as he turned back. A wicked smile was on her lips and that dimple in her left cheek showed.

"Didn't know we were on those terms yet."

And Ruby had the reputation of being the Ice Princess? *Damn.* He must be doing something right if she was being this flirty.

She shrugged. "It's my birthday. You're going to take me out to dinner. I figure I can at least give you a kiss. Especially for dealing with Troy that night. Never did thank you properly for that."

"Well, can't let it be said that Gabe Ramirez turned down an offer of a kiss from such a pretty lady." He ambled back to her. "I am C-19 safe, in case you were wondering."

"So am I." Those bright blue eyes twinkled mischievously.

"Figured as much." He chose to keep this first kiss cautious, delicately pressing his lips to hers, chaste without offering any pressure.

"Is that how a saddle bronc rider kisses a rodeo princess?" Oh, she was *definitely* flirty.

"That's for later," he said, a thrill washing over him at that prospect. "I'm no damn Troy Ridley to push myself on a woman too early in a relationship. Figure we needed to know each other a little better first."

She grinned. He'd scored with that one.

"See you later then."

"See you."

He wasn't so ecstatic that he didn't forget to be cautious as he went back to his car. It wouldn't do to get caught now.

Once he got back to his studio to change for that evening, he sent a text to Craig.

> Dinner date with the Princess tonight.

> You be careful. Remember what I told you.

> I will.

All the same, Gabe didn't feel like being cautious when it came to Ruby.

LORA'S STABLE WAS NEXT TO A WILDLIFE VIEWING AREA. HE COULDN'T SEE the barn because it was in a grove of Douglas firs that obscured everything except the front pastures, but the driveway entrance was in plain sight.

Keep that in mind, Gabriel.

At least his careful scouting had told him that this was the only discreet vantage point for anyone watching the barn.

His estimate of Ruby and Lora's arrival time was off by maybe half an hour, because he hadn't been in the lot for long before the truck and trailer with Lora's stable logo drove by. Then he waited for Lora to leave. Half an hour later, a car exited the driveway, going in the opposite direction. Gabe lingered ten more minutes to be safe, then cautiously drove to the barn.

He found Ruby taking care of the three horses who had been at the show, tossing a blanket on the one she'd been riding.

"She's a pretty girl."

Ruby didn't startle when he spoke, so he figured she had looked up when he came through the big barn door.

"Green as can be, but she redeemed herself this afternoon. Didn't place but she settled in a second class. She'll be placing soon enough. This show was just for experience."

He followed Ruby and the big mare to her stall. Sunshine nickered at him as she came up to the front of her stall, and Gabe rubbed her nose.

"Guess you remember me, eh, girl?"

Ruby handed him a horse cookie. "She's being a jealous treat hog."

He gave it to Sunshine, then scratched her nose some more. Ruby checked the other two mares and started wiping down tack. He joined her.

"You know the routine."

He nodded. "Donna—my grandmother—was pretty strict about us kids cleaning tack."

"So how dressed up do I have to get for dinner?" she asked.

"Not very. Depends on how much you want to go out wearing breeches, tall boots, and all after the show."

She chuckled. "I can change once we're done here."

After they finished cleaning tack, he looked closer at the other two horses. Ruby put things away, then took one mare to her stall, leaving a big chestnut mare who let Gabe know with pushes of her nose that she really wanted her head scratched.

"This girl's nice," he said as Ruby came back.

"Yeah. Lora thinks she's got a good amateur owner lined up to buy her. Apparently one of the Martinieres."

Oh fuck. Fuck. Fuck. Fuck.

He laughed hollowly. "No wonder I thought I saw some Martiniere bounty hawks drifting around."

He was in big trouble. Hopefully it was just Justine…but he had no idea how she was leaning in Family politics these days. He hadn't seen her since just before the trial, and Serg had been cagey about where their cousin's loyalties now lay.

Ruby put the last mare away. "We can go now."

"I can wait for you at the car."

She shrugged as she walked toward the other end of the barn. "I don't have any problems with you coming into my apartment."

"You sure?" Where the hell had she gotten the reputation of being the Ice Princess, if she was this open?

"I asked around. You've got a good reputation. I'm not worried."

"Okay." Well, she'd invited him—and she'd vetted him with other women on the circuit. He'd take her up on it. "Sorry. I've just spent the last few weeks dealing with—that little incident with Troy that your grandfather mentioned."

They entered the studio and he looked around. Neat, everything in order and in place. Monitors showing alleyways and stalls. Ruby unzipped her tall boots and pulled out clothes to change into.

"Oh?"

He exhaled. "Girl that he beat up took a turn for the worse. I had to be a grand jury witness. Troy's been charged with attempted manslaughter."

"Oh." She fled to the bathroom.

He kept looking around the studio. No fancy frills. Books, tablet, computer neatly laid out on the desk. Bed made. Muck boots on a mat by the door. Organized. A lot like his own small room except for the barn security monitors.

Ruby came out of the bathroom, her hair now down, and grabbed a pair of nice cowboy boots out of the closet. "I'm not surprised about Troy. He tried getting rough with me a few years ago. So I decked him."

"No wonder he doesn't like you."

She shrugged, pulling on her boots. "I'm one who got away. I chose to date another guy instead of him. Plus, we were bidding against each other at the auction where I bought Sunshine. I beat him out. He didn't like that." She straightened up. "Okay. I'm ready."

"Separate cars?"

"Only if you want to do it that way. Otherwise, I'm comfortable with you driving. I'd much rather not drive my truck into town if I can avoid it."

"Okay then."

Gabe resisted the impulse to take Ruby's hand or touch her as they walked to his car, but he turned on the full range of Martiniere manners that Donna-gran and his mother had pounded into him, opening the passenger door for her with a bow. Ruby giggled, flushing a little and the dimple in that left cheek popping out.

They chatted idly as he drove to the nice deli and bakery he'd discovered in Corvallis. Ruby ordered wine, and the server congratulated her on coming of age after looking at her ID.

So she's just twenty-one.

A year older than he'd thought. And his comment regarding being strict about age of consent scored another point—at least a flash of dimple.

He kept the chatter light and casual, pulling on the playboy Gabe persona he'd adopted when younger to distract Joey and Philip from his real goals. When Ruby rested her hand on the table while they waited on her complementary birthday cupcake, he dared to place his hand near hers. She delicately brushed an index finger across his knuckles, that wicked grin coming back, dimple deeper than ever.

Gabe fumbled his words, forgetting what he was saying. He wrapped his hand around hers as silence fell between them.

No. He wasn't dealing with a shy virgin here, but a woman who was definitely interested and not afraid to let him know it. How far would they go tonight?

He didn't think he was in charge. And he was quite happy to follow her lead.

They released their hands as their server and a couple more staff members brought out a chocolate cupcake with a single candle burning on it, singing "Happy Birthday." After Ruby blew out the candle, she cut the cupcake in half.

"Cake's meant to be shared," she said, in a husky voice that sent a frisson of delight through him.

He picked up the bigger half and offered it to her. Ruby nibbled it carefully, that wicked grin with the dimple returning as her tongue flicked at his fingers. He shivered, and traced her lips with a fingertip before withdrawing his hand. That grin spread as she licked her lips slowly, then picked up the other half of the cupcake and held it out to him.

He reciprocated, gently sucking on her fingertips while tickling them with his tongue. That widened her eyes and she quavered a little, the grin getting even bigger.

After he paid the bill, he bowed and offered his arm to her.

"Old-fashioned, but all the same, shall we?"

"Of course."

They strolled around the downtown, still talking idly, but he was intensely aware of her presence next to him. At last, they reached his car.

"I owe you a *good* kiss for your birthday, Ruby."

"Absolutely." Her voice was deep and husky now, almost a purr. She pressed into Gabe as he wrapped his arms around her and they kissed. Ruby's tongue teased against his lips and he parted them slightly, daring to meet her tongue with his.

He finally broke it off. "Much more of this in public and we'll be in trouble." He was glad his jeans were loose enough to camouflage the bulge in them.

"If we keep it up here, yeah," she said. "Let's take it to my place."

"You sure about that?"

"Not my first go-round, cowboy. I'm pretty darn selective; have birth control and disease protection. Plus, I have a weak spot for a nice guy with good manners who I might possibly rope into helping me do chores in the morning. Lora's taking the day off."

He laughed. "Well, if that's what it takes, I can sure live up to it." He stole another kiss, then opened the door for her.

As he drove off, she rested her left hand on his thigh. He placed his on top of hers.

He was relieved to see that there weren't any observers at the wildlife area as they drove by. Ruby directed him around to the back side of the barn—even better—and he parked next to a beater truck. She waited for him to open her door and take her hand, then pulled him to her for another kiss as intense as the last one.

"We'd better get inside," he said shakily when their lips parted.

Ice Princess? Like hell.

Ruby yelped as he swept her up into his arms. Surprise was replaced by a knowing smirk as he carried her to the door. Within two steps of the door closing behind them they were shedding coats and boots. Ruby pulled at his shirt and he took her hands.

"A warning. I'm pretty badly scarred," he said. "You may not want to see it. A bad car wreck."

Her lips tightened. Then she took his right hand, guiding it to her head until he felt the slight rough spot hidden under her loose, flowing hair.

"Beer bottle to my head." She stepped away, pulled off her shirt, and undid her bra. "Cigarette burns. And tire irons leave a mark as well." Ruby turned her back to him and he saw the old, faded scars. Not as bad as his, but....

He growled. "Who would dare—I'll make them pay."

She gulped as she faced him again. "You're a few years too late. My parents. And they're dead."

Gabe kissed the mark on her shoulder. "All right." He took a deep breath. He'd never shown his scars to a lover before now, but she'd shown him hers first. He pulled his shirt off and turned his back to her.

"Oh!" Ruby's voice trembled. Then her fingers brushed lightly against the marks on his shoulder blades, followed by light kisses along the length of those scars that made him gasp. He hadn't realized they were so sensitive. Her firm hands guided him around and they kissed again.

"I—it's been a while—may be out of practice," he whispered.

She chuckled, a deep throaty growl that grabbed him by the gonads, as she unbuttoned his jeans. "Not the only one, cowboy. And who says we don't have all the time in the world to get back into practice?"

Making love to Ruby was every bit as exquisite and marvelous as he hoped it would be. Afterwards, he pressed delicate kisses on her forehead, her brows, her eyelids and cheekbones and nose as she smiled, practically glowing with a softer purr in her throat.

Oh God, he was lost. Completely and totally lost. This woman owned him. He didn't dare—but he'd never met a woman quite like Ruby Barkley. For a moment he wondered what the Martiniere emeralds that he had inherited from his father would look like on this redheaded rodeo queen, then firmly shoved that notion away.

That life was gone. And he didn't dare risk this woman. No. Finally something was going his way. Even if it was only one night, he would have this memory. Ruby. His Ruby. Beautiful, brilliant, and one hell of a horsewoman. Why did he need emeralds when there was a Ruby at hand?

"Thank you," he whispered at last. "That was wonderful. Thank you."

She smiled even bigger, that sparky edge gone. "You're not as out of practice as you thought, Gabe Ramirez." She stroked his forehead, tracing a finger down the deliberate scar left by the plastic surgery that didn't quite alter his features. "And I agree. Wonderful. I'm looking forward to getting to know you one hell of a lot better."

He leaned his forehead against hers. "I don't have much to offer, I'm afraid. I'm broke, and I owe a lot of money."

Not much to offer unless I become Gabriel Martiniere again.

"That's all right. You've got manners, a good heart, and brains. I don't give a shit about anything else. It's what we make of it—together." She gulped. "Even if you have to take off because of the bounty hawks."

"I won't go without you knowing," he promised. "If I can."

"That's all I ask. Do your best."

Gabe took Ruby into his arms again.

No longer alone. To hell with you, Philip and Joey. I'll go to hell to protect this woman if that's what it takes.

Not that he thought she'd need much protection.

Except from Philip and Joey, that was.

This redheaded rodeo queen owned him now. And he didn't mind it one damn bit.

3 / FIRST CHRISTMAS TOGETHER

DECEMBER 2029

Sneaking out of his girlfriend's small barn apartment early in the morning was becoming a predictable pattern. A potential problem.

Gabe started the coffee before he got dressed. Not just to fortify him for the long day ahead at the Christmas tree farm preparing last-minute shipments for those who could afford real trees these days, but for Ruby as well, so she'd have it while doing the morning check and feed for the horses. At least she hadn't needed to juggle school and work during the last two weeks. The senior year ag robotics program at Oregon State was tough. One reason he'd started spending week-nights with Ruby was to give her a break while finishing the challenging fall term.

He'd become invested in helping her do well. Ruby had a vision of agricultural biobot design that made it oh-so-tempting to reveal himself. Gabe had spent enough time in the Martiniere labs to recognize something promising...and Ruby's designs were definitely talented. If circumstances had been different, instead of being Ruby's boyfriend, he would have been recruiting her for the Martiniere Group. She was just that good.

Coffee finished. Dressed (and noticing that Ruby had rolled on her side to watch as he pulled on his clothing, pretending sleep but her eyes were open enough for him to know). Overnight bag packed again.

Nuked the breakfast ratbar to make it more palatable. Time to kiss Ruby and go, before anyone else showed up—especially Justine.

He lingered over the kiss. With the weekend coming up, there would be too many people at the barn for him to stay with Ruby. This kiss needed to hold them until Monday.

"Morning." She reached up to pull him close. "Do you have to stay away this weekend?"

"Can't risk the bounty hawks," Gabe sighed. "But I will be with you for Christmas."

His cover was becoming more difficult to maintain the longer he stayed with Ruby. And since his cousin Justine had bought one of the high-end show horses under Ruby's care, there were too damn many Martiniere bounty hawks lurking around on the weekends, when she rode. Oh, they were supposed to be Justine's security—but he knew too damn much about how Martiniere security worked after spending time with the cousins in charge of it. And Serg Vygotsky had just explicitly warned Gabe about *not* trusting Martiniere security, unless it was under direct supervision from Serg or his father Piotr. Justine's security didn't impress him. Near as he could tell, a bunch of them were toadies spying on her for Philip?

Why the hell didn't Justine take her horse to California or Florida?

Granted, a new explosion of flu had shut down winter competitions in both places. And Lora Smith, the trainer and barn owner, was a damn good event trainer as well as being a former Olympian. But did that mean Justine had to park herself in Corvallis—or Eugene—or wherever the hell it was she was staying right now—and interfere with this most *interesting* relationship?

"Sorry," Ruby said, throwing aside the covers. "I'm surprised she's still here. I wouldn't expect a Martiniere to hang out in Western Oregon this time of year."

Well, there was *one* Martiniere hanging out here willingly, even if he was in hiding.

Gabe allowed himself a moment to savor Ruby's beauty, to tide him over the weekend. Natural dark auburn hair, with that faintly glowing pale redhead's skin. Lanky, long-waisted, muscular, long-legged. Enough curves to earn herself several rodeo queen and princess titles, coupled with equestrian ability that *could* take her to the highest levels in either rodeo or hunter-jumper—if she had the financing.

For the umpteenth time, Gabe wondered what her reaction would be if he told her who he really was—and it *was* tempting to reveal himself, to finance Ruby's talents.

Philip would kill you and take it away from her.

His uncle was why he didn't do that.

He kissed her again. "See you Monday night."

"Don't kill yourself working the trees."

He laughed. "I'll make sure I don't get taken out by a rogue bundle." The problem was real. He'd almost gotten clobbered by a drone hauling a bundle of trees yesterday.

"I'll kick your ass if you let that happen."

"Can't have that." He kissed her again and headed out the door.

A light frost coated the still-green grass and the gravel as Gabe walked to his sedan. The horses in the barn heard him, and began nickering demands for their morning hay and grain. He ignored them as he surveyed his little brown car. Beat up, old, but nondescript and, despite its appearance, mechanically sound. He examined the alarms around it, both cyber and physical. Even though this car couldn't be seen from off of the property, and there were multi-level sensors and security cordons around the barn to protect the expensive horseflesh inside, he wasn't trusting anyone.

Safe.

Another quick look underneath the car. No tampering. Lora's barn *should* be safer than his sleazy studio apartment, but it wasn't worth taking a chance.

"Gabie."

Gabe froze halfway through straightening up. *Fuck. Fuck. Fuck.* He did have both knife and derringer in his boot tops, but that wouldn't be sufficient defense if Justine had support.

Might as well face what's coming, damn it.

Gabe rose to his full height and turned toward his cousin.

Justine appeared to be alone, thank whoever, and dressed in running clothes. Didn't mean she wasn't armed—she was a Martiniere, and Philip's daughter, after all.

She brushed back her long brunette hair and smiled sadly. "I thought that was you."

He sagged against his car. "All right, Tine. Just do me a favor. Don't have your minions kill me where Ruby will find out. You owe me that much." He didn't know where Justine's loyalty lay these days, but given the number of Martiniere security staff flocking around her, he was willing to bet that Philip had somehow managed to override her husband Donald's influence.

"Gabie, *really*." Justine scowled. "Why do you think I'm here this early?" She glanced around. "I don't have much time. Ducked away from Daddy-poo's guards, but they'll figure it out soon enough. Luckily, I have a habit of slipping out to jog by myself first thing in the morning. Pisses them off."

Relief of a sort. So Justine was still somewhat defiant. An ally— or not?

He exhaled heavily. "How did you find out?"

"Caught a glimpse of you in Corvallis with Ruby," Justine said.

Oh God. He'd have to move on, damn it. And he'd promised her Christmas together. "Shit. And I thought I was being careful."

"So far it's just been me," she said.

"Yeah, but if you've made me then it won't be long before your entourage figures it out as well." He shook his head. "*Damn* it."

"I'm sorry. But I thought I'd better warn you." She glanced around. "Look. Don't get too spooked. We're heading to Paris for Family Christmas on Monday. That gives you time."

Family Christmas. He heard the capitals in her voice. Like every high-level Martiniere heir, he still thought in those terms despite nearly eighteen months on the run. The Family. The Group. The Martiniere— *Philip, damn it, not my father.* His fists clenched for a moment, then relaxed as he exhaled. Justine's leaving would give him a chance to say goodbye to Ruby before disappearing.

"Thanks for the warning."

Justine gave him one of her arched-brow, measuring looks. "Gabie. If you want to come back, there are ways. Daddy-fucking-dearest does not have a lock on the Family. Even if he *is* the Martiniere, you still have allies."

"So did my father. And now he's dead." His father Saul, Philip's twin, had been the Martiniere. Then Saul died in a plane crash, along with Gabe's mother Angelica and his sister Louisa. Gabe had been thrown on Philip's not-so-tender mercies—and bore the scars to prove it.

If only Donna-gran had been healthy.

His life would have been much easier under his grandmother's custody, instead of his uncle's. Or if one of his other uncles—like Gerard, for one, who had helped Justine escape Philip by marrying Donald Atwood—had taken charge of Gabe at age twelve.

Not that it mattered. Philip, as the new Martiniere, had ruled that he was taking custody of Gabe back then. Only Donna-gran, as the Matriarch of the Martinieres, had the authority to challenge Philip— and she had been undergoing a series of cardiac surgeries, unable to help Gabe.

"I'm just saying it's an option." Justine sighed. "Donald's getting sick of Daddy-poo and his controlling behavior. I'm transitioning from Martiniere security to Atwood security over Christmas. It will be different when I come back. But you'd best lay low this weekend."

He shrugged. "I'll be working my ass off."

She shook her head. "Manual labor, I suppose."

"Yep."

"It's a waste of your talents."

"But at least I'm my own person. Not dead, which is what your father really wants." Gabe sighed. "I have to get to work, Tine. Is Joey part of your entourage?" He hoped not. Justine's brother Joseph was as nasty as her father, only with cruder methods.

"God, no." She wrinkled her nose. "Joey still hates horses. Just like Daddy-dearest. He's still in Los Angeles." She paused. "Gabie. Be careful. If I could figure out your pattern…."

"I appreciate it, Tine."

He climbed into the car and drove off, regret already dumping on him.

Oh well. I'll say goodbye Monday night and leave early on Tuesday. So much for Christmas together.

And he'd been looking forward to Christmas with Ruby, damn it.

Another solitary holiday. Merry fucking Christmas. Loneliness crept up on Gabe as he drove, throttling his throat and making it hard for him to swallow. It was harder to think about being alone now that he'd had nearly two months with Ruby. Was living like this really worth it?

Maybe he should see if Craig Yellowhawk needed winter help on his ranch near Pendleton. At least he wouldn't be alone and he'd still be in the Northwest. And it was close to Thunder County and Ruby's home. He might find a means to see her safely again.

"You got tipped off?" Ruby looked tired and worried Monday night, even before Gabe brought up his need to leave sooner rather than later. Craig had been enthusiastic about Gabe joining him for the winter, so at least he had somewhere to go.

Gabe nodded. "I—uh—went to military school with one of Justine's cousins. She warned me." Close enough to the truth.

"Too bad she can't help you financially, so that you don't have to worry about the bounty hunters," Ruby said, her voice bitter.

"Let's not worry about it right now," Gabe said. He took her in his arms, brushing back a tendril of that lovely hair. God, he'd miss her. "Enough about my problems. What's bothering *you*?"

"Granma isn't doing well," Ruby said. "Gramps called me over the weekend. I was gonna have to tell you I had to go home for Christmas. Already told Lora. Leaving tomorrow."

"I'm sorry." And that was worrisome. I-84, the major freeway that passed near Thunder County, had raider problems every winter. Women traveling alone had disappeared. Been killed. Possibly sold into indentured servitude. "I'm gonna be worried about you on 84."

"I've not had issues before." But she still frowned. "Then again, I've not needed to go home over Christmas until now."

"Mmm." It bothered him that she was traveling that road alone, during the height of winter raiding season. "Maybe I should follow you until I turn off for Craig's." This way he'd be certain she got as far as Pendleton safely.

"Or you could go with me, then to Craig's when I come back. Gramps suggested that I bring a friend along for safety's sake. You'd still have to get out of here fast after we come back, but—we'd have Christmas together at least." She shivered. "And I could sure use your company. I don't think it's just Granma who has problems."

A few more days with Ruby. Including Christmas.

It was well worth the risk.

"When do we leave?" He had given notice at work and at his apartment. Everything he owned was in his car. He could throw it into the back of Ruby's crew cab. "I'll call Craig about the change of plans. We can pick him up when you're coming back here, and he can ride with me, so I'm not alone going to his place."

That eased her worried expression. "We'll leave as early as possible. I'll tell Lora that my friend's car is gonna be here. She'll be happy to hear I'm not traveling by myself. She's been fussing ever since I told her I had to go."

"Thanks." He went out to switch everything he cared about—not much these days—from his car to Ruby's truck. He wasn't going to tempt fate by leaving valuables in an unattended car, with no one staying at the stable for a couple of weeks.

His weapons bag came inside, like usual. He wanted to make sure that everything was loaded and ready. They might have an uneventful drive to Northeastern Oregon—or they might not.

Gabe planned to be ready. Serg and Piotr would kick his ass if he wasn't, and they found out. And while he was faster than old Piotr, he was definitely *not* faster than Serg.

THEY ROSE BEFORE SUNRISE TO DRIVING HARD, COLD RAIN. RUBY SCOWLED as they quickly threw hay to the horses and doled out the morning grain, then loaded what was left to go in the pickup.

"Hope to hell this doesn't mean freezing rain in the Gorge," she muttered as they climbed into the truck. "That could be a problem."

"It gets bad?" Last year he'd spent a lonely Christmas in a rough backcountry camp in southern Utah, spooked by someone tossing his cheap motel room in Las Vegas. And the year before had been his final Martiniere Christmas in Paris, where he'd been fighting with Philip, Joseph, and a couple of the cousins. Justine, Donald, Piotr, and Serg had kept Gabe from making things worse by getting him drunk as hell. Falling down, puking, pounding-hangover drunk, and starving himself so he didn't risk embarrassing himself should Philip decide to use his control words in front of the Family. His head still hurt when he thought about *that* Christmas.

He didn't know anything about the Pacific Northwest in winter. Paris, yes. The desert Southwest, yes. Los Angeles, yes.

Ruby nodded grimly as they drove off. "One reason why I've not planned Christmases at home while going to Oregon State, as much as the winter raider threat. The Gorge gets horrible ice storms. Blizzards. Even if it's just raining it can be pretty nasty. Weather changes fast this time of year."

He pulled up the road conditions link. "So far it looks good. Just wet."

"Let's hope it stays that way," Ruby said. "Then we can worry about raiders on the Plateau and weather over the Blues."

GABE PAID FOR FULL FUELING IN TROUTDALE, AT THE MOUTH OF THE Gorge, despite Ruby's objections. The wind-driven rain battered him as he filled the truck's tank. He used the time to assess the other travelers while Ruby grabbed snacks and drinks in the mini-market after using the restroom.

Three greasy, shifty-eyed men studied vehicles as they smoked cigarettes on the sidewalk in front of the mini-market. Raider scouts? Gabe didn't get back in the truck, but stood in front of it for whatever shelter it provided from that hard, buffeting rain as he waited for Ruby. She got too much attention from those drifters when she came out of the mini-market, even though she wore a shapeless insulated coverall and her hair was tucked up under a cap.

Raider scouts.

He made a big deal out of meeting her with a huge kiss and hug, raising his head to fix the drifters with a predatory glare, that Martiniere glower he used as a fight preliminary.

Just so you know what you're dealing with, boys. I may be in hiding and on the run, but I'm still a Martiniere with Vygotsky training.

"Something wrong?" Ruby asked, her voice low.

Oh God, he loved this woman. She'd picked up on the vibe without being explicitly told. If only he could have her as a partner while on the run.

"I think we're being scouted by raiders," he growled.

Her lips pressed together and she nodded.

Once they were back on the freeway and settled into the road, Gabe prepared, just in case it came to a fight. Clear pathway to driver's side back window. Meant stacking some of his stuff higher—which might attract raiders by itself, but couldn't be helped. Not if his instincts were correct and they'd been scouted. He wanted to be able to access the back windows quickly.

Rummage in my weapons bag. Pull out my favorite pistol, attach it to the glove box. Make sure refill clips are fully loaded and attached.

A moment's hesitation, then he did the same with his backup, before checking his disassembled light sniper's rifle in its case.

"Didn't realize you were loaded for bear," Ruby said, quickly glancing sideways before refocusing on the road, her lips tight as she wrangled the truck through standing water on the freeway.

"Military school training," he said. *And a Martiniere upbringing.*

"I have a weapon in the glove box," she said. "Might be nice if you can attach it within my reach with whatever it is that you're using for your pistols. What the hell is that, anyway? Looks like something from Vygotsky Security."

"It is," he said. "Serg Vygotsky was one of my classmates at Northview, and he was generous in handing out tech to friends."

He rigged up pistol and backup clips where Ruby could reach them, checking everything as he went along. Then he settled back in the passenger seat.

"If you're tired, I can drive," he offered.

She shook her head. "This truck has quirks. And I know where the bad spots are through this area. Hidden potholes that you won't see in this fucking deluge. Besides, you need to be ready in case there's raiders. Rest."

"Is there anything I can do?"

Ruby half-grinned. "Hand me a ratbar, will you?"

He dug in the bag of snacks. "Chocolate or blueberry?"

"Chocolate, of course."

Gabe unwrapped it and handed the bar to her. Then he settled in for a long and hopefully uneventful ride.

THE RAIN FADED OUT AFTER THEY TOOK A QUICK REST STOP AT BIGGS Junction and were well into the desert. But the wind switched so that it came from the north, blowing hard.

Gabe fed Ruby water and snacks as needed. This long, barren stretch of road reminded him of the Southwest, especially after they climbed away from the river.

A worried expression furrowed Ruby's brow as the freeway split past Arlington, eastbound lanes out of sight of the westbound ones. Perfect place for an ambush—and they'd both spotted suspicious characters at Biggs.

She kept glancing at the mirrors.

"We got problems?" he asked.

"Maybe. Couple of rigs pacing us since the Arlington exit. Might just be other travelers."

He looked in the side mirror, then fished out binoculars and peered through her tinted rear window with the small slider opening. Big black rigs with crash guard front bumpers. No front license plates. Security vehicles of some sort—or raiders.

Could be fucking Martiniere bounty hunters, too.

But he didn't think so. And as he watched, they accelerated, the one in the left lane rolling slightly ahead of the other.

Calm descended on him now that he *knew* it was going to happen.

Steady. Ready. Wait for them to come to you.

The repetitive self-talk along with breathing rhythm that narrowed his focus to his opponent, just like Piotr had trained him to do, shutting everything else out, slowing his perception of time.

"They're gonna crash us," he said. His voice seemed to come from far away, not part of that growing brilliant clarity which sharpened his concentration on his prey.

Gabe moved their water bottles out of the center console, grabbed his favorite pistol and slapped it on top of a box, picked up his rifle case, and climbed into the back, his movement careful and deliberate because it was far too easy to move too fast and fumble things in this mode. He was moving faster than his senses told him. He assembled the rifle, then opened the back slider window and driver's side back seat window.

Take out the rear rammer first. Then the side guy. Should be easy-peasy, Gabriel.

If they weren't well-trained Martiniere security, that was. But he and Ruby were fucked if that was the case. His training and practice against theirs.

He waited.

Steady. Ready. Wait for them to come to you.

Time slowed even further for him. Just as it should.

He waited for the right opening. Shoot too soon and the side rig would have enough warning to take evasive action. Shoot too late and the following rig would still crash them. And it all depended on how reinforced those windshields were. He couldn't quite make out the driver of the following vehicle, which meant good reinforcement.

Gabe watched.

Ah. Now.

He carefully slid the rifle into the back window opening. Switched on the sight. Focused.

No sign that they were Martiniere.

Good.

He aimed for where the driver of the rear vehicle should be, and shot. Had to empty the clip before the windshield shattered. That rig swerved off the road and crashed through a barbed wire fence before careening to a stop.

One down.

But that fucking side rig accelerated and smashed into the truck bed. Gunshots took out the driver's side mirror as Ruby wrestled with the wheel.

"Gabe...." Worry in Ruby's voice.

"I've got them."

Everything around him still diamond-sharp. Movement seemed too slow as he switched to pistol and side window. This time he didn't bother with precision but emptied the first clip quick as they bashed Ruby's truck again. They still kept coming. Ruby tossed him her pistol. He snatched it deftly, and emptied it. The windshield finally blew. Their pursuers swerved off of the freeway, this vehicle flipping and rolling down the canyon side.

Gabe studied the road behind them. No further pursuit. He closed the windows and climbed back in front, dragging the weaponry with him. "Raiders," he said. "For sure."

Ruby shivered.

"You doing okay?"

Breathe. Breathe. Disengage. Release.

The crystal clarity of his concentration faded and sound rushed at him, the truck motor sounding far too loud, causing a momentary panic when he thought it might have a problem, then realizing it was just an aftereffect of his intense focus on his targets.

Ruby nodded, but he saw blood on her lower lip where she'd bitten through it. "We'd better report it."

Her words broke the last of that disassociation between his movements and his perception of time.

"You need to be the one calling in. Is there a safe stop nearby?"

She nodded again.

Gabe flipped up the center console so that the front was now a bench seat. He slid over next to her, putting his left arm across Ruby's shoulders and pressing against her. They both needed this. She trembled under his touch, but that and the bitten lower lip were the only apparent signs of the impact that the raider encounter had on her.

God, I love you.

The woman of his dreams.

GABE TOPPED OFF THE FUEL TANK AT THE TRUCK STOP WHILE RUBY MADE the call. This time he took the wheel. Ruby squeezed up next to him, still occasionally quivering.

"Couldn't get through to the authorities," she said as they drove off. "Busy signal the whole time."

Gabe nodded curtly. He'd managed to mock up a substitute for the driver's side mirror, using duct tape from one of his boxes.

Don't need any more attention than necessary.

Now it just looked like a standard crashed mirror fix. He couldn't do anything about the fresh crash marks on the truck's side, or the bullet holes where the shooters had tried to take out the—fortunately reinforced—gas tank.

"We could stop at Craig's for the night if you want to take a break," he said. "Or even a rest stop."

Ruby shook her head. "Gramps and Granma will be worried." Her phone chimed and she flicked it on.

"Ruby? You all right? We heard reports of problems on the interstate." Male voice, worried. Gabe recognized it as that of Ruby's grandfather, Ron Ryder.

"We're fine, Gramps," Ruby said, her voice a little shaky. "My friend Gabe is traveling with me. He's driving right now."

"Where are you?"

"Almost to Hermiston."

"Did you see anything? There's been multiple raider attacks near Arlington. At least four dead."

Ruby drew a deep, shuddering breath. "We're okay, Gramps. Really. We can talk when we get home, okay? Gabe and I have it under control."

"This Gabe. Have I met him?" Ryder's voice shifted from worry to protective.

"Last summer," Gabe said. "Gabe Ramirez. Bronc rider. Little incident with Troy Ridley."

"Ah. *That* Gabe." The protective note in Ryder's voice faded. "All right. We'll have food ready when you get here."

"Thanks, Gramps." Ruby disconnected and burrowed further into Gabe's side. "I didn't want to tell them more and worry them. Especially Granma."

"They're gonna know something went down once they look at the truck." Crumpled metal along the bed, the broken mirror, and a couple of bullet holes. He and Ruby were lucky, awfully damn lucky.

"Better not to have them fuss while we're still on the road," she said with a shiver. "If I make it to Miss Rodeo Oregon next summer, they'll have enough to be concerned about."

"At least you'll have some support on the road then," he said.

"They'll still worry. But—we'll see how Granma is. I may not be able to do tryouts if her health gets too bad." Her voice quavered a little. "She's more important than a title."

The road was good enough that he put his arm around her for a while, doing his best to provide consolation.

———

RUBY SLEPT THROUGH THE BLUE MOUNTAINS ONCE DARKNESS FELL, BARELY stirring when they turned off at Grande City to head for Lakeside. Gabe woke her for directions when they reached Lakeside. Soon enough, they turned off down a snowy drive marked by a CENTURY FARM—RYDER FAMILY sign, heading toward a cluster of ranch buildings and an old white farmhouse that loomed larger as they drew close. Moonlight glowed on the snow and Gabe thought he saw deer in the fields—then cattle that raised their heads to watch the truck drive by.

"Welcome to the Double R," Ruby said, straightening up as they pulled into the barnyard. She shuddered and put her head in her hands as he parked the truck.

"You okay?"

She raised her head. "I'm worried about what I'm gonna see with Granma."

He took her in his arms. "It'll be all right."

The back porch light switched on. Ruby pulled away from him. "Better get inside before Gramps gets a good look at the truck."

"He'll figure it out."

"Yeah, but I'd sooner wait until morning to deal with what he'll say."

"Okay." He planned to manage that conversation if he could. No need for Ruby's grandparents to get more worried than necessary. "Go on ahead. I'll get the bags."

She nodded and slid out of the truck.

Gabe picked up his weapons bag, dropping the pistols and rifle case into it, then grabbed his overnight bag and Ruby's suitcase, following her up the trampled pathway to the house. *Not shoveled,* he thought. Surprising.

One thing to be done in the morning. Not a good sign, based on Ruby's worries.

Ron Ryder met them on the back porch, craning his head as he hugged Ruby so that he could look past Gabe at the truck. "Looks a little rough for wear. Good to see you, Gabe."

"We had a few issues," Gabe admitted, setting down the bags to shake Ryder's hand. "But we made it."

Ryder raised his brows even as a thin, reedy voice called from the kitchen. "Ruby? Ruby honey, is that you?"

Ruby slipped past Ryder and into the house. Gabe bent to pick up their luggage.

"How bad was it, Ramirez?" Ryder asked grimly. "I see bullet holes."

"We made it," Gabe said in an answering tone. "And neither of us got hurt."

Ryder studied him, then nodded curtly. He grabbed a cane that had been leaning against the wall and limped through the door. Gabe followed him into the kitchen.

Plain. Floors worn. Counters worn. Faded paint. But something simmering on the stove smelled damn good and wasn't a processed-food ratbar, the room was warm, and Ruby knelt by a frail old woman sitting in a wheelchair parked next to a Formica green and chrome table.

It wasn't the huge Hôtel Martiniere in Paris, but it sure as hell beat a lonely motel room somewhere on the road or even Craig's beat-up house. This cozy and shabby kitchen looked pretty damn good to him in comparison to what he would encounter in Paris with Philip right now. Even with a suspicious and protective grandfather who would doubtless be wanting to know what Gabe's intentions were toward Ruby. He was here. With Ruby. And they'd survived that damn attack.

He might even be able to enjoy eating during this Christmas celebration, instead of drinking his way through it with just enough food to keep him from passing out.

Gabe set the bags down again as Ruby beckoned him over.

"Granma, this is my friend Gabe Ramirez. Gabe, my grandmother, Ruth Ryder."

"Pleased to meet you, Gabe," Ruth said in a wheezy voice as she extended her hand.

"Pleased to meet you, Ruth." He gently shook her tiny, mostly bony hand, then, in a vestige of the Martiniere manners that Donna-gran and his mother had pounded into him, bowed and delicately kissed the back of her hand, just like he used to do for the elder women at the big Family Christmas.

Ruth giggled, just like the elders would. "Oh my. Ruby, this one's a sweetie."

"*I* think so," Ruby said.

"Unfortunately, we don't have an extra bed ready."

"We'll take care of it," Ruby said.

Ryder snorted. "Not to worry, they're probably sleeping together, Ruth."

Ruby flushed. "We'll take our things upstairs," she said. "Then we'll come back and eat. All right?"

"I can carry the bags. Just show me where to go," Gabe said.

"All right."

He followed Ruby through a swinging door and down a hallway. The rest of the house was noticeably colder than the kitchen. Ruby took him up several flights of stairs to a big bedroom on the third floor.

"This used to be Granma and Grandpa's room until she got so sick that they had to move to the first floor," she said in a low voice. She went over to a radiator under one of the windows and put her hand on it, frowning. "Not warm at all. I wonder if Gramps is having problems firing up the furnace?" She sighed. "Oh God, Gabe. I was afraid that things were getting problematic. Two more terms at Oregon State and then I'll be back here for good. But I don't know if they'll hold out until June. I didn't realize it was this bad. I thought their neighbors would contact me before it got too horrible."

He took her into his arms. "We'll figure it out. You need to finish that degree."

She sniffled into his chest, then gulped and looked back up. "Thank you for coming with me, Gabe. Not just for this but—"

"There was no fucking way I'd let you make this trip by yourself, based on what I've been hearing about raiders," he said. "And I was right. But. Wait until the morning before you start thinking of problems. The situation with your grandparents may not be as dire as it seems tonight."

Ruby pressed her lips together and nodded.

———

After a plain but filling meal of gruel with some meat chunks and a couple of parsnips and carrots, Ron put Ruth to bed. That was Ruby and Gabe's cue to retreat upstairs. Ruby dragged an electric heater out of the closet and fired it up. They dove under the heavy covers on the bed, snuggling close.

Ruby cried into Gabe's chest, whimpering about the incident and her grandparents, and he soothed her. At last, she settled and turned away, her breath coming smooth and even as she fell asleep.

Gabe rolled on his back, staring up into the darkness. He was exhausted, damn it. But his mind kept spinning, replaying the encounter with the raiders. Had he actually hit anyone? Killed one or more of them?

Another group of people looking for me.

On the other hand, if there was a big enough problem that Ryder had called them on the road once he'd heard about the incident, and Ruby couldn't get through to authorities, they might not be searching very hard for whoever it was that had shot those damn raiders. There had to be bounties on the raiders' heads as well.

And what if Ruby decided to drop out of college because of her grandparents? Much as it would give him an opening to stay with her —after all, she would need help on the ranch this winter—she needed to get that damn degree to get the financing which would allow her to do what she wanted. *He* had the degree that the banks would accept as a credential, but if he advertised it, he might as well call up the Martiniere bounty hawks and hand himself over to them.

Gotta be a solution to this situation.

Ron Ryder seemed to be mentally clear. Money could buy a resolution—but Gabe didn't have access to his Martiniere funds, at least not without causing more problems. Even if he went through Serg it was unlikely that he could raise cash fast enough to meet Ruby's needs. And, after seeing the farmhouse, the odds were very high that the Ryders didn't have the money to buy help.

Ruby's too damn smart to drop out this close to graduation. Gotta find a way.

Gabe tossed and turned, but it was clear he wasn't going to sleep. Too much to think about, plus the aftereffects of the adrenaline from dealing with the raiders. Well, his weapons needed cleaning. Maybe he'd go downstairs and do that for a while. Might just be the thing to calm his skittery mind with too much to fret about.

"Mmm?" Ruby muttered as he slipped out of bed.

He kissed her cheek. "Not sleeping well. I'll be back."

"Mmm." She exhaled and turned over, used by now to his wakeful nights. Gabe gathered up what he needed and pulled on his slippers and robe. Hopefully he and Ruby could get the furnace running tomorrow.

A light still showed under the kitchen door. When Gabe entered, Ryder sat at the table, scowling at a computer projection. Gabe set his bag down on the floor, next to the table, and went to the refrigerator. He'd grabbed a six pack of beer at their last stop.

"Want one?" he asked Ryder.

Ryder pointed to a glass half-filled with an amber liquid. "Get yourself a real drink and not that horse piss."

Gabe raised his brows and put the beer back. One of *those* situations. All right. He could handle it. Close enough to the Family drinking sessions. At least Ryder didn't impress him as someone who was a violent drunk.

Unlike Philip.

He remembered which cabinet held the glassware and picked out a squat square lowball glass like Ryder's. He raised his brows again at the weight of it in his hand. Good quality. Maybe the Ryders had some money after all. Or not. He didn't think Ruby would be driving a beater pickup and working for Lora Smith to get through college if they did. Might be a legacy from better times.

Ryder produced a quart jar. "Locally distilled by someone who knows what they're doing."

"Neat or with water?" Gabe asked as Ryder filled the glass.

"Neat."

He dipped a fingertip into the liquor and took a whiff. Nothing smelled wrong, but then again, as Donna-gran had always said when lecturing the young Martinieres about neurotoxins, it wasn't what he could smell that could kill him. He raised the glass to his nose.

"Cautious one, aren't you?"

Ruby had needed to growl at him to eat more at dinner, after Gabe had only eaten half a bowl, then automatically pushed it away.

Gabe shrugged. "I have my reasons." He sipped it. "Not bad." He set the glass down and pulled out his cleaning kit, then the pistols and the rifle case.

"So you two *were* mixed up in that mess on the Interstate," Ryder said.

"Uh-huh. Like I said, we made it, and neither of us got hurt." Gabe started with the now-disassembled rifle, swabbing down the barrel, the discipline of years of training taking over as he pulled each piece out of the case.

"One of Ruby's friends wasn't so lucky," Ryder said. "I wasn't gonna tell her until tomorrow."

That made Gabe pause, looking over at Ryder. "What happened?"

"Britt was beaten, raped, and killed," Ryder said, his voice hard. "Authorities found her up one of those little canyon roads between Biggs and Arlington. Traveling alone, on her way back from college."

Damn it, he should have asked Ruby if she had other friends who needed a ride.

"Shit. Ruby didn't say anything about friends needing a ride."

"She was coming from Eugene," Ryder said. "Overdue by two days."

So not when they would have been coming through.

Gabe exhaled and went back to work. Ryder watched him.

"After they found her body, the police found two crashed vehicles east of Arlington," he said. "Matches descriptions of rigs that were attacking women traveling alone or with small children. One vehicle matched the picture Britt's dashcam transmitted before it went dead."

"*Good,*" Gabe said. "Survivors?" He carefully squinted down the rifle's barrel, then put it back in the case. Pistols next. He picked up Ruby's first.

"Four bodies in the wreckage."

Gabe nodded, unwilling to say anything. Well, that was one answer. He doubted the authorities would be looking very hard for a shooter now. He'd taken care of a problem for them.

"Sounds like it was a nice little job of shooting," Ryder continued. "Took out both drivers."

Huh. His aim was better than he'd thought, despite lack of recent practice. Gabe focused on Ruby's pistol.

"You're not real talkative about what happened." Ryder paused. "That's Ruby's pistol, isn't it? You two had to shoot yourselves out of a situation."

Gabe sighed. "They tried to ram us. One from behind, one from the side. I took care of it."

"There's a reward. Doubly so if they connect the dead with Britt's murder."

"Not interested."

"I didn't think you were *that* well off. I talked to Vickie Chandler. You don't have the rep as a rider with money."

"I *don't* have any money." *Or at least right now I don't.* "That's not the issue. Fact is, I'm dodging bounty hawks. College debt, and I refuse to go into indenture." It was a good thing that Ruby's pistol was similar enough to his own that he didn't have to focus on safely cleaning it. His heart pounded hard. Ryder was too observant. Too knowledgeable. Too likely to make the connection between *Gabriel Martiniere* and *Gabe Ramirez*. Damn it, he should have been fussier about picking a name.

"I see." A long, pregnant pause. "You look like you know what you're doing with those weapons."

"Military school."

Ryder snorted, drained his glass, and poured himself another drink. "Tell that to someone without actual military experience, bub. You didn't learn that kind of shooting in military school. You've had training."

Years of it, in fact. But Ryder had blown through his first cover. Damn it.

"Serg Vygotsky was a friend and one of my classmates. I spent summers in training with him." Close enough to the truth.

"More like it," Ryder said. "But you didn't go with Vygotsky Security?"

"My degree is in microbials and agtech systems programming," Gabe said. "And the only position the Martiniere Group would offer me involved indenture." Another near-truth, both his degree and the work.

"I see." Ryder took a big swig off of his drink. "There's a lot more to you than appears on the surface, Gabe Ramirez."

"Just trying to get along and stay indenture-free." He finished Ruby's pistol and picked up his backup.

"And Ruby?"

Gabe sighed. He set down the pistol and took a big swig of whisky, raising his brows in appreciation at the second taste. Smooth, without a bite, of a quality his uncle Gerard would serve in the library for the men after Christmas dinner. The *good* stuff, that Gerard kept locked up, away from Gabe and Serg and the other cousins with a reputation for drinking hard over Christmas to hide their nervousness about Philip turning on them, using their control words to humble them.

Get drunk enough so you don't feel the Martiniere's wrath should he turn it on you.

Gabe shook himself and took another big swig, forcing himself to relax, damn it. That was then. He was in Thunder County. At the Double R. Philip was thousands of miles away, on the other side of the Atlantic Ocean. He needed to savor this home brew, give it the respect it deserved, instead of pouring it down his throat to anesthetize himself. Whoever the distiller was knew their stuff, all right.

"She means a lot to me," he said finally. "But I don't know if it's fair to saddle her with my issues. I've—I've gotta move on once she's back in Corvallis. Been tipped off that I got spotted. But I didn't want her coming here by herself—or going back alone. I'll be staying with a friend through the winter."

"I see," Ryder said. He drained his glass and switched off his projection. He placed the quart jar close to Gabe. "Put that back in the cupboard over the fridge when you're done, Ramirez. And don't worry about how much you drink. There's more where that came from. Figure that after the day you've had, you might just want a generous serving. Good night."

"Thank you."

"You got Ruby home safe. That's what is important."

"Good night," Gabe called to Ryder's retreating back.

"Good night," Ryder repeated.

THE NEXT FEW DAYS WERE A FLURRY OF WORK THAT KEPT HIS HANDS AND mind busy. It felt good to be working with Ruby and not needing to hide out. Letting himself enjoy the tasty morsels that Ruth Ryder tempted him with. A Christmas where he could actually eat without fear, and didn't need to drink himself into oblivion.

Gabe could almost forget the post-Christmas deadline bearing down on them.

Despite the impending separation after Christmas, he savored their lovemaking. Being able to pretend that this was a normal life. Reviewing Ruby's plans to convert the hundred-year-old former dairy parlor on the ranch into the sort of lab that would support Ruby's biobot design dreams.

Christmas Eve came soon enough. He and Ruby showered and

changed into nicer clothing before going downstairs for dinner. He had a brief moment of regret when he realized that the Martiniere emeralds—the one legacy he'd retained, now in an attorney's custody, to keep them out of Philip's hands—would look gorgeous on Ruby.

Could he go back?

Not as long as Philip lives and holds the power of the Martiniere.

Ruby was solemn and silent as they dressed.

"Gabe," she said finally, sitting on the end of the bed. "Can we talk a minute?"

"Sure." His gut tightened. Ruby had taken the news about Britt's death hard. But she hadn't said anything about that yet. He was learning that she preferred to process difficult losses before bringing them up.

She took a deep breath. "I've been talking with people around Lakeside. Vickie Chandler and the other neighbors. My friend Remy Trask, who's a lawyer. I've—got to do something about Gramps and Granma."

"You can't quit school," he said. "Not and be able to do the stuff in the labs that you're dreaming of. Even as an independent bot developer, you've got to have that damn degree for financing."

She swallowed hard. "I know. But—things are rough here. I can't— someone's gotta be at the ranch. Gramps can't do it all. Not take care of the chores and Granma both."

"Can you hire someone?"

Her lips tightened. "I—for Granma. Sure. But the ranch work— hands are very hard to find here in Thunder County. At least not anyone trustworthy. Gramps is just too old to keep up with it, and I'm afraid something will happen to him. And I won't bring in indentured workers." Another long hesitation. "I know you've got something set up with Craig. I know you don't have any money. I can't afford to pay you much, and I know you're worried about me being linked to you by the bounty hunters. But still—you working here might solve several problems."

"You want me to come here?" God, that would be an even better solution than wintering with Craig. He was a good friend, but Craig didn't have much money either. And it would keep Gabe close to Ruby, at least for a while. "But what do your grandparents think?"

She smiled. "Granma has a monster crush on you and Gramps thinks you're competent. That's the other piece. He wouldn't put up with just anyone on the place. But my boyfriend…would be different. And he likes your work ethic."

He leaned in to kiss her. "We'll figure out compensation later. Just being able to have a safe place to stay—and help you—is worth it to me. Just don't decide to come home by yourself, all right? Call. Craig and I will come get you."

"You'll do it, then?"

"Yes," he said.

———

GABE HADN'T EXPECTED PRESENTS, BUT ALL THE SAME HAD SCRAMBLED TO pick up some gift items from town. He got work gloves and a heavy scarf from the elders, and warm socks from Ruby. His own gifts were much the same—at least the public ones.

But the private gift to Ruby, up in what was now apparently *their* room, was special. It had eaten up almost all of his remaining cash. A pair of silver earrings that matched her lucky silver locket.

And after making love to Ruby, snuggling in close to her to keep warm on that cold winter's night, he decided that he wouldn't trade this for any of his Christmases in Paris as *Gabriel Martiniere*.

Perhaps this life as *Gabe Ramirez* wouldn't be so bad after all. Especially with Ruby in it.

4 / MARRIAGE

MAY, 2033

Ruby startled Gabe awake just before dawn as she ran into the bathroom. He slid out of bed, worried as he heard her puking.

Fourth day in a row that she's been throwing up first thing in the morning.

No fever. Ruby often felt better by mid-morning. But. Day before yesterday, when they were treating the fields for a new wheat pest that wasn't responding to the microbial treatments he'd whipped up, Ruby had stopped her sprayer to dry heave several times.

There were multiple things he could imagine this being, and only one was good.

If Philip's found a way to get to Ruby....

No. He couldn't think that. He didn't *dare* think that.

Gabe turned on the bathroom light and dampened a washrag, then knelt beside Ruby. When she finished, he wiped her face. She buried her head in his chest when he was done, trembling.

"We'd better talk to a doctor," he said. "I'm getting worried. Four days now."

"I'm—God, Gabe, that costs money."

"I know," he said. "But if you let this go, it could become more expensive."

Ruby gulped and raised her head. "My period's late."

He *had* noticed that. He *had* considered that possibility—the least troubling one. She was three weeks overdue. Ruby had been late before, but her period had always started by now. The puking was new. That meant—Gabe stroked Ruby's forehead, his hand quavering.

"Even more important that we know for certain," he said, his voice soft. "You shouldn't do any more pesticide spraying. At least until we're certain what's going on. We *both* know that."

Ruby frowned. "But it means more work for you."

He swallowed hard. "If you're pregnant and want to keep the baby, honey, it's for the best. Reduce the risk to both of you."

Did she want to keep the baby? They hadn't talked much about a future together after her grandmother had passed away last winter. Especially about babies. Ever since Ruby had graduated from Oregon State two years ago, they'd been together, except when she had needed to travel as part of her role as Miss Rodeo Oregon last year. They'd had too much time having fun rodeoing to talk about their future as a couple; had plans to do what little they could on the circuit this year, since her grandfather was becoming feebler.

But no serious talk about marriage or babies—yet. Part of that was his reluctance to bring up the topic. Ruby hadn't been inclined to say anything, either. The last time he'd talked to Serg, things hadn't changed with Philip. His uncle still wanted Gabe dead. So he continued to hide on the Double R.

Serg didn't even know where he was. Gabe kept his money drops to a minimum, scheduling them either for Pendleton or on the road when they were rodeoing. And Serg didn't follow the rodeo world, didn't react to any of Gabe's casual comments about it with any knowl-edge. None of the Martinieres were into rodeo, except him.

This possibility changed things. Time to stop playing. Time to grow up and figure out who he was going to be for the rest of his life. Was he going to be Gabe Ramirez or Gabriel Martiniere...and what did that mean for him and Ruby?

Ruby gulped again. "I'm scared. Babies are expensive."

"And precious." Gabe paused. "Do you want the baby? Damn the expense. Is this what you want? It's your decision and I'm good with either choice. Your body. I can't and won't force you to go either way."

She blinked, her eyelashes wet. "Yes," she said, her voice quavering. "I want to keep our baby."

"Shall we get married?"

"Oh, Gabe. Maybe we should wait and see—you don't have to marry me just because—"

"I *want* to marry you," Gabe said firmly. "Will you marry me, no matter what this turns out to be?" He couldn't turn back from this. Nor did he want to. He deserved this chance at happiness, in spite of what Philip had said to him over the years.

Didn't he?

She nodded, a tear trickling down her cheek. "Yes," she whispered.

He couldn't keep from grinning as he held her close. "Wonderful. I love you, Ruby Barkley. I'm honored that you'll marry my sorry broke ass."

That elicited a chuckle. Ruby drew a deep, shuddering breath, then pulled away. "I picked up a pregnancy test at the store yesterday. I was gonna check before I said anything to you." She got to her feet and pulled a box out of one of the cabinet drawers. "Want to wait and find out?"

"Wouldn't miss it for the world."

He leaned his head back against the cabinet while Ruby peed on the stick, closing his eyes for a moment to think and give her space. Marriage. Potential fatherhood.

Damn it, things would be much easier for Ruby if he returned to being Gabriel Martiniere.

No. They wouldn't. He'd be putting Ruby at risk, because Joey and Philip would see her—and their unborn child—as his weakness.

They'd done all right so far, with minor infusions of Martiniere money routed from Donald Atwood through Serg. The ranch was supporting the three of them—or would be once they sold this year's wheat crop, as well as the calves from the ranch herd. It could support a fourth. Might need to sell more heifers to cover expenses instead of keeping them for breeding stock.

Then again, when he'd met his friend Monty in town yesterday morning, the talk at the ranchers' table over coffee had been about a new virus that was causing cows and sows to abort. Gabe had listened closely because it sounded like something he'd heard about while studying at the University of Paris. If so, it was *bad*. It could cross over to humans.

Selling more heifers might end up being a necessity—they might not have much value other than meat if the virus turned out to be a problem. And what it might mean for them if Ruby *was* pregnant....

"Gabe?" Ruby's voice trembled and he opened his eyes. She held the stick out to him.

Blue circle.

"We're having a son," he whispered. *A son.* Furious joy pounded through him, because unlike Joey, he was going to have a wife and a son.

Fuck you, Joey. And fuck you, Philip.

He rose and took Ruby into his arms.

"You *are* going to see a doctor soon," he said firmly. "And no more spraying for you. Period. I don't care how much more work it means for me and if we have to sell heifer calves—you're going to take care of yourself."

He was *not* going to tell Ruby about the conversation at the ranchers' table just yet.

But he was going to make damn good and sure that Ruby saw a doctor, *fast*.

"Let's go tell your grandfather," he said.

"Should we?"

"Yes. Marriage. Baby. The whole thing."

Ron Ryder would insist that Ruby see a doctor and take care of herself. Gabe counted on that support from him.

"I—" Ruby hesitated. "What if he's pissed?"

"It's his great-grandson, honey. And he'll be thrilled that I'm making an honest woman out of you." Ron was clearly uncomfortable about Gabe's undefined role, especially since Gabe had been handling the ranch financials. Had hinted that he wanted to see them settled before he died.

"Okay," she gulped.

"Want me to take over the cooking completely, not just breakfast?" He noticed that she had started looking queasy while cooking, sometimes clapping a hand to her mouth and swallowing hard.

"That would be a help."

"All right. Consider it happening."

She sighed. "We'd better get dressed and tell Gramps. If I'm not spraying, then what can I do to make things easier for you?"

Gabe considered the tasks coming up. Ruby shouldn't be working around the cattle, or the feeder hogs, not until they knew more about that aborting virus and whether it jumped to humans. But if she took over the books, she'd be wondering about the infusions of money from Serg's cash drops. Gabe had been using some of that money to pay ranch bills, and some on gambling to raise more cash.

The books were the safest thing for her to be doing. He needed to give her a good story about them.

"Financials, hon." He sighed. "And you'll see unaccounted-for money." This would be the perfect time to tell her who he really was— but no. Too risky for her. "I came into a little cash from someone I helped out a few years back. He sends me money once in a while, and I've been slipping that into the ranch accounts to help pay my way. Especially now that we're building that biobot lab of your dreams."

"Oh Gabe. You should have used those funds against your loans."

"They wouldn't take it, honey. Nothing short of a full payoff will keep me from indenture." God, he hated this lie. It kept getting more and more complex.

But he disliked the prospect of what Philip and Joey could do to Ron and Ruby even more. And now…a child.

"I hate this," Ruby moaned. "The always watching."

"So do I, Rubes. So do I."

Then why are you still doing this? Why not come clean?

The question kept buzzing at him.

It wasn't just the issue of Philip's hatred and threats. He liked this life as Gabe Ramirez much, much better than the alternative would be if he returned to being Gabriel Martiniere.

Part of it was that the Family wouldn't let him get away with only collecting his funds if he became Gabriel Martiniere again. It wouldn't be just Philip wanting him to swear allegiance. The rest of the Family would be pushing for Gabe to become something more than an obscure rancher hiding out in Northeastern Oregon. And then there would be the power struggles. The scheming.

He feared that could tear him and Ruby apart.

Or worse, lead to the deaths of one or both of them. Even telling her could be risky. He'd been holding off until Ron passed away so that it was only the two of them dealing with any fallout from him becoming *Gabriel Martiniere*. Now, with a child coming….

"Let's get dressed and tell your grandfather," Gabe said. "Then you call a doctor and I'll fix breakfast. After I feed the stock, we'll go to town and get the license. No need to delay. What kind of ceremony do you want?"

At least Ruby wasn't a churchgoer. Gabe had dropped his Catholic faith after the deaths of his parents and sister. Calling out to God, Mary, and the saints hadn't protected him from Philip's abuses. So they wouldn't be dealing with that particular obstacle.

Ruby made a face as they went back into their bedroom. "I suppose I should invite Aunt Grace and her clan."

Gabe scowled but she was right, even though he'd figured out pretty fast that her father's family were a passel of shiftless mooches. And during their mutual sleepless nights, Ron had told Gabe details about the Barkley family. Ron hated Tony Barkley for getting Ruby's mother Beth into heroin and meth. But there was still a mystery about Beth and Tony's deaths. All either Ron or Ruby would say was that it had happened when Ruby was there, after she had been kidnapped from Ron and Ruth's custody.

Secrets of their own. And he was in no position to push them to tell him more.

"If you don't invite them, we'll be hearing about it for ages," he said. The Martinieres had their own versions of the Barkleys in subsidiary family branches, so he knew that dynamic.

"Yeah," Ruby sighed. "But I also want to invite the Chandlers and Reeds." Next-door neighbors, plus Vickie had been Ruby's rodeo queen advisor. "Some other friends from high school. What about you?"

"I'm gonna ask Craig to be my best man, but beyond that?" Gabe shrugged. "Our rodeo friends."

"Nobody from the Ramirezes?"

"Honey, they're all dead." An idea came to him to distract her from his family. "Why don't you call Vickie and plan a ceremony here at the ranch? I bet your grandpa would like that."

She grinned at that thought as she pulled on her bra, then tried to fasten one of her favorite snap-button shirts across her breasts. It gaped. "Oh no. Already," she groaned.

"Sweaters and t-shirts, hon." He hugged her.

Ruby remained solemn. "I'm not changing my name. And I don't want to tell anyone other than Gramps about the baby for a while."

"Not a problem."

Gabe was fine with keeping the baby a secret because after all, miscarriages *did* happen and this was Ruby's first trimester. As for her name, he already knew she didn't want to be a double R, even though she loved the ranch.

It's a damn cliché and I don't want to be a brand, she had told him. That was the only reason she kept her father's last name. And he didn't care, because even if he were to become Gabriel Martiniere again and use the Spanish surname protocols to honor his mother, Ramirez really wasn't *his* last name.

Though he doubted that he'd ask her to take the Martiniere name, either, if he went back to the Family.

Ruby Marie Barkley Martiniere?

No. It didn't fit his love.

She was *Ruby Marie Barkley,* through and through.

As always, Ron was in the kitchen before them, sipping on a cup of fake coffee. He usually rose before they did, and prepared it. Ruby headed for the coffeepot, started to pour herself a cup, then stopped, wrinkling her nose.

"Doesn't smell right," she complained.

"Same coffee I've been making every morning, girl," Ron said.

"Probably shouldn't be drinking it anyway," Gabe said. "I'll take that cup, hon."

"Hmm," Ron said, raising his brows. "So what's going on?"

Old man doesn't miss a thing.

After two years, Gabe had gotten used to Ron's scrutiny and detail awareness.

He put his arm around Ruby, careful to keep the coffee away from her. "Shall I break the news, or do you want to, Rubes?"

She raised her brows at him. He took that to mean it was his job to at least announce their engagement.

"I asked Ruby to marry me and she said yes," Gabe said. He tightened his arm around her and kissed her cheek. "I'm the luckiest damn man in the world."

"Oh? Congratulations. But. What's this about the coffee?" Ron's fingers tightened on the handle of his cup.

Well, *that* news had gone over better than Gabe expected. Looked like he'd called it right about Ron wanting to see something definite between them. Not surprising.

Ruby coughed. "And, well—Gramps, I'm pregnant. Test says it's a boy."

Ron was lifting his cup when she said it. He froze. Then he carefully placed the cup back on the table.

"Damn it, that's the way your parents started out, too," he growled.

"I'm not one to duck my responsibility to Ruby and our child," Gabe said. "Nor do I have any desire to get hooked up with meth and heroin."

Ron's lips tightened. "You *are* more responsible than Tony Barkley," he conceded. "But. That damned indenture contract hanging over your head could be as bad if not worse. What happens if they catch up to you? If I'm gone, the ranch is Ruby's. They could take it from her as well as grab you. How are you gonna fix that?"

Gabe took a deep breath. "We'll need a prenuptial contract to protect Ruby in that instance." Easy enough to say because only he knew the real stakes.

Another turning point. Another place where he could come clean. He paused, thinking hard about this aspect. He knew Ruby's losing the ranch wasn't a true risk, especially since no Martiniere interests were involved. But they'd have to deal with it as part of his cover. Keep his secret to themselves.

Ron and Ruby were good at keeping secrets. Maybe it would just be easier to reveal all. If Ron and Ruby were the only ones he told, there wouldn't be a need for him to go back to the Family. Though the temptation to collect his funds....

Ruby spoke before he could. "Remy Trask is back from LA, Gramps. She has a general legal practice. I was going to ask Remy to be my maid of honor anyway. I'm sure she can come up with something."

"I'll sign whatever's needed," Gabe said.

Saved.

If one could count that as salvation.

HE CALLED CRAIG WHILE OUT FEEDING THE STOCK. RUBY WAS DOING THE breakfast dishes before they went to town to get the license.

"Hey Craig. Got a job for you."

"What's that?"

"I need you to stand for me as best man."

"Best—*wha*?"

"Ruby and I are getting married. Soon. No date just yet, probably sometime in the next couple of weeks."

"Wha-wha-*what*? You. The Ice Princess. Getting married?" Craig spluttered. "How the hell did you manage that, Ramirez? For real?"

"For real."

"Will wonders ever cease. Damn. You and Ruby. Married. Well hot damn." Craig burst out with one of his deep belly laughs. "Let me know when and where, brother. Want me to put the word out?"

"Sure." Gabe laughed, sudden relief flowing through him. Relief and happiness. "We're getting the license today, and Ruby's talking to Vickie about planning the ceremony."

"Not wasting any time. You knock her up?"

"Ruby would kill me if I answered that question, and you know she would do it."

Craig chuckled. "All right. Just let me know when and where."

"Where—here, at the Double R. When—I'll tell you when I know."

"I'll be there, brother."

"Thanks, man."

Damn, this was just about the happiest day of his life. Gabe smirked at his phone, then put it away and got back to work.

Lonely no longer. A wife. A *son*. He hadn't expected this to happen when he first saw that redheaded rodeo queen on her palomino mare. But that warm glow inside of him made Gabe oh-so-glad that it had happened. Was happening.

If only his parents and sister were alive to meet Ruby, be around to see his son. That was his only regret.

RUBY GOT AN APPOINTMENT THAT AFTERNOON WITH A NEW DOCTOR TO Lakeside, Dr. Sheri Smith, who was setting up a general practice. Gabe went along because he needed to be with her.

"Call me Dr. Sheri," she said, glancing at the history her nurse had just taken. She bowed to them before leaning against a cabinet. Her mask flexed just enough to show that she was smiling underneath it, and the way her eyes crinkled made Gabe think that she smiled more than frowned. A good thing for someone working with kids and families. "So you're late cycling, Ruby, and a home test shows you're pregnant?" she asked.

Ruby nodded. "Yes."

Dr. Sheri eyed the chart again before looking back at Ruby. "How many days since you had your last period?"

Ruby's grip tightened on Gabe's hand. "Fifty-three days."

He did the quick calculation. *Almost four weeks overdue.* Not the three weeks he had thought.

"Are you usually cycling every twenty-eight days?"

"Most of the time. But I'll go long about once or twice a year—even when I'm not in a sexual relationship with someone."

Dr. Sheri nodded. "Which home test did you use?"

Ruby told her.

"Good. Those are usually accurate. And you said you've been throwing up for four days?"

Ruby nodded. Gabe patted her hand.

"Well, I've got the latest quick blood test. Let's just see what it says." Dr. Sheri brought out a pen and pricked Ruby's right index fingertip. Even before she finished ejecting the needle into one of the disposal cups, a bright blue display popped up over the pen. Dr. Sheri studied it, then sent it over to Ruby's record with a light tap.

"All right, Ruby," she said. "Yes, you are pregnant, and your hormone levels are consistent with you being six weeks along. Oh, and that test was right. You're carrying a boy."

Ruby exhaled. Gabe patted her hand again.

Dr. Sheri glanced at him. "You're the father?"

"Yes. Gabe Ramirez."

She frowned slightly as she looked back at the history. "Both living and working at the Double R Ranch. Tell me, do you have any breeding cattle or hogs on the ranch?"

Oh God.

Ruby blanched. "Is it—is it the abortion virus?"

Shit. She *had* heard about it after all.

"Yes," Dr. Sheri said, her brows furrowing.

Ruby gulped. Gabe answered for her. "We have a small cow-calf operation and three male feeder hogs. I told Ruby today that I'm taking over feeding. I heard about the virus yesterday."

Dr. Sheri's gaze softened, and this time Gabe was positive that she was grinning under the mask. "I am so happy to hear that you're taking those reports seriously, Gabe. Not everyone local is."

The rest of the appointment proceeded without complications.

THERE WAS A MINOR INCIDENT AT THE SIGNING OF THE PRENUPTIAL agreement keeping Ruby's interest in the Double R safe from indenture claims (or, as Gabe thought of it, free from any bullshit Philip might pull) while preserving some interest for him.

Something was familiar about Remy Trask that Gabe couldn't quite identify, but could place as an encounter before he came to Thunder County and the Double R. From the sideways look Trask kept giving him, it was clear she apparently had a similar feeling.

"Don't I know you from somewhere?" she asked outright, just before he signed the agreement.

Gabe shrugged, disregarding the icy tension that suddenly touched his gut. "Probably seen me around town."

"No." Remy brushed a strand of her brunette shoulder-length hair behind one ear and studied him, chewing on one earpiece of her narrow-framed black reading glasses. "I've seen you someplace besides Lakeside and Thunder County."

"Gabe rode saddle broncs on the Columbia River circuit," Ruby said, grinning. "There's some good pictures of him riding Skydancer. Those two have become a circuit legend."

"Maybe that's it," Remy said slowly. "But I could have sworn I've seen you somewhere else, Gabe. Ever spent time in Los Angeles? I used to work for the Feds there."

Oh shit. Philip's home was in LA, and then there was *US v. Martiniere Group.* Gabe had spent enough time in LA, after graduating from the University of Paris, that Remy might have seen him at some event. At the very least, she might have viewed him in a news clip.

But he didn't remember running into Remy at the trial. Anything else was deniable.

"Not really, unless you count something like Disneyland or Knott's Berry Farm," he lied, uncomfortable under Remy's scrutiny. Ruby gave him an odd glance. "I visited, but didn't spend that much time in LA. I lived in Tucson and Moab, couple of other small Southwest towns." He forced a laugh but it didn't sound right even to his ears.

Remy's lips tightened. "Well, maybe that's it. There's just something familiar about you."

Gabe shrugged. "I'm Hispanic. Lots of us down that way."

As he hoped, the race card deflected any further talk about recognition from Remy Trask.

But it didn't quiet his own sense of familiarity. He *had* met Remy Trask somewhere.

He just wished he knew where. If it meant that he was compromised and needed to tell Ruby and Ron what was really going on. Before it blew up in his face.

Two days later, Gabe dropped by Trask's office to leave a big manila envelope with her, triple-sealed with his initials across the flap. Maybe she would say something further that would give him some idea where they had met.

"What's this?" Trask glared at him as he stood in front of her desk. She read what he'd written on the envelope. "What the *hell* is this all about, Ramirez? What's going on that Ruby shouldn't know unless you're dead?"

"Family business," Gabe said, keeping his voice cold and hard, matching Trask's tone. "Doesn't affect her unless I'm dead. And I mean dead. Not disappeared. Not divorced. *Dead.*"

"Ruby's my friend as well as my client. If this is going to hurt her—"

"Knowing before I'm dead may hurt her much more."

Trask shook her head. "Who the hell *are* you and what the hell are you hiding, Gabe Ramirez? This is not the action of an innocent person."

"It's safer if you don't know," Gabe said. "But it's nothing illegal, okay? Let's just leave it at that. Just keep that safe for Ruby, please? If I'm dead she'll need it. Please."

Trask nodded. "All right, then. As long as it's not illegal."

"It's not." Gabe swallowed. "And I trust you to protect Ruby and her interests, a lot more than I would most attorneys. That is very important to me."

"Thank you." Her voice softened. "I appreciate your trust."

Gabe nodded and put his worn black Stetson back on. He exhaled hard once he was out of Trask's office. No further talk about where they might have met.

And that item was covered. If something happened to him, he could trust the Vygotskys to take care of Ruby and their child.

THE WEDDING WAS PART-POTLUCK, PART-CATERED. RUBY RODE SUNSHINE to the ceremony while Gabe rode a big chestnut gelding, Ranger, that he'd bought from Craig shortly after settling on the Double R. Remy and Craig held the horses while Ruby and Gabe said their vows. Ruby wore a pair of buckskin fancy chaps over black jeans, and a white Western snap-button shirt with an elegant fringed and embroidered buckskin jacket, plus her tan felt show hat. Gabe wore a matching shirt and black jeans as well. His favorite worn black Stetson had been banished in favor of a tan hat that matched Ruby's.

Afterwards, they rode to the barn. Before Remy and Craig showed up to deal with the horses, Gabe swept Ruby into his arms and kissed her again, marveling at his great good luck.

He was married to the woman of his dreams. And they were going to have a kid. Could anything get better than this?

If there *was* anything sweeter than this, Gabe couldn't imagine it. He'd never, ever, thought he'd be married with a child on the way. Not since the deaths of his family.

He had a new family now, and by God, he'd do whatever it required to keep them safe.

5 / FATHERHOOD
DECEMBER, 2033

ALL OF HIS INSTINCTS SCREAMED THAT THERE WAS A PROBLEM. GABE RAN his scanner around the isolated Forest Service campground in the Blue Mountains near Pendleton once again.

Nothing showed up. No cams. No mics. Nothing attached to the sturdy picnic tables. Just trees, what remained of the snowbanks after the latest chinook, the faint sound of occasional traffic from the distant highway, and a soft wind rustling the Ponderosa pines overhead.

And maybe that was the problem. No birds. Even this time of year he should hear and see some birds here. Maybe. He was still learning this ecosystem.

The real problem was that Serg was late, by more than a few minutes. Serg was *never* more than ten minutes late for a meeting, and it had been damn near half an hour. That spoke of complications. And Gabe's frequent checks of traffic apps didn't show issues along any of Serg's probable routes.

So. Something had gone wrong.

Gabe considered leaving. Serg was tough and could withstand a lot of torture, but if Joey suspected that Serg was in contact with Gabe, well…Joey was damn vicious. He *could* possibly break Serg.

This might be a warning that his cover as Gabe Ramirez had been blown. That Philip was even now sending Martiniere bounty hunters to capture or kill his rebel nephew Gabriel.

On the other hand—Ruby was due to deliver their son in three weeks. Gabe *needed* that cash Serg was bringing, desperately so. If there were any complications with the upcoming birth, neither he, Ruby, nor Ron had the cash or credit to pay for it easily. Not without risking debt secured by indenture. They barely had enough to get by now, thanks to the abortion-causing virus that had shut down the Double R's beef sales. They wouldn't have much money until this coming year's grain crop sold.

Gabe shuddered. To run or not to run? Serg hadn't sent a cancel code. That was the only reason he was still here and not scampering back to the Double R as fast as he could.

Motion along the road. He focused on it while pulling his pistol, holding it at his side, turning to narrow his silhouette as he hid behind a tree. Gabe exhaled with relief as a solitary vehicle came into sight, flashing its lights in a prearranged *safe* code. All the same, he waited until Serg got out of the electric truck, carrying a cloth bag, and was clearly alone. Then he holstered his pistol.

"Serg."

"Gabe."

They clasped forearms and pounded each other's backs before stepping back. Gabe studied Serg. He didn't look like he'd been in a fight.

"Having problems?" he asked.

Serg grimaced. "Followed out of Pendleton. Took me a while to shake 'em. This is gonna have to be the last cash drop, at least for a while, because Joey's getting suspicious. Justine and her husband are headed for a divorce. I think their separation is a cover for some things that Justine's doing, but I don't know that for certain. And while Donald is still on our side, he's got to lay low until the divorce is finalized. Justine says it's amicable."

"They did agree on seven years when they got married." Part of saving Justine from her damned father. Gabe blew through his teeth. Nothing he was entitled to know, these days. "All right." He wondered what cousin Justine was doing that she wasn't telling Serg—or that Serg didn't feel safe sharing with him. At least he'd have this stash. "Thanks for what you can do and have done, Serg."

"Whoever this woman is that you're with, Gabe, she must be pretty damn special. Is she the lady that Justine knew?"

Gabe shook his head, but from Serg's smirk he knew he wasn't convincing enough. "She's having my kid in a few weeks. A son."

"Congratulations." Serg studied him further. "Growing a beard, huh. Fatherhood?"

"Thought it might help with the disguise. Besides, there's a local winter beard tradition."

"Well, it'll be a help hiding who you are." Serg handed Gabe the bag. "There it is." He paused. "Donald doubled it; a draw from Justine's funds. I kicked in some of mine as well, since this has to be the last one. Twenty-five thousand dollars. A pittance, unfortunately."

Gabe peered in the bag, whistling softly. Ever since he'd stopped being a Martiniere he'd gained a greater appreciation for any amount of cash. Like Serg, *Gabriel Martiniere* would have considered twenty-five thousand dollars to be a trifle, throwaway money for a mildly extravagant weekend.

For *Gabe Ramirez*, it was a windfall.

"Twenty-five is a *huge* help, Serg." Twenty-five thousand dollars could hold them until the fall grain sales, if nothing went wrong.

Serg sighed. "Yeah. I can tell you need it. You're looking scrawny these days. Worse than you used to get at Christmas."

"Trying to route most of the food to the wife with the baby coming," Gabe said. He knew he'd lost weight, between shouldering most of the winter ranch work to spare both Ruby and Ron, and cutting back on his own food so there'd be more for them.

Serg winced at that. "Gabe. Look. Maybe you should come back to the Family. You do have allies. Is this really worth it? It'd be a better life for your wife and child."

"My father had allies. It didn't stop the plane crashing and killing him, my mother, and my sister. I don't want to risk *my* wife and child."

"You'd rather starve instead."

Gabe shrugged. "I've gotten used to living poor and on short rations. How likely is it that Joey has some idea that you're seeing me?" Time to change the subject. No going back. Not until he had more power, and that wasn't going to happen anytime soon.

"I think Joey's just trying to find a way to take control of security. As long as Dad and I stay safe, he doesn't have an opening. Justine's also been having followers tracking her movements."

His phone rang. Gabe glanced at the caller ID. Vickie Chandler. A chill washed over him. That meant problems at home.

"Gotta take this, Serg. Home stuff." He activated the privacy shield and turned away. "What's up?"

"Where are you, Gabe?" Vickie's voice was strained.

"Taking care of some business in Pendleton." God, at least he had the excuse of getting supplies.

"You need to get your butt back here fast. Ruby's in labor—has been for a while—and she won't leave the ranch until you get home."

"Damn it." Sometimes his redheaded darling could be so fucking stubborn. And this was three weeks early. "Put her on. She's gotta go to the hospital for the baby's sake."

"Gabe, I can't. She's too far along and she says you don't have the money."

"Damn it, tell her we have the money. I collected on a debt. I've got the money now. Cash. She can go to the hospital. We can afford it."

"I'll try," Vickie said, a dubious tone in her voice. "But she's close to being able to push. Eight centimeters dilated and fully effaced."

"I'm on my way." Gabe hung up and took a deep breath. Two hours away, and most of those on side roads. It wouldn't do any good to let his emotions get control, much as he wanted to fly to Ruby's side. Too easy to make a betraying mistake. Damn it, damn it, damn it.

He spun around. "I've gotta go, Serg. The wife's in early labor."

Serg nodded. "Got it. Give me five minutes to pull away followers."

"Wait. I need to give you something." He strode to his truck, pulled out the two envelopes, duplicates of the one he'd left with Remy Trask. He handed them to Serg. "Keep these safe. Don't open them unless I'm dead and you've confirmed it. Give the other one to Justine if that happens. They're—instructions for my wife. Just in case."

Serg eyed him. "Establishing her claim against the estate for the Family Trust?"

Gabe nodded. "For her and our son. A copy is with her lawyer as well. I signed prenups that should protect her from Philip, but she'll need the rest of this to collect anything from the Family Trust."

"I'll keep it safe."

"Thanks."

They shook hands again. "Good luck, Gabe." Serg ran to his rig, jumped in, and took off.

Gabe gave himself fifteen minutes instead of the five Serg suggested. Just to be safe. He took the time to carefully obscure his tracks with a rake he'd brought along for that purpose, making himself move slowly and precisely rather than rush. Then he dawdled while leaving the campground, checking for followers, the precious bag of money on the seat next to him. Instead of the main highway, he took several backroads to Thunder County. It added half an hour to his drive time, but it couldn't be helped. Not if he wanted to keep his loved ones safe.

Once he was through the river canyon and in Thunder County proper, Gabe floorboarded the accelerator and called Vickie.

"I'm in the County. Has Ruby gone to the hospital?"

"No. Dr. Sheri's here." He heard Ruby screaming in the background and his heart caught for a moment. He should be there.

He should be there.

Well, at least Dr. Sheri had come to the ranch. That was something.

"Can you contact Sheriff Rivers, let him know what is going on? I'd just as soon not deal with a traffic stop." Vickie was the leader of the Thunder County civilian Home Guard, and Jerry Rivers should be willing to listen to her, when he wouldn't acknowledge Gabe.

"Done." Vickie rang off.

It seemed to take forever to get to and then through Lakeside, the little town close to the ranch. Once clear, Gabe drove as fast as possible on the gravel road leading to the Double R. He raced up the driveway and skidded the truck to a halt next to the charger, grabbed the money bag, paused for a moment to plug in the truck, then sprinted toward the house. He galloped onto the back porch and stopped just long enough to kick off his hiking boots and hang up his coat.

Ron Ryder sat at the table, his usual place in winter since the kitchen was the warmest room in the house. "Where you been?"

"Business. Are they in our bedroom?"

"Next door."

"Thanks." Gabe tore up the multiple flights of stairs, money bag in one hand. He'd need to stick that in his safe tonight but right now he didn't want to wait. Besides, he needed some of the cash to pay Vickie and Dr. Sheri.

More screams from Ruby. Gabe burst into the bedroom they'd been preparing for the baby, even though Brandon would be spending his first weeks in the same room as them. Half-naked, Ruby sagged against pillows propping her upright in the middle of the bed so that her butt was at its end, eyes closed, breathing hard as Dr. Sheri knelt between her spread legs that were propped up on straight-backed chairs. Ruby's freckles stood out starkly across her far-too-pale face.

"Just in time," Vickie told him. "She's passing out between contractions, but the baby's starting to crown. If you can get up there and support her—"

"Got it." He dropped the bag by the bed, kicking it underneath, and climbed behind Ruby as she moaned, then doubled up, screaming again. "Hey, hey, hey, Rubes, I'm here. Breathe. Remember your breathing," he whispered, wrapping his arms around her.

Ruby groaned, then stiffened with a contraction.

"I'm here. I love you. Breathe with me." He could barely remember the instructions from the birth classes, and drew on his Martiniere training instead. Ruby gulped for breath, then followed his model.

"Atta girl!" Dr. Sheri's voice was soothing, steady. "Good, Gabe. Keep her breathing properly. Here he comes. Crowning now. Head clear. Couple more pushes, Ruby, and you've got it."

She collapsed against Gabe. "I'm here, darlin'. I'm here." His voice broke a little, because his love was *hurting* and he'd done this to her, and then hadn't been here when labor started. But she pressed her head against him. He kissed her cheek. "Sorry I wasn't here sooner. I didn't expect our boy to come this soon."

Another contraction.

"Push-push-push," Dr. Sheri was firm now. "Shoulders! Keep it up, Ruby, you're almost there!"

Ruby tightened hard. And then there was a faint little cry that grew louder and stronger.

"He's here," Gabe whispered in Ruby's ear. "Brandon's here."

"There you go." Dr. Sheri gently placed the still squalling Brandon on Ruby's belly. "Help her hang onto him, Gabe, until she delivers the placenta. He looks good for three weeks early."

Ruby gulped. "He's here." A sob choked her voice as it went deeper and she grasped him. "Oh, our little Branny. You're here."

Gabe steadied Ruby's arms as she held Brandon close.

Ruby quivered as she crooned wordlessly to their son.

"Dr. Sheri—" Gabe began, worried about Ruby's shaking.

"It's normal," Vickie said. She gently eased Brandon from Ruby's arms. "Let me get him cleaned up. Then you can hold him, Gabe, while we take care of Ruby."

Gabe clung to Ruby while Dr. Sheri and Vickie checked Brandon and dressed him. Ruby sighed and slumped against Gabe as he kissed her temples.

"If I'd known, I wouldn't have left today," he murmured to Ruby finally. "When did the contractions start?"

"Last night," she said.

"Oh honey. Why didn't you tell me?"

Ruby shook her head. "You'd have taken me to the hospital and—" her voice caught.

"Ruby didn't call me, Ron did," Vickie said, bringing Brandon back. "Her water broke, and she was on hands and knees in the kitchen, going through hard, frequent contractions when I got here. By then she was pretty far along. That's when I called you."

"It's all right," Gabe said. "I collected on a debt today. You could have gone to the hospital, Ruby." His gut clenched hard. What if something had gone wrong?

Fuck it. I should have gone back to the Family once I knew Ruby was pregnant. Then I wouldn't have risked losing Ruby and Brandon in childbirth.

But even as he thought that, the memory of the three coffins in the church at his family's funeral Mass came back. Being the Martiniere hadn't saved Saul's family.

Philip would not take Brandon's existence lightly. Gabe's son would be another high-level Martiniere heir—and competition for Joey. A threat to both Joey and Philip. Gabe tightened his grip on Ruby.

He did *not* want to see his new little family dead.

"Okay, Gabe. Here's your boy. Despite being a preemie, he's pretty good-sized. Easier on Ruby that he was early," Vickie said.

Gabe slid off of the bed and cautiously, carefully, took Brandon into his arms, studying his son's face.

Brown skin maybe a shade lighter than his, legacy of his Hispanic mother Angelica. Black hair—a common Martiniere inheritance. Brown eyes. And Brandon's features were clearly Martiniere, even at birth. Not much of Ruby. Another brown-skinned Martiniere like Gabe to piss off Philip's bigoted ass.

My son. Gabe stared at Brandon. *I'm a father now.* A rush of protectiveness and love surged over him. He would *die* for this child. His son. A little bit of him and Ruby in the world. His job to keep this child safe, help him grow up strong and bold.

Brandon deserved more advantages than he'd have as plain little Brandon Ramirez. And by God, he would find a means to give them to his son, damn it, without the toxic legacy of the Martinieres.

He just needed to figure out how to do that, without bringing down Philip's wrath on those he loved.

"I'm going to introduce him to your grandfather," he said to Ruby.

She nodded as Dr. Sheri and Vickie worked on her.

Gabe carefully carried his son—*his son!*—downstairs to the kitchen. Ron drowsed in his wheelchair.

"Got someone to show you," Gabe said. It was solid dark outside. Had he really been upstairs that long with Ruby? He thought he'd gotten here close to one o'clock.

Ron blinked and straightened up. Gabe knelt in front of the wheelchair.

"Ruby all right?" Ron asked.

"Far as I can tell, yes." Gabe eased tiny Brandon onto his great-grandfather's lap while holding him steady. "Meet Brandon Edward Mar—" he caught himself, because he *had* been thinking Martiniere. "Ramirez." Damn it, had Ron caught the slip?

"Brandon Edward?" Ron's voice quavered. They had chosen the

names of Ruby's dead uncles Brandon and Edward—both killed overseas during military service. Brandon Ryder in Iraq, Ed Ryder in Afghanistan.

"Yes. We thought it to be best." He was *not* going to saddle *his* son with any of the traditional Martiniere family names. Much as he'd like to honor his father Saul.

Dampness shimmered in the tough old man's eyes. "Oh. My." He reached out with a trembling finger to stroke Brandon's cheek. "He's a tiny little thing. I'd forgotten how small newborns are. We didn't get to see Ruby until she was walking, and she was our only grandchild." Ron exhaled. "A great-grandson. I wish Ruth was here to see him."

"Yeah. Same for my parents."

Brandon scrunched his tiny face, and whimpered.

"I'm so glad I got to see him," Ron said. "Brandon Edward Ramirez. A good solid name. But I think little Brandon wants his mama."

Gabe gathered Brandon back up. "I'll be back down to get you some dinner, okay? Should have thought of it sooner. Sorry."

Ron chuckled. "You were busy, and I managed to scrounge up something to hold me so I could take my pills." A rare smile twitched the corners of his lips.

The fact that the old man isn't complaining about dinner being late says something about how pleased he is.

"All the same, I'll be right back." Gabe carefully carried Brandon back upstairs as the whimper grew stronger. Voices coming from his and Ruby's room told him that Vickie and Dr. Sheri had gotten her moved into their bed.

Ruby had some color in her cheeks now as he and Brandon came into the bedroom. She was propped up against the headboard, talking to Dr. Sheri. Gabe didn't see Vickie but he heard her working in the other bedroom, cleaning things up. God, he hoped she didn't see the money bag.

"I think Branny needs his mama," he said.

"A little early, but he might want to nurse," Dr. Sheri said. Gabe lingered to watch as Ruby held Brandon to her breast. He latched on quickly.

"Good," Dr. Sheri said. "Pretty strong for a preemie. Might not be as early as we thought."

"What did Gramps say?" Ruby asked.

"He teared up when I told him Brandon's name," Gabe said.

Ruby smiled. Then she looked down at Brandon, and Gabe's breath caught. She—*they*—were so damn beautiful together.

"I'd better go down and get your grandfather fed," he said, his voice tight. "He found something to eat so he could take his pills. But I'd better give him more."

"I'll stop and check in with him before I go," Dr. Sheri said. "Save you a visit. Be right behind you."

"Thanks." Gabe diverted to the other bedroom. Vickie was gone and the bed was stripped—she had probably taken the bedding to the laundry room. The bag of cash was untouched. Gabe sighed with relief, retrieved it, then went downstairs and dropped it in his office before going to the kitchen.

"Sorry it took me so long, Ron—Ron?"

The old man slumped in his wheelchair, his left side sagging. Gabe shook him gently. Still breathing, but….

Gabe whirled to find Dr. Sheri. At least they already had a doctor in the house.

THE NEXT FEW WEEKS WERE A BLUR, BETWEEN NEWBORN, SICK ELDER, and winter ranch chores. Vickie Chandler stayed on as Ron's hospice nurse when he returned to the ranch the day before Christmas.

Gabe risked one last contact with Serg to send Brandon's baby picture. He was less cautious about sending the news to Craig and his other rodeo friends. Dribs and drabs of cash gifts popped up in Gabe's PayMeCash account—he'd never dared to use it for cash drops from Serg. Too insecure, but it made gambling and the occasional payments from friends easier.

Then his PayMeCash suddenly acquired another $25,000, along with a note.

Congratulations on the future Martiniere-in-waiting. Babies are expensive. PV.

Twenty-five thousand dollars. The traditional present sent by Family heads to the Martiniere when his first son was born. Gabe almost sent it back to Piotr. Brandon was not going to dance to Martiniere expectations, not if *he* had any say in it.

But Piotr *was* right about baby expenses, so Gabe thought better of that decision.

All the same, Gabe withdrew the funds—$35,000 in all—and closed the account, letting Craig know that he'd done that and to pass the word along to their friends. Safer that way.

ANOTHER LATE NIGHT, AND BRANNY WAS NOW A MONTH OLD. GABE *HAD* thought that he'd sleep better now that they had a baby. Brandon was waking them regularly but no, Gabe's insomnia still popped up like clockwork, every third night.

"Gabe," Ron called as he passed by Ron's bedroom.

"What's going on, Ron?" Gabe checked the monitors. Ron's improvement meant he didn't need round-the-clock supervision, and Vickie tentatively suggested that Ron *might* be able to get around in his wheelchair again soon. He'd regained his speech quickly post-stroke. Walking was still challenged and would probably never return. But Ron could move around in bed without help, at least.

"You running baby errands right now?"

"Nah, just wakeful. Ruby's finished feeding Branny and they're both asleep. I'm not."

"Good." The old man wheezed and shifted his position to sit up more. "Want to talk."

"Sure." Gabe pulled a chair up next to the bed.

Ron eyed him, and nervous tension tightened Gabe's muscles. He *had* thought the stroke had wiped out Ron's memory of that slip of the tongue he'd made when introducing Brandon. But what if it hadn't?

"I know your secret, boy. Have suspected for a while. Time to talk about it."

Gabe swallowed hard. "I slipped a few weeks back."

Ron shook his head. "Nah. I had doubts before then, *Gabriel Martiniere*, and that slip confirmed what I was thinking. You've been pretty cagey about it all along. Figured you had your reasons."

"My uncle and his son will kill me if they can." There it was. Flat, no gloss. "I've wanted to protect you, Ruth, Ruby—and now Branny." He paused. "Where did I make the mistake? Besides that slip of the tongue." He'd have to fix that. If he could.

"What happened to those raiders when you and Ruby came here that first Christmas wasn't the work of a man who'd only had summer training with the Vygotskys. Or military school. I did some checking around with my connections once you and Ruby looked pretty serious. Found out that Gabriel Martiniere and Gabe Ramirez were roommates at Northview Military. That made things interesting, especially when Gabe Ramirez's history got kinda foggy after he was sent to Brazil, before he suddenly popped up on the rodeo circuit." Ron coughed again. "But it wasn't just that. I'm around you daily. Everything I see of you matched up better with *Gabriel Martiniere* than Gabe Ramirez, especially as I got to know you. Your experience. The everyday things you do—caution about food and drink, for one. Programming skills. Defense and security skills."

Gabe sighed. "Have you said anything to Ruby—to anyone else?"

"Not a word until now. You gonna tell Ruby?"

"She's safer not knowing." Gabe stared at his hands. "I'm not kidding. Better for her that she's honestly innocent of who I am, should Philip and Joey catch up to me. One reason I was on board with that prenuptial agreement was to protect her in that instance. There's a sealed envelope on file with Remy Trask that spells it all out if necessary. Only to be given to Ruby upon my death. Certain things will—come to her should that happen."

Including the heirloom Martiniere emeralds that he had inherited from his father, in part an indicator of family power. He'd sent a matching envelope to the Seattle attorney who held the emeralds for him.

"How long do you think you can keep up this dance, boy?"

Gabe looked up. "As long as necessary, for Ruby and Brandon's sake. I *have* thought about going back. It's something I consider on a regular basis. But Ron, my family is fucking toxic. I'm deadly serious about Philip and Joey wanting to kill me. I have reason to believe that my uncle caused my family's deaths—I don't know why he spared me."

"You don't think Ruby can deal with it? She deserves to know."

"I go back and forth about that," Gabe said slowly. "Right now—no. Too much for her to handle. At some point I'll tell her."

"And that debt?"

"Nonexistent. A cover to explain why I'm in hiding, because if Martiniere bounty hawks run across me, they *will* take me." Gabe let a wry grin briefly tweak his lips. "But protection against indentured debt also works to keep the Double R out of Philip's hands, should something happen to me."

"You've chosen a hard road for yourself, son, considering your upbringing. But you hide it well."

"I've been running defensively since I was twelve." Gabe looked down at his hands again. "That part is second nature. I'm a threat to Philip's dynastic plans, as the son of the previous Martiniere. As long as I'm alive, as long as he and Joey are alive, I'm a potential challenger. Especially now that I have a son—and from all I've heard, Joey doesn't. The Family is very traditional in that respect."

Philip and his dreams based on being descended from the Medicis as well. And the Napoleon connection. He'd be King of France, given the opportunity.

"Are you saying you could be the *head* of the Martiniere Group?"

"Yes."

Ron shook his head. "And yet here you are, a dirt farmer on a ranch barely in the black. Damn. You must love my granddaughter one hell of a lot."

"I do."

"And no wonder you've been so good at financial management."

"I was raised to manage large subsidiaries," Gabe said. "But yes. If I returned to the Family, I could be the Martiniere-in-waiting, the potential head of the Martiniere Group and the Family. At the cost of putting a target on every one of us." He sighed. "I *can't* go back, Ron."

He stood. "Going to get a drink. If we're gonna talk about this further, I've got to have a drink."

It was a relief to finally be able to talk to *someone*.

Even if he should be having this talk with Ruby, not Ron.

Still, he dreaded the prospect.

In the kitchen, he poured himself a generous shot of the whisky that Monty distilled, instead of his usual beer. Gabe stared out the window at the barnyard, at the partially-completed lab that he and Ruby were building, in order to develop the biobots they were planning to create and grow in easily dispersed growboxes.

Ron's disclosure stirred up all the old questions. Was it really fair to Ruby—or Branny—for him to continue to hide who he really was? Put them through more hardship than was necessary? Piotr's gift plus the message suggested that there were elements in the Family who would welcome him back.

But the cost. Dear God, the cost. The paranoia. The threats. Watching their backs every second of the day, questioning everything around them. And what the Family would demand of Branny. He couldn't do that to Ruby. To Branny.

Gabe tossed the shot down his throat and poured himself another before he returned to Ron.

"You've been thinking, son," the old man said. "So I stirred something."

"Yeah." Gabe sipped the whisky, staring into its depths. "It's still— God, Ron, the life of a Martiniere is not all bonbons and indulgence. Ruby and Branny wouldn't want for anything, and that's what I keep coming back to, that makes me second-guess my choice. But the Family would demand that Branny to be subject to the same sort of mind control that—" he swallowed hard, fighting back the old compulsions that restrained him.

"So what you testified to was true." Ron's lips tightened.

Gabe exhaled as the compulsion released and nodded. "More than that. Those habits of mine about food and drink. Necessary in the Martiniere life. It was pounded into me from earliest childhood, and the lessons weren't always pleasant." He took a bigger gulp of his drink.

"Sounds rough," Ron said.

Gabe nodded. "Always on guard. And it wouldn't matter if I said I didn't want to be the Martiniere, that I just wanted access to Family privileges and nothing more than a life with Ruby here on the ranch. Philip's opponents would simply turn their attention to Brandon."

"I hadn't thought about that."

"I think about it all of the time, because that was the position I was in while growing up." He finished his drink. "I've kept loose contact with my cousin Serg. Vygotsky."

"So that part was true."

Gabe chuckled dryly. "I *did* spend the summers training with Serg, but it was the training that all Martiniere heirs get from Vygotsky Security. When I sent Serg a picture of Brandon—all he knows is that I'm married with a kid on the way, not where I am—I got the traditional Martiniere head of family cash present from his father Piotr. Twenty-five thousand dollars. As far as the Vygotskys are concerned, I *am* the Martiniere, apparently." He shook his head.

"That's how the hospital bills have been getting paid."

Gabe leaned back in the chair. "That wasn't all. Serg has been providing me with cash drops. That's where I was when Ruby went into labor—getting the last one for a while, because Serg was being followed."

Ron coughed. "But if you've got the Vygotskys on your side—"

"They are a very small branch of the Martinieres, and even though they're running the Family's security subsidiary, it wouldn't be enough support to keep Ruby and Branny safe. Too many loose cannons looking for a chance to wrest Family control to their divisions. It would be a life of less want—but much more danger. And that's what has held me back ever since I realized I loved Ruby. I didn't want to subject her to the danger." He looked down at his empty glass again, marshaling his thoughts. "If I could claim the Family money without the Family baggage, I'd do it in a heartbeat." His voice caught. "I've buried one family already, when I was twelve. I do not want to bury another."

"That's a tough decision to make," Ron said softly. "And damn, son, I understand things better now." He sighed. "All right. An old man just wondered. I think I'm ready to go to sleep, now."

Gabe stood and rested his hand on Ron's wrinkled one. "Thank you, Ron. I didn't realize how much I needed to talk about it. Especially after Brandon's birth."

"You've done good. Just—keep them safe, all right?"

"All right," Gabe promised. "On my honor as a Martiniere."

It had been a long time since he'd said those words. They felt right.

Ron smiled and shifted sideways, closing his eyes.

RON DIED DURING THE NIGHT.

Gabe bolstered Ruby through the funeral, burial, and the details of the estate transfer.

He kept thinking back to that last talk with Ron.

But it didn't change his conviction that he'd made the right decision.

6 / AG SUPERSTAR

JULY, 2034

Two o'clock.

Gabe snapped up his comp display to check the time and winced. He used his forearm to brush away the sweat dripping into his eyes as he drove the crawler at its highest speed along the track leading down from the big Homestead field at the top of the ridge between the Double R and the neighboring Reed ranch, raising a small dust cloud.

Late for lunch, but it couldn't be helped. He'd run into an issue with the center pivot irrigation line in that damn Homestead field, *again*, and it had taken him a while to get the problem figured out and fixed. Declining water pressure, and the programming that drove the line had glitched, triggering a chain reaction of things going wrong that needed to be repaired in the correct order for that pivot line to work. And it routinely went out every few days.

> Do you need help?

Ruby had texted at one point.

> No, it's too damn hot up here for Branny and
> no wind to speak of.

he had responded when he finally reached the sector of the field where he had connectivity. Overly humid for this arid high-elevation climate—he sure hoped that meant a thunderstorm with plenty of rain was on its way.

But much as Gabe tried to convince himself that he saw the faintest hint of clouds edging over the Thunder Mountains to the south, it just wasn't happening. And nothing in the forecast. Both Ruby and Branny were better off at the house, shaded by trees, with plenty of water. Homestead field was no place for a seven-month-old.

We need more help.

But there was just no money to spare for additional hands at the moment. At least now he was off the hook for a few hours. There were other chores to do but he wanted to take a break after working in the hot sun. Have some lunch and perhaps....

A wry grin pulled at his lips, softening as he cruised into the barn-yard to hitch the crawler up to charge and spotted Ruby in the garden harvesting produce. A big sun hat and coverup hid her upper body and she must have had her braid tucked up into the hat. But the coverup didn't conceal her long, slender, muscular bare legs—mmm, those beautiful, beautiful legs. Ruby must be wearing one of her bikinis.

There were *some* nice things about having just the three of them on the ranch.

Brandon's playpen was in the shade with the border collies Spot and Snip lying watchfully by it. Both dogs raised their heads as Gabe parked, but neither barked—they'd become very protective of Branny soon after his birth, and their silence suggested that he was napping.

Ruby picked up the basket next to her and headed out of the garden as he walked toward the house. She went through the gate and closed it—too many deer around to grow unfenced produce. Gabe brushed himself off so he wouldn't be too dusty, then quickened his steps to meet her.

"You got it beat?" she asked. That smile of hers still sent his stomach flopping like he was on a roller-coaster ride...and tightened other parts of him.

"Finally." He peeked into the basket, then took it from Ruby and set it down before he embraced her. Mounds of lettuce, chard, and spinach. Salads in their future. "Water pressure settings needed adjusting, and that kicked off other problems. Had to do a bit of programming on the fly." Mmm. She wore his favorite floral bikini underneath the coverup. It was enough to take his mind off of his growling stomach, especially since Branny was asleep.

Like minds. Her lips parted and they kissed deep and hard before she pulled away.

"Go put the basket in the basement and get some lighter clothes on," she ordered. "Your sandwich is in the fridge. Branny just went down for his nap, and I've got some things to show you."

"Mmm, so I see," he said, eying her. She freckled all over in the summer, and he loved it.

That sly smirk of hers with one corner higher than the other flashed quickly at him, along with his favorite dimple. "Only one of those things I want to show you requires Branny to be asleep. Go hydrate. Change clothes. Eat. I'll be waiting."

AFTER PUTTING THE BASKET IN THE MUCH COOLER BASEMENT, GABE gulped down a big glass of water, then retrieved the plate with his cheese sandwich and a few slices of wrinkled apples out of the refrigerator. He carried it upstairs, taking big bites as he climbed the steps. They were still on short rations, but the garden produce was starting to come in. And in a few weeks, they could butcher the feeder hogs.

Need to check the hog mud wallow water this afternoon, Gabe thought as he changed into cutoffs and a long-sleeved shirt he didn't bother to button.

A few final bites of the sandwich as he went downstairs, put the plate in the sink, then filled his water bottle. Gabe headed back outdoors. It *was* cooler in the shade of the big Jeffreys pines, or at least it was less stifling. Ruby lay in the shaded hammock strung between two of the trees, poring over a comp projection. Her hat and coverup rested on the grass next to the hammock, beside her slip-on sneakers.

Gabe glanced at the playpen. Brandon slept on his back, arms and legs spread wide. He only wore a cloth diaper, its pale white stark against his light brown skin. Gabe dropped his water bottle next to

Ruby's and kicked off his sneakers. Ruby snapped off her display as Gabe eased into the hammock next to her. She purred as he kissed her, her hands deftly undoing his buttons and zipper as he unfastened her top and slid down her bikini bottom. It took careful adjustments in the hammock but before long she was on top and he could admire her as they made love.

Afterwards, they catnapped together in the hammock, not bothering to pull on their clothing. The hammock and Branny's playpen would remain in the shade for another couple of hours.

One advantage of just us here on the ranch.

Especially on nasty hot days like this. Soon enough, he'd have to get up and go back to work until the sun finally set, just like Ruby would. For now, it felt good to rest naked in the shade of the big pines during the hottest part of the day. Branny was teething, and that meant none of them got a good night's sleep. When their son napped, Gabe and Ruby tried to steal what slumber they could.

Ruby stirred. "Hey. I may have found a new funding source that could help us finish up the growbox design, maybe even let us hire some help."

"Oh?" Gabe opened his eyes.

The lab was ready and waiting, but building the growboxes to cultivate biobots was the next step—and spendy. They couldn't move ahead until they got prototype growboxes built. Complicated technology, especially since their growbox schematics combined cultivating the biobots with using the growboxes to transport the bots to the fields, for simplicity's sake. Marketability depended on that combination of easy cultivation and field transport, and developing inexpensive but durable growboxes was tougher than designing the bots.

"Yeah. Game show competition, the AgInnovator. Different levels, but the most interesting one is called the Superstar Innovator." She snapped her fingers to bring her comp display back up. "Aimed at promoting new tech innovations in agriculture. If we win the Superstar, then that's two hundred thousand dollars a year for ten years."

"Huh." Gabe scrolled through the display. "Requires yearly recertification, and the payout stops if you show losses for two years in a row. Sure you don't want to do the Star Innovator or the Innovator instead? A much lower bar to qualify, and not as rigorous to requalify."

"We meet the criteria for the Superstar and it's likely to be less competitive in the early stages because the qualifications *are* so high," Ruby said, chewing her lip thoughtfully before speaking again. "And —this would put us over the top when it comes to the lab. The big issue would be the risk of exposing you to the Martiniere bounty hawks during filming—but since I'm the majority owner of the Double R, we might be able to slide by with you in the background."

Gabe scanned through the display again. It *was* tempting. If they could get the growbox prototypes working, maybe he wouldn't need to fight that damn Homestead pivot line so hard. Ruby's bot design was supposed to carry a load of microbials that enhanced drought resistance.

If.

"It's probably worth the risk," he said finally. "You're the better looking of us, anyway, and if you play up the rodeo queen aspect, then that might give us an edge."

"Probably would be better if I'd won Miss Rodeo America," she fretted.

"Eh, it was stolen from you anyway," he crooned. "That's my story and I'm sticking to it."

Before she could say anything more, Brandon began to whimper. Ruby sighed and pulled on her bikini bottom. "So shall I go ahead and apply?"

"Don't see why not," Gabe said as he dressed. "It's worth a try."

After all, he had no idea how long it would be—if ever—before he could get another cash drop from Serg. The connection had pretty much dried up. Serg hadn't sent Gabe an all-clear that it was safe to get back in touch again. Justine was still in the middle of a high-profile divorce from Donald Atwood, and who knew how that affected the situation within the Family?

One thing Gabe was certain of, however. His uncle would be *pissed* about Justine's divorce, and if Philip was pissed, then that meant Joey would be as well. Perfect timing for Gabe to do something like the

AgInnovator, because Philip and Joey would be distracted by Justine's drama.

Or so he hoped.

- - -

OCTOBER, 2034

IT WAS NERVE-WRACKING TO BE BACK IN LA FOR THE RECORDING OF THE AgInnovator. Once Ruby's application had been accepted, the Double R biobot/growbox proposal shot to the top of the list. Gabe did his best to keep in the shadows, but part of their appeal was *young couple with a baby, ex-rodeo queen developing easily cultivated and transported biobots that any rancher or farmer can grow.* Branny earned them a lot of social media votes—a huge part of the competition, as well as the strength of their proposal. No one else had babies. And Ruby still had the looks that had helped her earn her rodeo queen titles. But his exposure was getting riskier all the time.

Plus, Gabe didn't like the AgInnovator owner, Georgy Batineau. He drooled over Ruby too damn much. Batineau reminded him of some of the sleazier elements who lurked around Philip and Joey. On the other hand, Batineau *had* been helpful when the biobot prototype came out shimmering bright red, suggesting that they title it the RubyBot to make it sound catchier than the "Double R bot". And Batineau hadn't pushed for Gabe to be more visible, suggesting that Gabe lurking in the background with Brandon would earn them more votes. Gabe tempered his criticism of Batineau because he *had* made good suggestions, which most likely made the difference that got them into the finals.

So. Here they were, in the Green Room, finalists waiting to go into the studio to hear who had won. An outbreak of a new Covid variant in Los Angeles meant masking, testing, and isolation. Gabe didn't mind that one bit. A lot easier for him to hide his face if he had a mask covering it and a Stetson on his head. He was also nervous, now that they'd reached the finals. Justine's divorce had just settled, which meant—Philip and Joey might not be as distracted as he had hoped. Gabe had sent out a feeler to his last contact email with Serg to try to get a read on the situation, only for it to bounce. What the hell was going on?

Ruby tapped her fingers nervously on her chair's arm. Gabe jiggled Brandon on his knee, doing his best to keep Brandon distracted so he wasn't fussing at their masks or Gabe's Stetson. His gut cinched down tight. They were close. So damn close. All the same, if they didn't make it, then at least they had the paperwork all prepared to go to a bank for a loan. He had started to think that would be a preferable option. No more monitoring or cameras.

One of their competitors, Mariah Meyers, really worried him. She had the kind of easy tech tracking blockchain chips for farm-to-table production that would garner audience appeal. And while Ruby still possessed that rodeo queen glamor, he feared that Mariah's polished, sophisticated, urbane look would draw more audience votes. Her outfits were bespoke, high-end designer. He recognized the quality—it was what the Martiniere women wore. *Somebody* had invested a lot of money in Mariah, because her appearance sure didn't match her story of rising from working-class origins.

Ruby's rodeo outfits were lovely and right on brand, but would they play to the mostly-urban voting audience? Or would Mariah's polish dazzle them?

Maybe they should have gone for the Star Innovator or the regular Innovator.

And speak of the devil—Mariah Meyers minced toward them. Neatly-sculpted, shoulder-length white-blond hair that clearly was the result of weekly salon visits. Sleeveless, form-fitting white sheath dress that sparkled, with an elegant matching mask. White stiletto pumps. Something about Meyers screamed *Martiniere-owned* to Gabe, but he couldn't explain why. Perhaps because she resembled the indentured, body-modded hookers that his cousin Joey preferred. God only knew she looked enough like the entourages he'd glimpsed around Philip and Joey to set off every fucking alarm bell Gabe possessed.

"So this is your little cutie," Mariah crooned, squatting in front of Gabe and Brandon. "Hey, there, kiddo." She poked at Brandon.

"Hey!" Gabe snapped. "Social distance."

Brandon wailed at Gabe's sudden sharp tone. Mariah flinched back.

"Yes, that's our son," Ruby said as Gabe stood, pulling Brandon close to his chest to soothe him.

Mariah rose. "That's going to be hard to compete against," she said. "Unfair advantage."

"I'm not planning to take him on stage," Gabe said. He hummed wordlessly to fussy Brandon as he jiggled him.

"Oh really?" Mariah arched her chiseled brows as Georgy Batineau joined them.

"You're not taking this little guy on stage?" Batineau said, eying Ruby lecherously.

"I'd just as soon not have him in the studio, with the Covid," Ruby said. She ran her fingers through her hair and adjusted her tan Stetson with Thunder County Days insignia embroidered on the crown. Vickie Chandler had donated matching Thunder County Days masks to Gabe and Ruby especially for the AgInnovator.

"You wouldn't have to have him out there for long. You might want to consider that, Ruby. Right now, it's a three-way tie in the clicks."

Gabe and Ruby exchanged glances. Gabe shrugged in surrender.

"Sure," he said. "But we'll stand in the back near the door for ventilation's sake, and only come forward during the introduction."

"That works." Batineau beamed at them. "Star Innovators up in five. Ten minutes for you."

He strode away.

Mariah smirked at Ruby. "May the best woman win." She minced off.

"We'll see about that," Ruby growled. "You sure about this, Gabe?"

"I'll keep my hat low and Brandon high on my chest," he said. "With any luck everyone will be looking at the kid. We can pull it off, Rubes. I know we can." But his voice carried a confidence he didn't really feel.

Your wife and child are your weak spot, Gabriel.

Couldn't be helped, now.

With any luck, he'd find a way to keep Ruby and little Branny safe from Philip.

It was time to go into the studio. Ruby patted Gabe's shoulder and Brandon's back before stepping out with Mariah and the other competitors. Brandon fussed and Gabe murmured softly to him as he paced back and forth behind the others, doing his best to prevent his son from erupting into a full-voiced squall. He winced as he spotted a camera focusing on him and Brandon and bent his head so that his face was more obscured.

Applause. Gabe hadn't been paying attention to Batineau's patter, but suddenly one of the assistants—an indentured with a blue-green AgI ownership diamond tattooed on her hand—stopped in front of him.

"They need you out front," she said. "For the announcement."

Gabe inhaled sharply. Did that mean—

He strode out and stood behind Ruby, half-turned away from the cameras blazing on them.

"And I'm thrilled to announce the winners of our Superstar Innovator," Batineau said.

Winners, plural.

Gabe's gut tightened even more. That ruled Mariah out—confirmed by her angry glare toward them. But there was another couple in the mix besides him and Ruby....

"Our rodeo queen and her husband are your Superstar AgInnovators for 2034, with the RubyBot! Give Ruby, Gabe, and their baby Brandon a hand!"

Brandon erupted into a full-voiced squall and Gabe was happy to focus on his son as the cheers rose. If he tried to kiss Ruby right now, he wasn't sure he could keep his hat from flying, and besides, he didn't like kissing through masks.

It was a relief to know that social distancing would keep them from any big post-show parties. There were interviews to do the next day, but Gabe let Ruby handle those, hovering in the background with Brandon.

One interviewer tried to press Gabe to say more.

Ruby intervened. "My husband is a very private person, and I respect his wishes. I speak for both of us."

At last, they flew back to Portland, then drove as far as Craig's ranch near Pendleton to spend the night, rather than chance the Blue Mountains after dark during an early winter blizzard.

"You two," Craig said, shaking his head as they shared a congratulatory drink once Brandon was put to bed. "So what are you going to do with all that money?"

"Several growbox prototypes," Gabe said.

"And hiring help," Ruby added. "Then figure out where to house them."

"What kind of help do you need?" Craig asked.

Gabe and Ruby exchanged glances. They'd been talking about that while driving from Portland—what they could afford, what would free both of them up the most, what got them the most bang for the buck.

"We need a lab manager," Ruby said. "Not so much a programmer but someone with a stronger biology background than we have." She grimaced. "Bot programming, Gabe and I can handle. The bio part is our challenge. We can design it, but managing the growth mediums in the growboxes...."

"And a ranch manager," Gabe added. "I'm doing my best to keep Ruby from getting overloaded. Sometimes I've got to pull her off of programming to work the fields."

"We need you on programming as well," Ruby said.

"You said housing's available?" Craig rubbed his chin thoughtfully.

"One small two-bedroom house and a bunkhouse," Ruby said. "Left over from the old days. We'd have to clean up the bunkhouse and modify that for one person, unless they want to share the house."

"I do know of a couple," Craig said. "It's an odd combination of skills, and they just got married. Remember Charlie Thompson, Gabe?"

"Pretty decent roper," Gabe said. "Good person."

Craig nodded. "He got together with an ag biologist and they're having problems finding jobs in the same area. Martin McVey-Thompson. Let me talk to them."

"I've heard of McVey," Ruby said slowly. "I'd grab him in a heartbeat for the lab."

"I'll give them a call," Craig repeated.

THINGS CHANGED QUICKLY AT THE DOUBLE R ONCE CHARLIE AND MARTIN moved in.

But perfecting the growboxes, even with good money, proved to be a challenge. There were no leisurely midday breaks in the hammock that summer, and it wasn't just lack of privacy. Toddler Brandon didn't sleep as much, and Gabe and Ruby kept wrestling with the programming and the growth mediums for the RubyBots.

Busy times. But good, in their own way. Working hard, both mentally and physically. Raising Brandon. Sneaking out to ride Ranger and a couple of the other horses, sometimes with Ruby, sometimes with Charlie.

All the same, the growboxes and growth mediums continued to be a problem.

OCTOBER, 2035

SCHMOOZING WAS MUCH MORE IMPORTANT FOR THIS SUPERSTAR production, especially since they didn't meet the development progress benchmark. Barely missed, but it was a problem. Next year was make or break—otherwise, while they'd be able to keep the first three years of cash, there wouldn't be any more coming.

This time around, there also weren't any masks or social distancing. Vickie Chandler's middle daughter Renee took time away from college to watch Brandon in their hotel room the night of the Superstar events—a dinner beforehand, the taping, and the afterparty.

Gabe slunk around in the shadows as best as possible at all of the events.

It didn't help Gabe's nerves that Philip showed up for the afterparty.

Nor that he saw Ruby talking to Philip while he dodged his uncle.

"What did Martiniere want?" he demanded of Ruby as they took a rideshare back to their hotel room.

Ruby frowned thoughtfully. "It was weird. He was very interested in the base programming, not the RubyBot itself or the growboxes. He got kinda angry when I told him the coding was proprietary, and I wouldn't share it with the Martiniere Group or anyone else. It didn't make sense, especially since he supposedly was interested in distribution and not manufacture. And he kept touching me." She shivered. "He's a nasty, awful, lecherous old man. He gave me the creeps."

Gabe wrapped his hand tightly around hers.

Why is Philip putting the moves on Ruby?

"Do you think he might be trying to steal our coding?"

"By itself the coding's not that unusual," Ruby said, chewing her lower lip. "The RubyBot's value is in the biobot variants, the growth medium, and the growboxes. It's a package. What on earth would he want with our codes?"

"I sure as hell wish I knew," Gabe muttered. His heart pounded hard in his ears.

Fuck. Fuck. Fuck.

His lovemaking that night was driven by fear, seeking comfort in Ruby's arms.

What the hell do I do now?

THEY TOOK BRANDON WITH THEM TO THE FINAL BREAKFAST EVENT THE next morning, planning to leave for the airport right after that. Philip sat two tables away from Gabe and Ruby, with Mariah Meyers (who had earned her own Superstar title that year) and Georgy Batineau. While Gabe focused on Brandon and Ruby, he did his best to watch Philip out of the corner of his eye. From what he could see, both

Batineau and Philip flirted with Mariah, the ensemble occasionally breaking out in intimate-sounding chuckles.

Luckily more attention was on Brandon rather than Gabe or Ruby. His big dark brown eyes, curly black hair against light brown skin, and cheery temperament entranced a lot of people. Branny flirted with all the adults at the table, as polite as an almost-two-year-old was capable of being when he was the center of attention.

"Daddy, gotta go pee-pee," Brandon announced in a loud, high-pitched voice when breakfast was almost over.

Ruby rolled her eyes, smiling as Gabe forced a grin. Philip was looking at them.

"I guess Daddy's got a job to do," he said softly, and gathered Brandon out of the high chair.

Normally, he'd let Branny walk, but he wanted to get out of Philip's sight as soon as possible. The scars on his back ached as he carried Brandon out of the banquet room, as if Philip's gaze had opened them up all over again.

He took Brandon in the stall to pee, and got him cleaned up.

"Wanna walk," Branny said as they left the restroom.

"Branny, I don't think—"

"*Gabriel.*" Philip's voice came from behind them.

Gabe stiffened, then swept Branny up into his arms. He strode away from the bathroom as Brandon struggled to get down, whimpering his way into a tantrum.

"Shh, not now, Branny," he murmured. Just a few steps away from the door. Just a few steps, if he could get Branny calmed down—

"*Gabriel.*" A sharper tone. The next one could well be his code phrase, and if it were…oh God, Branny was in his arms. If Philip wanted to grab him….

Gabe whirled to face Philip as Branny's cries grew louder. "You stay the *fuck* away from me and my family. Hear me? *Stay the fuck away.* I'm not challenging you. *Leave us alone.*"

Gabe's harsh tone silenced Brandon.

Philip raised both hands. "Gabriel. Br—"

"*Lilith!*" Gabe snapped. A long shot that the code Piotr had given him would work, but if it paused Philip for even a moment, that would give him enough time to return to the comparative safety of the banquet room.

Philip paused, then shook his head. "Gab—"

But the momentary break gave Gabe time to bolt into the banquet room. Things were breaking up and Ruby was standing, talking to someone he didn't want to take time to acknowledge.

"Let's go," he said to Ruby as soon as he reached her side.

She glanced at Gabe, taking in his expression, and nodded.

He made sure they left from a different door. Ruby didn't ask questions, fortunately, but snuggled Brandon on their way to the airport, leaving Gabe with whirling thoughts.

Philip knows who I am now. He knows who Ruby is and that I have a son. Fuck. Fuck. Fuck.

What do I do?

7 / FALLING APART

NOVEMBER, 2035

WHAT THE FUCK DO I DO NOW?

Those seven words loomed over everything Gabe did. Popped into his mind when he woke to watch Ruby sleeping. As he went through parenting tasks with Branny. While wrestling with growbox coding. Analyzing the growth medium. The long walks and rides he took (while watching out for potentially dangerous drone overflights) to wrestle with his dilemma.

And the media attention from their failure to meet criteria didn't help.

"Gabe, what's wrong?" Ruby asked while they were cleaning up after dinner, two weeks after their return from the Superstar. Branny played with trucks on the kitchen floor so they had to be careful as they worked. "You're as nervous as Sunshine used to be before a bad run."

Gabe swallowed hard. "I'm worried about Martiniere's interest in the RubyBot," he said finally. Brief, without getting into all the nuances. "I've been poking around to see if this is part of an investment pattern. He has a habit of buying out competitors. I just can't figure out how the RubyBot fits into that."

Ruby nodded, worry lines easing on her face. Good. He'd given her something to focus on besides his behavior.

"I've been thinking about that as well," she said. "You're right. It really doesn't fit his pattern. Unless the Martiniere Group wants to expand into our packaging—but that doesn't explain his interest in the base RubyBot coding." She frowned again. "Gabe, would he know that you're pursued by his bounty hawks?"

"No," he lied.

"But he could find that out if he wanted."

"Yeah," Gabe said. "Which is why I've been researching further security additions. We need to secure our fence lines and extend surveillance to include drone overflights. Prepare for weaponized drones, because Martiniere may try to cripple us before approaching with a cut-rate offer for the RubyBot. Martin has a good system going at the lab, so I'm not as worried about that."

"That's why you've been buying more sensors. Okay. What about the house?"

At least she wasn't dismissing his concerns as excess paranoia.

"The sensors are already installed." He was glad to have this excuse to talk about what he wanted to do. "But if we could spend an afternoon highgrading the programming that would be great. And keying controls to you as well as me."

Ruby wiggled her fingers to bring up her screen and check her schedule. "Tomorrow work for you?"

"Tomorrow would be *wonderful*."

"Then tomorrow afternoon." She eyed him. "All the same, you've been really snappish since we came back from the Superstar."

"Just worry," he admitted.

She rested a hand on Gabe's arm. "If we have to, we'll find a way to pay off your indenture."

"Thanks," he said.

Ruby turned to their son. "Hey Branny, time to pick up toys," she said.

"Do I hafta?"

"It's bedtime," Gabe said. "Hurry up and get your bath. I'll tell you a story."

Brandon pouted, but gathered up his trucks and put them in the five-gallon plastic bucket repurposed from barn storage.

"I'll be up in a few," Gabe said to Ruby as she herded Brandon off.

He sighed and stared out the kitchen window.

If only the issue was as simple as paying off an indenture.

If only he could reach Serg. At this point, he'd bring Serg to the ranch to secure everything—and tell Ruby the truth.

Serg's lack of response worried Gabe more than he could admit. It was one reason why he didn't tell Ruby everything yet. Why make her worry more than necessary, especially if they couldn't access helpful tools?

He considered contacting Justine, then decided against it. She was in the news often enough for him to be assured that she was safe. After her divorce from Donald Atwood, Justine had gone out of her way to be visible as a social butterfly, dating a higher-up in the Martiniere Group and a high-end Los Angeles real estate agent.

But that gave him no idea where she stood when it came to Philip.

Perhaps it was time to reach out to Piotr.

Tonight.

After Ruby and Branny were asleep, because God, he didn't know how much longer he could take this uncertainty without cracking.

GABE GOT UP FROM HIS DESK AND WENT INTO THE KITCHEN TO POUR himself a stiff drink, still shaken by what little he had learned.

Vygotsky Security was gone. Completely. No trace of it anywhere on the above-ground internet, and very little on the dark web. He'd found references within dark web archives, but nothing new since six months after Brandon's birth.

Fuck. Did Piotr sending me that money betray him to Philip?

Or had Piotr taken Vygotsky Security completely underground? In which case....

Problem was, things could happen within the Family, *big* things, and no one outside of it would know. Piotr, Serg, and Vygotsky Security could be dead and gone. Gabe didn't want to entertain that possibility, but it *was* one.

He tossed down the first drink and poured the second, taking it back to his office. He didn't need to get too drunk.

He was screwed no matter what. The most positive option was that Piotr had taken Vygotsky Security completely dark. But that meant contact codes changed randomly in two-to-six-week intervals. Gabe had been out of touch just long enough that none of his codes would be allowed. That would explain why he hadn't been able to contact Serg.

Maybe.

Gabe flipped over to tracking Justine. She would know if Serg was safe. He'd not probed too deeply into her activities before now because she was just too damn visible for him to risk contact, not unless he wanted to resurface.

A warning flared before he could poke around too far in Martiniere database accesses that he somehow still possessed. Yellow lights flashed.

"You have triggered Donald's Little Divorce Present to the Martinieres," Donald Atwood's recorded voice droned. *"Further investigation of Justine Martiniere's records will result in your systems becoming infected and destroyed. This is your only warning."*

A Y/N prompt flickered. Gabe tapped the N, then initiated a deep scan of his own systems to ensure that there were no trackers, nothing to identify who had been probing, much less infect the house systems.

Something was definitely up within the Family. But Gabe let himself smile, a little.

Was this just Donald being protective of his ex-wife?

He didn't think so.

What are you doing now, Tine?

This meant that *something* was happening deep within the Martiniere family. And that despite the divorce, Donald was still protecting Justine. A real divorce, or something strategic, part of something sneaky Justine was up to? He could see both Donald and Justine scheming to do that.

That ruled her out as a contact. Best that he not insert himself into the middle of whatever was going on with them. Justine would help Ruby if he were dead, but more than that—no, he'd better not try working through her. Unless he went public.

Gabe returned to examining other records involving Justine. He thought he recognized Serg's profile in a recent picture of her, and augmented it.

Yes.

So Serg *was* working with Justine.

That still didn't help Gabe, but at least his *favorite* cousins were alive, and to all appearances free.

What the fuck do I do now?

He *really* needed to talk to someone in the Family to see what was happening. Another possibility occurred to him. Gabe searched out his grandmother Donna. Was she still alive?

It took some digging, but Gabe discovered that Donna-gran lived at her estate near Quebec City, occasionally sponsoring event riders and horses. Few pictures of her, and what there were didn't show any improvement in her health status from what it had been before he'd gone underground. He didn't want to poke around in the Martiniere databases again—who knew what would happen next? Those damn databases were securely protected, and that alert from Donald's programming might be enough to awaken attention that Gabe wanted to keep dormant.

So, no contact with Donna-gran. Especially since it appeared that she was still sick. Not a good idea to access her.

Damn it. Do I tell Ruby or not?

What the fuck do I do now?

SUDDENLY, THE SLIGHTEST THINGS AROUND THE RANCH IRRITATED GABE. Fighting with the damn furnace because the nearest repair person was in Grande City, and booked out for several weeks. The perpetual obstacle of growth mediums not working well with the damn stem cells. Sometimes even Branny or Ruby.

Gabe paced the house at night. His main relief was the weekly run to Pendleton to pick up growth medium supplies. He occasionally stopped by Craig's place for a visit, just to talk to someone who wasn't Ruby, Charlie, or Martin.

"You're really on edge," Craig said on the Monday before Thanksgiving, as he and Gabe drank coffee in the kitchen of his small house. "Everything all right with you and Ruby?"

Gabe sighed. He and Ruby had been sniping at each other. His fault to begin with, but now the slightest thing not right exasperated Ruby. Shoes out of place. Flecks of hay in the kitchen. Misplaced lab equipment. Programming glitches.

Something was eating at her as well.

"I wish I knew," he said finally. "We've been at each other's throats more often than not lately."

"Maybe the two of you need a break from the kid," Craig said.

"Maybe," Gabe said reluctantly. Branny was the only constant in their lives right now, cheerful, seeming to ignore his parents' testiness.

Craig side-eyed him. "Usually when I see someone as touchy as you are right now, there's another person involved. Or something big blowing up."

"Another person?" Gabe considered the possibility for a moment, then rejected it. "Ruby's not that way. Neither am I." He paused. "Oh hell. Philip Martiniere started bugging Ruby about the code underlying the RubyBot when we were at the Superstar taping. Neither one of us can figure out why he wants it. That has us both on edge because —" Well, he didn't really have to say more. Craig knew the cover story that Gabe was on the run from Martiniere bounty hunters.

"Think he might be backchanneling her?" Craig asked.

That possibility hadn't occurred to Gabe. "I'd think she would tell me," he said slowly.

"She might be trying to cut a deal to free you."

Oh fuck. That would be even worse.

"I hadn't considered that," he said slowly.

He'd have to think about the right way to phrase a warning to her against doing that.

"WHY THE HELL ARE YOU SO LATE? I'M WORRIED!" RUBY SNAPPED WHEN he entered the kitchen that evening.

"I stopped to see Craig and the traffic was nasty over the Blues."

Gabe inhaled sharply because her tone yanked at him somehow. Almost as if she were accessing his mind control programming. "And Martin and I were taking extra care unloading this batch of medium. We're thinking that handling might be part of the problem."

Ruby scowled. He slipped by her and went to his office. At least Branny was down for the night, looked like. And he was in no mood to argue, especially since it looked like he was going to have to forage for dinner and he had a pounding headache. Traffic *had* been problematic with the upcoming Thanksgiving holiday, combined with a wet, gloppy, icy blizzard. He'd been worried about the growth medium freezing in the back of the truck, and had waited for Martin to check it before coming up to the house. While he'd gotten ahead of the storm, it had caught up to him about halfway to Lakeside. He had needed to creep along the road because of horrible visibility.

He heard her footsteps behind him.

"You could have called," she growled. "God damn it, I worry."

"I was all right! Things just take time!"

"You're no fucking angel—"

Without thinking his hand lashed out and he slapped her.

Oh fuck. She'd triggered his control codes.

Ruby landed a hard fist on his left cheekbone, followed by a punch to his gut that doubled him over. Gabe grabbed her hands and she kicked him, barely missing his crotch.

"Ruby, Ruby, Ruby!" He managed to wrestle her to the floor, doing his best to keep her from kicking and hitting him. "What the hell is going on?"

"I was fucking scared, all right!" she yelled. "I thought the bounty hawks had gotten you!"

Shit.

He sighed and eased up, rolling off of her and lying on his back.

"Sorry. Not just for not calling but for hitting you. I shouldn't have done it. I'm really sorry." Plus she'd gotten him *good* on that cheekbone. Maybe a little higher, in the eye.

Ruby propped herself up on her elbow, looking down at him. "And what the hell was *that* all about?"

Now was the perfect time to tell her who he was, but he couldn't.

His throat locked up involuntarily and he recognized the mind control programming at work.

What the hell?

He'd been able to talk to Ron. But not Ruby?

He coughed. "Pre-indenture conditioning," he said finally, when his throat unlocked.

Wait a minute. Ron had guessed it. He hadn't had to say the words first. Was that the key? How the hell could he ever tell Ruby who he was if his mind control conditioning locked him up? Write it down? He might have to resort to that option.

"Pre-indenture conditioning?" Puzzlement replaced anger as she stared at him. "I've not heard of that before."

"A Martiniere thing." Damn it, his own programming working against him. That had to be it.

"Aw, fuck, Gabe. I wish you'd told me."

"Just avoid using that word in an angry tone, okay?" He exhaled, shuddering. Why hadn't this come up before? Had Philip somehow gotten to him at the Superstar events?

Or had Philip somehow managed to program Ruby?

No. He had to stop being this damn paranoid. He had to *stop*. Gabe groaned and threw his forearm over his eyes, wincing at the contact. Ruby had probably given him a black eye.

"The a-word?" she asked.

He nodded.

She eased his arm away from his face. "Ah hell. I gave you a shiner all right."

He blinked, aware of the swelling. "Let me look at you."

Flushing that was already fading.

"You're all right." He sighed with relief. "Guess I just walked into a door."

"Gabe. Oh God." Now she sounded more contrite than ever. Ruby leaned over and kissed his face gently. "I'm so sorry."

"I hit you first. It's my fault."

"I didn't know that was a trigger."

"It shouldn't be, from you."

"Gabe, what the hell is happening to us?"

"Philip may have found a means to implant a trigger in you that sets off my programming, back when he talked to you at the Superstar reception," he said bleakly.

"No. Gabe, no." Her kisses became more frantic. She rolled on top of him, and, well…nature took its course.

But it was hard, angry, fearful sex, not the gentle lovemaking that had been their norm until now.

THEIR ARGUMENTS BECAME MORE PHYSICAL. NO MORE FISTS, BUT SHOVING and kicking, loud voices and yelling. Most of the time it led to sex.

Not lovemaking.

Sex.

Rough, hard sex, fueled by a mix of anger and fear.

DECEMBER, 2035

THE FIRST ULTIMATUM CAME A WEEK BEFORE CHRISTMAS.

> Gabriel. We need to talk. PJM.

Gabe deleted that message and blocked the source. That night he and Ruby actually made love instead of the aggressive fucking that had become their norm.

The next morning, Ruby woke him with puking. And her period was late.

This time the circle was pink.

GABE DROVE HIMSELF HARDER IN THE LAB AND ON THE RANCH. HE checked and rechecked their security. He didn't ride Ranger or drive crawlers on top of ridges when checking stock and fields, staying below the ridgeline, flinching whenever he thought he heard a buzz that could mean the approach of a drone.

The second ultimatum came between Christmas and New Year's.

> Gabriel. If you won't come to me, I'll come to you. PJM.

Gabe deleted the message and blocked that source as well. He tried sending distress messages to Piotr and Serg.

No response.

JANUARY, 2036

GABE ALMOST BROUGHT MARTIN WITH HIM ON THIS RUN TO PENDLETON. But Martin wasn't feeling well, and Charlie had his hands full with feeding the stock and keeping an eye on his husband. Gabe didn't want Ruby taking care of Martin, not while she was pregnant, so that ruled out bringing Charlie along instead. Too many bad bugs going around these days.

A nasty storm running faster than the forecasts shut down the freeway and alternate routes over the Blues after he crossed over. The wind-driven icy snow came down hard enough that Gabe didn't want to risk driving out to Craig's. Motel rooms were at a premium, but he managed to get a space in one of the downtown hotels with secured parking.

Once he checked into his room, he called home.

"Rubes. I'm not gonna try to make the run tonight." He sighed. "I'm sorry."

"The medium's okay?"

"I'm picking it up at the labs tomorrow instead of today. Talked it over with Jerry and he has no problem with that. Better than worrying about it freezing in the parking lot."

"Thanks for calling, Gabe. I was getting worried."

"Jerry and I kept watching the radar and road reports to see if there might be a window for me to load up and leave before dark. Not happening. It's just too big a storm to risk the drive. Should be better in the morning."

"I'm glad you didn't try to push it." Her voice softened.

"Daddy?" Branny's voice chimed in. "You gonna read to me tonight?"

"Afraid not, kiddo. But tomorrow night for sure, okay?"

"Okay."

"You think it'll be clear tomorrow?" Ruby again.

"Honey, if it's at all possible I'm going to be on the road home first thing," he said. "Stay safe. Please."

"I will." Her voice caught a little. "And you as well. It's storming hard—"

The line cut out and a brief flurry of panic surged through him. Gabe tried again. Nothing.

Fuck. But he got the same result when trying to call Craig. A quick switch to news revealed that phones were down region-wide.

All right, then. Nothing to worry about unless it continued into tomorrow. Ruby knew how to manage storms on the Double R, and she had Charlie and Martin to help. Gabe sighed and slumped back on his bed. He hadn't prepared for an overnight stay. No spare clothing and—most important—no food. No drink other than the water bottle he'd brought with him. *Stupid.*

He considered his dinner options. The closest supermarket was on the other side of town, a walk of several miles one way. The rattling of icy snow against the window discouraged him from considering a drive, much less walking. A night like this meant fewer people on the street. More vulnerability if someone wanted to grab him.

The hotel restaurant and bar should be safe enough.

Bar, he decided. *Less visibility.*

Besides, he wanted a couple of drinks, and if he sat in the right place, he could observe the preparation.

The bar was almost as crowded as it might be during the Round-Up, but the restaurant was even worse. Gabe found himself a seat at the end of the bar and ordered a straight-up whisky with water back, plus fries and faux chicken nuggets.

He was halfway through the nuggets and fries, skimming through the news on his comm, when someone sat next to him.

"Fancy seeing you here," Mariah Meyers said.

Gabe concealed his flinch. "What brings you to Pendleton?"

A predatory smile that made his stomach lurch spread across her face. "Checking out operations in Hermiston to pitch a tracker contract, of course. Flew in just ahead of the storm. And you?"

"Supply run and got stranded. Doesn't happen often." He shrugged, and sipped his whisky. This whole glass hadn't tasted quite right, but he'd been watching the bartender pour, and it had been ages since he'd had anything but home-distilled whisky to drink, so nothing was amiss except his taste buds. He thought.

"And how are the beautiful Ruby and your darling child?" Her mocking tone didn't match the words as her hand brushed against his.

Gabe blinked as things blurred slightly. He shouldn't feel like this after one drink. Fatigue and stress?

"They're doing just fine, thank you." His tongue felt heavy. Damn it. Someone had gotten to him. But how had that happened, and why hadn't he felt it until Mariah sat next to him?

That touch. But how did it happen without it affecting her?

"Worse luck for you, my dear *broken angel*."

Gabe froze, unable to move, unable to speak as Mariah's predatory smile widened. She reached out to stroke his cheek, then his neck. Something pricked there, right over his jugular. The world blurred even more around him, as if he'd had several drinks instead of the one.

What the hell did she just inject me with?

"All right, *broken angel*, come with me," she purred, then tucked her arm into his.

He couldn't resist as she guided him out of the bar. The duration of the code word effect without triggering a more dramatic reaction, and his ability to move under her direction, was something he'd *never* experienced under mind control before. More theoretical applications that he'd heard about but not seen in actual practice. And he couldn't fight it, couldn't do a damn thing.

She led him to a bigger room than the one he was in.

"Take your clothes off and get on the bed," she ordered.

The one resistance he was able to maintain was keeping his t-shirt on.

Only Ruby got to see his scars.

<hr>

IT WAS THREE IN THE MORNING, ACCORDING TO THE BEDSIDE CLOCK display, when Gabe finally came to himself. Mariah slept naked next to him. Gabe shuddered, a momentary fantasy of strangling her popping up, then fading as quickly as it surfaced. That wouldn't solve anything.

He ducked into the bathroom and wiped down with soap and washcloth. He didn't want to shower in Mariah's room, but he didn't want to put his clothes on without a spit bath at least. Who knew what the hell was on his body?

That done, Gabe staggered to his room. He thrust his fingers down his throat to puke in case he had something bad in his stomach, just like he'd learned from Justine all those years ago. Even though he thought it was the injection and the body contact, not anything he'd taken by mouth. Then he took a long shower, sobbing as his awareness sharpened from the haze blurring his senses.

Mariah was working with Philip. *Had* to be. And what he and she had done last night—had it been recorded? He had no doubt that it probably was.

Fuck. He was royally screwed now. And shit. No protection last night. Entirely possible that Mariah had introduced not just potential venereal disease, but additional control nanos into his body. More theoretical work that he remembered from Philip's labs.

He didn't dare touch Ruby. Not until he was cleared. That meant he had to disclose everything.

Gabe sighed. After he got out of the shower, he searched the room until he found a notepad and pen. He started to write *Ruby, my real name is Gabriel Mar—*

Spasms wracked his body, snapping the pen in half, ink spilling over what he had written. He barely managed to crawl to the bathroom in time to vomit sour stomach fluid into the toilet, then dry heave.

At last Gabe collapsed against the wall, breathing hard, hurting all over.

This is new.

After all, a couple of years ago he'd been able to confess his identity and write down instructions in that letter he'd left in Remy Trask's custody. It held all the information Ruby would need to make a claim for support to the Martiniere Family Trust upon his death, including a certified copy of his real birth certificate, the forged one from Serg and Piotr, and a copy of their marriage license.

This left him out of options. Mariah must have managed to load him with more control triggers.

There was the pistol secured in the room safe.

But that would cause problems for Ruby if she tried to make any claim on the Trust…an explicit suicide restriction which would keep her from collecting. And the publicity connected to the Ag Superstar would be horrific.

Not a way out.

Yet.

GABE WAS AT THE BIOGROW SHOP FIRST THING IN THE MORNING. THE storm had passed and the roads were opening up. Slowly, but opening. Gabe tried to call Ruby on his way home, but the phones were still down.

By the time he reached the Double R he felt sicker than hell, feverish and dizzy.

What did Mariah do to me?

He managed to help Charlie get the medium offloaded, then staggered to the house, waving Ruby off when she hovered.

"Isolate best," he groaned. "Keep you and Branny safe." Then he collapsed in Ron's old room.

He knew he was running a high fever. That Dr. Sheri showed up at least once, masked and gowned, and at some point, hooked him up to an infusion. That Vickie Chandler was there, checking his lines and vitals, helping him with a bedpan.

But he'd never been this damn sick before. Not even as a kid.

Faint memories of Branny whimpering outside the door, "I wanna see Daddy!"

And Ruby's voice, tight and tired and worried, "You can't see him, Branny. Daddy's bad sick."

He didn't want to fight it. Maybe this was the best solution. Death from illness. No one could call this suicide. And if he died from whatever this was, it might just keep Philip from harassing Ruby and Branny, while giving her access to the Martiniere funds that would keep the two of them safe and healthy.

***

GABE GOT BETTER. HE WOKE ONE MORNING, MIND CLEAR AT LAST, BUT weak. Besides a saline drip into one arm, a thick PICC line had been inserted into him—a process he didn't remember. And he was by himself in Ron's old room. Why hadn't Ruby taken him to the hospital? Money? Avoiding media stalkers? They hadn't had much attention this year, but that could change.

"Hey," he said, voice hoarse. "Anyone around?"

Ruby bustled into the room. She blinked. "You're awake," she gulped, and burst into tears, sinking into a chair next to the bed and taking his hand, burying her head in the bedsheets.

"Rubes. Hey Rubes." His voice shook.

"You almost died," she whispered, raising her head. "Too sick to take to the hospital, because you screamed every time that we tried to move you. It was—" she shook her head. "A combination of diseases. And psychotropics. Dr. Sheri found an injection site on your neck. Fits the pattern of some local raiders out of Pendleton—thank God they didn't get you. She's been pumping as many antibiotics and other meds into you as she dared. It's been two weeks, Gabe."

"It was—" and his throat closed down. He choked, coughing, trying to regain his breath.

He couldn't even say Mariah's name.

Fuck.

And Ruby didn't seem to have heard that he'd tried to say anything as she fretted over his coughing.

FEBRUARY, 2036

IT TOOK ANOTHER TEN DAYS BEFORE GABE WAS BACK ON HIS FEET. His endurance was shot to hell. He wasn't able to make the weekly run to Pendleton until the end of the month—and then he took Ruby and Branny with him, ostensibly for Ruby to give him a break from driving. And they spent the night at Craig's.

He tried to write a confession to Ruby on his computer. The resulting seizure flattened him for a full day.

The whole night with Mariah was blurry in his memory, and Gabe wasn't sure just what had happened. *Had* Mariah actually dragged him to her room and ordered him to fuck her? Especially some of the things he fuzzily thought they had done that made him shudder?

By early March, Gabe and Ruby were back to fighting. And he was going to Pendleton alone once more.

There were blank spots in his memory, and sometimes Gabe startled into alertness just before reaching Lakeside, only then realizing that he didn't remember a damn thing about the trip. But the compulsion kept him from saying anything, and he went completely numb when he tried to think about it.

APRIL, 2036

> This is your final warning, boy. I know when
> you go to Pendleton. Meet me there or else
> your wife learns what you've been doing, as
> well as the media. PJM.

GABE GULPED AT THE PICTURE THAT ACCOMPANIED THAT MESSAGE. Clearly him and Mariah. T-shirt still on, but...unmistakably him. Unquestionably her. And the date was last week.

He shuddered. Now he understood why he had those blanks in his memory. And since he couldn't tell Ruby the truth, he was fucked. No options, except that pistol—*no.* Not unless he was completely cornered with no hope of escape.

If he walked away unharmed from a meeting with Philip, that was.

> Name the place.

The address sent to him was on an isolated back road near the Umatilla Reservation, but not on it. The date for their meeting was April 1st.

April Fool's Day. Not fucking ironic at all.

The location was right on his route if he chose to bypass Grande City by taking the backroads. So Philip had been tracking him. Not surprising.

Gabe did a satellite view search. Near as he could tell, the only building on the site was a big metal hayshed with open walls. Damn near perfect for an ambush and murder.

And yet, he didn't dare duck this meeting.

That morning before he left, Gabe gave Branny an extra-big hug, and the same for Ruby as she washed breakfast dishes. She stiffened, then eased.

"What's up, Gabe?" she asked.

I might die today, was what he wanted to say. Instead, he buried his nose deep in the junction between neck and shoulder. Hopefully this lavender and mint scent of her might be the last thing he would remember.

"I wish we could break out of this rut we're in," he said instead. "I feel really bad about my part in it. All of this stuff. I'm so sorry, Ruby."

She sighed and turned to face him, still within his arms. "I'm sorry too," she said. "Maybe we should check out counseling."

"The hardest thing is finding someone we can trust with my history." He exhaled. *In more ways than one.* "But I'm willing to try. For us. For Branny's sake and—" he rested his hand over the slight rounding between Ruby's hips. "Her sake."

He kissed her, lingering.

At last, he pulled away.

Hopefully he was leaving Ruby with a good memory after all the bad things since October. If he didn't come back.

"If—something does happen to me?" he said, still standing within the circle of her arms, looking deep into her brilliant blue eyes. "Remy Trask has an envelope for you. Only to be opened on my death. Nothing else." He choked, not wanting to break into tears. "Not disappearance. Not divorce. Death. Confirmed death. Only. No matter what happens between us after today."

"Gabe?" Ruby's voice quavered.

He leaned his forehead against hers. "No matter what happens next, I have loved you. Oh, have I loved you. Even during these awful last few months. I love you. No matter what you hear. No matter what I say after this morning, it doesn't erase this fact. I love you and always will. For real. Not an April Fool's."

"*Gabe.*" Tears in her voice. "Can't you tell me what's going on?"

He shook his head numbly.

She gulped. "I love you too."

Gabe tried one last time to tell her the truth about himself, but his throat tightened and he coughed, unable to speak.

Fucking mind control.

HE WAS FOLLOWED ONCE HE TURNED OFF THE HIGHWAY AND ONTO THE back road that took him to the meeting with Philip. The drivers didn't even try to hide it—not that it would be possible in the wheat lands. Gabe's hands tightened on the truck's steering wheel.

Have I done everything I could?

He had sent one final distress message to Serg and Piotr, telling them that he was cornered and forced into a face-to-face meeting with Philip.

No response, which was what he expected. If they were fighting for their own survival within the Family, it would be risky for them to help him. The only means he'd have for getting aid would be to challenge Philip as the Martiniere—and he didn't have the support needed to do that. But at least Serg and Piotr knew what was going on, and his death would open up their channels to Ruby.

He'd told them that much.

> Ruby Barkley is my wife. Brandon Ramirez is my son. Please answer any comms in their names. Please protect them if something happens to me. Exploit the Ag Superstar media to bring Philip down.

At last, he saw the red-roofed shed with the partially-covered metal sides. A big black SUV was parked next to it. Gabe swung the truck around in the lot and parked next to the entrance. Not that it would do him any good because there was no damn way to get out of this situation if he had to run. Not by himself. It was too open and isolated—and anyone hearing gunshots this far out would reasonably assume either target practice or varmint-hunting.

The other rigs pulled in next to Philip's SUV, except for one that blocked the driveway and not his truck. Gabe's lips tightened. One possible break. His truck could climb through the gravel road's bar ditch easily enough. He'd taken it through worse in the Thunder Mountains. Blocking the driveway wouldn't stop him if he wanted out bad enough.

Philip doesn't have country boys on his team.

That might be worth something if he tried to make a run for it, and actually reached the truck before getting shot down. While the back road apparently dead-ended on Forest Service land adjoining the reservation, he'd checked out the old jeep trails in the area. *He* could get through if needed, and he'd tossed a chainsaw in the back just in case he needed to create blockades or swamp a rough trail.

But he doubted he'd get enough lead time to exercise that option unless he drove off right now—and running wouldn't solve anything anyway. Nothing more than a final, desperate option to escape dying. If he even got that opportunity.

Gabe exhaled. Checked the weapons in his boots and his sleeves, as well as his holstered pistol. Then he stepped out.

Philip stood next to his SUV, surrounded by his security, his arms crossed. A signet ring that Gabe remembered all too well from past beatings was on his left ring finger. He needed to avoid it if he could—the damn thing often carried toxins and psychotropics.

Multiple weapons trained on Gabe as he walked away from the truck. Without being told, Gabe put his hands on top of his worn black Stetson and kept moving.

Security stopped Gabe before he got within thirty feet of Philip. They frisked him, taking his holstered pistol and the knives and derringer in his sleeves. They got the boot derringer but not the knife, and they missed the knife in his pocket. At least they put the hat back on his head. Then they cuffed his wrists, cinching them down as tight behind his back as possible.

Gabe raised his brows at Philip when they did that.

"So you're that scared of me," he taunted, faking bravado. "Even with the control words."

His uncle answered with a matching raise of brows. "You're in damn good physical condition and I doubt you've forgotten your training. You've always been quick as a rattlesnake. I'm not."

"Your control codes have a pretty damn good effect."

"True. But only a fool depends on those alone, and that counter of yours works on me. And before you get any wild ideas—my security has orders to shoot you if you try using it." Philip jerked his head toward the shed. "Let's go there."

"Can I at least get these cuffs loosened?"

"No."

Gabe followed Philip. Security remained at a distance, their weapons fixed on him. The shed was empty. Gabe took a deep breath, looking past Philip to the winter wheat fields, green appearing amongst the stubble, wondering if this was going to be his last sight. Before darkness. Forever.

Philip turned to face him. "So. You've managed to do all right for yourself."

Gabe forced a laugh. "Is that all?"

"Did you think that was all? No. You made a big fucking mess for me with the Family, boy, and it's not been easily fixed. I want you to repair it for me. Reprogram that algorithm you screwed up. Then retract your testimony in front of the whole Family and the press. Tell them you were wrong. Do that and I'll restore your income. You won't be able to become the Martiniere but you'll be comfortable."

"Really." Gabe wanted to laugh at the news that the nasty little program he'd used to derail Philip's plans was working and that Philip hadn't found a solution yet. But he didn't.

Philip glared at him. "Yes. Really. You screwed things up. I want you to fix them."

"The answer is no. What you were trying to do—what I suspect you're still doing—is wrong. I refuse to be a part of it. And besides, that court settlement was nothing more than a slap on the wrist. It sure didn't stop you from doing whatever you damned well please with indentureds. You made sure of that." He tensed, expecting gunshots.

"Then what about repairing that algorithm?"

"Still no." The longer it took for his uncle to recover the possibility of creating mind controlled indentureds capable of programming outsiders through voice commands, the better.

Philip shook his head. "Gabriel, Gabriel, Gabriel. The Family is deeply divided and you caused it."

"*Good.*"

Philip flinched but continued. "I expected this response, but had hopes that your parenthood would make you more reasonable."

"You keep my family out of this," Gabe snarled.

"Oh, that possibility ended a *long* time ago, Gabriel." Philip bared his teeth in a humorless grin. "So, here's another option. I want the base code for your RubyBot."

"It's not mine to give. Ruby designed it. It's her idea. I just helped with the coding. Besides, why would you want it? You have similar designs that could achieve what you need that probably work better than the RubyBot. Its value is as an integrated package, not the base code." A sudden flash came to him. "Philip. It won't work with artificial intelligence. Nor will it translate well to augmented body mods. It doesn't function that way. I ensured that."

"That's not what my experts say."

"They're fucking wrong. *I* wrote that code for the RubyBot. *I* made sure it wouldn't work with anything brighter than our field bots. And you know damn good and well I'm capable of doing that."

He met Philip's glower straight on. Pale, icy blue eyes that lacked the warmth of Ruby's deeper blue.

"And as for my family," Gabe continued, his voice cold and hard. "I signed a prenuptial agreement before my marriage. It gives me only ten percent of the Double R and any intellectual property devised as a product of the Double R labs. On my death, everything goes back to Ruby. You can't get control of the Double R or its IP through killing me. I *have* ensured that Ruby will obtain the keys which will allow her to make a claim against the Family Trust should I die."

"So she knows about you."

Gabe shook his head. "Your little blonde tool's tricks made sure I couldn't tell Ruby. She knows nothing about who I really am or anything about the Family. I've kept silent for Ruby's safety all along. But Serg and Piotr have been informed who she is to me and that I'm here. If something happens to any of us...."

Philip flushed red and slapped Gabe. Gabe kicked at him, connecting with a shin. Philip yelped and four security guards descended on Gabe, knocking him off his feet and kicking him.

"Get him up," Philip growled.

Security yanked Gabe upright, restraining his legs. Philip slugged Gabe in the gut. As Gabe doubled over, Philip hit him in the face, grinding the signet ring into Gabe's nose. Gabe reeled against the men holding him as Philip hit his nose over and over, until it bled freely.

That awful, sneering, *pleased* smile Gabe knew too well from his beatings in the past spread across Philip's face as he pummeled Gabe.

Finally, he stopped. "You leave me no choice, boy." Philip's smirk deepened as he pointed his right index finger at Gabe. "Either you divorce your woman or something happens to your family."

Gabe snuffled back the blood dripping from his nose. "Divorce won't change the agreement I signed. Divorce won't cancel my death instructions."

"No. But," Philip said slowly, dragging out his words. "It will devastate and shred you. It will hurt you so much more than even the most painful death I can concoct. And I will take great pleasure in inflicting that sort of agony on you."

"*Why?*" Gabe groaned.

"Why not?" Philip's voice hardened. "You have one week to file for divorce. Then everything starts." He turned to one of the security persons standing behind him. "Once I'm in the car, Captain, you can cut him loose." He glanced back at Gabe. "Gabriel. I wish I could say it's a pleasure doing business with you, but alas, my only pleasure is personal. You have one week."

"I hope you *choke* on your damned pleasure, you motherfucker," Gabe snarled.

Security shoved him to the ground. One of them put a knee on his back. Gabe snuffled and struggled to breathe as they hit and kicked him some more, rubbing his face into the dust. Then his hands flew free and the knee lifted off of his back. Another series of kicks in the gut doubled him over. By the time he could rise to hands and knees, the last SUV pulled out of the lot.

Gabe shook his head and collapsed on his side. It took several attempts before he felt able to get back on his hands and knees. He tried to stand, and fell over. He lay on the ground for a while, breathing hard. Then he tried again, this time crawling until he reached the side of the shed and could use a post to pull himself upright. He leaned on the post for a while. His nose still bled.

Finally, he had enough strength to stagger away from the post and stumble to the truck. His weapons had been thrown into the light skiff of snow next to the driver's side door. He wouldn't need to replace them. But he'd better damn well check to make sure they hadn't been messed with.

Not now, though. He *hurt.*

Gabe wiped his nose and slumped against the side of the truck, leaning his head back and swallowing the blood running down his throat. It was taking too long for the bleeding to stop. Philip had done something more to him. Probably connected to that damned ring.

Fuck. Fuck. Fuck.

He wasn't in any shape to drive very far. Certainly unable to pick up that damned growth medium today, especially if any media was loitering around. Definitely unable to drive home.

And oh God. Divorce. He couldn't—especially not with another baby on the way—*oh God. No. No. No.*

Gabe screamed as loud as he could, pushing every ounce of rage, frustration, and terror he felt into that anguished roar. Sobs racked his body and he buried his head in his hands, leaning against the truck for who knew how long, until he was just too tired and hurting to keep crying.

Then, moving slowly and painfully, he gathered up his weapons. Put them in the back of the crew cab. Crawled into the truck and called Ruby.

"Rubes," he said when she answered. "Not coming home—tonight. Beat up—pretty bad. Going to Craig's. Should be better tomorrow."

"Oh God, Gabe. Should I call the sheriff?"

"No. Don't. Won't do any good. Just draw attention—that we don't want."

A moment's pause. Then, "Is it tied to what you said this morning?"

"Yes." He could at least say that. "Not over—either."

"Bounty hawk-related?"

"Yes." Oh God, if she could just figure it out. Not that he'd given her any clues in the past. Not enough to put things together, and she didn't have her grandfather's Army experience to notice that his security skills didn't match what she knew about him.

"We need to pay it off, Gabe."

"Won't—make any difference. Beyond that. Personal. Won't matter if paid off." He gulped. "Stay safe, Ruby. Don't—try heroics. Protect Branny. I'll be home tomorrow."

He hung up before she could answer, and called Craig.

8 / DIVORCE

APRIL, 2036

It hurt Gabe's soul to see Ruby run to the truck when he pulled up next to the lab to unload the growth medium. She held Branny. He rested his head on the steering wheel, groaning and shaking his head.

How could he do this? How the *hell* could he do this?

Philip was right. The process of divorce *was* going to shred him, damn it. He suspected that Philip hoped he would commit suicide—which would cut Ruby off from any Family Trust claims. It would have been better for Ruby and Brandon if Philip *had* killed him.

Which was the only reason that he'd walked away alive from that damned empty hayshed yesterday. He had stacked all the cards so that *Philip* wouldn't win if he were killed.

But Philip had figured out how to get around his maneuvering. *Fuck.*

Ruby passed Branny to Charlie and opened the truck door. "Gabe. Oh God, Gabe, you look like hell."

"Better than I did yesterday," he said, exhaling. At least he'd been able to wash up and borrow decent clothes from Craig, even if they didn't quite fit.

"I've got this, Gabe," Charlie said. "You go to the house with Ruby. She's right. You look like hell."

Gabe coughed. He didn't have the will to argue right now.

He half-slid, half-fell out of the truck. Ruby caught him, braced against his weight. God only knew she'd had enough experience helping him walk after they'd tied one on after a night's rodeo performance. But what really broke his heart was when Charlie set Branny down and his son took his free hand.

"I help you too, Daddy."

Gabe gulped and blinked back tears. With Ruby's help and Branny's hand in his, he hobbled to the house. Ruby guided him to the downstairs room that he'd been in while sick. She helped him into bed.

"Is there anything I can do?" she asked.

He shook his head. "I tried—Rubes. I really tried. Everything. Everything to protect you and Branny. And I fucked up. I fucked up so bad. Just—protect yourself and Branny. Stay safe. Please. For me. Just stay safe."

The kiss she placed on his forehead broke him. He burst into tears.

"You need me to get away from you for safety," he gulped. "I'll— leave when I get better."

"Oh Gabe. *No.*" She sniffled. "We'll face it together—whatever this is."

"I fucked up, Ruby. I really did."

"Nothing's so awful that we can't work it out."

What could he say to that level of trust?

HE TRIED TO FIND SOME WAY TO GIVE RUBY A CLUE ABOUT WHAT WAS going on. But experimentation revealed even tighter strictures on what he could say or write than he'd had before.

Clock's ticking, boy. Five more days. PJM.

Now he couldn't even hint to Ruby that Remy Trask held the documents that would tell her who he was. The lockdown was just that hard. At one point, Gabe went out to the corrals and buried his head in Ranger's mane. God damn it, he'd miss this horse as well as his wife and son. And the daughter to come.

You're a weak, lovesick fool, boy. Two more days. Is any woman really worth it? PJM.

Gabe spent as much time with Branny as he dared over that last week, memorizing his son's features, his quirks, his Branny-sayings. How Branny bounced up and down in his crib, arms outstretched, when Gabe got him out of bed first thing in the morning. Sounding out his letters—*already*. The way Branny mimicked Ruby's serious face when he focused on fitting his big puzzle blocks together, tip of his tongue nesting in the right corner of his mouth. Branny had his father's looks but Ruby's mannerisms. He was a smart little kid, and it tore at Gabe's gut that he might not be able to see Branny grow up.

At night he did his best to memorize Ruby's scent, that lavender-mint fragrance that was always hers. The firm, warm, pleasant sensation of her skin against his fingers that made him smile.

Gabe's plan was to make one last trip to Pendleton to pick up the growth medium, come back late, unload the medium, then fabricate a reason to go to Grande City that evening. He had packed a duffle with everything he wanted to take, except his weapons and data, tossed it in the back when Ruby was busy with Branny.

He wouldn't divorce her but he'd leave, and hope that was good enough to satisfy his uncle. It was pretty damn likely that their separation would be blasted all over the media. He could just see the headlines and posts now.

And maybe, just maybe, death would come his way without it being from his own hand. That was the best option he could hope for now.

Everything went to shit that last morning. The bot grow was touchy, and Martin was down sick again. Someone had to supervise the grow, and Ruby was late coming to the lab.

He called up to the house, anxiety and the desire to *just get it over with, damnit,* making him irritable.

"Where are you? This grow needs more medium. Gotta go to Pendleton to get more. Why aren't you here to monitor the grow?" She *knew* that Martin was sick and that he couldn't leave the grow, much less let it go longer without supervision. "I thought you were on your way with Branny."

Ruby gulped, her voice tight and tearful. "Branny's bad sick, Gabe. I've got to take him to the hospital. I think it's that new flu. I called, and Dr. Sheri says don't mess with the office, take him straight to the ER. I can't do the growboxes. Can you pause things?"

Oh God. They'd gone to a birthday party this weekend. Had to be where Branny picked it up—didn't it? Gabe stared at the growboxes. He needed to stay.

He didn't dare stay.

"I can."

"You'll be back in time to restart before the stems go bad?"

"Yeah, yeah, I should be back if you aren't." Damn it. Another thing.

"I don't know, Gabe. Kiddo's in rough shape. I'm scared."

And he had to fucking leave her, *today. Damn it.*

"He'll be okay, darlin'. Trust Dr. Sheri. She'll pull him through. I'll be back in time. Or you will."

He hung up and paused the growboxes. Then he took one last look around the lab. So much of his labor had gone into it. The RubyBot was a good product and would eventually work. God, he hoped that Ruby could pull it off by herself. But if anyone could do it, she could. His beautiful, brilliant Ruby. Gabe choked and rested his face in his hands, fighting back tears.

Damn you, Philip. Damn you to fucking God damn hell.

He gulped and rubbed his eyes.

By the time he got to the truck, Ruby and Branny were already gone.

So that was our last conversation. Gabe swallowed hard.

Before he pushed the button to start the truck, he put a block on his phone. He couldn't take talking to Ruby anymore, especially when he'd have to come back home and pick up his weapons and comp. That confrontation would be bad enough.

At least Dr. Sheri would take care of Branny.

He didn't dare consider any other possibilities.

AN AUTOMATIC ROUTINE TOOK OVER AS GABE DROVE INTO PENDLETON. After picking up the medium at Biogrow, he steered off to a nondescript diner connected to a cheap motel. He thought one of the vans in the lot looked like a media vehicle.

This time it looks like I remember the programming, he thought bitterly. Well, Philip had plenty of opportunities to modify the mind control programming as part of beating him up during that damn meeting. Just had to get some blood flowing—probably why Philip's security left his face alone until Philip punched him in the nose with that damn signet ring. One last jab from his uncle.

Part of his damn pleasure in watching me suffer.

As he walked into the door, the woman behind the counter grinned at him.

"She's in the back, Mr. Ramirez."

Damn it, they know my name, and why I'm here.

And lordy, was this place ever a dive. His body knew where to go even if his mind didn't.

Mariah looked up from her seat on the far side of a booth. He slid in across from her. At least she was shrunk in on herself, almost shame-faced. Was it his expression?

"I'm sorry," she said in a low voice. He thought she was going to say more, but then her eyes flicked away from him. Before he could react, his cousin Joey dropped onto the seat next to him.

"Good to see you again, *broken angel Gabie,*" Joey said, his sarcastic tone almost a match for his sister Justine's. Gabe swallowed hard. He couldn't move, damn it. "So you're still pushing your boundaries."

"I'm leaving her today," he finally was able to say.

Joey smirked. "Too late, cuzzie. You're gonna lose everything you hold dear. They're as good as dead."

"NO!" Gabe shoved Joey off of the booth's bench seat. He thought he felt a jab on his hand as he ran past Joey, heading for the back door. An alarm blared as he blasted through it but he didn't care, running hard for his truck. He was vaguely aware of camera bots following him, but he didn't pay attention to them. Only one thing mattered.

Are Ruby and Branny all right?

His vision seemed to narrow as he raced for the freeway, accelerating as fast as he dared.

Ruby. Branny. They were at the hospital. Nothing could happen there, could it?

Gabe gulped, half-sobbing as he drove. Only the faintest sense of self-preservation kept him from speeding through Grande City after turning off the interstate. Same for the small towns between Grande City and the canyon leading into the Thunder Valley. He raced directly to Lakeside Memorial Hospital, brushing past staff when they tried to keep him from the ER.

"Ruby?" he bellowed. "Ruby!" He raced down the line of beds—and spotted Dr. Sheri. A sheet covered a Branny-sized body and she was pulling a sheet over Ruby's head. She looked up at his yell, her face turning angry and accusatory.

"NO!" Gabe screamed, and turned to run back through the staff grabbing at him. He raced through the parking lot and jumped into the truck. The world around him whirled and glowed but he didn't pay attention to that. Instead, he sped to the Double R. Dumped off the medium in the labs without taking any particular care. Galloped up the stairs to sweep up whatever he had forgotten, primarily every damn gun he owned. On his way out he hit his office to gather up his comp and data.

Charlie stood in the doorway of his office. "What the hell are you doing, Gabe?"

"They're dead!" he screamed at Charlie. "They're fucking dead and

it's my fault, damn it! Maybe if I get out of here, they'll be all right."
He gulped, unable to keep from bawling. "Maybe they'll be all right."

Charlie grabbed at Gabe as he shoved through the door. "No, Gabe, they're *not* dead, just real sick."

Charlie wouldn't let go of his arm. Gabe dragged Charlie through the hallway to the kitchen before yanking free and whirling to face him.

"No," he gasped. "They're dead. I saw them! Sheets over both—" he choked. "Pulling the sheet over Ruby's head. And Branny—oh *god*, Branny—"

"They're *not* dead, just very sick. I just talked to Dr. Sheri. Gabe, we need you here."

"They're dead!" he wailed. "I saw them. They're dead, damn it, and the only thing that will bring them back is *if I leave*." He hated to do it, but he clobbered Charlie to shut the man up and keep him from interfering. Then he ran out the door.

Another frantic drive. Gabe stopped at a cheap motel in Grande City and checked in for the night, thankful that it was computerized and not with a nosy desk clerk who might notice his tears. Yeah, his presence would be registered. Like he really gave a shit now. No more necessity for those routines. God, he'd *welcome* the bounty hawks with open arms now. At least he seemed to have momentarily avoided the media cams.

It was only habit that made him drag his weapons duffle into the room with him and drop it beside the bed. He sat on the side of the bed, sobbing, rubbing his face.

Joey's words kept echoing in his head.

You're gonna lose everything you hold dear. They're as good as dead.

At some point his hands automatically went to the duffle and unzipped it. Pulled out his .45. As his hands slowly cocked the pistol and raised it shakily toward his mouth, a car horn honked in the lot. A fleeting doubt rose.

Charlie had said they were alive. *Alive.* Killing himself wouldn't help them now. If they were dead that would be different. He'd bet that Remy Trask would open the envelope in that case. Perhaps he should send her new instructions.

If I die and Ruby and Brandon are already dead, then open the damn envelope.

He fought against his muscles. His hands stopped inches from his mouth. Slowly, carefully, Gabe reversed the weapon. Ejected the magazine. Then the bullet in the chamber. Dropped everything into his bag and zipped it back up.

The room door opened. He looked up, numb, unwilling to react, hoping that whoever had come to kill him would make it quick, because he *hurt*, damn it. Ruby and Branny might still be alive, but they were lost to him, and right now he didn't want to think about life without his love and his son.

Mariah stood there. She grimaced and crossed the room to sit at his side, pulling him close. He broke into sobs again. She didn't say anything but pulled him close. Gabe was certain that since she was here, Philip was surveilling him, probably laughing his head off to see how he'd broken his nephew.

I hope you're enjoying the fuck out of my pain, you motherfucker, he thought savagely. *Because one way or another, I will pay you back for this. Even if it kills me in the attempt.*

Mariah finally shook him. "This isn't where you need to be," she said finally, her voice surprisingly flat, devoid of the control tones she had used to manipulate him before.

Not that he cared. He let her guide him through picking up the bags again and carry them out to his truck. Didn't resist when she eased him into the passenger seat.

He closed his eyes while she drove, and turned onto his side away from her as much as the seat belt allowed, still crying.

The next thing he was aware of was waking in the middle of the night in a strange bed, his head on Mariah's belly, sobbing from a nightmare about Branny's still body in a little white coffin.

GABE LOST TRACK OF TIME, THINGS COMING TO HIM IN BITS AND PIECES. Sex with Mariah that felt forced, a duty that he'd been shoved into.

Long blackout spells. Seeing mediacams following him in public. Blearily staring at his phone with a message from Charlie's number.

> Gabe. Where are you? Ruby.

He blocked Charlie's number.

GABE DID REMEMBER DRINKING. A LOT OF DRINKING, IN PENDLETON dive bars, with Mariah crawling all over him. Pictures popping up on websites all over the place.

Ag Superstar Dream Marriage Falling Apart, Other Woman is Ag Superstar Winner.

Another message arrived during one of those nights.

> Gabe. What the hell is going on? Ruby.

This time from Martin's number.
Gabe blocked that one as well.

ANOTHER MESSAGE, FROM VICKIE CHANDLER'S NUMBER, IN THE MORNING.

> Gabe. Your son is crying because he's still sick and he misses his daddy. Please call. Ruby.

Once again, he blocked the number. At this rate he was pretty well screwed in Thunder County. He'd burned those bridges for certain.

STILL ANOTHER MESSAGE, FROM REMY TRASK'S NUMBER, THE NEXT morning.

> Gabe. I miscarried our daughter and the bots crashed. Goddamn it, please call me. I know you're still alive because of the damn media. Please tell me what is going on. Please.

He didn't dare block that number. Gabe stared at his phone, then sighed, deep and hard, finally typing.

> Do not try to contact me. Do not try to find me. You're safer without me. Please listen. Don't contact me. I can't come back.

He sent that message.
The answer came swiftly.

> Fuck no.

He groaned.

> File for divorce for your own safety, Ruby. If you won't, then I will. What happened to you was a warning to both of us.

Gabe took the lack of response to be his answer.

He managed to duck Mariah's supervision and the mediacams long enough to go to the Catholic church in Pendleton. He lit a candle and said a prayer for that lost little daughter. Even though he still didn't believe anymore. Gabe collapsed on the prie-dieu before the rows of flickering candles and cried. At some point, a hand gently touched his shoulder. He looked up to see an older woman, dressed in Marian blue, gazing down at him. She looked like his mother.

Mama?

He wanted to hug her, but no, he didn't dare.

She smiled sadly, and signed a cross on his forehead. Then she walked out the door. Gabe gulped, oddly soothed.

He still didn't believe, but it sure as hell matched stories he'd heard as a child about apparitions of the Virgin Mary. Even if she was just an older parishioner who had recognized him from the media and not of supernatural origin, the gesture calmed him, at least temporarily.

Maybe there was hope after all.

MAY, 2036

ANOTHER DRUNKEN NIGHT IN ANOTHER FORGOTTEN BAR. MARIAH ON HIS lap, squirming and kissing as he stared at the television projection in the corner, trying to focus on whatever basketball game it was while pouring as much whisky as he could down his throat to keep him numb. And ignoring Mariah and the ubiquitous mediacams.

"Goddamn it, Gabe!" Ruby was suddenly there, yanking Mariah off of his lap. "What the *hell* do you mean by screwing this bitch all over the place, in every fucking dive in Pendleton?"

He stared at Ruby as the cams swarmed around them. She'd lost a lot of weight, skin drawn down tight over her face, dark circles under her eyes, pencil-thin braids hanging on each side of her face. She looked haggard. Older.

He coughed. "You look like hell."

"So the fuck do you." Oh, she was pissed. She slapped him, hard. "What does she have that I don't?"

He lacked the energy to fight, just shaking his head. Between what he couldn't say and everything else, was it really worth it? He couldn't explain what was going on.

"God damn it, *answer me*." Tears brimmed in her eyes. Oh God, she was *pissed* if she was on the brink of tears.

"Leave him alone, Ruby!" Mariah snapped.

Ruby whirled to face her. "And you. *You*." Her voice shook as she raised a fist. "I should beat the crap out of you. My son's lost a father, or don't you give a shit about that?"

Mariah blanched and backed away, shaking her head. Then she fled.

Ruby turned back to Gabe. "Well. You told me to file for divorce."

She tossed an envelope into his lap. "There it is. I hope you're fucking happy now, with *that bitch.*" She stomped out of the bar.

Gabe exhaled. Then he shakily got to his feet, paid his and Mariah's bar bill, and staggered to Mariah's apartment, cams trailing behind him.

That night he slept on the couch. Mariah didn't say anything about it.

He looked at the papers the next morning. Per the prenuptial agreement, all he was getting was ten percent of the Double R's income and any intellectual property that came out of it. And the truck he was driving, which he'd purchased with his own funds.

There were no provisions for visitation with Branny, and full custody to Ruby.

Gabe sighed and called Remy Trask.

"Your attorney should be the one talking to me," Trask said sharply.

"No money for a lawyer. I'm not contesting the divorce, except for one provision."

"And that is?"

"I want to see my son."

A pause, and then a sharp, bitter laugh. "Here's my instructions from Ruby. Gabe doesn't get to see Brandon until and unless he has nothing to do with that damn bitch Mariah Meyers. He needs to be living in a place of his own, not shared with her."

"It's not enforceable."

Another sharp, bitter laugh. "After the pictures Ruby's seen of the two of you, buddy, you'll be lucky to be able to get within a quarter mile of your son. Your choice. Your son or *that woman.*"

Fuck. Philip sent the pictures to Ruby.

Gabe sighed again, despair crashing down hard over him. "All right. It will take me a couple of days to set it up. I'll contact you with a new address. Branny's more important to me."

As he hung up, Mariah came into the living room. "I'll be moving out," he said.

"I was going to tell you it's time to move on." A crooked smile briefly spread across her face. "It's been fun, but my work here is done."

"All right." He wasn't going to call this fun, not at all. "Give me a day or so to pull things together."

He wasn't going to wonder what she meant by *my work here is done.* It was pretty damn obvious from the way she had acted that he was nothing more than a job to her, a task that she somehow owed Philip. A side gig that she could work while setting up her programs in Hermiston.

CRAIG WAS HIS NEXT CALL.

"I've really fucked up," Gabe said. "Ruby's divorcing me. Do you need a hand on the ranch? I'll work for board. I just need to get my ass out of the situation I'm in, and away from mediacams. An acceptable place that Branny can visit."

"Aw, fuck, Gabe, I'm sorry to hear that about you and Ruby. I was hoping all the coverage was just hype." Craig paused. "And you know damn good and well I always need a hand with Moondance. It's a pretty place, but a lot of work for an old man. Come on out."

They chatted for a couple of minutes longer.

When Gabe hung up, he felt as if a weight had been lifted off of his shoulders. The future still looked bleak without his gorgeous, brilliant Ruby.

But at least he could see Branny. And Craig was good company.

GABE CALLED REMY TRASK AGAIN ONCE HE HAD SETTLED INTO HIS OWN spot on Moondance. It was a separate little shack from Craig's rundown main house and would be freezing in winter unless he did something about it. He'd have to take meals with Craig, but from the way his friend's kitchen and pantry looked, Craig needed someone to step in and cook, anyway. Another means by which he could pull his own weight.

"I've got my own place now, such as it is," he told Trask. "Ruby will know the situation." He took a deep breath. "I'm working for Craig Yellowhawk on the Moondance Ranch near Blue Bucket. Living on the ranch. Ruby knows Craig and I think she'll find him acceptable company for Branny to be around."

"And Meyers?"

"You can tell Ruby that that damned bitch is *gone*. I hope to never see her again." Except for one last appearance at the Superstar.

Trask snorted. "I will do so with pleasure."

"Thank you." He exhaled. "And Trask?"

"Yes?" Her voice sharpened.

"That—item—I left with you. For Ruby. Protect it. Seriously. If something happens to me, it's safety insurance for Ruby. If something happens to Ruby and Brandon and I die—open it. Publicize what you see. Please."

"What the *hell* is in it, Ramirez?"

He gulped, gasping hard for breath. "I—can't—tell. Mind controlled. Pre-indenture." He choked and gagged, finally regaining control.

"Are you all right? Is it—Martiniere tech?"

"Yes," he rasped. "Pushed—the line."

Silence. "*Fuck.* All right, then."

She'd worked for the Feds in Los Angeles. He wondered how much she knew about *US v. Martiniere Group*. Enough to make a correct guess, at least.

He hoped.

Gabe and Craig settled into a routine. He cooked and cleaned for Craig in the main house as well as keeping up with the ranch chores, working with the pivot sprinklers and checking the fields, running the harvest equipment and supervising workers. Craig didn't run stock except for a couple of horses—nothing of Ranger's quality, and Gabe wasn't going to ask Ruby for Ranger. He wasn't entitled to take anything from her.

Gabe worried about his old friend. Craig hadn't seemed this frail six years ago, certainly not this feeble. Yeah, he was in his sixties, but Craig had taken care of himself—at least since Gabe had known him. He shouldn't be this impaired.

"What's going on with you?" he finally asked one moonlit night, as they sat around the firepit placed on the rocky outcrop at the tip of the ridge that overlooked the valley and Craig's lower fields. "What's making you so sick?"

Craig sighed and took a swig off of his flask. "Radiation exposure from working at Hanford in my twenties. There was an accident. I was lucky at the time but it appears it's catching up with me. Leukemia." He grimaced. "The tribe's doing what they can for me…damn it, Gabe, I'm really sorry about you and Ruby. But you living here means I can stay on my place. That's what matters to me now. I want to die on this land."

"Fuck. Damn it, Craig." Another reason to wish for his Martiniere connections, because maybe he could help his friend. "I'm really sorry."

"Eh, life happens." Craig shrugged.

Gabe looked down at his hands. "You've got the same sort of connection with the land that Ruby has. I—will you be willing to teach it to me?" His voice trailed off.

He didn't want to think about a future. At some point he needed to plot vengeance on Philip and Joey. But the pain was too raw, too near to contemplate what to do in the sort of calm, cool-headed manner that such action would require. He needed something else to consider for a while.

Craig smiled. "Gabe, I'd love to do that." He shook his head, face settling in regretful lines. "My daughter Sophie isn't interested in the place. She and her husband are settled in Seattle and don't want to ranch, even as silent partners."

With that conversation, a new partnership began, Gabe as Craig's apprentice. Craig took Gabe into the forest first, talking about the inter-actions between ecosystem elements. Taught Gabe to just *be* there, listening to the land. How the birds said their own names in *niimiipuu*. Learning the great trees that Craig's grandparents had planted, and the ones that needed to be replaced due to changing climate, and how to tell when to do that.

It was one thing for Gabe to have the knowledge from his studies in the classroom and on farmland in Europe and the US. Had started to see the practical application on the Double R.

But it was another thing to listen to someone whose people had been on the land for millennia, and had learned to live with the land, not subdue it.

And that was still another thing wrong with the approach that Philip and the other Martinieres frequently took. They wanted to conquer the land.

Not exist with it.

Gabe deepened his research into microbials. Moondance appeared to be an even better site for working with them than the Double R, given its greater ecosystem variety over a smaller acreage, and how Craig had managed the ranch over the years. Listening to Craig talk about the land gave him a more precise conception of how he might go about the process of creating the best ones for the smallest micro-climates.

Now he just needed funding to make it work.

BRANNY CAME TO MOONDANCE EVERY OTHER WEEKEND ONCE CHILDREN'S Services approved Craig's ranch for visitation. At first, it wasn't Ruby who brought Branny to the transfer spot in Grande City. Sometimes it was Martin, or Vickie, or even Trask herself. The mediacams clustered around them, but they gradually faded away.

Those weekends with Branny were the brightness in Gabe's life now, especially when they sat around the firepit.

No stories until wintertime, Craig said. *When winter comes, I'll tell you stories, Branny.*

But when Branny went back to Ruby, darkness collapsed around Gabe again. Despite Craig's presence, he was lonely once more, back to being Gabe Ramirez the footloose cowboy.

Except that he couldn't be footloose anymore. Even with the challenges that learning Moondance from Craig brought, Gabe still missed married life. He missed Ruby. He missed the Double R, and his son in the bedroom next to theirs.

And processing the damn divorce seemed to be taking forever.

OCTOBER, 2036

THE SUPERSTAR WAS HORRIFIC. IT WASN'T JUST THE DIVORCE HANGING over him and Ruby, or the media hype about their divorce in progress. Mariah gloated over both of them because she'd hit her marks for her second year. She embraced her role as the relationship destroyer. She flirted openly and outrageously with Georgy Batineau and Philip.

Gabe avoided them and Ruby as best as he could. Until he and Ruby got drunk at the afterparty and had a ghastly, screaming, fight. Which, of course, got them lots of headlines and clicks, trending in popular social media.

He had another blackout, coming back to himself in Pendleton, drinking in a dive bar once again, Mariah in his lap as Ruby barged in, screaming at them. With more media coverage, naturally.

Once he returned to Moondance, Gabe checked himself over carefully. Nothing on his neck. He ran his fingers around his groin…there. A tiny bump, that if he hadn't known better, he would have thought was a bug bite of some sort. Gabe rummaged in his things until he found a small hand mirror in his things and looked. Yes. No question about it. Once again, he'd been injected with something.

Mariah's still playing Philip's game, he thought grimly, with a shudder.

Well, at least there would be no more Superstar. He and Ruby were out of the competition, and he was glad for it. That chapter in his life was closed. He could only hope that media interest in him would fade away now.

NOVEMBER, 2036

CRAIG CAME BACK FROM THE POST OFFICE WITH A REGISTERED LETTER FROM Ruby. Gabe raised his brows, surprised, when Craig handed it to him. Then dread clutched his gut. What now?

The envelope contained a check from the Double R ranch account. $100,000 dollars. And a note.

Technically, I only owe you ten percent of this AgInno-vator payout, but even though you turned out to be a son-of-a-bitch, you worked your ass off to get us there. It really wasn't your fault that we lost that third year. And you're Branny's father.

The divorce finalizes on December 15th.

Gabe rubbed his forehead. He really wished he could remember what happened before everything blew up. Why had they divorced? He had vague memories of Mariah, Philip, and things going wrong. Of wanting to tell Ruby about who he really was, but not being able to do so.

The blackouts had finally stopped. They only seemed to happen around Mariah.

He drew a deep breath. Maybe he and Ruby could try again, now that Mariah was gone.

Gabe picked up his phone—he'd unblocked all the numbers except the ones that Philip had used to contact him. One thing he had finally figured out over the long, lonely summer was how to tell Ruby who he really was, and why Philip was such a threat.

Gabriel Martiniere was dead and gone. Lost forever.

Only Gabe Ramirez remained.

Gabe tentatively tapped out his message.

Thank you. You didn't have to do this, and I respect you for it.

He hesitated.

> Can we meet at the Southfork Restaurant in Grande City and talk? Just talk. We do have our son's future to think about.

Her response came quickly.

> I'd like that.

Maybe there was hope. The divorce wasn't final. Maybe he could beg his way back into her life.

<hr>

BUT SOUTHFORK BLEW APART, LIKE EVERYTHING ELSE CONNECTED TO RUBY these days. She showed up angry about Mariah and it escalated to a stupid fight, both of them yelling and throwing fists at each other, tussling and knocking over tables, until the cops arrested them. Which brought another flurry of media interest.

The charges got dropped, but they were both banned from the restaurant.

And Gabe found himself in another cheap ass motel room, drunk off his rear (*though he could have sworn he hadn't drunk that much, he really hadn't, but that damn bitch Mariah had shown up and somehow he was drunker than a skunk*), his hands wrapped around a .45 pointed toward him, guiding it to his mouth seemingly of their own will.

Once again, a horn honked outside his window. Gabe startled. His hands dropped and he threw the weapon on the bed. He sat for a moment, swearing that if that damned bitch Mariah walked into the door again, he'd shoot her. Or something.

After fifteen minutes, he picked up the pistol with shaking hands, unloaded it, and tucked it away. Then he went to bed.

He woke up alone that morning. No punctures. None of that drained post-coital sensation he experienced after fucking Mariah.

At least he had that.

December, 2036

THE DIVORCE FINALIZED WITH NO FURTHER DIRECT COMMUNICATION FROM Ruby. They settled into a routine of exchanging Brandon in Grande City, surrogates for Ruby once again handling the transfer until media interest faded. Gabe and Craig established their own patterns. When Branny spent the weekends with them, Craig told traditional Cayuse and Nez Perce winter tales. Branny nestled in Gabe's arms as they sat by the woodstove, enthralled by the stories.

Gabe rocked his son and wished that Ruby was there as well. That would have made everything complete and whole.

But he had fucked up that possibility, big time.

9 / REBUILDING

2037-2041

The next few years passed quietly, without fanfare or media excitement except the occasional *what are they doing now* retrospective. Between learning the seasons and flow at Moondance, and developing his microbials, Gabe deliberately worked at appearing to be nothing more than Craig's ranch hand, while developing long-term plans. *Boring* was his goal, and he strove to make Gabe Ramirez the most dull, dreary-appearing person possible.

Craig's daughter Sophie brought her kids to the ranch during summer vacations. Sophie's husband Tom worked with Gabe to fix the old house and make it more comfortable and accessible for Craig.

During the summer of 2037, the four of them worked out the details of eventually transferring Moondance to Gabe. Gabe put half of the Superstar money from Ruby into a down payment, and negotiated credit for unpaid work on Moondance toward further payments.

"I wouldn't be making an income on the ranch if Gabe wasn't here," Craig said one evening as they sat around the firepit, kids asleep in the nearby wall tent that Gabe had put up for them so they could have outside adventures. He'd join them as the adult in charge once he was ready to go to bed. "It'd all go to hired hands and even then—" he shrugged. "The help would eat up most of my money."

Silence as they digested Craig's words.

"I thank you for being here," Tom said, raising his beer to Gabe.

"I needed a place to stay and heal," Gabe said, nursing his own beer. "A safe place for my son to visit out of the media spotlight. I owe Craig, big time. But I'm also growing fond of Moondance. A chance for me to start over."

"Is Ruby going to be a problem in this transaction?" Sophie asked. "Will she make a claim on you for Moondance?"

Gabe shook his head. "She's washed her hands of me. If it wasn't for Brandon, we wouldn't have any contact."

Except for his share of the Double R's income. But Gabe had sent back the last quarterly payment, and asked Ruby to keep future amounts as child support for Brandon. What he saw of her ranch financials as a ten percent owner didn't look good, and he could survive on the remaining Superstar cash. Not that he needed much. Moondance provided enough income to keep him and Craig going. His needs were simple these days and—Branny's well-being was his priority.

Sophie smiled. "He *is* a nice kid."

Gabe had asked Ruby if Branny could spend extra time on Moondance while Sophie and Tom's kids were there. She agreed to it, since Branny didn't get much exposure to other kids at the Double R and, in her words, *she wasn't about to make nice to her Barkley relatives just to provide companionship for their son.* Neither of them mentioned the danger of media stalkers if Branny went off of the Double R or Moondance to hang out with other children. But that awareness hung in their discussions.

Gabe heartily agreed with Ruby on that decision about the Barkleys, so Branny now trailed after Jeff and Penny and Ginny, the elder three watching out for four-year-old Branny.

At least Branny was one area of agreement between him and Ruby.

"Mostly Ruby's doing," Gabe sighed. Ruby *was* a good mother. Donna-gran wouldn't fault her great-grandson's manners, and he did his best to apply a Martiniere veneer to Ruby's work when he could.

Not that he expected Branny to need the higher-level faux politeness that went along with the Martiniere life. Gabe wasn't ready to contemplate challenging Philip yet. Too much of what he felt was raw and emotional, and that would interfere with what he wanted to do. He needed to be cold and calculating when it came time to act.

And, honestly, Gabe wanted to destroy Philip. Not challenge his uncle.

But burning down the Martiniere Group wouldn't work, either. There were too many innocents involved whose only crime was the name of Martiniere. His vengeance needed to be precise and targeted. As of yet, Gabe hadn't figured out how to pull it off.

Sophie cocked her head. "Don't short yourself, Gabe." Her eyes narrowed. "So, when are you finding yourself another woman?"

Gabe laughed hollowly. "I'm done with romance." He tossed down the last of his beer.

"That's a shame," she said. "Lots of women would be proud to have a man like you in their lives."

"Ah, Sophie, if only you knew," Gabe sighed. "I'm better off alone."

He was *not* going to put another woman in the same situation as Ruby. Not that he wanted someone else in his life. Ruby couldn't be replaced. Some nights Gabe stood at the edge of the rocky point, firepit burning behind him, and screamed into the valley below, because ripping Ruby out of his life still ached. Still burned deep inside.

He loved Ruby like he had never loved anyone else. Except Branny.

November, 2039

"HEY GABE," CRAIG SAID, AFTER RETURNING FROM A FUNDRAISER AT THE tribal casino. "Got something for you."

"What's that?" Gabe looked up from the screen where he was scanning through the Moondance financials. If he were lucky, he *might* be able to set up a lab this winter to develop a potentially commercial version of his microbials by spring planting. Definitely could by the time he needed to plant winter wheat next year.

Craig smirked, waving an envelope at him. "Won all-expense paid tickets to the National Finals for two in a raffle. Includes transportation and lodging."

"We ought to have some fun."

"*We*? No, buddy. This is for you, and whoever you want to bring along."

"You sure about that?" Gabe took the envelope from him, scanning through the details. Tickets every night for the National Finals Rodeo, *good* seats. Suite at the Dreams Come True casino. Meal credits. Direct flight from Pendleton to Las Vegas. "I mean, you won it after all."

Craig laughed, gesturing at his wheelchair. "And it would be a right royal pain for me to make that trip. You've been working your ass off for three years. It's time for you to have some fun." He turned serious. "You've been carrying a torch for the Ice Princess long enough. It's time to move on, buddy."

Gabe contemplated the tickets instead of snapping back at Craig for that comment about Ruby. Six-year-old Branny was too young to go to Vegas. He didn't think of anyone else to take along—unless Ruby?

Could he do something with her without that damn Mariah or Philip interfering? Or the media hyping it up again?

Always worth a gamble.

December, 2039

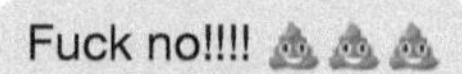

He scowled at Ruby's response to his tentative feeler.

She's still really pissed at me. Can't blame her.

He would have to miss a weekend with Branny to go to National Finals, but Craig was right, he needed the break.

"Can't I go?" Branny pleaded. He'd heard enough rodeo stories from Craig and Gabe to develop an interest, along with looking at Ruby's queen sashes and barrel racing trophies.

"Too young, son," Gabe said. "But I'll bring you back a souvenir. Maybe we'll go to the Round-Up next September."

He ended up selling the extra travel voucher and tickets, but kept the fancy suite for himself.

Coming to Vegas, after three years of doing nothing but ranch-related chores in Pendleton, dazzled Gabe. He looked around the suite when he arrived, taking it all in. It had been *years* since he'd experienced such luxury. It was gaudier than anything Martiniere, save the family chateau near Versailles, and the Hôtel Martiniere, his uncle Gerard's Parisian mansion. How long had it been since he'd stayed someplace this nice?

At least ten years.

He had a nest egg for gambling and other expenses. And for whatever reason, he was under the radar when it came to media attention, which had been a worry. By himself, he must be boring and not worthy of their interest.

Good.

The first thing Gabe did after he settled in his suite was to go to a high-end menswear store and pick out a couple of good suits, with shirts and ties to match. Ten years since he'd worn quality suits fitted to him. He couldn't afford bespoke suits again. Not yet.

But looking good was part of Gabe's long-term plan. It was time. If he was serious about launching Moondance Microbials, he needed to have the look down for talking to bankers and promoting product. No more fucking gamified financing dependent on social media clicks and scandals. That had been the mistake he and Ruby had made. He wouldn't make *that* mistake again, at least not for anything longer than one year.

Now Gabe's dreams were about making it on his own. The microbial route seemed to fit the market, and if he played his cards right, he'd make his own success.

He wanted to show his uncle that he didn't need to be a Martiniere to succeed. Wanted to rub in Philip's face that he had managed to recover despite Philip's attempts to destroy him.

That would be an excellent beginning to his vengeance.

Once Gabe's suits were ready, he hired discreet escorts for the nights he wasn't at the NFR. The sex and companionship were okay, but nothing spectacular. He remained detached and polite throughout, but it was clearly transactional.

It seemed like his inner self was encased in ice.

Perfect for what he needed to do.

Relationships were a liability.

He was not ready to risk his heart to someone else.

December, 2040

Moondance Microbials did well enough in its first year that Gabe paid his way to Vegas and National Finals for a second year. And he continued to avoid media attention. He indulged his gambling habit, lost a little, won more, let himself engage more escorts.

On his way back this time, he flew to Seattle before returning to Pendleton, to negotiate further financing. Sophie joined him, to represent Craig's interest in Moondance.

Gabe noticed one of the assistant bankers, Rachel Alvarez, who was a friend of Sophie's. She had a pleasant laugh and made useful marketing observations. Her long dark hair was often up in a French twist, and she wore bright blue and green couture dresses in jewel tones that accented the beauty of her brown skin. Long-legged and long-waisted, but gentle in speech and soft around the edges. In many ways, she was the opposite of Ruby.

Not that he was looking for company, even when they went out for drinks with Sophie. At least not any companionship that didn't involve some sort of transaction.

Safer that way.

And after Gabe returned to Moondance, he scheduled a vasectomy, now that he could afford it. He was not going to risk leaving any more hostages to fate. Dear as Branny was to his heart, there would be no other offspring of his running around for Philip to exploit.

Worrying about one child was enough.

JUNE, 2041

CRAIG DIED IN HIS SLEEP TOWARD THE END OF MAY.

Rachel came to Moondance with Craig's daughter Sophie on a quick overnight trip to finalize the ranch's transfer. Craig had waived the remaining payments and bequeathed Moondance to Gabe. When the three of them sat around the firepit that night, Sophie excused herself early, leaving Gabe and Rachel alone on the rocky point, nursing beers.

Sneaky, Sophie, sneaky.

He'd wondered if she was playing matchmaker, damn it. No. It wasn't going to happen. His heart still belonged to Ruby.

"You know," Rachel said at one point in their conversation. "You've got to do something about that house. This property would have better value with a nicer residence on it."

"Yeah, yeah, I agree," Gabe said. "But it was what Craig wanted to live in, and it was the family home. Until now, replacement hasn't been a possibility."

"It's falling apart. You'd have to pump a lot of money into the place to keep it livable for more than a few years. Meanwhile—" she waved her hand. "This site would be absolutely *gorgeous* with the right house on it. If it were me, I'd not waste doing more than the bare minimum of maintenance on what you have now. Spend the money on building a showplace instead."

Gabe sighed. "Not worth the expense for just me. My son's mother has full custody of him. Besides, why would I want to build a showplace?"

Rachel cocked her head and smiled. "If Moondance Microbials takes off, you'll want to entertain investors."

"There are perfectly good hotel spaces in Pendleton."

"Ah, but Gabe, the personal touch is what wins investors over. The right house, located on this point, could make a difference."

Gabe shook his head. "I've already been down that road with the Ag Superstar. And you saw how that turned out."

"Totally different." Rachel leaned back in her chair.

"In any case, I don't have the money to hire an architect, much less build a showplace."

"Mmm." Rachel steepled her index fingers and tapped them against her chin. "I know somebody in training who'd love to do the design for a project. Pro bono."

"Oh?" He raised his brows at that. "Who would that be?"

Rachel stared into the fire for a few moments, then looked back up.

"Me. I don't intend to stay in banking forever, Gabe. My father got me this job when I wanted to move to Seattle. It's been a good background for what I really want to do. I may not go into design myself, in the long run, but I want to develop real estate, the sort that's cutting edge. But sound structures. And Moondance has exactly the sort of potential that could help me establish my name, at a reasonable expense."

"So a business proposition," he said slowly.

God. He'd have to be careful. This was how Ruby snared him in the first place—a brilliant, beautiful woman with a dream.

Rachel nodded. "I'd like to work up a proposal if you're amenable. I'd be willing to invest in building the house. Just let me stage it and use it for promotion."

It *would* be nice to be able to entertain investors on site.

"Then I'd have to figure out how to entertain people for my purposes as well," he sighed. And yet...the thought was tempting.

What if I could bid on hosting a Martiniere family meeting? Oh, wouldn't that be sweet?

Rachel cocked her head and grinned at him. "Oh, I think advice on how to do that could be arranged...for a fee."

Transactional. He had to keep *this* relationship transactional.

Safer that way.

AUGUST, 2041

WHEN IT WAS TIME FOR THEM TO REVIEW RACHEL'S PLANS IN FURTHER detail, the summer wildfire smoke was bad enough that Gabe didn't know if Rachel would be able to fly into Pendleton. But no cancellation notice had popped up by the time he had to leave Moondance for the airport to pick her up, so he grabbed an extra mask before putting his own on.

He hid behind a pillar because Mariah was the first person off. But she walked right by without looking at him. A relief. Then Rachel exited the plane, sneezing. She wore a bright blue summer dress in the same lapis shade that had caught his eye back in December.

"There's sure a lot of smoke," she said.

Gabe offered her the mask he'd been carrying. Just in case. "This will help."

Rachel took it with a smile and immediately put it on, fitting it to her face.

"Ah. One of the *good* masks. Thank you, Gabe."

He shrugged and took hold of her roller bag. "Things get dusty when I'm working the fields. I always have a few good-quality masks around. Mask-wearing was one of Craig's big safety issues, and I got into the habit of doing the same."

"I should have been thinking ahead," she said as they left the terminal and went through the parking lot. "Especially since we're starting to get this smoke in Seattle."

He opened the passenger door for her before tossing the bag in the back seat. "It's better up on the ridge at Moondance. Back in the trees it's not bad at all. The smoke seems to concentrate in the valley and unless the fire's right behind the house, that ridge stays reasonably clear."

"What kind of wildfire risk do you have?"

"Craig worked with the Confederated Tribes on land management and I'm keeping up that tradition," Gabe said. "Controlled burns on the forested areas with thinning, and fire lines around the property borders. I do hope that wildfire safety is one thing you're keeping in mind while you design."

"Oh, absolutely," Rachel said. "And seeing this gives me more ideas for HVAC filtering. Dust, too, you say?"

"Lots of dust during plowing and harvest seasons," he said. "Or when we have high wind events. Similar dispersal patterns as the smoke."

They chatted the rest of the way back to the house while he thought ahead. He'd made an effort to spruce up the spare room in the main house. But Gabe was well aware of how shabby the house looked, the uneven floors, even the stained grout along the seams in the shower stall and the way the stall's bottom flexed.

Rachel *was* right about his need to do something different. And the microbials were doing well.

"I have to run a fire check up in the woods," he said as they went into the house. "Do you want to come with me?"

"It'd be helpful to see more of the property," she said. "I won't be but a moment changing."

Rachel was true to her word, and emerged from the spare room dressed in a sleeveless white blouse, loose-fitting light blue long-sleeved shirt, and green hiking shorts as well as boots, a scarf restraining her long black hair. As he drove the crawler along the fence line, Rachel peered at the woods, asking questions about the plants and trees.

Then she was quiet on their return to the house. Air purifiers meant they could shed their masks once they were inside. She pulled up her comp when they got back. He started dinner.

"There's a lot more here than I thought," she said finally. "Lots of potential. I only saw the flatlands in June, with the grain fields."

"I thought about running stock on the forest property at one point," he said. "But there's just not that much return on cattle these days. One of the local sheep ranchers leases the forest land in spring for early grazing. She has them off by June, taking them up higher. That helps with the fire hazard, as well as the controlled burns in late fall, once we've had some rain. And I don't have to manage stock."

"That tour helps me tweak the proposal," Rachel said. "Want to see it after dinner? I'd thought I'd wait until tomorrow to show you what I've been doing, but I'm pretty excited about it after looking at the forest. Designs incorporating footpaths and trails would make this place even more attractive. I think you could appeal to the executive retreat market. Plenty of open-air space for hiking and running. Can you work on that creek a little bit? Make it more visually appealing?"

"Needs negotiating," Gabe said. "Water management is one area where I collaborate with the tribe."

"All right." She smiled at him. "Some of the additions I just made need to be fleshed out further. But I can show you the outlines."

RACHEL PULLED UP THE ROUGH DESIGNS AFTER DINNER. AT FIRST GABE thought it was too big.

"Not for entertaining," Rachel said.

"Keeping a house that size warm in winter will be a challenge," he said. "We get some big winter storms. Wind and snow, hard winds from all directions. That's one reason why Craig's grandparents built back in the trees."

Rachel nodded. "I've calculated sun exposures and wind stresses up to one hundred fifty miles an hour. I'll need to look closer at the site, but...I planned to do that tomorrow. Here. Take a look at the rough walk-through of what the inside will be like." She pulled virtual goggles out of her bag and handed them to Gabe.

He still wasn't completely convinced, but...the thought was tempting. He liked what he saw during the virtual tour. Sleek, modern design that was nothing like he'd grown up with.

"It's still pretty big for one man," he said finally.

Rachel shrugged. "The way I've designed it, you can shut off sections not in use. It's also useful for separating out family area from visitor areas. Each suite has dedicated mini-split controls so that they can be kept at an optimal condition for energy-efficient usage. This isn't just a residence. It's a function space."

They talked late into the night about the possibilities.

And when Rachel left the next afternoon, Gabe had signed a tentative design agreement, conditional on final plan approval, permitting, and financing. But he had enough information to go to the county planning department to start the process.

GABE RESEARCHED RACHEL'S BACKGROUND BEFORE SIGNING FINAL agreements. She was fronting a large chunk of the new house/Moondance redevelopment construction costs, and he wanted to make sure she was good for it.

The Alvarezes were rich, with most of their money coming from real estate, construction, and banking, plus a small security subsidiary connected to Rachel's oldest brother Rafael. An extended family without the long history of the Martinieres, but from an equally respectable Cuban and Mexican heritage, at least as far as banking, real estate, and finance were concerned. She had grown up in San Diego, in different circles from the ones he had run in as a Martiniere in Los Angeles.

There had been an ex-fiancé, Cameron Hawthorne, from Boston, another banking and real estate family scion.

However, Rachel could definitely pay for her share of the development she proposed. And her finance sources would more than guarantee any loans he needed to build this huge new house.

Anything more than that?

No, he told himself. *Keep it transactional.*

Still, he invited Rachel to go to the Round-Up with him and Brandon. She needed to meet with him and the Pendleton bankers to finalize their initial development plans. Might as well see if she had any interest in rodeo and horses as well. After all, that would be a potential promotional market segment for what they were visualizing Moondance to become.

Eventually.

A twenty-year plan. Had he and Ruby ever thought that far ahead?

No, he admitted to himself. There had always been a transient element in their plans, an unspoken realization that he might need to disappear someday.

Well, disappearance was not in the cards now. For better or worse, he was permanently at Moondance.

———

SEPTEMBER, 2041

"I THOUGHT YOU WERE JUST TAKING *ME* TO THE ROUND-UP," BRANDON sulked after Gabe told him about Rachel's impending visit. He had picked Bran up before meeting Rachel at the Pendleton airport.

"Hey. Rachel and I are business partners," Gabe said. "She's never seen a rodeo before, and that's a market segment for our long-range plans. I need to talk to her about the new house this weekend. She's designing it."

"But why does she have to go to the rodeo with *us*?" Brandon's lower lip stuck out in a pout that reminded Gabe of Ruby. "Especially if she's only a business partner. Mom doesn't go out with any of her business partners."

"It's a different kind of business, Bran," Gabe said patiently. Almost eight-year-old Brandon had insisted that he be called Bran or Brandon. No more Branny. And he'd gotten moody this summer. Sophie and Tom hadn't come over to the ranch, so Brandon spent more time with Ruby instead of Gabe. Less time with his father had clearly not set well with Brandon. "Some businesses require more socializing than others. Rachel's in banking and real estate. Totally different from what your mother has to deal with."

Brandon grumped some more, glaring out the truck's window.

"Bran," Gabe finally sighed. "What on earth is wrong?"

"I want you back home!" Brandon burst out. "I want you and Mom to be back together! Not you at stupid Moondance and us at the Double R. Not you going out with other women."

"I'm not *going out* with Rachel," Gabe said. "And as for me getting back together with your mother—you need to talk to her about that.

She's pretty much slammed that door shut hard and locked it." He paused. "Bran. Please. Be polite to Rachel. This is your future, too. I'm turning Moondance into an event and retreat site. Rachel is the one designing it."

Brandon grumbled, but didn't say any more, still sulking. Gabe sighed.

Damn it, he'd definitely sired another strong-minded Martiniere man.

He made a note to himself to ask Ruby if Brandon was being difficult for her. Tonight, while he was still thinking about it, and might need to head off further issues.

Bran's mood didn't improve by the time they got to the house. Gabe stepped outside after Brandon went to bed, to call Ruby.

"What's wrong?" Ruby snapped, without preliminaries.

"God, Ruby!"

She sighed and her voice softened. "Look. It's been a rough week. And Bran's been a real brat for some reason."

"Then it's not just me. I wondered. He nearly ripped my head off when I told him that my architect was going to the Round-Up with us, and he's still sulking."

"Sounds about right," Ruby said. "And—architect?"

"Craig's old house is falling apart and I need to do something about it. One of my Seattle bankers is working toward an architectural degree, and offered to design a new one as one of her class projects."

"Her?"

"Rachel Alvarez," Gabe said. "A friend of Craig's daughter Sophie. It's a pretty big design, but means I can hire the place out for events and retreats. Her family's experienced in real estate as well as banking. She wants to try some experimental work. Hey, she's fronting a big chunk of the cost, and she gets some of the income once the house becomes a working facility. Hard to turn an opportunity like that down."

Ruby snorted. "Probably a better deal than Gramps and Granma remodeling the house here for vacation rooms just before the pandemic hit. You're closer to Pendleton, for one thing."

"Yeah. So, what do you think is going on with Bran?"

"It might be school. He *has* been grumping around about maybe you and I ought to get back together. It started right after school did."

"He said something like that to me too." Gabe paused. "Want to join us at the Round-Up tomorrow night?"

"Like hell," she growled, her voice hard again. "The sooner our son figures out that we aren't getting back together, the better. And you need to tell him that." She hung up.

Gabe sighed. Well, he'd tried. He could honestly tell his son that his mother had no interest in a reunion.

Still, a little bit of himself shriveled up. There had been a tiny piece of Gabe's heart that had held out some hope. That maybe, just maybe, Ruby was as lonely as he was, and would be looking for another chance to renew their relationship.

Looked like the answer to that question was a firm no.

Not that he had any plans for another woman in his life.

Even Rachel.

NOVEMBER, 2041

"DO YOU HAVE THANKSGIVING PLANS?" RACHEL SOUNDED HARRIED. They'd taken to calling each other several times a week, mostly for Gabe to give Rachel updates on the progress of the house construction. But this was an out-of-sequence call from her.

"Not much, really." Ruby had Bran for Thanksgiving this year and he had Bran for Christmas. Thanksgiving would be just another lonesome day on Moondance Ranch.

Rachel sighed. "My family is coming to Seattle. I think my future architectural and real estate career is the primary point of discussion. Along with a man that Mama wants to hook me up with."

"Oh." Well, he could play the boyfriend if Rachel needed. "Do you need me to provide support? I can fake being a boyfriend."

"Would you mind horribly, Gabe? Not the boyfriend fake but as my co-investor in the Moondance property development."

Gabe knew this dance well enough from his Martiniere days.

"I have no problems with that. How formal should I plan to be?" His investigation of the Alvarez family suggested that he needed to dress up for dinner at a family gathering. Business casual at the minimum.

She burst out laughing. "Oh Gabe. You are one of the few men I know who doesn't run screaming from the prospect of formal dress. That's the problem with Seattle. Too many men here still buy into flannel chic." She made a face. "Throwbacks to the 1990s."

"Hey, I don't own anything dressier than my business suits. Just wanting to know in advance, so I can rent what's required to fit in and not look like a hick. Even if I am one."

"Your suits are just fine, Gabe. And thank you."

They chatted further. A thought came to him after he hung up.

Rachel's background was closer to how he had been raised than Ruby's was.

Gabe dismissed that notion with a shake of his head. He and Rachel were business partners, and nothing more than that. He still loved Ruby, and if she ever relented, he'd be back at the Double R in a heartbeat.

That was, if his fucking uncle didn't do something to prevent it.

Now that he was thinking about backgrounds, though, he had to wonder. Philip hadn't shown any inclination to bother him after the divorce. What *would* happen if he openly courted someone like Rachel instead?

After all, while the Alvarez family wasn't as wealthy as the Martinieres, they also weren't people that Philip could screw over without facing consequences. Rachel had the power of money and family behind her. *Bankers*, no less. One tenet of Philip's was that *you never screw around with bankers.*

Ruby didn't have that clout in her background.

Stop it, he told himself. *You have no interest in this woman beyond a business partnership. No woman is safe in a relationship with you.*

And the thought made Gabe briefly bitter, because he was still lonely, and missed having a companion he could depend upon.

HERNAN AND ERICA ALVAREZ, RACHEL'S PARENTS, WERE GRACIOUS AND polite people of the ilk that Gabe remembered from his Martiniere days. He didn't trust them as far as he could throw them as a result. From the moment he entered Rachel's penthouse condo, Gabe felt Erica's eyes measuring him as a marriage prospect for her daughter. Another familiar element from his past.

He stifled a wry thought that if it were *Gabriel Martiniere* and not Gabe Ramirez showing up right now, both parents would be falling all over themselves at the idea that their daughter had attracted such a catch. But thanks to all of the publicity around his divorce, he was tarnished goods. That might explain the caution in their interactions with him.

Not that it mattered. Gabe was here as Rachel's business partner, not her boyfriend. Though apparently the unattached potential date hadn't shown up. Gabe half-wondered if his presence made the difference.

Hernan wore a bespoke suit. Gabe could probably still name the tailor that Hernan had gone to in Paris. Italian shoes—more expensive than Gabe's decent-quality dress ones. Silk tie and pocket square similar to his. Light-colored shirt with French cuffs. And the same was true for how Rachel's brothers Rick and Rafael dressed.

Dinner conversation was polite. Rachel tensely supervised the serving staff she had hired for this occasion, but did so with a grace that made it seem easy—except that Gabe realized he now knew her well enough to see beyond the nervous façade. When Rafael and Rick slipped into a conversation in Spanish, Gabe joined after it was clear they were discussing him. He called Rafael *Rafe*, like the rest of the family. Perhaps a bit of showing off on his part, but he also wanted to make damn good and sure they realized he understood what they were saying.

Points scored, plus a quick approving smile from Erica. Rachel hid a giggle at her brothers' startled reactions, which amused Gabe. He'd demonstrated his fluency in Spanish to her already—they'd forced Brandon to practice his Spanish and French that weekend at the Round-Up. That had jollied Bran out of his sulk, especially once he realized that the three of them could snark about the crowd and other things without being understood by many of those around them.

Ruby had muttered about that afterward because Bran brought attitude home. But she had enough French and Spanish from high school and college studies to kick Bran's butt when he snarked at her, thinking he could get away with something.

After dinner, Hernan stretched and rose. "Perhaps we should talk a little bit about this wild plan of Rachel's, hmm?"

And allow you and her brothers to quiz me about my intentions.

"Certainly," Gabe said. "I brought my comp with the projections. But perhaps we should wait for business discussions until Rachel's finished with her duties?"

Send a clear signal that he was *not* the mastermind behind these plans, and that he wasn't going to support any notions of excluding the "little lady." Like Philip would.

Hernan arched a brow at him. "Cognac and cigars, until she can join us?"

Oh God, this is just fucking like being in Paris with the Family.

Gabe scaled his understanding of the Alvarez family social status up even more notches. No, Philip would *not* fuck around with trying to hurt a woman from this family, even if they were Hispanic. He might manipulate Hernan, but he would not touch the women of the family.

A brief frisson of anger wafted through Gabe. How much of Philip's desire to force his divorce had been shaped by Gabe's marriage to someone Philip didn't consider worthy of a Martiniere connection? His goddamn uncle was a fucking snob as well as a bigot.

"Certainly," he responded smoothly, tucking away that anger for later. No one here would understand it—unless Hernan had already figured out who he really was. Entirely possible.

And he didn't care about *that,* as long as Hernan and Rachel's brothers kept his secret, open as it was now.

Perhaps he should rethink the likelihood of a relationship with Rachel. The Alvarez connection would be enough to discourage Philip from harassing him further—and perhaps keep Brandon and Ruby safe as well. Hell, Hernan and Philip might already be talking. Even though Philip wanted Gabe out of the family, preferably dead, a disowned Martiniere married into another wealthy family could be seen as a positive alliance. And Philip might think that said alliance would be worth working through in-laws to persuade Gabe into giving ground to what Philip wanted.

Gabe would be happy enough to play that dance for a while without promising anything of significance, especially if it allowed Brandon to grow up in peace.

Possibilities. Always possibilities. And he was still a Martiniere capable of exploiting opportunities that came his way. He might just have landed a prospect bigger than he had originally thought it was.

Gabe followed Hernan, Rafe, and Rick into a separate room—clearly Rachel's home office. Sliding doors opened onto a balcony with a view onto one of the Seattle-area lakes. Hernan opened the doors, then activated a smoke extractor and a privacy screen. Gabe noted the security tell-tales in the screen. Vygotsky, or something close to that quality. The Alvarezes had the money for the best. Very possible that Serg and Piotr knew he was here.

Hernan doled out the snifters and poured the cognac. Rafe passed the cigars—Cuban, highest quality. More things to note. Rafe was clearly the designated family heir. Gabe needed to pay more attention to Rafe than to Rick.

After a puff and a sip, Hernan focused on Gabe.

"All right, then," he said in Spanish. "You are not what I anticipated when Rachel told us about her business partner. Nor from our investigation into your background."

"I grew up around Vygotskys and their kin," Gabe said, continuing in Spanish. Oh, he was going to have to be *very* careful with this interrogation. Give just enough information but not too much. Conducting this conversation in Spanish would help. Even though he spoke everyday

Spanish more frequently at Moondance than the Double R, using the more formal language was advisable in *this* talk, and he had to be more mindful in his choice of words due to lack of recent practice in Castilian Spanish.

"So we have learned," Rafe said. "But there are—shall we say, discrepancies in your background?"

Gabe puffed on his cigar, then sipped the cognac to keep from coughing. It had been a *long* time since he'd smoked tobacco this good. The nicotine rush went to his head, his heart pounding, his thoughts racing.

"Yes," he said smoothly. "And due to pre-indenture mind control programming, I can't speak about that."

That earned him arched brows all around.

"That indenture status," Rafe said slowly.

Gabe waved his cigar dismissively. "Not an issue. Dealt with during my divorce." Another puff, another sip. Another nicotine jolt. Tip off the ash.

"So you are no longer at risk, then." Rick this time.

"No. My issues with a certain family are not tied to any indenture status."

"Your name has come up in connection with that of a particular missing Martiniere heir," Hernan said as Rachel came into the room. "Can you say anything about that?"

Puff. Sip. Think. Tip ash. Slow the racing thoughts with another sip.

"I am under some rather stringent mind control programming as a result of my past," he said finally. "I can neither confirm nor deny that status."

His eyes met Rachel's, noting her quick smile, and he wondered at the timing of Hernan's question. Had it been intended so that she could hear his answer?

"Asking me to say anything more explicit will result in some rather —unpleasant—and uncontrollable reactions on my part," he continued. "For all intents and purposes, I am what you see before you and in my financials. Gabe Ramirez. Owner of Moondance Ranch. As a result of my divorce, a ten percent owner of my ex-wife's Double R Ranch. Developer of Moondance Microbials. And a forty percent interest holder in Rachel's Moondance Resort proposal. Divorced with a son. The rest of my past stays in my past."

Another puff. Another sip. Tipping off even more ash. Meeting Rachel's eyes again before she gracefully crossed the room to pour herself a cognac, then light a cigar of her own before taking a seat next to him.

Hmm.

Prospects danced through his thoughts as he and Rachel described their plans for Moondance. And at the end, there were no more critical comments about *Rachel's wild plan.*

There *was* an invitation to join the family for the Apple Cup at Husky Stadium on Friday and the Seahawks on Sunday, both in premium skyboxes.

Gabe accepted both invitations. He had expected the possibility if this talk went well. It would be the accepted behavior from someone in a business partnership with a family member and—he suspected there could well be more in play. That he was being scouted for an alliance with the Alvarezes that went beyond business.

Back to the big leagues, Gabriel.

Philip would support this relationship, if only because he would see it as a means to control a wayward family member.

Not that Philip's approval mattered. Unless it kept Ruby and Brandon safe.

RACHEL PULLED HIM ASIDE BEFORE THE FAMILY SAID THEIR GOODBYES FOR the evening. "Stay," she whispered. "Papa is going to want more details, but he's willing to invest in startup costs. I told him we'd give him a proposed budget tomorrow before the game."

Gabe wondered if that was her only intention, but he wasn't going to say anything as long as family was around. A familiar dance from when high-society Parisian mamas were throwing their daughters at him during his studies at the University of Paris.

"Sure," he said.

Rachel heaved a big sigh once the door closed behind her family. She kicked off her stilettos. Gabe followed suit with his shoes.

"I love my family but they *are* high maintenance," she sighed again. "I've become enough of a Seattleite that I don't care to live like that all the time." She extracted a hanger from the coat closet. "Would you like to hang up your jacket and get less formal?"

Gabe laughed and slid out of his jacket, giving it to her. As they walked to her office, Rachel undid her hair. It fell in a silky black cloud halfway down her back, and he suddenly itched with the desire to run his fingers through it. The luminous blue of her dress highlighted her hair's blue-black shimmer.

She picked up the cigar butts in her office, wrinkling her nose and setting the ashtrays outside on the balcony. "Papa and his cigars."

Gabe shrugged. "I noticed you smoked one, too."

Rachel pursed her lips. "Have to impress Papa and the boys that I'm as capable as they are. Now. Here's what I have so far. Let's go over it." She sat on the loveseat, patting the cushion for him to sit next to her, and popped it up.

They spent a couple of hours on the spreadsheet, and had another glass of cognac while working. After saving their final results, Gabe slumped against the back of the couch.

"Whew." He contemplated the rest of the cognac in his glass—he'd actually not been drinking much while working. "I'm surprised I'm thinking this well. Still full from dinner and wanting to take a nap. That was good, Rachel."

"I'm glad you liked it." Rachel turned sideways on the couch to face him. "And I appreciate your coming." She grimaced, wrinkling her nose in a way that he was starting to find cute. "Mama was much more amenable to leaving David in San Diego after Papa talked to her about your coming for Thanksgiving."

"David?"

Again with that delightful nose wrinkle, followed by a sigh. "Old energy money. The Johnstons. Mama's been throwing him at me for years. Mutual disinterest, but we play along to keep the parents happy."

"I see." Oh yes, definitely *that* sort of family. Rachel might be as much of a rogue from her family as he was from the Martinieres. Only she hadn't acted on it.

And it would give Philip and Hernan something in common—dealing with the problematic younger generation.

She deftly loosened his tie, her hand remaining on his chest afterward. "Maybe you should get a little more comfortable."

"I need to check in at the hotel."

"You flew in today?" She raised her brows.

"No. Late last night and stayed by the airport. I have reservations downtown for the next three nights. I didn't worry about leaving my things in the rental car, since you have secured garage parking."

"Ah." She leaned closer, resting her elbow on the back of the loveseat. "I have space for you to stay here. If you're interested."

A wistful Ruby memory flitted through his thoughts. But that bridge was well and truly burned. He *was* lonely. And the way Ruby had rejected his last overtures pissed him off. He loved the woman, but he couldn't carry a torch for her forever.

"I could be," Gabe said cautiously. "But there's always a risk mixing business and personal life."

Her smile was wide, open, and straightforward. No sly dimples. No sharp edges.

"I'm always up for a gamble," she said. "And besides, I am in no hurry to make any commitments. I have my own past to deal with."

She kissed him.

He kissed her back.

Later that night, after their lovemaking, Gabe lay awake, one arm tucked behind his head as Rachel snuggled into the crook of his other arm, sound asleep.

This felt good. Not as great as with Ruby, but still—that black hole deep inside of him wasn't the deep pit it had been until today.

He had a lot to think about.

Maybe he'd see if Rachel wanted to attend National Finals with him. He wasn't going to give up his liking for rodeo. And that would be another test of where things were headed with the two of them.

DECEMBER, 2041

GABE AND RACHEL WERE HIGH-PROFILE ATTENDEES AT THE NATIONAL Finals Rodeo. She liked gambling as much as he did, so they hit the poker and dice tables. It wasn't at all like rodeoing with Ruby, where he had to keep his head down for fear of Philip. Gabe and Rachel *played*, where he and Ruby had been intense and deadly serious, even when having fun.

He was ready to play after everything he'd experienced over the past twelve years. Almost forty years old. Time to relax.

Then it was back to Moondance for Christmas with Bran. He had an invitation to spend Christmas with Rachel and her family in San Diego, but declined for Bran's sake. Too soon in this relationship to introduce his son to Rachel's family, especially since Bran was resentful of his involvement with a woman other than his mother. However, Gabe accepted Rachel's invitation to spend New Year's in Seattle with her.

An early snowfall was deep enough for Gabe and Brandon to spend most of Christmas Day cross-country skiing in the forest. Gabe packed a thermos of cocoa and a light lunch. They spotted deer, elk, and a shy bobcat. Then they came back to the house and ate a big dinner. Brandon crashed after stuffing himself—it pleased Gabe to see his son eat freely, without the same fears he'd gone through about being embarrassed by a vindictive adult. Eating as much as he wanted at Christmas without fearing that Philip would use his control words to make Gabe physically embarrass himself was still a novelty.

Gabe poured a stiff drink and sat in the darkened living room, staring out the window at the snow falling again.

Next year, if everything went right, they'd spend Christmas in the new house.

Alone except for his son?

Too early to say—yet.

RACHEL MET GABE AT SEA-TAC AIRPORT ON DECEMBER 30TH, RIGHT AT the security turnstiles. Her smile and then her kiss banished the grayness of the drizzle outside.

"I thought about calling you Christmas Day, but then thought it might not be a good idea," she said.

"You probably could have called in the evening without a worry," Gabe said, wrapping his free arm around her waist as he pulled his roller bag. "There was enough snow for us to go skiing. I got Bran good and tired, then stuffed him with a nice dinner. It was good father and son time." He paused, waiting to say more until they negotiated the outer doors and headed for the parking lot. "I thought about calling you, but wasn't certain how that would fit into family time."

"You should have," she said. "But thanks for the text." Her mood seemed a little off, and he wondered if he should have tried to call anyway.

Eh, he was rusty at this game. Rachel was a more traditional woman than Ruby, and he needed to remember that. More flowers. Jewelry—though Ruby had liked the jewelry he bought her.

Her mood lightened as they got into her sporty two-seater. Gabe sat back and watched her drive. Rachel handled the sports car deftly, driving fast and precise. He wondered how she'd handle his big truck on a rough road—that was where Ruby's driving excelled.

Rachel sighed once they got to her condo. "I'm sorry, Gabe. I'm just a little distracted. Always am this time of year."

"What's wrong?" He started unpacking his roller bag as they talked. The present he'd bought her was on the bottom.

"It's my mammogram," she said softly. "There was a shadow. I go for more scans on the second of January."

Gabe froze. He carefully set down the sweater he was preparing to hang, and went to her. "I'm sorry. Do you need someone here for support? I can push my travel date back."

She leaned against him and sniffled a little. "I should be used to it by now." A false laugh. "I had breast cancer six years ago, Gabe. It's probably just the implant. I should have gone for a full mastectomy instead of a lumpectomy, but—" Rachel looked up at him. "It's just—scary, you know? Every year on the anniversary of my diagnosis. And this year—I have a bad feeling."

"I can stay if you want," he said softly. He had noticed the scars, but didn't want to push for more information.

She nodded and leaned into him for a moment. Then she pulled back. "Let me get dinner started. I imagine you're hungry and tired."

"I can help."

"It's nothing major." Her smile came back, happily without that shadow.

Once she was gone, Gabe extracted the present from his bag. He managed to sneak it on the table next to her plate, noticing that there was a similar-sized one by his as well. Then he changed his flight back to Pendleton.

Dinner was light, with present opening afterward. His present was a nice set of cufflinks, onyx with his initials in gold. He'd gotten her a bracelet of blue topazes to match her favorite dress color. Afterward, once Rachel had cleared the dishes and cleaned up—she wouldn't let him help but he could stand there and talk—they sat on a couch, facing the bay view.

Gabe put one arm around Rachel's shoulders. "I moved my flight to the morning of the third," he said.

"Thank you," she said, exhaling. "It's silly of me. I've been clear so far. But every year this nails me. Hard. Because one day…."

"You don't need to minimize it," Gabe said.

Rachel stared into her wine, then looked back up. "I can't have children, Gabe."

"And that's an issue? Rachel, I had a vasectomy several years ago. For—reasons. Much as I love Brandon, I didn't want to be responsible for any more children coming into the world."

"At least you have Brandon," she said, a wistful note in her voice.

"Even if he is a stubborn little butthead at times."

She laughed. "I just wanted to get that out of the way. Before we got any deeper into the personal relationship."

So it was going to be one of *those* talks. Gabe inhaled, thinking about what he wanted to say.

"I've got some big stuff to get out of the way, too," he said quietly.

"The divorce?"

"Yeah. Nothing about it was as cut and dried as the publicity made it seem."

Rachel pressed her lips together tightly. "I followed the story. It happened at the end of my chemo. It kept me distracted. Given *that question* my father asked, and your answer, I had to wonder. The man I'm getting to know doesn't seem like the Gabe Ramirez that was all over the scandal social media. Daddy was very concerned about your reputation. Joey Martiniere chased after me for a while, and wouldn't take no for an answer. Had to get Philip involved. Daddy didn't want to deal with another situation like Joey."

"I meant what I said about the speech constraints."

Joey's been after Rachel, and she turned him down.

That added to her attraction.

"So that was a factor."

"Yes." He considered what to say next. "I didn't want to leave Ruby like that. I really didn't." He sighed. "Rachel, I enjoy being with you. But I'm pretty messed up. I've tried to get Ruby back, in part because Bran wants it. If anything, she's become even more angry at me as the years go by. I don't blame her. I was a shit, even if what happened wasn't all things I could control. I—still love her. Deeply. She's the mother of the only child I'll ever have. And I'm afraid that all I have to offer someone else is leftovers in comparison."

"Your leftovers are more than some men can give in the first place."

Rachel's upper lip curled. "My ex-fiancé—Cameron—broke off our engagement when I told him I couldn't have children."

"What an ass. There's more to love and marriage than biological children."

"And that, Gabe Ramirez-who-is-actually-someone-else-whose-name-he-can't-say, is why I'd happily take your leftovers over anyone else's full love. You're a good man and not an ass, unlike too many men of our social class. Besides, I'm a gambler." Her voice caught. "I don't know when cancer will grab me back again, but I know the odds for my variant. It *will* return. Someday. So I'm going to live my life to the fullest. I want to play—and I think you do too."

Then she kissed him.

"Are you gambling on a relationship with me?"

"Yes," Rachel said, voice quavering. "Though I don't think it's that much of a gamble." She stroked his forehead. "I just get the sense that you need to play. I need to play, too." She chuckled, but Gabe heard the break in her laugh and wrapped his arms around her.

She clung to him. Was there desperation in the way she held him tight? Gabe wasn't sure, not that it mattered.

They spent New Year's Eve at a party with her colleagues and friends. Both of them laughed their way through the evening, being brilliant and witty and sparky as they danced and drank their way into the New Year. A model, well-dressed, cultured couple, a perfect image of ascending social and financial power.

Then Gabe held Rachel as she sobbed with fear and worry once they were back at her condo. Comforted her the next day, and rejoiced with her when her scans came back clear.

And on the third, watching her walk away after she kissed him goodbye at the security turnstile, he realized that perhaps the ice around his heart was melting a little bit.

Rachel wasn't Ruby. But maybe that was what mattered.

COURTING RACHEL WAS NOTHING LIKE COURTING RUBY.

For one thing, instead of a protective grandfather, Rachel had a protective father and brothers Gabe had to negotiate.

Rafe showed up at Moondance in mid-January—oh, he went through the formalities of asking for an invitation—and prowled through the building site, now in early preparation stages, then sent a report back to Hernan. But it was clearly an inspection of Gabe and his prospects by Rachel's oldest brother as much as checking on the Alvarez investment.

Gabe took Rafe out to a good steakhouse in Pendleton before putting him on the plane to San Diego. He drank just enough over dinner to venture the question he'd been considering for a while.

"Rachel said that you had to run off someone from a certain family."

Rafe rolled his eyes. "*That* ass. Yeah, back when Rach was eighteen. He came onto her at a party. She'd heard plenty about him already from her friends. She said no. I stepped in before security did. There was a fight."

"It wouldn't be the first time," Gabe murmured, and sipped his whisky. He would have been in Paris by that time, his junior year in college. Otherwise—he wondered if he would have been called in to make amends to the Alvarezes. The *polite* Martiniere scion squiring Rachel around, instead of the ass.

"He wouldn't stop, either. It took several years, but Dad finally went to his father after I threatened to do more than beat the crap out of Joey." Rafe laughed and switched to Spanish. "I was running with a tough crowd then, you know? And they aren't afraid of the Martinieres. Still are good friends, and I hired them for Alvarez Armory."

Gabe got *that* message loud and clear. "Just wanting to know what the circumstances were," he said. "If it weren't for the mind control—" He shrugged.

"Mmm." Rafe squinted at him. "Dad doesn't approve of that set of friends or their methodology. I'm not so picky. Especially when it comes to dealing with *certain people*. I'm not satisfied with how things came out with Joey."

"We could have some mutual interests in dealing with *certain people.*"

"I think we could, indeed," Rafe said, smiling. "Especially if we become more closely related."

Gabe bared his teeth in a grin. "I look forward to that possibility."

Oh, this whole relationship was becoming *much* more interesting.

February, 2042

Gabe spent a *lot* more time in small planes than he liked as part of this relationship. Rachel enjoyed both downhill and cross-country skiing, and the better resorts were closer to her than to him. She came to Moondance one weekend in January while Brandon was visiting. Bran was tense but well-behaved. Going skiing in the woods helped him relax a little bit around her, though he still privately grumped to Gabe about *replacing Mom.*

Rachel and Gabe spent Valentine's Day weekend touring wineries and galleries in Walla Walla. Exploring amenities that they could use to promote Moondance, of course.

"It's nice getting out of the rain and mist," Rachel said over dinner on Saturday night.

"Weather doesn't always behave over here, either," Gabe said. "But Moondance is usually above the temperature inversions, so not as much fog."

Rachel smiled. "I'm looking forward to spending time there when it's done." She paused. "Gabe. Do you ever like to go to science fiction conventions?"

"I've never been," he said. "Why?"

She took a deep breath. "I—kind of like going to them. There's some high-level gaming that goes on, and even though money's not involved, it can be a lot of fun."

"What kind of gaming?"

"All kinds. Cards. Board games. Dice. 3-D figures. LARPS. Full-body immersion video. And more."

"I'd have to learn about it."

"I can show you. And if Bran's interested, maybe he'd like to come along."

"What? Kids too?"

She nodded. "There's a convention in the Tri-Cities in mid-March. Third weekend."

One of his regular weekends with Bran. "I'll talk to him."

AS IT TURNED OUT, BRAN KNEW ALL ABOUT THE TRI-CITIES CONVENTION. When he learned that going was a possibility, and that Rachel was friends with some high-level gaming executives from Seattle, he got even more excited about it.

Gabe found the whole scene fascinating. Elaborate costumes and role play, including weapons—granted, blades, not guns, but he found himself drawn to the different fighting demonstrations. Some of it was good, while others weren't. But oh, the blades, especially the well-designed ones…he ended up buying several knives for both himself and Bran, and talking with Bran about practicing with them. It was a perfect cover to teach his son about edged weapons.

Even better, after the Tri-Cities convention, Bran was much less irritable on the subject of Gabe dating Rachel.

APRIL, **2042**

THERE WAS NOTHING SPECIAL ABOUT THIS WEEKEND. A SUNNY SEATTLE Saturday spring day, and both the Olympic Mountains and Mt. Rainier glistened free from clouds. For once, Gabe and Rachel stayed put in her condo, not darting around the city or doing something. Just spending the weekend together. Gabe was tired from ranch work—the past week had been a real crunch to get everything done before he caught his flight to Seattle—and Rachel had been busy with presentations.

They curled up together, Gabe with an e-book about his Medici ancestors; Rachel with a game. Gabe in pajama pants and loosely belted robe; Rachel in a soft, shimmery blue negligee. Both of them barefoot. He'd put the tablet down and was drowsing, his head in her lap, soaking in the warmth radiating from the sun shining through the big picture windows. Rachel occasionally ran her fingers through his hair.

For the moment, concerns about Moondance, Brandon growing up safely—even Philip—seemed remote. Gabe rolled onto his back to look up at Rachel until she finished her game sequence. She smiled, and switched it off, bending over to kiss him.

"I could live like this for a very long time," she said.

Gabe grinned. He raised his head. "Why don't you join me?

Rachel laughed and slid next to him. He held her tight, showering her with tiny little kisses all over her face.

"Did you really mean what you said?" he finally asked.

She looked down, then smiled back up at him. "Yes."

"As my wife?"

An even bigger smile. "Yes, Gabe."

<hr>

THERE WAS A FAST BUT INTENSE BLOWOUT WITH RUBY WHEN SHE discovered that Gabe wanted Brandon to be his best man at the wedding.

"How the *hell* can you do that to him?" she screamed over the comm, bristling with rage.

"I gave him a choice whether to do it or not. I wasn't even going to make him come if he said no." Gabe wasn't sure if going to video when she called was such a good thing after all, given the Double R's connectivity. Her agitation made her pace, which kept the connection jerky.

Besides, he was more than a little bit irritated with his ex-wife.

She'd rejected every damn overture he'd made to patch things up. And now she pitched a fit about him remarrying. What the hell did she want from him? He wasn't about to become a damn monk. Not like the austere life she apparently had chosen.

"The fuck, Gabe. Why." She stopped pacing and glowered at him, chin thrust out, red hair braided into two plaits that bounced and jerked as she moved. "Or were your words all those years ago about loving me forever just more of your bullshit?"

Gabe exhaled. There it was. Damn it, the woman expected him to carry a torch for her the rest of his life, without giving him any encouragement that things would get better between them.

He reined in his anger and spoke quietly. "I'm tired of being lonely, Ruby. And you've made it pretty damn clear that we no longer have a future together. I'm moving on. You *are* the mother of my son. I will always love you, and Rachel understands that. But I can't do this anymore. I just turned forty. I want a damn fucking life, and if you refuse to be part of it, then I've got the right to do as I please. I've tried. I've asked. Your answer is no. So what the fuck am I supposed to do?"

She winced, pressing her lips tightly together. A curt nod.

"I'll make sure he's there in time for the rehearsals," she conceded. "But don't expect me to attend."

"I wouldn't. Though you would be welcome."

Were her eyes glistening with tears as she switched off the comm?

Not that it mattered. Ruby had made her choice, and he had made his.

July, 2042

THEIR JULY WEDDING WAS THE FIRST BIG EVENT AT THE COMPLETED Moondance house. Bran solemnly performed his tasks as best man, proud in white tie and tails, already becoming darkly handsome at almost nine years old. He escorted Erica Alvarez to her seat proudly, then walked down the aisle as Gabe's best man, with Sophie as Rachel's matron of honor.

"He's a son to be proud of," Hernan said to Gabe during the reception.

"I am proud of him," Gabe said, watching as Brandon politely danced with one of Rachel's bridesmaids. Bran didn't have the polish he would have possessed if he'd been raised as a Martiniere...but Ruby wasn't doing all that bad a job with him, either.

Sophie grabbed Gabe's hand before he and Hernan could talk further and dragged him onto the dance floor.

"Did I do a good job of matchmaking or what?"

"This was your idea?" Gabe snarked at her.

Sophie shrugged. "I saw two lonely people who might just have a few things in common. And Craig was worried that you were just gonna lock yourself up on the ranch and become a hermit doing microbial research. I made a promise to my brother, and I take those seriously." She smirked. "You look the happiest I've ever seen you."

He deftly spun her. "I *am* happy."

Though there was a faint wistful sorrow that Ruby was not a part of his joy.

Gabe dismissed that thought as being unfair to Rachel. Bygones were bygones.

And if he couldn't have the redheaded rodeo queen of his heart, then at least he could have a beautiful and elegant wife who understood the quirks of his upbringing, and didn't need explanations about his Martiniere background to love what he was.

Lonely no longer.

11 / BRANDON

OCTOBER, 2043

THINGS RAN SMOOTHLY THAT FIRST YEAR OF HIS SECOND MARRIAGE. GABE and Rachel continued to play, aided by Rachel's money, adding jet-skis to the mix as well as a ski boat. They kept Rachel's Seattle condo for city vacations, but lived mostly at Moondance.

Moondance Microbials grew slowly. The income was sufficient for Gabe to make payments toward Alvarez Investments' share of the building cost of the new ranch and lab.

Moondance Resort was slow to develop. Not unexpected.

Brandon got moody in the fall, a year after the wedding. His usually outgoing personality became quieter and more restrained; withdrawn and prickly, like Ruby at her worst. But Bran's behavior also reminded Gabe of what he'd been like after his parents' death.

What was eating at Brandon? Gabe wasn't in a hurry to ask Ruby— she was struggling with a water rights battle in Thunder County and already had a lot to deal with. And Bran wasn't talking. Not to Gabe, not to Rachel.

Was Bran's behavior was connected with what Ruby was going through now? Or was it something else? After all, Bran had been moody last year in the fall. Was it a sign of a problem emerging? It wasn't just Ruby's Barkley relatives who had mental health problems that emerged at this age. Those problems existed in the Martinieres as well.

He didn't see enough red flags to contact Ruby about it. Yet.

Then Ruby called him, late one Thursday evening in October. Gabe and Rachel were watching a *Star Wars* movie—Gabe hadn't seen them before, so Rachel was taking him through the series.

"Double R Ranch Lab," the identifier said.

Gabe raised his brows. "I'll be back," he told Rachel. Why a call from the lab? Was something wrong with Ruby?

Rachel paused the movie. "Go ahead. You can take it here."

Gabe hoped this wasn't something weird. "Accept."

Ruby appeared, lab in the background. "Gabe." She spotted Rachel, and her jaw tightened. "Rachel. I need help." She sighed. "Calling from the lab because Bran can't hack into it—more secure than my cell. I'm having problems with him."

"We have as well. He's been awfully moody of late and he won't talk," Gabe said. "I had thought he'd adjusted to me remarrying, but now I'm worried."

Ruby shook her head. "Don't think that's it. Or at least I *wish* that was it, and not what I'm afraid of." She swallowed hard. "He's flunking out of school. Won't go to his sports. Is begging me to let him attend online school instead of regular school. Won't talk to a counselor. I asked if he'd go to school if he were staying with you, and he melted down at the thought of leaving the ranch. It's just—everything's come to a head with the water rights fight, and I have to find some solution so I'm not worrying about him too. He spent today in bed. Yesterday he left school once he got there, and sneaked home. And I can't get him to do anything around here."

"Fuck." Gabe stared at his hands. "Did he get a ride home, at least?" That was a hike of at least ten miles from Lakeside Elementary to the Double R, maybe less if Bran took off cross-country. Still seven miles.

"No," Ruby said grimly. "And from the look of his pants, he wasn't sticking to the road."

Gabe blew hard. "Damn it."

"He's been pretty happy about the two of us," Rachel said slowly. "Unless we're doing something that bothers him, and he won't talk to us about it."

Ruby shook her head. "I don't know. I'm—things are really rough here with the water rights fight. I think that's why he doesn't want to leave me alone. But it would be safer and easier for me if I didn't have to worry about him, especially if he's gonna run away from school. I'm —I don't dare go to town alone. For him to run off from school like that scares me."

"No fucking shit, Ruby. If things are that bad—God!" Gabe inhaled sharply.

"Do you need protection? Because my brother's company is available," Rachel said. "Family connection. No charge."

Ruby shook her head as her eyes shimmered with tears. "Thanks, Rachel, but I—I don't want to escalate. Yet. I hope this water rights thing is all that's going on with Bran. I'm terrified that it isn't. I just keep thinking about my father—his family—is this how it started?"

Gabe rubbed his face, remembering all he had learned about the Barkleys. Tony Barkley, who had murdered Ruby's mother and almost killed Ruby. The insanity that was Ruby's Aunt Grace. And other family members who revolved in and out of jail. He'd been around Thunder County long enough to know that Ruby was viewed as *the only sane Barkley worth a shit.*

Ruby's fears were entirely possible. Add those to what he knew about similar issues in the Martinieres...and him. The wild streak that had landed him in Northview Military Academy had started when he was Bran's age. Granted, beating the crap out of Joey for torturing and nearly killing Justine's cat wasn't the same sort of thing, but...Gabe remembered those days, when he had wanted to lash out at the world. God. Had his son inherited *that*? Or Tony Barkley's—whatever?

"Oh God," Gabe said slowly. "He's young, but within the age range when mental health problems start showing up. Look, Ruby. I'll pick him up tomorrow. If you'll give us permission, we'll take Bran to Seattle for evaluation. Put all of our minds at ease, and begin treatment if necessary."

"I—already talked to Remy about the paperwork. She recommended I hand this off to you, with everything else I have going on." Ruby gulped. "Here's the thing. I don't think he'll leave with you willingly. He might run if he saw your rig. Branny's gotten pretty good at crossing rough country fast and staying hidden." She swallowed hard. "Charlie and Martin think they can get him to come with them. I'm packing up some of his things tonight. The rest of his stuff can come over later. They'll be over first thing in the morning, along with the paperwork. If that's all right with you."

"That's more than all right," Gabe said. "And with the water rights —is there anything I can do?"

Her expression hardened. "Not a damn thing that would make it better. If anything, you'd make it worse. I'm serious about not wanting to escalate."

"We'll expect Bran in the morning, then." What else could he say?

"Thank you." Ruby hung up.

Gabe sighed. "It looks like we're going to become full-time parents. For a little while, anyway."

"I'll get him set up with specialists and—whatever else we need," Rachel said softly.

"Thank you," Gabe said. "Let's give him a day or two, okay? Figure out what's going on."

"I'll call Rafe and tell him not to come tomorrow morning."

"No. Tell Rafe what's going on. Maybe he can help us keep an eye on the kid."

Rafe *had* sent Gabe an *interesting* message about the activity of *certain persons* in Thunder County. Gabe wanted to learn what that was about.

And maybe Rafe could help him with Bran.

BRAN SCOWLED IN A CREDIBLE IMITATION OF GABE'S OWN MARTINIERE glower as he marched between Charlie and Martin to the big house's front door, their arms locked in his so he wouldn't bolt. Gabe greeted them with his hands on his hips, glaring down at his son. Charlie had to shove Bran when he wouldn't go through the door.

"So, what the hell is going on, Bran?" Gabe demanded once they were inside.

"Not telling," Bran snarled, lips tight. "Not gonna stay here either. Mom needs me."

"What your mother needs is for you to be where you're supposed to be, do what you're supposed to do, and stay the *fuck* safe!" Gabe snapped. "You're not staying in school; you're not doing your chores—how the *hell* does that help her?"

Brandon shook his head and looked down at his feet.

Gabe exhaled. *His* father Saul hadn't taken his behavior seriously when *he* was ten. And whatever was going on with Bran was a lot more dangerous than what Gabe had done to Joey. If Ruby didn't dare go to town alone, then Bran cutting school and going home on foot cross-country was much worse.

Especially given whose son he was. The more Gabe had thought about it the night before, the more shaken he'd become. He wasn't convinced that Joey's minions were out of Thunder County. And with Ruby having problems due to the water rights fight, well, that would be an excellent cover for *something* to happen to Brandon.

He wouldn't put it past Philip to try to hurt Brandon. Things had been too quiet for too long.

Rachel came from the family wing of the house. They'd set up the suite next to theirs for Bran, including extra security options that Ruby wouldn't have. She handed Gabe a smooth steel bracelet with the Alvarez Armory arrow and shield insignia carved into it. Rafe had produced the needed tech and taken Rachel through the programming steps that morning. All three of them agreed that Rachel needed to be the one orienting Brandon to his new limitations. In the past year, he'd accepted correction better from her than from Gabe, and if he was having mental issues—Rafe might not be the best idea, either.

"All coded."

"Thanks." Gabe stepped forward and took Brandon's left hand. Before Bran could yank his hand away, he snapped the bracelet onto his wrist. "There. That's a tracker and restraint. Unless I allow it, you can't leave the house. And if you do get out, I can find you."

Brandon yanked at the bracelet, becoming more frantic as it wouldn't budge. "What is this—*jail*?"

"Protective custody," Gabe said bitterly. The bracelet keyed into the household security system that Rafe had installed during construction. It would lock doors and windows if Bran tried to leave without permission. He'd been wrong about the security source at Rachel's condo—it was an Alvarez Armory installation, one of Rafe's companies, and nearly as good as Vygotsky Security.

Gabe had to wonder because there were definitely Vygotsky Security elements in Alvarez Armory products. How close a connection did Rafe have with Serg? Hadn't been one fourteen years ago. But a lot could happen in that much time.

"Come on, Brandon," Rachel said quietly. "Let's get you set up in your room."

"Since I have to stay in this *jail*—but I'm not talking to you!"

Rachel shrugged. "That doesn't matter to me. I just want to make sure you're coded in properly to the accesses you *can* have."

More grumbling, but Brandon followed Rachel down the hallway.

Gabe exhaled and turned back to Charlie and Martin. "Thank you. I hope Ruby's not alone on the ranch."

"Vickie's with her while we brought Bran over," Charlie said grimly. "The fight isn't with our neighbors. It's with some new people up the line at the Hot Mountain Ranch. They've been picking fights with everyone, but Ruby worst of all. She's the only single woman standing up to them."

"Some of the nastiest verbal attacks are coming from family," Martin said. "And they may be behind sabotage in the fields and water lines."

"Barkleys."

Charlie nodded. "Grace demands that Ruby sell the place to someone who knows what they're doing."

"Like hell! Ruby's damn good at what she does!" Gabe shook his head.

"We know that Bran's getting hazed at school," Charlie continued. "That happens off and on. But it's been getting worse in the last week. We took him out behind the barn to show him some moves."

"Does Ruby know?"

"He melts down if we hint at telling her about his getting beat up at school," Martin said. "The only way we got him to come here was to threaten to tell her what *we* knew. And he's not telling us everything. He won't show us how bad he's hurt. This is above and beyond the bullying he's experienced before. He gets hysterical when the subject comes up." Martin glanced at Charlie. "We had to promise that we wouldn't tell Ruby. It's weird."

"All right. Thank you." This whole scenario made Gabe even more suspicious. "I might know of a means to take care of this fight with the neighbors. Secretly. But I may need to get into contact with you two to set it up. Personal numbers okay?"

"Call mine, not Charlie's," Martin said. "Ruby's hot-keyed to Charlie's number for security's sake. Keep that line clear."

"Good."

"Yeah, well, we'd better get back," Charlie said. He handed Gabe an envelope. "Here's the paperwork you need."

"Thanks again," Gabe said. He took the envelope to his office and locked it in his safe, then headed for Brandon's room. Rachel met him halfway there.

"It's like he's not the same kid he was a month ago," she said quietly.

Those words sent chills through Gabe. Had Philip gotten to his son somehow?

I've been too complacent.

He strode past Rachel and into Bran's suite.

"Whaddya want?" Bran snapped from the office chair in front of his desk, his back stiff and straight, knees curled into his chest. He stared at a computer projection hovering over the desk.

Gabe put his hands on his hips again. "For one thing, you can show a bit more respect. Not just to me but to Rachel. Take whatever this is out on me but don't draw Rachel into it. She doesn't deserve that from you."

"I don't want to be here! I want to be at the Double R!" Bran buried his head in his knees, huddling tighter but still keeping his back straight. Untypically straight and stiff, especially for a kid who was normally athletic and lithe.

"That's not an option. Your mother is scared to death that something's going to happen to you because you aren't where you're supposed to be. So am I."

Despite his blank, hard, face, wetness formed in the corners of Brandon's eyes as he raised his head to glare at Gabe.

"I need to be with Mom. I need to protect her."

"You're a fucking distraction in a dangerous situation right now. Do you want her to get hurt because she has to worry about you? Because that is what is going on. She sent you here to be safe, so that she could do what's needed to stay out of trouble, without fretting about you."

"You don't understand."

"Don't I?" Bran wasn't moving right, holding his shoulders stiff and wincing every now and then. "I was on the run from indenture bounty hawks all those years I spent with your mother. Maybe I know more about this situation than you realize." Gabe eyed him. "Turn off your comp and stand up."

"What?"

"You heard me. *Now.*" He pushed a touch of Martiniere control tones to see how Bran would react—just guessing. At his age it wouldn't be word-specific, not yet, especially from an authoritative adult…control words came at puberty.

His son stiffly, jerkily, clearly resistant, got to his feet. He slowly switched off the comp, arm shaking as he fought the compulsion.

Gabe's heart sank, pieces coming together. The way Bran moved confirmed his greatest fear. There was more than schoolyard bullying going on.

Someone got to Bran. Programmed him. Fuck.

He needed Serg, *now.* As locked down as Gabe was, he couldn't do one damn thing about this on his own if Bran had received Family-level programming.

And Bran was hurting. His right shoulder was a bit crooked and he held himself tightly. Charlie and Martin wouldn't have roughhoused the kid like that. Not anything that would have lasted this long.

"Take off your shirt," Gabe said.

Brandon shook his head, tears now spilling down his cheeks. "You don't understand, Dad. You just don't understand."

Gabe drew a deep breath, then exhaled. Slowly unbuttoned his shirt and dropped it to the floor, then pulled off his t-shirt. He'd left the Double R when Branny would have been too young to remember seeing his scarred torso, and hadn't exposed him to it since.

Gabe touched the burn scar on his chest. "I got this at age twelve." The long, wavering scar from a bullwhip. "Age thirteen." Another scar. "Seventeen."

He turned his back to Brandon, hearing his son gulp.

"Ages fourteen, fifteen, sixteen, eighteen, twenty-one, and twenty-four," he said flatly, staring at the full-length mirrors on the closet doors, past his reflection to Brandon's. His son still stood stiffly as he shook with sobs, eyes wide, gaping at Gabe's back. "Still think I don't understand?"

"Dad—" A groan. But no more defiance in his voice—now Bran was nothing more than a very scared kid, his shoulders heaving as he cried.

"So maybe I understand one hell of a lot more than you think," Gabe said quietly. He turned back to his son. "Take off your shirt, son. Please." No command tone in his voice this time, just anguish.

"It's not Mom. It's not Mom," Brandon blubbered as he slowly unbuttoned his shirt.

"I wouldn't think it would be your mother. Or Charlie or Martin." Gabe kept his voice nonreactive as Bran struggled with his t-shirt. He didn't dare help. Bran was proud, like him. No assistance, unless he was asked.

Oh God, he thought as Bran finally yanked off the shirt. Tell-tale bumps on his ribs, indicating breaks. Healed or still healing? Bruises over his belly that extended into his pants.

"Turn around."

Brandon gulped as he complied. "They said that if I told, I'd be taken away from Mom. That she'd go to jail. Along with Charlie and Martin—they called them *perverts!*" His voice screeched with outrage. "Maybe send you to jail too. Dad, please—the teachers were getting snoopy. I *had* to cut school because the counselor wanted to talk to me."

More bruising and bumps on his son's back. Whoever did this

knew what the hell they were doing. No marks on Brandon's arms or face.

"I've seen enough, Bran," Gabe said softly. "Don't try to put your shirt back on." He went to the closet and fished out a robe—something Rachel had gotten for Bran to wear around Moondance. "This will be softer."

Brandon accepted the robe, nodding, still sniffling. Gabe held it for his son as he worked his way into it.

"Who are *they*, Branny?"

Brandon closed his eyes for a moment, shuddering. "Friends of Cody and Steve."

"Barkley?"

Bran nodded. "But there's others." He gulped. "I—I hear things sometimes. Trying to hide at school. At the games. In the grocery store. Around town." A faint note of pride in his voice. "I'm good at blending in and not being noticed." He shivered. "But the adults. I heard them talking about Mom in the store parking lot. They're gonna hurt her, Dad. They're gonna *hurt* her. Maybe even kill her!"

"Your mother is a hell of a lot tougher than you give her credit for," Gabe said. "And who wants to hurt your mother?"

"The new people. From the Hot—" His eyes widened and he choked, struggling to say more. His hands raised to his throat. "Agk…"

"Don't," Gabe said quickly. "Don't push it, Bran. You've been programmed for mind control. If you try to say more it will just hurt you. I *know*."

Bran sniffled and wiped his eyes, swallowing hard.

"I'm going to call Rafe and Rachel in now."

"Do they hafta know?"

"They can help." Gabe met Brandon's eyes steadily. "Not just you, but your mother. She doesn't want me to give her a hand, but I think she's in over her head with this mess, because she doesn't know every-thing behind it. I do. I can make sure she gets what she needs to fix it, but Rafe has to know. Just as Rachel needs to get a doctor in to see you." He gestured at Bran. "I'm worried about how hurt you are. You need medical attention. I'll have Rachel take care of you—and Rafe and I will do what we can to help your mother."

Brandon gulped. Then he flung himself at Gabe, hanging on hard as he sobbed.

Gabe was careful not to touch Bran's back as he comforted his son.

Damn you, Philip. Damn you to fucking hell.

No doubt in Gabe's mind that his uncle was part of this.

And if Ruby's kin were involved, too...well, he had no qualms there about doing what would be required to get them to back off and leave Bran and Ruby alone. Not after the stories he'd heard about the Barkleys from Ron Ryder.

GABE'S FIRST PRIORITY WAS TO MOVE RACHEL AND BRANDON WHERE Brandon could get medical help without risking reports to authorities, and ensure that they were safe. After Rachel and Rafe saw Brandon's battered body and listened to what Bran had to say, they agreed.

Rafe got a crew from Alvarez Armory to guard Moondance. Rachel called their father and somehow chartered a private flight from Pendleton to Seattle. Gabe secured the ranch. At least this was fall. He'd just finished the harvest. No need to supervise microbial grows. Once he knew that Bran and Rachel were safe, then he and Rafe could act.

But until then, Gabe was a custodial parent with all those responsibilities. To his shock, Ruby had temporarily transferred all custodial responsibilities to him—*and Rachel*—until the end of the school year. That spoke of her desperation and fear. It *did* make taking Brandon to Seattle a lot simpler.

He called Remy Trask to confirm his understanding. "I've got the paperwork for Brandon. I just wanted to confirm what it says."

"Ruby's desperate, Ramirez. There's been shots fired." Was that anger or fear on her face as she frowned at him? "Better that he's with you if something happens to her."

An icy chill ran down his back. "I'm getting him out of here to a safe location. I didn't know about the shots. Charlie and Martin didn't tell me."

Why the hell can I say Martin's name but not Martiniere?

"Happened this morning on the ranch, and that fucking Sheriff Rivers won't lift a finger to help her. I thought you might want to move him out of the area, either to Seattle or San Diego. Figured it was a good idea to make it easier for you to do that. Ruby's counting on you being able to keep Brandon safe." Trask raised her hand before Gabe could speak. "Don't tell me details. I don't need to know. What you need to know—the people leading the charge aren't Thunder County people. New owners of the Hot Mountain Ranch. Some of Ruby's family are involved but they aren't the movers." Her scowl deepened. "Ruby would be pissed if she knew I told you this much, but I thought you'd better be aware."

Gabe nodded curtly. *Thank God, Trask isn't under mind control.* Her freedom to talk demonstrated that.

"Thank you. Ruby doesn't want me involved any further, but—I have connections that can help with the situation. Once Brandon's secured."

"I don't want to know about it."

"Ruby shouldn't know either."

"Agreed." She hung up.

Hernan met them in the plane. "Your mother and I agreed that I should stay with you and Brandon," he said to Rachel. He glanced at Gabe and Rafe. "I'm assuming there are plans?"

"We'll talk in a safe place," Rafe said.

Nervous silence dominated their flight. As soon as they got settled into Rachel's condo, a doctor showed up to examine Brandon. Gabe and Rachel stayed with him. Luckily, there didn't appear to be any internal injuries other than cracked ribs. Gabe had been worried about that.

"You say that kids did this?" the doctor asked tensely—Gabe hadn't gotten her name.

"Down in Oregon," Rachel said.

"His mother and I are divorced," Gabe said. "She begged me to get him out of the situation and temporarily transferred custody to me and

Rachel. Law enforcement isn't involved and won't be. Neither will school authorities. It's—complex."

"Some of these blows were dealt by some awfully big kids, then."

"High school," Bran choked. "Cousins." He stuck his lower lip out. "And I *won't* talk to authorities."

That startled Gabe. As far as he knew, the only Barkley cousins were around Bran's age. No. Wait. Some of Grace's grandchildren.

"All right then," the doctor sighed. "Here's what we need to do."

Gabe ducked out as the doctor gave Rachel instructions. He went into Rachel's office to call Ruby. Bran still didn't want Ruby to know about him being attacked at school, but at least Gabe could reassure her that their son wasn't having mental problems.

"Bran's safe and out of the area," he said when her image appeared. "He isn't going to run. I've got a tracker on him. That's all I can tell you—and that what's going on is not a mental health issue."

Ruby closed her eyes for a moment and exhaled, relief softening her expression. Then she opened them again, her face drawing tight once more.

"Then it's related to the water rights fight."

"I'm afraid so. Trask told me you've been shot at."

"Just this morning."

"Ruby—"

"I can *deal* with it, Gabe! A lot of it is family bullshit. Just—I know I can depend on you to keep Branny safe, better than anyone else. Please. Keep him safe."

"I can do that."

"Thank you." She closed the connection.

BRAN WENT TO BED AFTER A LIGHT DINNER, UNDER PAIN MEDICATION. Gabe, Rafe, Hernan, and Rachel gathered in her office. They spoke in Spanish.

"I think our concerns have just intersected," Rafe said. "The buzz I'm hearing is that indentureds and lower-level security affiliated with that family we don't mention have been directed to a holding in Thunder County. There's concern about that."

"Your source?" Gabe steepled his fingers.

"Somebody within that particular family."

Gabe paused. He swallowed, tensing in anticipation. Nothing ventured, nothing gained.

"How well do you know Serg Vygotsky?"

To his relief, Serg's name didn't trigger any reaction from his programming.

Rafe raised his brows. "You know Serg?"

"Very well." Gabe met Rafe's eyes steadily. "You've used Vygotsky Security tech as a foundation for a lot of your products. Close enough that at first, I thought Rachel's condo security had been provided by Vygotsky. So how well do you know Serg?"

"We've worked together on some contracts," Hernan said. "Our collaboration started ten years ago. Shakeups were happening within the Group, and Piotr Vygotsky came looking for alliances. Because of our situation with Joey, he thought we might possess some useful mutual interests."

"So, you know Serg well enough," Gabe said. *And it started before Rachel and I got together. That would have been about the time Serg cut off comms with me.* "What's going on with those indentureds and security at the Hot Mountain Ranch?"

"None of us know for certain," Rafe said. "It doesn't match any known Group holdings or interests. Serg came to me because he has an unspecified interest in Thunder County."

"I can specify it. Ruby. And Brandon. At my request," Gabe said. "And he most likely knows that I'm married to Rachel by now?"

"Yes."

Gabe sighed. "I can't contact Serg directly. But I need to see him as soon as possible. There are—multiple issues tied to this situation. Proprietary things that only he and I can talk about. If we can meet tomorrow at Moondance, that would be ideal."

"Let me see what's doable." Rafe pulled up a shielded comp projection.

Gabe continued. "Hernan. Thank you for staying with Rachel and

Brandon. One thing you both need to know. Bran has been subjected to —the same sort of mind control I've experienced. I confirmed it for myself. Don't question him about what's happened. There may be partial triggers which can be violent. I need to get Serg or his father Piotr in to deal with it."

"Violent?" Rachel asked. "How violent?"

"I don't know if it would be self-directed or at others." Gabe firmly pushed back the sudden memory flash of slapping Ruby after she said a partial code. "I don't think they programmed code words into him. Not the norm until after puberty. But that doesn't mean there won't be triggers."

"You seem to be quite aware of the mechanics of—that particular family's proprietary structures," Hernan said cautiously.

"And I will *not* be forced into revealing details of how to do it, even if I *could* speak freely," Gabe said. "Remember the choices I've already made. A certain criminal corporate Federal case."

"Papa." Rachel frowned at her father. "Enough."

"I understand," Hernan said. "Just—checking."

"All right. Back to Serg. We'll handle the Thunder County situation. I also want him—or Piotr—to deal with what's been done to Brandon. They may be able to undo it."

Unlikely they'll be able to ease my strictures—but it would be worth a try. Not doing it here, though. Not around the innocents I love.

"And then?" Rachel asked. "What about school?"

"Let's give Bran a week to recover," Gabe said. "With any luck, we can go back to Moondance by then, if Rafe and I are successful. Right now, I don't want any pressure on him."

"Serg can be at Moondance at ten am," Rafe said, shutting off his comp.

"Good." Gabe ran a hand through his hair. "I'd like to leave early tomorrow morning, if we can schedule another charter. I need to say goodbye to Bran—I don't think I should just disappear, and I don't want to wake him up tonight."

Rachel kissed his cheek. "I'll get the charter set up now, hon."

"Thank you." And part of it was that he wanted a night with her before he left.

He hadn't cherished Ruby enough when he had her. He wasn't going to make that mistake with *this* wife.

"Be careful," Rachel murmured sleepily as Gabe slid out of bed and dressed.

He sat on the side of the bed and kissed her. "I will, darling. You and Brandon stay safe."

"With Papa here? Have no worries, Gabe. Between our security and what he can do, I'm not concerned…and we won't leave the condo until we get an all-clear from you and Rafe." She smiled at him. "This is not my first time dealing with a security lockdown. Papa slept at my bedroom window with a shotgun and Rafe the same at the door when Joey Martiniere was a threat. That also wasn't the first time they had to do it."

Joey, you fucking ass. And yet, a slight tendril of glee stirred within him. *I ended up with a woman you wanted that damned bad. I'm sure that's eating at you but good.*

Which—could be another piece of this puzzle.

"Then you're prepared for this sort of situation." Gabe bent to kiss her again. Another advantage of marrying into a family similar to his. Ruby was tough, but there were just some things difficult to explain unless they'd gone through it. Then again, Ruby would be on her feet, getting dressed, preparing to go with him, once she was certain that their son was safe.

"It's a perfect time for me to start a quilt for Brandon," Rachel said drowsily. "I'll talk to him about it today. We can pick out fabric and design. And that will be safe for us to do. He might even tell me more without being prompted." She smiled and turned onto her side. "Good hunting, my dear. Come back safe."

"I will," he promised.

Brandon's room was his next stop. His son still slept, looking a lot younger than almost ten. Gabe bent over and kissed Bran's forehead.

"Branny. Wake up for a minute."

Brandon's eyes popped open. He shot up, wild-eyed and uncertain, disoriented, gasping for breath. Gabe rested his hand on Brandon's shoulder. "Hey. Hey."

Brandon blinked at him, calming. "Dad?" He lay back down.

"You're in Rachel's Seattle condo. She and Papa Hernan are going to stay with you and keep you safe. Rafe and I are off to do some things to help your mother. Okay?"

Bran nodded, relaxing under Gabe's hand. "Wanna come too."

"Not this time. Besides. You've done your part. Now it's time for you to stay safe. Heal up. Listen to Rachel and Papa Hernan. That's the best thing you can do right now—so that neither your mother nor I have to worry about you." Gabe paused. "You'll see a bracelet like yours on Rachel. It's a tracker. Just in case someone tries to grab either one of you. Not that you are leaving the condo until we've—done what we're going to do."

"You're gonna help Mom?"

"I am going to make those people pay for hurting you, Bran. And threatening your mother. I promise you that."

"*Good.*"

Gabe kissed Bran's forehead again. "Go back to sleep, now, my tough warrior son. I'm proud of you."

That earned him a smile. Then Branny closed his eyes, nestling back into his covers.

SERG ARRIVED AT MOONDANCE WITH A CONTINGENT OF VYGOTSKY Security staff. Gabe strode out to meet them. He and Serg clasped forearms, then pounded each other on the back.

Serg sighed, stepping back. "God *damn*, it's good to see you alive and doing well, Gabe."

"I'm locked down pretty hard. I'm surprised I could even say your name to Rafe. My—relative—got to me."

Serg nodded. "We couldn't respond to your distress messages because we were on the run ourselves. That got resolved, but—everything went to hell about the time that I saw you last. It settled about the time you got divorced."

"The only reason I'm alive and walking today is because of those envelopes I gave you and Piotr," Gabe said.

"Got it," Serg said. "And now you've got this issue—and it's of concern to us as well."

"Let's go inside and talk further, where things are secure," Gabe said.

Gabe took Rafe and Serg downstairs, to his office. He switched the shielding to its highest levels before he spoke.

"The problem has two prongs to it. First, we need to deal with the Family—" Gabe paused carefully before continuing.

No reaction. *Good.*

He continued. "The Family and their connections to the people harassing Ruby in Thunder County. They've hooked up with Ruby's unsavory relatives, who would love to bring her down hard using the vehicle of a water rights lawsuit." He'd spent time looking up the details of the Thunder County water dispute last night so that he could explain it in detail to Rafe and Serg if necessary. "Normally, this would settle pretty fast because overall, it's a minor dispute, but if someone wants to be difficult...well, there have been gunfights over water rights in the West."

"Are you the reason for the Family connection?" Serg asked.

"Probably," Gabe said. "It's an opening to go after Ruby and Brandon without being obvious that's what's going on. Even though I've kept my head down, focused on my own business, not made any plays. Our—relative—told me in that face-to-face meeting that he wanted to see me broken. Destroyed."

"Hurt you by hurting them," Rafe said.

"Exactly. This was after I thwarted his original plan. At first, I think he intended to kill me." Gabe swallowed hard. "He locked me down instead. Had me beat up, then hit me several times in the face with his signet ring, until my nose bled."

"Ah," Serg said, nodding. "Nano delivery into your system. But why didn't he kill you? I'm glad he didn't, but—"

"I told him that on my death, Ruby gets access to keys to make a claim against the Family Trust as my widow. I wrote those provisions so they still hold even after divorce. I had programming residuals that tried to force two suicide attempts—that I remember. I've lost a few months' worth of memories from that time, consistent with recorded instances of memory tampering tied to mind control programming." Gabe gestured at Rafe. "I haven't modified those keys to include Rachel. She has family resources. Ruby doesn't—and she has Brandon to raise."

"All right," Serg said slowly. "Makes sense. How much do you know about Gabe, Rafe?"

"Pretty damn good idea who he really is," Rafe said.

"How much do you want to disclose, Gabe?"

Gabe shrugged. "He's my brother-in-law. I'm all right with *you* being explicit. Just—not too many Family name mentions. It might encourage me to get casual myself and—the last time triggered seizures."

Serg frowned. "The issue is that Brandon is a potential heir and Philip knows that you've made provisions for him to claim his inheritance. Competition for Joey, just like you are."

"Uh-huh. Me marrying Rachel has a further component." Gabe eyed Rafe. "Rachel told me this morning that things got so bad with a certain relative that at night, Hernan sat at her bedroom window with a shotgun and you at her door. How rough did it get?"

"That's how I met Serg," Rafe said. "I went to Vygotsky Security for help. I knew they had gone dark to evade—the Family. Dealing with the situation lasted for a good two years. So yes. We never fired a shot, but it was close."

"All right. You know your way around the Family."

Rafe nodded.

"Where *do* things stand within the Family, Serg?"

Serg sighed. "Philip almost got deposed right before your divorce. Uncle Artie in France made a play for Family control, with our help. Donna-gran pitched in. Joey and Philip managed to beat Artie back, but it broke down into warring family factions. Philip got to you before any of us could have, or we would have pulled you in as the Martiniere-in-waiting, to be our standard bearer. He kept us far too busy to respond to your distress call—and then after, I wasn't sure what, if anything, you'd be able to do. We were fighting for survival, and just didn't have resources to spare."

Gabe tapped his fingers on the desk. "Okay. Now I know how things fall into place. Is this a Joey operation? Or—our other relative?"

Interesting. He could say Joey's name, hadn't even thought twice about saying it. That said volumes about Philip's perception of Joey's effectiveness.

"Joey is the main organizer," Serg said. "Not sure how involved Philip is. The supervisor on site reports to one of Philip's managers, but *anything* Joey does these days has that level of monitoring going on. At the minimum, Philip has approved it."

"Okay." Gabe twined his fingers together, thinking. "And then there's my other problem. Someone has managed to program Bran. I don't think it's the deep programming. I can't do anything about it because of my own lockdown. I need you or Piotr to free him." Gabe took a deep breath. "Then I need to have you see what you can do to ease my strictures."

"How bad is it for Brandon?"

"He can't name his attackers without starting to choke. I was able to compel obedience by using general tones. I don't think there's a keyword."

Serg nodded. "And you?

"Full lockdown. I cannot say, write, or type my real name. I can say similar names but even attempting to say it causes problems. Same for the name of the woman who expanded the parameters, as well as our relative and the Family name. It appears to be tied to intent on my part. Depending on what I am trying to say, the result is anything from mild muscle spasms to seizures significant enough for me to break writing instruments and cause blackouts. A partial mention of my keywords in an angry tone triggers an involuntary violent reaction. It needs to be said either in anger or by someone trained in tone use."

"Damn it." Serg scowled. "You *are* out of play. Completely."

"Yes."

"Can my father gain access to Brandon? Dealing with this is more his specialty." Serg turned away from them and called up a shielded screen, inputting quickly.

Gabe looked at Rafe. "Can we get Piotr to Brandon, or vice versa? I'd like to have the names of Bran's attackers from him before we start our move, if possible."

"I'll contact Dad." Rafe pulled up a screen. "Serg, sending you the access codes. Dad's guarding Rachel and Brandon. Have Piotr escorted by Rick."

A few moments while that action was coordinated.

"Done. My father will be there this afternoon," Serg said. He sighed. "His accesses might not be enough for your issues, Gabe. That might only be able to be changed through Philip—or Donna-gran, as the Matriarch, if she has the strength. But we can try."

"After we take care of Thunder County issues first," Gabe said firmly.

His grandmother still held the title of Matriarch of the Martinieres. Good to know.

PIOTR TEXTED THAT EVENING.

> Complete reversal. Minimal nano dosage. Here are the names you wanted. Not everything happened at school or at the hands of children.

Gabe scanned Piotr's notes, and then the list. Besides the kids, there was no one he recognized. He called Serg and Rafe to his office, then handed the list to Serg.

"Part of Joey's staff, damn it. Including the supervisor who reports to Philip's people." Serg glanced over at Rafe. "Good news is that we've dealt with this crew before."

"I want to talk to that supervisor," Gabe said grimly. "He may have laid hands on Bran, he may not have, but he's responsible for that stuff. He's going to answer to me."

Serg eyed Gabe. Then he nodded.

They set up their final plans.

Gabe reserved dealing with the Barkleys for himself and a small team from Alvarez Armory. His plans required coordination through Charlie and Martin to get the proper government authorities involved.

When he was done, Thunder County would damn well be safer not just for Ruby and Brandon, but for a bunch of other people.

———

Gabe wore a full-face mask, and played the role of a bounty hawk swooping down on the assorted problematic Barkleys. Easy enough to scoop up the ones with outstanding debts, restrain them, then hand them over to the *real* waiting hawks. The family had clearly been depending on Sheriff Rivers' lax enforcement and Lakeside's distance from population centers to avoid capture.

Charlie pointed Gabe toward an ambitious Thunder County deputy, Sharon Wilhite, who'd been chafing under Rivers and was running for election to replace him. She was happy to cooperate with bounty hawks willing and licensed to enforce arrest warrants. That handled another big chunk of the Barkleys.

Grace Barkley sputtered and fumed as her son and his wife were hauled off to jail. Children's Services removed their kids. That included the older ones involved in attacking Brandon. That just left Grace and her daughter Jeannie, and if Gabe could have found a way to drag them away, he would have.

Grace glowered at Gabe as she and Jeannie sat in the kitchen of their decrepit rental double wide, under close watch by an Alvarez Armory team. Gabe kept his pistol handy. Just in case.

"You can't do this!" she screeched at intervals. "It's not fair. We're just trying to get along—"

Gabe bit back the retorts he wanted to make, waiting for the all-clear from Serg at the Hot Mountain Ranch.

It came during another one of Grace's periodic tantrums.

"Shut up," he growled.

"Who are you to tell me—" Grace sneered.

She gasped as Gabe pulled off his mask.

"I'm telling you what I should have said ten years ago, and laid down the line then," he growled. "Shut the fuck up, Grace."

"Ruby. Ruby put you up to this."

"No. You and your family did this to yourselves." Gabe handed his weapon to one of the Alvarez team and strode toward Grace. She cowered back as he towered over her. "When you chose to join in with others harassing Ruby as part of this water rights fight, when your grandchildren decided it was fun to beat the crap out of Brandon and help outside people hurt him—*that's* what did this to you. Your choices. You fucked with my ex-wife and my son, and I *do not* tolerate that. You've been nasty to Ruby for years, and it will stop. *Now.*"

Grace blubbered incoherently. Gabe glanced at Jeannie. "I'd recommend you two find a new place to live, away from Thunder County," he said silkily.

"You can't do this—" Jeannie blustered.

"Can't I?" Gabe gave her his best Martiniere feral grin. "Gabe Ramirez is not exactly who you think he is, Jeannie Barkley. And you had better fucking think more than twice about causing problems for Ruby or Brandon ever again. I don't have to live in this county anymore. I don't have to consider the implications and impact of my actions here on my business. And I *will* protect my son and his mother."

Especially since I am no longer afraid of Philip fucking Martiniere.

"Is there anything else?" Captain Sanders of Alvarez Armory asked Gabe.

Gabe glowered at Jeannie and Grace. "Understand me?" He pushed a menacing tone.

Both women nodded, wide-eyed.

"Then we're clear," Gabe said.

He settled into their van with a sigh, as they headed for Hot Mountain to wrap it up.

On the one hand, he didn't feel all that good about threatening women. That was a Joey trick.

On the other, when Gabe remembered the amount of misery Jeannie and Grace had caused Ruby over the years, perhaps he didn't feel that bad after all.

Serg met Gabe as he climbed out of the van. "We've got Philip's man isolated in the machine shed, like you asked," he said.

Gabe bared his teeth in anticipation. "Perfect location."

"Gabe, what are you—"

"I'll leave him alive," Gabe growled. "But I fully intend to send a message to *our relative.*"

He was not surprised to recognize Philip's man as one of his assailants from seven years earlier. The captain of Philip's security force, if he remembered correctly. The man was zip-cuffed in a chair, face paling as Gabe strode into the shed.

Yes, motherfucker. You know who I am.

Rafe idly pointed a rifle at the man. He chewed on a cigar clenched in his teeth, fully on alert despite his apparent casualness.

"Undo the cuffs," Gabe ordered, his rage building.

Serg hesitated.

"Undo them," he repeated, glaring at the man. No name. But he didn't need the man's name.

The minute the man's hands and feet were free, Gabe backhanded him, knocking him off the chair and onto the floor. He followed up with several hard kicks to the man's gut, sending him rolling onto his back. The man whimpered as he crumpled onto his side again in a desperate attempt to protect his belly, eyes wide as he stared at Gabe.

"You can dish it out but can't take it, huh? Including beating up a kid. *My son,* God damn you." Another kick to the man's gut. "Get on your feet, asshole. Or can you only fight when your opponent can't strike back?"

"Please," the man begged shakily as he staggered to his feet. "I didn't know—"

"*Bullshit.*" Gabe slammed him up against a wall, gripping the man's shoulders. "You knew damn good and well who that kid was. You knew damn good and well who I was seven years ago."

The man tried to kick Gabe. He spun the man around and slammed him face first into the wall, twisting the man's right arm behind his back.

"You *listen* to me, motherfucker," he snarled. "I know who you work for. And that son-of-a-bitch may think he's shut me down with his mind control bullshit but *he hasn't.*" Gabe slammed him into the wall again, at full strength. "You motherfucker. You should have never put yourself in my path after what you did to me seven years ago. Especially after doing the same damn thing to *my son.*"

Another hard slam against the wall, as hard as Gabe could do it.

"Please—" the man snuffled, turning his head sideways, blood flowing from his nose.

"The only thing saving your pathetic hide from me beating you to death very, very slowly is that I need you to carry a message. Understand?"

The man nodded, coughing.

"You make *sure* this message gets to the big boss. The *head* man. Understand?"

Another nod.

"Tell him that he *does not touch* me or my family. Got it? Tell me."

"Don't touch you or your family." The man's voice shook.

"Good. There's more." Gabe leaned closer, his voice going quieter and silkier, but no less menacing. "You tell him that Gabe Ramirez remembers. Is coming for him. Sooner or later, just like a phoenix, I will rise from the ashes. Again. And when I do—he will regret what he has put me through...." he let his voice trail off. "Tell me."

The man repeated what Gabe had said.

Gabe slammed him against the wall two more times, then stepped back. Even though the man sank limply to the floor, Gabe was careful to back away out of his reach before he turned to face Rafe and Serg. Rafe grinned at him. Serg looked shocked.

"Dump this worthless piece of shit on *my relative's* front door," Gabe said to Rafe. "He's the captain of his security force—or was seven years ago."

Then he marched out of the machine shed to stare at the Thunder Mountains, now dusted with a scattering of snow. His breath came fast, hands clenching and unclenching. The memories of *that* April day came back hard and clear, especially the one when he'd looked over the wheat fields and wondered if that would be the last thing he'd ever see before that final darkness.

Release. Release. It's done now.

Gabe made himself breathe slower, let the rage fade away.

"Damn. Gabe," Serg said, coming up next to him.

"Seven years ago, that man led a detail that beat the crap out of me, under the tender supervision of *our relative*," Gabe growled. "I thought I was going to my death. It was the beginning of my world going to hell, instead. And then he beat the crap out of Brandon. The final straw."

Gabe exhaled, shuddering, trying to ease the fury that threatened to rise again at the memory of his son's beaten body.

"The motherfucker is damned fucking lucky I left him alive," he continued. "If I hadn't wanted to send a message to *our relative*, he'd be dead."

Serg didn't say anything more, but left Gabe alone.

Gabe didn't rejoin the others until he was certain he could control his anger.

RAFE TOOK OVER THE REST OF THE HOT MOUNTAIN OPERATION. THE actual owners had been bullied into compliance thanks to debt owed to the Martiniere Group. Rafe planned to pull together a financing team to clear them from Martiniere obligation.

But before they separated, Rafe took Gabe aside.

"Let's talk," he said. "I think we might have some mutual interests that would benefit Alvarez Armory. Not now. When all this is over."

"Be happy to," Gabe said.

Gabe went back to Moondance with Serg. Piotr waited for them there. Gabe had wanted to do his deprogramming work at Moondance —if it could be accomplished.

It was an excruciating forty-eight hours of scans and seizures. And when it was done, he'd only gained enough release to do small things. An improvement, but not enough.

"No more," Piotr said finally. "The nano count in your bloodstream is far too high to safely clear. It is going to take time for them to degrade to a harmless level for deprogramming you. Maybe twenty years at the earliest. I cannot touch the base programming otherwise.

That is something only Philip or Donna can do—and Donna is not in any condition to do it."

Gabe grimaced. "So that means I'm sidelined when it comes to the Family."

"Yes." Piotr shook his head. "Damn it. I was able to slightly strengthen your counterdefenses, and you will be able to use more control tones. A little gain, enough to protect yourself further. Your code words are less volatile than they were, barring another infusion of nanos."

Oh well, he hadn't honestly expected release from the programming to be a possibility. He couldn't have everything.

"Maybe someday," Serg said before he and Piotr left.

"Maybe." Gabe shrugged. "Stay safe, cousin. I wish I could be of direct use to the Family, but it doesn't look like that's going to happen."

"Things could change," Serg said. "Keep in touch."

"I will. But I'm not going to be a player, Serg. Safer to keep contact down except in an emergency."

"I'll still keep hoping." Serg paused. "Watching you in all this— there's no question in my mind. You are the one who should be the Martiniere right now. Not Philip. Not Joey. You."

Gabe snorted. "What should be and what the reality is are often two very different things."

"That's for sure." Serg clapped him on the shoulder and left.

Gabe got back to the Seattle condo on Sunday afternoon. On the way back, he texted Ruby.

All clear now. Does it work to have Bran call you at 7 pm on Sundays, regularly?

Oh God, Gabe, yes!

Starts tonight.

He refused to let himself think about the fact that this was the first time he'd gotten a happy text response from Ruby since their divorce.

Rachel and Bran were playing a video game when Gabe entered the condo.

"Dad! Dad!" Bran jumped up and crashed into him, bouncing back with a wince. He looked up at Gabe, face now solemn. "Did you make them pay?"

"Yes. I personally beat the crap out of the man that you said had hurt you the worst. And your cousins are…in the custody of the state."

"*Good.*" Glee briefly flitted over Bran's face. Then concern. "Is Mom all right?"

"I haven't talked to her but yes, she's all right. She's expecting you to call at seven tonight."

"Great! Gotta get back to the game."

Gabe half-smiled, watching his wife and her stepson play. Bran almost seemed back to his normal self. He sighed and carried his duffle to the bedroom, noticing a new quilt on Brandon's bed as he walked by his room. The one that Rachel had talked about making? Possibly.

The bed in their room looked awfully good, so he crashed onto it, kicking off his shoes and letting himself nap on top of the covers, not even bothering to pull up the crocheted afghan folded at the foot of the bed. Damn, he was *tired*.

It was dark when Rachel woke him. "Bran wants to know if he should call his mother from his room or somewhere else."

Gabe startled and checked the time. Almost seven. He hadn't intended to sleep this long.

"Your office," he said sleepily. "Highest security. Need to keep that going for a while—no trackers on our current location. Just in case."

"I'll set it up." Rachel kissed him and switched on a reading light. Gabe didn't move. He was tired, damn it. He counted back the days… how long had this actually been?

A week at all-out speed.

No wonder he was tired.

Rachel returned and lay down next to Gabe, pulling up the crocheted afghan to cover them. "Good hunting?" she asked.

"Excellent hunting," he said. "Except that Piotr wasn't able to do much to ease my lockdown."

She smiled at that. "Maybe I'm being selfish, Gabe, but I don't want to lose you to your real family. And I think I would." She kissed him, then nuzzled down to rest her head on his chest. "Do you have any idea how soon Ruby will want Brandon back?"

"I have no idea," he said. "She still has to deal with that water rights fight, but at least it should be on a less acrimonious footing."

"Dad?" Brandon appeared in the doorway. "Mom wants to talk to you."

Gabe sighed. "I'll be right there." His whole body ached as he got out of bed. He needed a day or so's rest after everything—especially Piotr's deprogramming attempts.

As he walked down the hallway, he ran his fingers through his hair to make it appear less disheveled.

"Hey," he said as he entered Rachel's office. Tears ran down Ruby's cheeks. Gabe collapsed into Rachel's desk chair, slumping back.

"Thank you, Gabe," she gulped. "That's our old Branny. Thank you."

"He'd been programmed," Gabe said. "Just like I was—still am."

Ruby absorbed that with widened eyes. He wondered if he'd ever told her about that. Wait. Yes, he had. After he'd slapped her.

"The trigger you hit that time has been defused," he added. At least that was one thing.

She shook her head. Then scowled slightly. "You got involved, didn't you." Statement, not a question.

Gabe considered for a moment. "Yes. There were factors that went beyond you and Brandon that needed to be dealt with." He shrugged. "It had to be done, and I had the connections to pull it off."

The scowl softened to a grimace. "Aunt Grace is still in hysterics. But she and Jeannie are moving in with John down in The Dalles. And Sharon Wilhite's campaign for sheriff has kicked off with a bang."

"I *enjoyed* telling your Aunt Grace what the fucking score was," he admitted. "She's made your life hell over the years. But I couldn't say or do anything until now. Didn't have the backup to do it." He sighed. "It would be safe for Bran to go back to the Double R in a few weeks— if you're comfortable with that. But he's going to need to make up schoolwork and there should be some follow-up counseling."

Now it was Ruby's turn to sigh. "There's still a lot of complexities that I have to work out with the water rights. And there'll be blowback from your activities. Bran needs to stay clear of that. I—Gabe, I wouldn't know what to do about the counseling part. I hate to ask, but would you continue with the agreement as arranged?"

"We can do that."

"Thank you."

"Maybe you should have him for Christmas this year instead of me," he said. "We'll do Thanksgiving."

She nodded fiercely, tears trickling down her cheeks again. "Thank you, Gabe."

"Do you want to talk to Bran some more?"

"Yes," she whispered.

Gabe got up. Bran waited in the living room.

"Your mother still has more to say," he told his son.

Bran ran past him. Gabe watched him go with a smile.

And then he went back to Rachel.

12 / ALVAREZ ARMORY

A week after Bran went back to live with Ruby again, Gabe was working in the forested part of Moondance, checking the springs and fences after his grazing lessee had moved the sheep out for the season. He already missed having Bran at his side. Sure, it took longer to get stuff done, but besides work, he'd been teaching Bran part of the Martiniere heir self-defense regime, with Rafe's help whenever he dropped in. Work in the forest was good for developing situational awareness—

Gabe's skittering thoughts abruptly shifted from *missing Bran* and the prospect of asking Ruby for partial custody as well as expanded visitation rights.

There it was again. Movement in a brushy section of the forest, on or near the crawler track.

He switched off the chainsaw that he'd been using to cut up the aspen that had fallen on the fence around one of the springs.

Flash that disappeared, just where the crawler track dipped into a thicket of lodgepole pine.

Flicker of light on a crawler canopy.

Gabe slowly pulled off his ear protection, set the chainsaw on the ground, and picked up the rifle he usually carried when working alone these days, checking around him just in case.

Nothing else moving, and the lodgepole thicket was the most

obscured area nearby. It might be Rachel coming out to share lunch. He was just out of connectivity range, so he had let her know his approximate working location today. A simple farm safety precaution even for non-Martinieres. That might be her.

Usually, though, Rachel would let Gabe know about the possibility of her eating with him before he left the house. And she had a marketing project due today. It would not be her normal pattern to join him for lunch when one of her freelance jobs was approaching its deadline.

Gabe squatted behind a tree trunk and angled the rifle toward the opening where the crawler track came easily into sight. The vehicle stopped as it emerged from the trees.

"Gabe? Hey Gabe!" Rafe's voice. Rafe emerged, hands apart from his body and held wide so that Gabe could see he was unarmed.

Gabe laughed with relief and disarmed his weapon. "Over here, Rafe." He stood up and walked back over to the aspen, placing the rifle nearby.

Rafe scrambled back into the crawler. Gabe added a couple of wood chunks to the stack he was making while Rafe parked next to Gabe's vehicle.

"I stopped by the house, and Rach said you were out here," he said.

Gabe dusted off his hands before bumping fists with Rafe. "Yep, wanted to get some of this work done before we get too far into fire season."

"Bran visiting his mom or has he gone back for good?"

"For good," Gabe said. "Might try to get partial custody. We'll see how things settle with Ruby. And Rachel." He eyed Rafe. His brother-in-law usually didn't drop in like this—he'd call so that either Rachel or Gabe could pick him up at the Pendleton airport.

"I can give you a hand, if you'd like," Rafe said.

"Sure. I need to finish cutting up this tree, then fix the fence. If you could stack the wood as I cut it, that would be great."

"Got gloves?"

"Should be some in the crawler, either mine or the one you drove out. There's ear protection in my rig."

Gabe started up the chainsaw once Rafe had put on his protection.

He mulled things over as he finished sawing the trunk into lengths that would work for the fireplaces at Moondance. This might just be a casual visit. Rachel would probably have sent Rafe out no matter what, just so she could finish her work.

But he didn't think that was the case. Not an unannounced visit. Out of pattern for Rafe.

And then there had been that comment about *mutual interests* when dealing with Bran's issues last fall. Rafe hadn't said anything about that since then.

Gabe finished cutting and shut off the chainsaw. He pulled off his ear protection and joined Rafe in stacking the final chunks.

"So now what?" Rafe asked.

Gabe studied the fence, a set of wire panels attached to wooden posts. The fallen tree had taken down one panel, but it looked like he could straighten and reattach it.

"Gonna try to salvage the panel and nail it back to the posts," he said. "This is just to keep the sheep and elk from mucking up the spring and chewing the aspen grove down to nothing."

"Got it."

They set to work. Four hands got the job done faster than two.

"What's up?" Gabe asked as he hammered the panels back in place. "A social visit?"

"Not exactly. This a good place to talk?"

"About as good as my office. No connectivity unless someone's running a drone."

"And my alerts would tell me if that happens. Good." Rafe sighed. "I mentioned a few months back that we might have some mutual interests. I've been wanting to bring you into some of the things I've been doing, but," he shrugged. "The timing hasn't been right."

"What's been going on?" Gabe pounded the last heavy staple into place. "Whew. I'm ready to take a break. Close enough to my lunchtime."

Rafe chuckled. "Rach made sure I had a lunch packed before pushing me out the door so she could work."

They went back to the crawlers. Gabe secured his tools—no more chainsawing for the rest of the day, anyway, under fire regulations—

and checked the angles on the vehicles' rooftop solar chargers. Then he grabbed his lunch. The two men plopped onto the close-cropped grass in front of the crawlers.

"So," Rafe said, after they had finished their sandwiches. "Here's the deal. Alvarez Armory has a particular market—providing defensive services to small organizations under threat by commercial militias. We do a little government work, such as patrolling freeways in remote areas, but most of what we do is emergency service. Farm cooperatives. Water districts. Small municipalities. Usually places where one bigwig decides that he wants to be the Boss, and hires heavies to push folks around."

"Mmmhmm," Gabe murmured. He took a big swig of ginger water. Rachel made a lot of it as the summer heated up. The flavor hit the spot when he was working outside, and he tended to stay hydrated better because he drank more. Ruby used to make something similar when they worked the fields.

"We're seeing a change in that pattern," Rafe said. "And it worries the hell out of me because I don't understand how it's working."

"How so?"

"Instead of heavies, there's an influx of indentured workers. Past incidents have involved agricultural sector and sometimes construction workers. Not this time. This case is heavy with clerical staff in government offices. They push out the local folks and take over those jobs. Then they—switch their bosses."

"Switch their bosses?" Gabe frowned.

Rafe nodded. "Turn them to support particular local leaders and policies. It's usually not as gross and obvious as a complete one-eighty attitude change in county and city electeds. It's usually shifts in certain policies favoring corporate investments and developments." He paused. "What I see looks one hell of a lot like Martiniere Group mind control. But I don't know enough to identify it for certain. Could it be possible?"

"I'd have to see it in action to be sure." Gabe picked up a fallen Ponderosa pine twig and started fiddling with it as he thought. "Are there noticeable verbal cues?"

"I think there are. But I'm not positive. The electeds generally have an indentured staff person hanging around."

"Who holds the contracts?"

"Ostensibly the city or county government for the clericals—those are the ones I can track; the others are privates."

Gabe pursed his lips thoughtfully. "Private would require specific access authorizations for you to track down."

"I didn't know that."

"What about the ones you can track?"

"This isn't one hundred percent because they're coming from general labor pools, and there's a pattern of multiple origins, but—at least a third of the clericals trace back to the Martiniere Group."

"I see." The twig snapped. Gabe absently kept breaking it until the stick was in tiny pieces. "What specifically do you want me to do? Given that I have certain limitations."

"I've got a contract with a small water cooperative on Diné Free State land," Rafe said. "Mostly Diné and Hispanic people. A larger private group is trying to take them over and privatize the cooperative. Valois Investments."

Gabe snorted. "That's my particular relative." Philip had a tendency to name corporate subdivisions after the long-distant French royal ancestry he prided himself on. Obscure French royal ties or Bonaparte names on a corporation usually traced back to Philip's control.

"I can't find the connection."

"I can. It's well-buried but I know the links."

"See? Already I know more than I did five minutes ago. I'd like you to take a look at the records as well as the clips I have of some of the before and after behaviors. At the very least." Rafe paused. "Look. Dad and Rick think I'm tilting at windmills by having Alvarez Armory take on these situations. They think I should focus on corporate security, and I do just enough of that work to pay the bills. But these are good people, Gabe, and they're being abused. They've worked hard to get what they have set up so far. I just hate—"

Gabe held up his hand. "Yeah, yeah, not a problem, I'll do what I can. How much documentation will you need from me, considering I can't explain how I know these things? That's my big concern."

"My clients know that my source is well-placed but can't be revealed," Rafe said. "Gabe, I don't have to prove a case in court. I just have to provide enough evidence to convince some very frightened people about the source of their problems, and help protect them from a certain family. Any countermeasures you can suggest would be useful."

"You said this isn't the only incident of this type?"

Rafe nodded. "But this is the toughest one I've had to work on. Look. I'll pay you a consulting fee. I'm not asking you to do this for free."

"All right." Gabe stretched. "I need to spend another hour checking fences and springs before I can knock off for the day. If you hop in my rig, we'll come back for this one. We can talk further."

"Sounds like a plan," Rafe said. "I'll get my things out of the crawler."

Gabe noticed that one of the items that Rafe brought over was a semi-automatic rifle very similar to his own.

One thing he kept mulling over as he waited.

Why was Philip doing this? Or was this a Joey project?

Either way, he didn't like the sound of what Rafe was describing.

GABE LIKED WHAT HE SAW EVEN LESS AS HE SPUN THROUGH THE RECORDS Rafe had called up for him that afternoon. He still remembered enough of the Family accesses and associated companies to trace the complex transfers of indentured rights back to their source.

Those clericals are fifty percent Martiniere Group in origin. At least.

With more time, he'd most likely be able to identify an even higher percentage. And—someone in the labs had finally figured out and countered the sabotage algorithm Gabe had created within the indentured mind control programs before his testimony. No wonder Philip was *pissed* at him. Given what little Gabe could see from the clips Rafe had provided, the sophistication of indentured programming was back up to what it had been fifteen years ago, when he'd left the labs to testify.

At least the sabotage worked for that long.

And his little algorithm had worked well, for Philip to take until now to finally get performance back to a standard Gabe recognized from his time in the Martiniere labs. But what the hell was Philip—and this had to be a Philip project, too well-planned to be Joey's job—trying to accomplish by taking over a small water co-op like this?

Gabe tapped his fingers on his desk. He didn't like where that line of thought went, either.

You were trained to become the Martiniere. If you were taking these actions as the Martiniere, where would they lead?

No matter how Gabe tried to dodge the notion, it all came back to the simple conclusion that Philip was building a political foundation to run for office. And not just an ideological foundation, but one which would establish Philip as a regional strongman, if not a dictator. Control of water resources over a desert region, including Southern California.

Fuck.

He wondered how much Serg and Piotr knew. What Justine was doing.

And if Gabe were still married to Ruby, and didn't have a reason to know Rafe Alvarez, would he even have been aware of this? Or would he have been able to communicate and work with Serg and Piotr? So many unknowns, but—

Perhaps his uncle had actually done Gabe a favor by forcing him away from Ruby. Had laid the foundation for his own defeat instead of Gabe's.

He just couldn't leave me alone to be with my family in peace. Fucker. But he will pay for that.

Time to pull Rafe away from his visit with Rachel and *talk.*

RAFE AND RACHEL WERE OUT ON THE BIG DECK.

"Uh-oh," Rafe said as Gabe sat down, facing him. "I don't like the expression on your face, Gabe."

"You shouldn't," Gabe said grimly. He glanced at Rachel,

wondering how much he dared disclose around her. "We need to go to a more secure location, but I can tell you this. The number is closer to fifty percent than one-third. And if I spent more time and dug deeper, my estimate is that further data will likely bring that number up to seventy percent."

Rafe groaned. "Aw, crud. That is not the news I wanted to hear."

"Didn't think so," Gabe said. "Anyway, I still have questions. Maybe we should go down to my office." He looked back over at Rachel. "Sorry, dear. Rafe asked me to do some research for him."

"That's all right. I don't need to hear about it," Rachel said. "And now that I've got the McKinley project sent off, I think I'm just going to sit out here in the sun and rest."

"You have been going at it hard," Gabe acknowledged. He bent to kiss her before leading Rafe down to his office.

He and Rafe didn't talk until Gabe had raised his shields to the highest levels.

"All right, Gabe. How bad is it?"

"It's pretty fucking bad," Gabe said. "I'll have to observe behaviors on site to be certain, because normally indentureds aren't given the ability to program non-indentureds. It's possible, but I sabotaged that program years ago. It's taken them until now to undo my programming. But." He raised a finger. "That percentage I gave you? It includes hidden indentureds, not just indentureds whose contracts have bounced around several owners in order to hide their origins. I went down the whole list of clericals you gave me. A lot of hidden indentureds on that list, that you wouldn't identify unless you knew how to look for them."

"Hidden indentureds?" Rafe raised his brows quizzically. "I've not heard of that."

"It's a Family thing," Gabe said grimly. "Another thing that was supposed to be sabotaged, that is now back in existence. You have to know where to look to find those links."

"So how the hell can my clients counter them?"

"Can you get Vygotsky Security on this job?"

Rafe shook his head. "Serg tipped me off about this and suggested I talk to you. They're in a difficult spot right now. More turmoil within the Family. His exact words were, *Tell Gabe that Joey is being an ass and thinks that Aunt Marguerite is tippling with the bourbon.*"

"Aw, *shit*." Gabe exhaled. The code words *Aunt Marguerite, tippling,* and *bourbon* meant that Joey and possibly Philip suspected the Vygotskys of actively working with *him.* They couldn't act in this situation without being at risk. And there were deeper meanings tied to *Aunt Marguerite* and *bourbon,* especially given Philip's penchant for venerating the Martiniere family descent from a bastard Valois French royal line, and their Medici ancestors.

Rafe raised a brow. "Not good news, then."

"Serg basically told me that his hands are tied and I have to do it." There was more to the message than that, but he wasn't going to tell Rafe that Serg wanted Gabe to challenge Philip, that things were *just that bad* in the Family.

Bourbon. No fucking way am I activating that protocol right now. Maybe I should have Rafe tell Serg that I thought Aunt Marguerite had a thing for rum instead.

No. Invoking their ancestors whose bad behavior had been one cause of the Haitian Revolution wasn't a good idea, either. There were protocols associated with that history as well—and he wasn't in a position to burn it all down.

"That's going to make things more complicated," he continued. "I can't come at the situation as directly as Serg can. But I'm going to need to go onsite to script it out."

"How soon can you do it?" Rafe asked.

Gabe considered his to-do list. "I'll need a day to put things in order here so that I can go, and let Rachel know. Can you get me a plane ticket?" He wasn't supposed to have Brandon until the Fourth of July, so he wouldn't need to be juggling time with his son and this job, at least for a couple of weeks. Leaving the ranch wasn't optimal, but he could hire one of Craig's cousins to monitor irrigation and the fields temporarily. The microbials—well, he was in a lull there. And things like checking fence and the springs in the forest just needed to get done sometime this season.

"We're driving," Rafe said. "Not perfect, but it draws less attention."

"Got it."

———

ONCE HE WAS ONSITE AND ABLE TO OBSERVE INTERACTIONS, IT TOOK GABE a couple of days to craft countermeasures to the mind control programming done to the assorted water co-op officials by the hidden indentured workers—a variant of his original destructive algorithm. Surprisingly, the programming backdoor he had used before was still present, effective, and to all appearances unguarded.

They didn't completely figure it out.

That was a relief. As was testing his boundaries, and finding that yes, he could still work with the data and test the countermeasures. Piotr's intervention had won him that much more freedom.

Gabe also identified and devised countermeasures to the psychotropics being fed to the officials by their hidden indentured assistants, to make them more susceptible to programming. Part of his work included training and briefing this cohort of Alvarez Armory staff on defeating mind control attempts and keeping themselves safe.

Cracking the algorithm on the mind control used on the hidden indentureds took a couple of days longer, because that was more complex and he couldn't work directly with them, plus he didn't want to signal to anyone in the Martiniere labs that *Gabriel was here.*

But he got it finished. A deceptively simple set of code phrases that could be uttered by any of the Alvarez Armory staff or the officials that had been previously under Martiniere mind control influence.

And the Family influence went beyond the co-op to a number of local jurisdictions. By the time all was said and done, over one hundred indentureds, both hidden and open, had walked away from their contracts. They disappeared into the indentured underground either in Canada or Mexico, where regulations managing indenture contracts and preventing abuses were tighter than in the US.

Gabe counted that as a big victory against his damned uncle.

———

"YOU SURE YOU WANT TO GIVE ME THIS MUCH?" GABE ASKED AS HE looked at the amount of cash in the briefcase that Rafe pushed across the motel room's table to him.

Rafe laughed and saluted Gabe with his glass of champagne. "Gabe. I got an extra bonus for cleaning out the region. You earned it for me. And you've given tools to protect my people against Martiniere mind control. I appreciate your work. Couldn't have done it without you."

Gabe closed the briefcase. "Well, I won't argue." He'd need to recount the money, but it looked like he might just be able to move up his purchase of a new seeder for Moondance. This payment could put him over the top for being able to afford a down payment on that piece of equipment.

"I'm just surprised you can't use the same deprogramming for yourself."

"The Mar—" Gabe choked, then doubled up, spasming hard. His champagne glass went flying as he crashed to the floor. He couldn't think, and everything *hurt*.

Then the paroxysms stopped, and he staggered to the bathroom to puke. When he was done, he dragged himself out and splashed his face, breathing heavily.

"Gabe. Jesus. Are you all right?" Rafe loomed behind him.

"Just—careless." Gabe sighed and straightened up. "And frustrated. I can fix others but I can't fix myself, damn it. But that's an example of this—" he waved his hand, not even wanting to say *mind control*. "Stuff in action."

He could *think* about the Family. But that was it.

If only he could figure out the algorithm that controlled *him*. Why he could say the name of Ruby's lab manager Martin but not— Martiniere.

At least he could fix others. That was one small consolation.

***

JULY, 2044

. . .

GABE SPLURGED ON CELEBRATING THE FOURTH THAT YEAR, ESPECIALLY since not only Brandon but Rachel's family plus Tom and Sophie came to Moondance to celebrate. It was already too dry to set off fireworks, but Gabe staged an elaborate laser light show off of the big deck which sent everyone into raptures of oohs and ahhs.

Hernan pulled Gabe aside at one point. "Thought you weren't revealing anything about your ties to a certain family's mind control programs."

"I'm not," Gabe said. Something about Hernan's behavior put him on high alert.

"That's not what I heard. Something about you helping Rafe out on one of those goddamn side projects of his."

"You'd have to talk to Rafe about that," Gabe said.

Hernan scowled. "Don't encourage him to tilt at windmills. Understand?" He poked at Gabe's chest.

"Message received," Gabe said noncommittally.

He's your father-in-law. You can't punch him out for being an ass about Rafe's social justice activities, much as you'd like to. For Rachel's sake.

"Good." Hernan walked away.

Gabe frowned after him. Where had Hernan heard about his involvement with Alvarez Armory?

GABE AND RAFE WERE THE LAST ONES AWAKE THAT NIGHT.

"So your dad said something *interesting* to me," Gabe said as he and Rafe leaned on the deck railing, sipping beers and staring out over the valley below. "Apparently I'm not supposed to encourage you to tilt at windmills."

"Rick asked me a lot of questions about that latest action we did." Rafe took a swig off his beer. "I'd like to know how they found out you were involved, because I haven't said anything."

"Rachel?" Gabe frowned. He'd been careful about putting the cash into a bank account, had opened a new line of credit with the farm co-op and put most of his payment into that, planning to use it to order a new seeder after he sold his grain this fall. He didn't *think* Hernan was tracking their bank accounts, and most outsiders didn't know how the co-op's finances worked. "I've been cautious with the money."

"I asked her. She hadn't said anything to Dad or Rick."

Either that meant someone had recognized his coding, or else he'd improved the Armory's performance significantly enough that Philip had put two plus two together. Or Hernan had figured out the co-op accounting system.

No. Philip had figured it out somehow. That made the most sense. Gabe took a mouthful of his beer. He didn't like the way this was going. He'd thought Philip would leave the Alvarezes alone. Unless this was a long-cultivated relationship between Hernan and Philip—entirely possible.

"I didn't think that my relative would have put the pieces together this quickly," he said.

"You think that's it?" Rafe asked.

Gabe contemplated his bottle, wondering just how much he wanted to say. At last, he sighed. "If your father has any business interactions with my relative, then he's at risk for light programming. Yes, this is a message from my relative."

"He wouldn't—your relative, that is—program my father, would he?"

"Hell yes." A sardonic chuckle escaped Gabe. "My relative would manipulate anyone and everyone to achieve his goals. And as we saw, that includes politicians and business associates. And family." His throat tightened and he coughed, recognizing a light compulsion.

Just how does this damned algorithm work, anyway?

"To hell with him and my father then," Rafe said. "We're doing the right thing." He paused. "My staff has been applying the things you've been teaching them. I appreciate that, Gabe. And if there's another opportunity—"

"I won't turn it down unless I have a damned good reason—and *damned good reason* does not include being warned off. By anyone." Gabe finished his beer.

"Glad to hear that." Rafe finished his. "I'm headed for bed. Night."

"Night," Gabe echoed. He padded through the great room and

checked the security panel before joining Rachel. She stirred as he slid into bed and snuggled up close to him.

"Hope I didn't wake you," he murmured into her upturned ear.

"No, I was just drowsing."

He thought that was it, until she spoke again.

"Papa seems to be concerned that Rafe is getting stirred up with social justice crusades again."

"Well, that *is* part of what Rafe does with the Armory," Gabe said.

"Mmhmm. Papa's been fussing about that aspect of the Armory from the beginning. Mama was complaining about it. He's been grumping about it more than ever in the last week."

Me, Rafe, and Rachel. Covering all the bases.

Was this something Philip would push an associate like Hernan to do?

Hell, yes.

"You wouldn't have happened to have mentioned me going off with Rafe last month to anyone, would you?" Better to know now. And —it suddenly struck him that he would never have needed to ask a question like this of Ruby.

Rachel turned to face him. "I have always figured that what Rafe does, especially with the Armory, is his own business. And that includes *you* doing Armory things with Rafe."

"Do you have a problem with it?"

"I don't know for certain what you're doing, nor do I really want to know," she said. "But I know my brother, and I know you." She stroked his temple. "I am absolutely not opposed to social justice crusades. You two are doing the right thing. Papa is a hidebound conservative. Not me."

Gabe closed his eyes. "Thank you." He hadn't wanted Rachel to be in opposition to what he was doing with Rafe.

Rachel turned back over to snuggle against him again. "Just—be careful, all right? Don't get hurt."

"I will be careful," he promised.

———

Gabe got involved with two more Alvarez Armory actions in 2044. For one, he provided logistical support from Moondance. An outside militia had moved in on a small town in Texas, and it was more than the town's defenses could handle. His job on that project was routing supplies to the Armory unit and performing remote scout work to identify where the outsiders were getting their supplies so that the Armory could cut their supply lines and bring the conflict to a reasonable resolution. It felt *good* to be exercising his Martiniere-trained planning skills again.

No indentureds involved in that campaign, and only a peripheral link to the Family. In this case, the offenders appeared to be nothing more than smugglers looking for a new base—a big enough group to form a militia.

The other situation involved retrieving hostages from mind-controlled abductors. Gabe went face-to-face in that campaign, and managed to free the hostages through negotiation and a little bit of his own use of mind control programming. Neither he nor Rafe identified who was really behind the abduction of a small-town mayor's family, but they suspected the same group of smugglers.

Once the mayor had her family back, she didn't care who had done it.

"We're in a rough area," she told Gabe. "It comes with the territory. I'm more concerned about precedent. If these assholes think they can kidnap my family and I'll pay ransom or let them take over the town, then we'll never stay independent."

Gabe wasn't satisfied, and did the research once he was back at Moondance. Soon enough, he found the connections he was looking for. The smugglers had been bouncing around between assorted game-related names and had settled on the Horde. After a quick check with Bran and Rachel about popular games with obscure social media channels, he found the discussion line. The Horde bounced around to avoid detection, using code words to trigger switching between different servers and once he'd figured out the names and the patterns, it was easy enough to connect them to the kidnapping. And there might have been a connection to the Family. *Might.* Gabe couldn't quite decide.

Christmas was in San Diego that year. Gabe pulled Rafe aside to give him the Horde file. But there were no further discussions with either Hernan or Rick about *social justice windmills*, and he was grateful for that.

By 2048, Gabe and Rafe had fallen into a pattern. Gabe did most of his work for the Armory remotely. Patterns had changed. Instead of waves of indentureds moving in on small government organizations, civic leaders were invited to attend specific training conferences that had loose ties to Martiniere Group-funded think tanks. On their return, they instigated policies that aligned with the tenets of the political party that Philip was aligned with, the Real Truthers.

It was a slight and delicate shift. But it led to more attempts to privatize and control natural resources such as water and energy distribution, linked to Philip's private subsidiary company.

And more private militias tied to the Real Truthers appeared. Gabe started spending time in the field, fighting alongside Rafe.

Gabe and Rachel held fundraisers for the New Democratic Party at both Moondance and the Seattle condo. Rafe joined them.

Rick and Hernan hewed to the right wing of the Honest Republicans. Not as bad as the Real Truthers—but too close to the left wing of the Real Truthers for Gabe's comfort level. Erica confessed privately to Rachel that her sympathy was more with the centrist Classic Democrats or the left wing of the Honest Republicans, but she didn't dare let Hernan or Rick know.

Gabe had seen too much of this in-fighting in the Family. That his in-laws were drifting into the same pattern worried him.

"You need to be careful," he cautioned Rafe during one of their meetings while cutting wood in the Moondance forest. "I'm not the only one with relative issues."

"I'm always careful," Rafe laughed. "Dad and Rick are full of hot air."

Gabe hefted his maul high and split the round of white fir. Last of the Moondance white firs—higher temperatures had finally killed the big ones like this old tree. He replaced them with pines, where he could.

"I just—watch your back, Rafe."

Rafe turned solemn. "It's one reason why I've never married, Gabe. I've seen too many family hostage situations. Pisses Dad off that I won't give him an heir, especially since Rick likes the playboy life, but...no."

"Wiser than I was," Gabe admitted. At least he and Rachel didn't have children. While he wished that the daughter Ruby had miscarried had survived—it was probably for the best that he had only Brandon to worry about.

"I learned from what happened to you, even before you and Rachel got together," Rafe said. "Serg got drunk one night and spilled it all."

"Shit." He didn't *think* Serg would be that careless—unless—

"There's another reason why I haven't married, Gabe. Or Serg."

Gabe shook his head, grinning, putting the pieces together. "I can just imagine the explosions, though. Especially with Serg's connections."

"It'd be just as bad on my side," Rafe said. "And we keep it low-key, but—if and when something happens, there's a file keyed only to you, in the Armory files, to send to Serg." He sighed. "I can trust you. Damn glad I have a brother I can trust."

"Same here," Gabe said.

Rafe was the brother he'd always longed for. That he had a personal connection to one of Gabe's favorite cousins just made it better.

13 / IN SICKNESS AND...?

MARCH, 2050

FORTY-EIGHT YEARS OLD THIS MONTH, GABE THOUGHT AS HE SHOWERED after he and Brandon came in from working the Moondance fields. This summer he'd be married to Rachel for eight years. Longer than he'd been with Ruby.

Brandon was sixteen this year. Most of the time, Gabe got along well with his son, but there were those moments when they argued during visitations, more frequently over the past year than before. Bran was just as intense and driven as Gabe had been at the same age, only without the angst caused by an abusive uncle and the loss of his family. When Bran got a notion in his head, it was hard to shake him free from it. He wasn't interested in robotics like either Gabe or Ruby—his focus was on media production. And what good would that be on either ranch?

Damn it, Dad, media is an important job these days! Bran would yell, his jaw jutting out like Ruby's would in an argument.

For what? Nothing's centralized anymore. Are you planning to become somebody's mouthpiece? I don't have the funds to back an independent project!

It's not like that, Dad! And then a slammed door. Sulking. Eventually —an apology.

But Bran was still determined to go into media production. And

Gabe just couldn't see how that would fit into any decent future for his son.

Gabe rubbed his left shoulder as he stepped out of the shower, still deep in thought. Bran was visiting during spring break. Unfortunately, weather timing this year meant Gabe had to spend more time planting than visiting or having fun. Bran wasn't about to work on Moondance except for rare occasions—he already did plenty on the Double R and viewed his visits to Gabe as a vacation. Which—Gabe had to grant the boy that. His son was becoming a decent ranch hand, and Ruby definitely relied on him.

But damn it, when the boy got a bee in his bonnet about something —at least Bran embraced the fight workouts with Rafe and Gabe. Sometimes that was an excellent excuse to bust his son's chops, though Bran was getting faster and sneakier. A good thing. At some point Bran would need to hold his own against Martinieres, and he caught Gabe and Rafe unawares part of the time. That boded well for his future.

And Gabe had talked Bran into being his assistant on a couple of Alvarez Armory actions. That was one way for his son to learn what a Martiniere heir should know, and Rafe was amenable to helping Gabe educate Bran. Understanding logistics was a big piece, and Bran could learn mind control manipulation through the Alvarez systems—apparently Serg had offered his input to tweak the systems that Gabe had set up for Rafe.

Ruby was teaching Bran bookkeeping as well.

Gabe toweled off, a faint smile coming to his lips at the thought of Bran's growing skills, in spite of his obsession with media production. At some point he needed to figure out how to communicate to Bran what his Martiniere connections were. Through Serg? A possibility. *He* might not be the future Martiniere, but his son…and perhaps that prospect might shift Bran's focus from media production.

But not right now. Gabe had busted his butt all week so they could go to the big Tri-Cities science fiction convention this weekend, leaving tomorrow. That had been enough incentive for Bran to run a seeder for Gabe to make sure they got things done in time. Long hours in the field for both of them all week, though. Maybe that was why he was so tired.

Gabe pulled on sweats. It had taken Rachel a few years to relax about dressing for dinner. But as she got a sense of the rhythms of ranching, she became less strict about formalities when it was just family at Moondance. Dinner tonight would be at the kitchen table, not in the dining room.

He padded down the hallway and into the great room, wincing. His left shoulder hurt worse than ever, radiating into his fingertips. Gabe rubbed it again. He'd taken the cranky seeder with the crummy steering, not the new one he had purchased with his first Alvarez Armory earnings. Maybe he should have had Bran drive it instead. But the old seeder required a knowing, delicate touch or it would keep breaking down. Better that he used it. Even if it left him sore and achy.

"Bran? About ready for dinner?" he called back down the hallway when he didn't see his son in the great room.

Brandon popped out of his suite. "Just getting there, Dad."

Suddenly it felt like he'd been clobbered hard in the chest. Light-headed.

"Dad!" Bran yelled, racing toward him.

He was on the floor. How had that happened?

Bran knelt beside him. "RACHEL! CALL 911! SOMETHING'S WRONG WITH DAD!"

Gabe winced. Bran was *so loud*. He grabbed at his son's arm as more pain pulsed through him.

"Avenge me," he choked, staring up at his son. "*Avenge me.*"

"Dad, what the hell are you talking about?" A catch in Brandon's voice.

"Papers. Your mother's lawyer. If I die...."

More pain, filling his awareness and blanking everything else out.

A LOT OF FUZZINESS. PEOPLE WEARING GOWNS AND MASKS, ASKING questions he couldn't remember the answers to. Beeping noises. Things attached to him. Bright lights. Constant, unfamiliar background sound. Periods of awareness and nothingness. And he *hurt*. Different from that slam in the chest, but it still hurt.

Gabe winced. "Wha—?" He raised one hand to shade his eyes. Shaky. Weak. *Wrong.*

"Dad." Brandon rose from the chair next to the bed. "You're in the coronary unit."

"Noisy. Bright."

"Can't do anything about the noise but I can turn down the lights." Bran reached over and tapped something on a control pad. The glare eased. Gabe dropped his hand.

"Thanks."

"You've been in and out of consciousness over the past few days," Bran continued. "We've had to reorient you every time you wake up. Rachel's taking a break to check on things at the ranch so I'm here. We're taking turns. She's found a temporary ranch manager."

"Don't know why she hired a ranch manager. I should be back shortly," Gabe said.

"Not from this, not that fast," Bran said. "You had a bad heart attack. We almost lost you."

"Aw, shit." Gabe drew a painful breath. "I'm sorry I fucked up the convention for you and Rachel, Bran."

"It would have been worse if you'd died," Bran said, his voice quavering. "I'm—going to be coming over every weekend to help Rachel with the ranch management. Already talked to Mom about it and she approves. I don't know the microbial business—I'm sorry, Dad, I should have paid more attention. The last fields got planted without them."

"Hey. Thanks for what you could do."

He was getting tired again. Gabe closed his eyes, unwilling to think about much. It was so hard.

NEW REALITIES. EVEN THOUGH HE'D KEPT FIT, THAT HADN'T BEEN GOOD enough. Stress and hard living—and possibly those damn nanos and that damn mind control programming. Rachel changed Gabe's diet and he cut back on drinking.

The new ranch manager came as a couple. Tim and Kathleen

Vanhorn. Kathleen split her time between the lab and the fields. There wouldn't be problems with microbial production now, not with Kathleen learning the procedures.

With Gabe's slow work toward recovery, though, the already struggling aspect of Moondance Resort got sidelined and never started back up. On the other hand, the house was convenient for family visits, parties, and fundraisers.

Gabe and Rachel had problems with sex. Normal enough, or so the doctor said. Fixable if he took a pill.

But she was not quite as open as she had been before his heart attack. A normal fading over the years—or self-protectiveness?

Gabe couldn't decide. And Rachel wouldn't talk about it.

He was afraid to push her, frightened of what she might say.

BRANDON EARNED A SCHOLARSHIP TO THE UNIVERSITY OF OREGON'S media program. Gabe wished he could send Bran to the University of Paris, following family tradition. There just wasn't any money to do that, though. Oregon was spendy enough, even with in-state tuition rates, and the scholarship only covered a fraction of the cost of tuition, books, housing, and other college expenses. Hernan had discreetly let it be known that he didn't support Rachel financing Brandon's college. As Rafe and Gabe worked together more frequently, Hernan had become more disapproving of what he called *Gabe's bad influence on Rafael*.

Ruby remained distant at Bran's high school graduation. Gabe threw a big party at Moondance to celebrate, but she didn't attend.

Have a nice life

was the message that she sent him on Bran's eighteenth birthday in December. Along with a deposit for his ten percent share of the Double R's income. And Ruby blocked her personal number so he couldn't contact her.

Gabe sent the money to Brandon. Their son needed it more.

December, 2053

Decembers were always an edgy time as they approached Rachel's annual mammogram. She had gotten to the point where she went to the appointment on her own, at least for the first one, and Gabe accompanied her for any follow-ups. But it had been a few years since there even was a shadow on any of the scans. Still, just in case, Rachel's Seattle doctors handled the annual check.

Gabe was in his office in Rachel's condo, working on another campaign for Rafe, this time running logistics for a battle against yet another indentured militia that had chosen to harass a small Black-owned agricultural cooperative in Arkansas. Back in October, he'd also won an Innovator to finance the next stage of microbial development, so he was making those plans as well. Everything was on track for a good spring in 2054.

"Gabe." Rachel's voice was tight and strained as she entered his office. He looked up, his heart sinking as he saw her distraught expression, eyes swollen from crying.

"Oh, honey." He saved his work and got up. First scan, so maybe it was just another one of those occasional shadows that disappeared by the time the doctor did a more detailed scan. He hoped.

But Rachel wasn't usually this emotional about a shadow on the mammogram. She'd gone through the process enough times.

It's bad. Has to be.

She went into his arms. "It was big enough that Dr. Achren did a needle biopsy. The—the cancer's back."

"Oh, honey," Gabe repeated, holding her tight.

Rachel gulped. "It's a more aggressive type than the first one." She burst into tears. "They—they're doing other tests. It may have metastasized already."

"I'm here," he whispered to her. "I'm here."

"Love me," she pleaded. "Just love me. Don't run away. Please. Don't run away."

"I'm staying right here and I will keep on loving you," he promised, holding her tighter. "No matter what. I'm here."

Gabe hadn't thought that anything could be as horrible as losing Ruby the way he did.

But God. Oh God. This.

GABE DID THE BARE MINIMUM TO KEEP MOONDANCE ROLLING AND HELP Rafe. Rachel had to be his priority.

When her gorgeous, beautiful hair started falling out during treatment, Rachel asked Gabe to shave her head. He cried along with Rachel as he did it, and showered her poor bare head with kisses when it was done. Then he helped her pick out cute hats to wear around the house to keep warm. He assisted her through the hell of surgeries, chemotherapy and radiation treatments.

Rafe visited frequently, but the rest of the Alvarez family not at all.

"That's what they did the last time Rach had cancer," Rafe told Gabe one night as they sat on the deck on a warm June night. Rachel had gone to bed. "Her ex-fiancé Cameron, Mom, Dad, Rick—they left her to face it all alone. Except for me." He grimaced. "God. Pisses me off. Dad doesn't like it when we're not perfect."

"I—know the feeling," Gabe said. There *had* been a time in his early life where perfection hadn't mattered, where he'd felt loved by his family. But that had ended with the plane crash that killed them.

Since then, it had only been during those few short years with Ruby, and now with Rachel, that he'd felt the same degree of acceptance.

"I'm so glad that Rach has you," Rafe said. "Keep her safe."

"I vowed to be by her side in sickness and in health," Gabe said.

And meant it. He'd messed things up with Ruby.

He was *not* going to do that with Rachel.

A few days after that conversation with Rafe, Gabe went looking for Rachel to ask her a question about a potential financing discrepancy he'd come across while reviewing their payment records. The drawback of the big house was that with only two people living there, it was sometimes hard to find each other. The condo was a lot easier in that respect, though he felt like a caged bird in the urban setting.

At last, Gabe heard Rachel crying, and followed the sound to her quilting studio. Rachel slumped over her big quilting work table, head buried in her arms as she sat on her tall stool, body shaking with sobs.

"Honey. What's wrong?" Gabe wrapped his arms around Rachel, easing her upright. She turned to keep crying into his chest. He saw scattered bits of fabric where she'd been placing them to piece together.

"I can't do it," she wailed. "I can't visualize the block layout even with the pattern in front of me, Gabe! My mind just won't work!"

"Maybe you just need to take a break and come back with a fresh perspective?" he offered, aware that the words sounded stupid even as he said them.

Rachel shook her head. "I've been doing that for a week. I can't even get one simple star block to come out right. *One block.* Of a design I *know* I have down solid! I used to piece big blocks like this for a whole quilt top in a day—now I can't even do one a week! I can't concentrate on *anything* anymore!"

Oh. That might be the answer to his question about the financial discrepancy.

"It's all right, honey," he soothed. "Once the chemo's done it'll come back."

"But what if it doesn't?"

Gabe couldn't answer that.

God. He'd thought what he and Ruby had gone through during their divorce was hell. But that divorce had been fast and clean by comparison.

This slow erosion and suffering of the woman he now loved was much worse. Especially since he hadn't been a witness to what he'd done to Ruby. Conversely, he was observing what the cancer did to Rachel on a daily basis.

After comforting Rachel without asking his question, Gabe went back to their financials, now grimly aware that he needed to check *everything* she had entered recently. When he was done with his review, the results were ugly.

They had a big hole in their finances and it was getting worse. Hernan was tightening down on the money available to Rachel. Going outside of the Alvarez family for a loan was going to be difficult—and they were going to need more cash for her medical expenses.

Gabe sighed. Gambling had always been for fun and not a serious funding source.

Now it was time to figure out if his knack for picking winning sports teams could actually earn something.

SEPTEMBER, 2054

"YOU MOTHERFUCKER!" HERNAN SCREAMED AT GABE THE MOMENT HIS projection solidified.

"What the—Hernan, what's wrong?" Gabe racked his brain to figure out just why his father-in-law would be so angry at him. The call had popped up out of nowhere, since Gabe had set that connection to open without needing him to respond. Normal setting when there was an Armory action, so Rafe could call for help if needed. He was clearing out a nest of Philip's devotees up in Northern Idaho—in a town called North Fork, with a religious-based compound, Heaven's Reach, that Rafe and Gabe suspected was a cover for a hidden Martiniere research lab. A new pattern that Gabe had discovered.

"You Martinieres. You evil, manipulative Martinieres!"

"I don't understand," Gabe said.

"Rafael is dead," Hernan said icily. "Killed as part of one of your little *actions*. And this message was sent to me, to pass on to you." He flung a video link at Gabe.

Gabe tucked it away in a safe file, until he could review it with every damn safeguard possible, chills tightening his gut.

Rafe dead? Oh my God.

This latest action wasn't supposed to be that dangerous, and Rafe had dismissed Gabe's offer to help when he needed to go on site.

Rachel's cry behind Gabe startled him. "Oh no. Rafe's dead? Papa, what happened?"

"Ask your fucking husband," Hernan snarled. "Rafe was killed during one of their damn half-assed, tilting-at-windmills campaigns!"

Gabe inhaled sharply.

Rafe had said it was easy.

"What happened?" he asked. "I offered to go onsite with Rafe. It wasn't supposed to be a difficult situation!"

Hernan shook an index finger at Gabe. "Your motherfucking uncle *targeted* Rafe. Lured in. You were supposed to be there. You were the actual target. Rafe was a secondary. It's all in that damned link I sent you."

Gabe slammed his fists on his desk. "Damn it, damn it, damn it!" He gulped. "Hernan, I am so sorry."

Hernan drew a deep, sobbing breath. "Not another penny of Alvarez money goes to you, motherfucker. To Rachel, yes, as long as she lives. But not another penny of Alvarez money otherwise."

"What about the funeral?" Rachel asked. "And Mama?"

"I don't want to see either of you ever again, except at the service. Period."

"The field unit," Gabe said slowly. "They're still active?"

"They are finishing out the contract," Hernan said.

"Then I'm going." Gabe pulled up the data on that Armory unit. "I'll wrap it up. My last job for Alvarez Armory, then it's all up to you and Rick, Hernan."

"Gabe—" Rachel said.

"I'll be back in time for Rafe's funeral," Gabe said. "It won't take long. And I'll send you the final report on that action, Hernan."

"If we're lucky you'll get killed as well." Hernan switched off the connection.

Rachel gulped behind him. "Gabe," she said again. "No. Please."

Gabe rose and took her in his arms. "I'll be careful, honey." He was already mentally flipping through alternatives. Serg. He'd call Serg in for this—for vengeance purposes. He needed to send Rafe's file to Serg, like he'd promised.

Brandon. Bran would want in on this, because he'd been close to Rafe. Bran was playing around with the notion of working security to support his media production goals, and Gabe had trusted Rafe to school Bran while not risking him.

Who else? Too bad he wasn't on speaking terms with Ruby. Gabe would bring her into this fight otherwise, would have brought her into the Armory a couple of years ago. Brandon's toughness didn't just come from the Martinieres. Should he have Bran ask? Ruby might be a good support for Bran.

Wait and see.

Serg. Bran. Maybe some others.

"But if they're gunning for you—" Rachel frowned at him.

"I'm old and sneaky enough and I'm going in forewarned," he said. "And I'm not going alone. I'm calling in Serg and Bran. They'll both want revenge." He took Rachel's head in his hands as she blinked back her tears. "Those assholes will pay for killing Rafe." He shuddered. "And if that message from my relative is what I think it is—it looks like it's time for me to send another message back to him."

"Gabe. Oh Gabe, *no.*"

He kissed her. "Honey. Get Sophie to stay with you while I'm gone, okay? I'll ask Tim and Kathleen to be here, too, so you aren't alone. I'm sorry, but—I need to do this. For Rafe." He sighed. "I'm going to open that damned file. You may not want to be here."

He fully suspected there would be graphic pictures. If not a video, then stills. If he could spare Rachel that—

Rachel gulped. "I want to see it."

"Hon. It's likely to be pretty explicit. I'm trying to spare you."

Her jaw tightened. "If so, *I want to see what they did to Rafe.* It will help me understand why you have to go. And why my father is so angry."

Gabe swallowed hard. "All right. But tell me if it becomes too much."

She nodded.

THE STILLS WERE JUST AS GRAPHIC AS GABE FEARED FROM THE REPORTS he'd read about what that damned North Fork commune did to betrayers and opponents. They'd butchered Rafe like they would a hog or cow. Rachel squeezed his hand hard as they scrolled through the pictures, moaning softly.

No wonder Hernan was so fucking pissed.

What was left of Rafe at the end....

Then Philip came on screen.

"Gabriel, Gabriel, Gabriel," he said, shaking his head. "When are you going to learn that you can't win against me?" He bared his teeth. "And Hernan. Let this be a lesson. I warned you that Rafael's and Gabriel's actions against Martiniere Group interests needed to be stopped. The body was *supposed* to be Gabriel, but as usual, he's being a coward who runs away from his responsibility."

Gabe flinched because there were *definitely* trigger tones in that statement. Not just for him.

Philip continued, sneering. "The orders to my people were to eliminate Gabriel first, and leave Rafael alone—unless Gabriel wasn't there. Then Rafael, as a warning. This—" he gestured. "Whole crusade against Martiniere interests needs to end. Now. With the death of your son, I sincerely hope that you appreciate the folly of letting Gabriel pursue his futile attempts to thwart my plans. And Gabriel? You are no fucking phoenix rising from the ashes. You are not even a Martiniere anymore. You are a fucking brown-skinned mud person who has managed to pervert everything this family has stood for. Go crawl back into your hole, *boy*, before I feel the need to swat you down as if you were nothing more than an annoying fly. Run away—*again*."

The video ended, and Gabe shut it off, vision narrowing as rage flooded him. He stormed out the balcony door and gripped the railing, bellowing incoherently into the valley below Moondance.

Some of it was Philip's triggers.

But even more was his own frustration. He *should* have ignored Rafe's disclaimers and gone with him this time. He'd ignored the undertones in what Rafe said because he was eager to grasp at any excuse to be with Rachel. Her cancer. His heart.

And now the man who had been like a brother to him was dead.

Because of him.

My fault. My great, grievous, maximum fault. Another one of my goddamned fuckups. When will I ever learn?

Rachel's arms wrapped around him. "Gabe. Gabe. *Please.*" Her voice choked. "Stop it. Please."

The catch in her voice halted him. Gabe shuddered, breathing in deep gasps, not letting go of the railing until he had control of himself. Then he turned to Rachel.

"Honey. I am so, so, sorry," he murmured.

"That motherfucker," she said. He startled, because Rachel so rarely swore, unlike Ruby. She scowled. "That evil, evil racist son-of-a-bitch. Why my father ever thought that Philip Martiniere respected him—" She exhaled. "And the degree that he hates you. Both of them. Philip and my father. You're right, Gabe. You have to go. But—*don't get killed.* Please. I need you."

"I'm planning to take Serg and Brandon with me," he said. "I intend to come back. Dying will just satisfy that motherfucker."

A faint smile played on her lips. "Don't get Bran killed, either. Your ex-wife will blame me if that happens."

"Bran's more likely to come back in one piece than me," Gabe said. "But I mean to bring all of us back, safe and whole. Just so you don't have to worry about Ruby in a rage, as well as your father."

That brought a bigger smile from Rachel.

Serg brought a small group of hand-picked Vygotsky Security fighters who had known Rafe. Gratis. All wanted vengeance for Rafe's death.

Brandon was Gabe's shadow—his assistant, his backup, his

enforcer, his protector. Acting like the Martiniere-in-waiting would be if Gabe were the Martiniere.

Gabe led the sorely-depleted Alvarez Armory team in tracking down and killing the leaders.

When it was done, Brandon made a variant on the video that Philip had sent, featuring Rafe's killers. Gabe sent copies to Philip and Hernan.

But Gabe added a message for Philip alone.

> I may be down but I'm not defeated. Time is on my side. GMR.

It was the first time he'd signed his initials on anything he'd sent to Philip—and there was a double meaning. They *could* just mean *Gabriel Marcus Ramirez*.

Or they might also mean *Gabriel Martiniere Ramirez*, a Spanish surname protocol to honor his mother.

Most people wouldn't pay attention to that sort of detail, but Gabe knew that Philip would. He hoped the bastard spent at least a little bit of time trying to figure it out.

HERNAN AND ERICA WERE STIFFLY POLITE TO GABE AND RACHEL AT Rafe's funeral. Brandon came as well, a silent follower at Gabe's side.

They were in San Diego just long enough to honor Rafe. Gabe handed the chip with his final report and the Alvarez Armory authorization codes to Hernan and Rick, along with his resignation from Armory control, immediately after the service.

Then the three of them left.

Gabe never saw his in-laws again.

2054-2057

. . .

Several years passed.

Rachel was in remission.

Then she wasn't.

And then she was. The cancer advanced further each time. Metastasis. And though the treatments beat it back, with every occurrence, Rachel lost a little bit of herself that never returned.

Brandon graduated from college with honors and went to work for the AgInnovator. That was another point of conflict between him and Gabe.

"Why AgI?" he asked Bran.

"It's done well for both you and Mom." At this point Ruby had won not just a one-year Innovator but a Star Innovator for five years, completing it successfully. Gabe had gotten two Innovators himself. "It's a good place to start."

But it meant that Bran was working in Los Angeles. Too close to Philip for Gabe's liking.

Gabe and Rachel managed to stay afloat financially—just barely.

It seemed like every time that Gabe managed to get them ahead of the bills through gambling wins, Rachel suffered a health setback. From the quarterly statements, he saw that Ruby wasn't doing any better on the Double R, in spite of her AgI money. Then again, the Double R was a bigger operation than Moondance, always had been.

Serg occasionally sent Gabe a note, but that was the only news Gabe heard from the Family. All he really wanted to hear. Keeping ahead of the bills and coping with Rachel's health was almost more than Gabe could handle at this point in time.

And yet. Watching summer sunsets on the big deck while Rachel sat in his lap was priceless. Snuggling with her in front of the fake fireplace in their bedroom suite, as a nasty winter blizzard pounded against the windows, was another moment Gabe cherished.

Especially as he sensed that Rachel was slipping away from him, bit by bit, daily.

March, 2057

. . .

"HAVE YOU EVER THOUGHT ABOUT TRYING TO MAKE CONTACT WITH RUBY again?" Rachel asked suddenly, over dinner. She no longer had the energy or the appetite to cook, so Gabe did it. He'd prepared synth-pork to go with rice and rehydrated peaches—just about one of the few dishes that she could stand to eat more than a few bites. She was scary thin but at least her hair—now silver—had grown to shoulder length. Gabe still found Rachel beautiful in a different way from before cancer, but he couldn't overlook the toll it had taken on her.

"Can't say as I have," Gabe answered. "Her last message to me was pretty much final. *Have a nice life* doesn't sound like someone who wants further contact."

"I was just thinking it might be nice to share Brandon over the holidays. Sooner or later, he's going to find someone to be part of his life and we'll want to do family things together," Rachel said wistfully. "I'd really like to know Ruby before that happens."

Gabe eyed her. Rachel hadn't said one word about missing her family after Rafe's funeral. Was that behind her sudden interest in Ruby?

He reached out and rested his hand on hers. "Are you missing family?"

"Sometimes. But—" Rachel exhaled. "I just think it might be a good idea. Brandon sent me some old pictures of you two from the AgI archives. He was awfully cute when you won. I'd like to see more."

He didn't have many pictures of Brandon from before the divorce. And Bran was the closest thing to a child that Rachel would ever have. She'd loved her role as his stepmother—that would be a means for her to connect with Ruby. Gabe tightened his hand on hers.

"If you want to contact Ruby, you have my approval, not that you need it," he said softly. "But I think it would be better from you than from me. Tell her about those old pictures. She might not have them either."

Rachel smiled. "I'll do it soon. Maybe I can smooth things over enough for the four of us to celebrate Thanksgiving and Christmas together. If not the Fourth."

"She'll definitely have more time by then." A reprieve, of sorts. He had time to get used to the idea of his ex-wife and his current wife talking to each other.

Not that he disapproved.

It *would* be nice to be able to share Brandon with both Ruby and Rachel.

14 / G9

APRIL, 2057

AT FIRST, GABE WASN'T VERY CONCERNED ABOUT THE INITIAL REPORTS OF A new virus arising in the Southwest during the first week of April. He was old enough to remember Covid-19's first appearance, but this bug, dubbed G9 for some reason he hadn't figured out, didn't seem to be that virulent. Ever since Covid and the horrible flu that had waylaid Ruby and Brandon during that—godawful divorce year, occasional concerned flurries in the popular media popped up when a new virus appeared. Anxiety over *is this another Covid?*

This bug appeared to be spluttering out pretty quickly. After an initial hotspot of cases, reports died down. Gabe kept an eye on it because it was in a region where he and Rafe had spent quite a bit of time countering Martiniere schemes. He *knew* what the socioeconomic conditions were there, and just how screwed up recordkeeping could be.

From all reports, however, it seemed to be just another scare. Nothing to get too excited about.

All the same, he watched the spread of G9 carefully, because of Rachel's vulnerability.

269

Gabe was alone on Moondance that final week of April. Rachel had gone to town. One of her quilt groups had a regular sew day, and Rachel was feeling stir-crazy. Plus, sewing with other people helped her work around the problems she still had with fuzzy thinking. Gabe was finalizing his bets for the upcoming weekend. If he pulled this one off, then he and Rachel would be in good shape until harvest.

"Brandon Ramirez," his comm chimed. Gabe didn't keep anyone on auto-open anymore. Not since that last call from Hernan.

"Hey Bran," Gabe answered. "What's going on?"

His son's expression was grim as his projection solidified. "Dad, have you been watching the spread of G9 in your area?"

"It wasn't that bad, the last time I looked."

"Check it again. We're shutting down production on the AgI temporarily while we switch over to new sanitation protocols," Bran said. "The spread's taken a big leap here in LA. And Mom—I was supposed to visit her this weekend. She called me just now, told me not to come. Thunder County is locked down hard. Restricted access in and out. A hotspot just popped up on the county border with Idaho and Washington." He swallowed. "It's moving fast, Dad. Scary fast. A new variant is what I'm hearing."

"Shit." He *hadn't* been checking that closely, depending on alerts from county health. And if that hotspot was flaring, then—*it was here.* "Damn it, Rachel's at a sew day. We haven't closed down yet."

"I thought you'd better know, for Rach's sake," Bran said. "Things we're hearing about the spread here, just from our ag connections—it's a lot worse in rural areas right now, because it's jumping to birds, mutating, and then back into people. Information I'm privy to that isn't on the general news media. Dad. You two be careful. Please."

"We will," Gabe said, planning to call Rachel as soon as he hung up. "Thanks for the warning. You be careful, too."

"I am," Bran said. "I'm more worried about you and Rachel than Mom. She's not health-compromised like you two, and Thunder County is darn good about locking down. Not like other places."

"All right." He heard a door close upstairs, and then Rachel's quick, light steps along with the drone of her wheeled sewing bag. "And Rachel just got home." It was early. He hoped things had been all right with the quilt group. It wasn't even lunchtime. Very early for Rachel to be back—unless something had gone badly wrong.

"I'll let you go." Bran disconnected.

Gabe saved his work and went upstairs. Rachel was in her quilting room, unloading the bag that carried her sewing machine and supplies. She looked up as Gabe entered.

"We decided to cancel sew days for an indefinite period and get together online instead," she said. "Sarah—her son called just as I got there. She died. G9. And there's a flare nearby."

"Bran just called. Thunder County locked down—Ruby let him know because he was supposed to visit her this weekend. AgI is temporarily suspending production to change protocols."

Rachel nodded. "It's bad, Gabe. Kenny told us it came on fast and hard, and it was an awful way to go." She blinked. Kenny's mother Sarah had also been struggling with cancer, and she had provided Rachel with a lot of emotional support.

"Oh, honey."

Gabe wasn't sure if he was the first one to reach out or if it was Rachel. They clung to each other.

We've survived a lot together already. Heart attack. Cancer.

We will survive this as well.

MAY, 2057

PENDLETON WAS THE NEXT LOCAL HOTSPOT FOR G9.

Moondance was too far out of town for food deliveries except via shipments. Gabe repurposed one of his lab biosuits to do whatever errands that needed to happen off-site, and told Tim and Kathleen Vanhorn to feel free to use the lab resources so they could keep safe while working at the ranch.

Everything went through decontamination in the lab before it came to the house.

It wasn't enough.

"I don't feel well," Rachel said on the morning of May 7th. She poked at her breakfast oatmeal, usually a favorite. "My head hurts and I'm not hungry."

Gabe popped out of his chair to feel her forehead. Sometimes she just had these days—but with G9 hovering over them, he wasn't taking any chances.

"You don't seem to be running a fever." He went over to the drawer where he kept Rachel's medical support supplies, and pulled out a thermometer. G9 manifested with fatigue and a sudden high fever.

He sighed with relief when the reading showed Rachel's normal morning temperature.

"All good, hon."

"I want to lie down." She made a face. "And here I was hoping to use my long-arm sewing machine to finish that quilt today—finally."

"Eh, you can do it tomorrow. Go on to bed, I'll fix you some soda water and bring crackers." What he usually did when she felt off like this.

"Thanks."

Gabe felt a little woozy as he put saltines on a plate and ran the carbonator to spritz up Rachel's water. But sometimes his meds affected him like that first thing in the morning.

After setting plate and glass on Rachel's nightstand, he decided to join her. Napping suddenly sounded good to him. She was already sound asleep, curled up on her right side.

His head was starting to hurt, and it was hard to focus.

Gabe lay down next to Rachel on his right side, snuggling close to her.

Rachel's moans woke Gabe. Her slight body radiated heat. His headache was worse, and the world around him shimmered in bright lines. If he didn't know better, he'd think he'd been slipped a psychotropic of some sort.

Focus. Don't think about this being G9. Not yet.

Even though this *was* a G9 symptom.

"Rach. Rach," he said softly.

"It hurts, Gabe. All over."

"You're running a fever." He crawled from under the covers, feeling like he'd gone through another of Philip's beatings.

No. God, no.

Their symptoms matched the onset of severe G9.

He grabbed the thermometer out of his nightstand and took her temperature.

102 F.

No. God, no!

It was hard to think about anything as the weight of impending doom crashed over him.

Gabe held the thermometer to his own head, hands trembling so much that it was difficult to keep them steady. Colors pulsed around him but he did his damnedest to ignore the distortion of vision. After all, he'd been dosed enough times with psychotropics. He should be able to manage this....

101.5 F. Fuck. G9.

"Gonna be sick," Rachel groaned. Gabe stood to help her, and collapsed because he wasn't sure which way was up. Rachel staggered out of the bed. She fell on the floor halfway to the bathroom, vomiting. Then she managed to pull herself upright and stumbled to the bathroom. She started puking again, between inarticulate cries.

Gabe rolled to hands and knees, crawling after her. He couldn't stand up and *she needed his help.*

Rachel lay in her vomit, seizing. After the seizure, she gasped for breath. Gabe cleared her mouth with an index finger so she wouldn't choke, and took Rachel into his arms.

"Keep breathing, Rach. Keep breathing." Her eyes were dull and she didn't seem to see him.

Oh God. This is G9.

Gabe forced himself not to panic. He snapped his comm open and called 911.

"Nature of the emergency?" the autoresponder asked.

"G9 infection. Gabe and Rachel Ramirez. On Moondance Ranch." He gave the address.

"Are both of you sick?" Human voice now.

"Yes."

Another convulsion wracked Rachel's body. She didn't gasp for breath when it stopped.

Oh God, she's not breathing!

"Fevers—over 101 degrees. Can't—talk. Wife has stopped breathing. Seizure."

"Are your doors locked?"

Gabe took a moment to snap the autolocks open. "Open—now. Starting CPR."

He had to ignore the voices because there were *so many* of them now, including Philip. And Ruby. And whoever was yelling at him from the comm.

Gabe focused on compressing Rachel's chest. Compressions. Breath. Compressions. Breath.

She wasn't responding.

"Oh God, Rach, *don't die!*" he begged as he worked and the universe distorted around them.

He wasn't at Moondance. He was at the Double R, and the body he was working on was Ruby's.

No.

Blink. Back at Moondance, and *Rachel still wasn't responding.*

The Double R and Ruby again.

"No!" he screamed, still working on compressions and breath, even though he wasn't sure which woman he was working on. "Rachel. Ruby. No. Don't die on me! No!"

I told you, boy. I told you that I'd take everything you ever loved. Philip's voice.

"No, you fucking bastard!" It was Ruby he was working on now.

Breathe. This time Rachel.

But she didn't respond. *She didn't respond.*

Hands on his shoulders. "We've got her, Mr. Ramirez." A familiar voice, someone he encountered regularly in the community. But he couldn't see who it was through the biosuit. Gabe tried to reach for Rachel but hands pulled him away.

More voices as he tried and couldn't focus on the questions being asked.

What's happening with Rachel?

Rachel's poor body jerked as the paramedics used a defibrillator on her. He winced.

"No response," he heard clearly.

Another attempt. And another.

Finally, the words he dreaded. "Patient pronounced dead at 11:45 am, May 7th, 2057."

Gabe burst into sobs. He was barely aware of being strapped onto a gurney and rushed to a waiting helicopter.

NIGHTMARES OF RACHEL AND RUBY DYING IN HIS ARMS, SOMETIMES ONE, sometimes the other, sometimes both at the same time.

Hammers pounding in his head. Burning up. Hard to breathe. World pulsating around him.

Not seeing any humans. Just biosuits.

Fighting for air.

He wasn't going to let a fucking disease beat him. Not when he hadn't finished with Philip.

But this was much, much worse than anything else he'd experienced. Even the heart attack. Even the beatings from Philip.

HE WOKE WITHOUT THE ACHES AND PAINS. NOT EVEN BURNING UP.

Breathing was a lot easier.

Had he made it past the worst of the G9? And what had happened to Rachel?

Still no humans around him. Just biosuits. And they didn't seem to hear him talking.

ANOTHER WAKING. SOMEONE IN A BIOSUIT SAT NEXT TO HIS BED, STUDYING a projection.

Gabe moved a finger. Tried to talk.

"Dad?" Bran's voice. He snapped the projection shut and leaned over the bed so that Gabe could see his face through the suit. "It's me. Brandon."

"Hey," Gabe exhaled. He sounded weak to his own ears.

"You had a moderately severe case of the G9," Brandon said. "Still contagious, but another forty-eight hours and you should be safe."

Gabe winced. "That was *moderately* severe?"

"Not bad enough for the Chan Protocol treatment," Brandon sighed. "And we still don't know what the aftereffects are going to be. Hopefully you don't develop post-G9 syndrome."

"Rachel." He didn't know what to ask. Had he hallucinated her being pronounced dead?

"I'm sorry, Dad." Brandon's voice was heavy. "She was dead on arrival."

Gabe moaned and closed his eyes. Not a hallucination, then. "Funeral arrangements?" He was sure Bran would do the right thing.

"Not in our hands," Brandon snapped, cutting his words short and sharp. "Hernan and Rick took custody of her body before I was able to get here. They left a message. Stay the fuck away. Both of us."

"Aw, shit," Gabe groaned. He exhaled. "Did they take anything from Moondance?"

"Tim and Kathleen said that no one has come to the house except me," Brandon said.

Gabe sighed, raggedly. "Tell Kathleen and Tim—" what? He wasn't sure. "A memorial here, at least. No matter what her family does. She has—*had* a lot of friends."

He'd have to do something in Seattle as well. But the weight of dealing with *everything* was just too much right now.

June, 2057

GABE WASN'T RELEASED FROM THE HOSPITAL UNTIL MID-JUNE. BEFORE then, he directed Brandon to clear the Seattle condo, ship personal items to Moondance, and sell it. He needed the money to pay their medical bills, especially since Rachel's death shut off the Alvarez funds. And with Rachel dead, he had no reason to maintain a residence in Seattle—hell, he didn't have the cash to do that.

Whenever he asked Bran about his financial status, his son wouldn't answer, except to say that things were being taken care of.

Gabe was too weak and tired to investigate further.

IT BECAME CLEAR DURING GABE'S FIRST WEEK AT HOME THAT HE WAS developing post-G9 syndrome. Brandon worked remotely and stayed with him, helping Gabe with daily affairs and through the early stages of physical therapy. AgI was still temporarily closed due to G9, and Bran was scouting for a big twenty-fifth year competition to be held in February, 2059, with a new category that was going to be bigger than the AgSuperstar.

Gabe couldn't sleep in a bed anymore without choking from sinus drainage, much less rest in the bedroom that he and Rachel had shared. Every time he went into their old room, he remembered that last nightmare of a morning.

Brandon got Gabe a sleep recliner and put it in the room that Bran used when visiting. That worked better. He also got one for the great room.

Tim and Kathleen moved into the small caretaking apartment that was across the hallway from his and Brandon's bedroom.

But Gabe had screaming nightmares that woke both him and Brandon.

And when Bran wasn't there, Gabe roused either Tim or Kathleen with his yelling.

August, 2057

THE G9 BURNED OUT QUICKLY, THANKS TO THE DEVELOPMENT OF A NEW vaccine. One effect of the post-G9 syndrome was that Gabe's left side was weaker than his right, his left leg slightly withered and smaller than the other.

You may never regain the muscles lost, he was told.

It was pure serendipity when he discovered another post-G9 effect. He hadn't thought about it until he came across an old picture of Rachel in a bikini, one she'd given him early on in their relationship. He'd always found it arousing and had used it as a masturbation stimulus during their times apart.

It was still beautiful. But nothing stirred. He remained flaccid, though God, he was excited enough.

He took his pills. A couple of hours later, he tried again.

Nothing.

Hidden away in his files was an old picture of Ruby in a bikini.

Still nothing.

He reported that effect to his doctor, trying to stay as clinical as possible.

Unfortunately, that's one side effect we can't fix, was the response. *It may improve with time, or it may not.*

Another thing the G9 had stolen from him.

Not that Gabe was planning to get together with another woman ever again. He'd destroyed two relationships—if he hadn't been such an ass and put vengeance at a higher priority than his wife, then Rachel wouldn't have been estranged from her family and spent her last years away from them.

He still felt guilty about that. Until he confronted Philip and won, he wasn't going to risk a third love. While Philip wasn't connected with Rachel's death, he was tied to her estrangement from those she had loved.

This situation just made that choice easier.

---

*2057-*ᴇᴀʀʟʏ *2058*

"Mᴀʏʙᴇ ʏᴏᴜ ᴏᴜɢʜᴛ ᴛᴏ ʀᴇᴄᴏɴɴᴇᴄᴛ ᴡɪᴛʜ Mᴏᴍ," Bʀᴀɴᴅᴏɴ sᴀɪᴅ. Hᴇ ʜᴀᴅ popped in for the Labor Day weekend to keep Gabe company. "The two of you seem awfully lonely to me."

Gabe shrugged. He'd been lonely before. By now, he could live with it. But if Ruby was willing to try again—despite his vow to not seek another relationship, a desire to see her, talk to her, hold her rose within him. Even if he couldn't make love to Ruby, he found himself craving affectionate contact—from her.

He missed his redheaded rodeo queen, even more now that Rachel was gone. And the nightmares about Ruby and Rachel dying in his arms had only gotten stronger and more frequent. He wanted to make sure that Ruby was all right.

"And what does your mother say?"

Bran's silence was his answer.

Gᴀʙᴇ ᴋᴇᴘᴛ ꜰɪɢʜᴛɪɴɢ ʜɪs ʙᴏᴅʏ. Hᴇ *ʜᴀᴅ* ᴛᴏ ᴅᴏ ɪᴛ ɪɴ ᴏʀᴅᴇʀ ᴛᴏ ʙᴇ ᴀʙʟᴇ ᴛᴏ farm again, much less finally avenge himself on Philip. The income from the sale of Rachel's condo wouldn't last forever—and he was surprised that Hernan and Rick hadn't swooped down to take those funds away as well.

By spring, he still needed a cane to walk, but at least he was able to cultivate microbials and handle the spring planting along with Tim and Kathleen.

It was becoming clear that Moondance was becoming too much for a single man his age and with his disabilities to handle. The house was just too damn big, and even with Tim and Kathleen's help, the work was more than he could do with post-G9 syndrome. Moondance deserved someone who could focus on it, turn it into the showplace that he and Rachel had once dreamed of creating.

In the same position as Craig was when I came along, he thought wryly at one point. And close to the same age as Craig had been at his death.

MAY, 2058

THE FIRST ANNIVERSARY OF RACHEL'S DEATH WAS HARDER THAN GABE HAD expected. He scrapped his careful cardiac diet devised by Rachel—destroyed by post-G9 syndrome anyway—and got thoroughly drunk.

Kathleen shook him awake. He'd fallen asleep in the great room's recliner.

"You were screaming," she said, face crinkled in puzzlement. "Why were you screaming about the Martinieres?"

"What was I screaming?" Gabe asked.

She shook her head. "Martiniere was the only thing I could make out. Is it tied to that work you were doing with Rafe?"

Gabe shrugged. "I have no idea." He reached for his cane, using it for support to get back on his feet. He was determined not to use any of the chair's lift functions, focusing on strengthening his core muscles. He *had* to get them stronger.

And it was interesting that he *could* say the family name in his nightmares. Or was saying it what caused his nightmares?

He forgot about that incident when he woke the next morning with a raging hangover.

Brandon called him a little later that day. "I've found where Hernan and Rick put Rachel," he said. "They cremated her and didn't bury her in the family plot. She's in Los Angeles, not San Diego—that's why I had a hard time finding her. I can take you there, if you'd like."

"I would," Gabe said.

A few days later he and Bran made that pilgrimage.

The marker made no mention of their marriage. Birth and death dates only, under the name Rachel Alvarez.

Gabe left red roses, feeling somewhat sick. She deserved better than this plain marker. If he could ever get back on his feet financially, he'd erect a better memorial.

But at least he now knew where to find her remains.

And even though he still wasn't practicing faith anymore, Gabe had Brandon take him to the nearest Catholic church. He lit a candle for Rachel and knelt before it. Words couldn't come to him this time—just regrets.

He *had* to get better so that he could defeat that damn uncle of his.

Bran contacted him a few months later, to tell him that Hernan, Erica, and Rick had fallen to the G9. The Alvarez family was in shambles as a result. Gabe grinned mirthlessly when he read that Alvarez Armory was now part of Vygotsky Security, and wondered if that was Serg's doing.

He *should* feel regret that his in-laws were dead.

But after what they had done to Rachel, he didn't care.

SEPTEMBER, 2058

"HEY DAD," BRANDON SAID WHILE THEY SAT ON THE DECK NURSING drinks as the sun set on Labor Day. "Have you considered trying out for the AgSuperhero next February?'

Gabe scowled. "What happened with the Superstar pretty much put me off of anything more than the Innovator."

"This one is different," Brandon said. "Three point seven five million dollars a year for five years. And it's like the Innovator, in that you never have to requalify again."

"Hmm." Gabe considered it. "But Moondance Microbials needs so much financing to be competitive that I'm not sure it's worth the effort."

"You wanted to expand the lab before you got sick. This would give you the funding to do that."

Gabe studied his hands, flexing them as he thought. That money would not only juice up Moondance Microbials. It would also finance the fixes needed to make the place more attractive to a potential buyer.

"Isn't there a conflict of interest since I'm your father?"

Bran shook his head. "While I'm involved in recruitment, I'm locked off from the judging and that aspect of production. I already asked Georgy Batineau. He's all for trying to get you and Mom back on the show."

Ruby. He'd get to see Ruby again.

"So is she going for it?"

Brandon flashed him a bright grin. "Mom's already signed on."

Despite himself, Gabe couldn't help but meet Bran's grin with one of his own. "Then I'm up for it as well."

"I'll send you the info packet," Bran said. "You'll need to hurry. Entries close in two weeks."

"I can do that."

It only took him a week to put his application together, with Tim and Kathleen's help. Once he sent it off, Gabe allowed himself another night of hard drinking. He'd pay for it in the morning, but that didn't matter. A fall thunderstorm had blown in, wind and rain pounding against the big west windows of the great room. Gabe was now strong enough to wheel the recliner in the great room over by the windows so he could watch the lightning.

Once it faded, leaving a steady rain pounding against the windows, Gabe went to bed in the recliner of his and Brandon's shared room, drink in hand.

He woke in the middle of the night, rousing from a nightmare where he was screaming *I am Gabriel Martiniere*. To his surprise, he hadn't stirred Tim or Kathleen awake. But the memory of yelling his name in the dream was vivid, and Gabe was just drunk enough to try.

"My name is—" he held himself tense, before uttering the rest of it. "Gabriel Martiniere."

Nothing.

Could it be?

Gabe staggered into the bathroom and went to the slider that opened onto the balcony. Rain still pounded against the glass door, a torrential downpour that meant he'd better check the streams and ditches for flooding in the morning. Perhaps that was why Tim and Kathleen hadn't heard him. He slid the door open. No need to disturb them further.

"My name is Gabriel Martiniere!" he bellowed into the storm, shaking a little as the deluge drenched his pajamas.

No reaction.

"My name is Gabriel Martiniere!" he screamed triumphantly. "I was betrayed by Mariah Meyers! My uncle Philip Martiniere deserves to die!"

Nothing more than quivering from being soaked to his skin. Gabe slammed the door shut, laughing hysterically. He sank to the floor, leaning against the slider, unable to stop cackling even as tears flowed.

It was over. *It was over.* Whether it was the G9 or something else, *he was free.*

At last, the sobbing mirth let go of him. Gabe rested his head against the glass.

This changed *everything.*

But dear lord, the price.

I will win the AgSuperhero or die trying. I will get Ruby back.

And when the time is right, I will strike at Philip.

God damn it, this time, he would *win.*

He would live long enough to become the Martiniere. Not for long —he didn't possess enough strength to keep up with that job for more than a couple of years post-G9. But long enough to make Philip and Mariah *pay* for what they'd done to him, Ruby, and Brandon. And Rafe.

And then he would hand the title over to his son.

Gabe grinned into the darkness.

I'm going to win, Philip. And when I do, it will be marvelous.

15 / AG SUPERHERO

GABE SPENT THE REST OF SEPTEMBER PLOTTING HIS CAMPAIGN. ONE THING he decided early on was to exaggerate the post-G9 syndrome effects. And his overcoming G9 to work on the ranch would make for a good, heart-tugging story. He drafted his supplementary materials to dramatize the effect that Rachel's death from G9 had on him.

But he asked Kathleen and Tim to check what he wrote before sending it to AgI. He'd become more dependent on them for day-to-day operational decisions since he'd been sick.

"I'm not being overdramatic, am I?" he asked during their review meeting.

"No," Kathleen said firmly. Tim nodded in agreement. "You two were married for fifteen years, and you were very much in love. Especially when Rachel's family stopped talking to her after she got sick. I notice you didn't mention that."

"I don't want to bring up that whole mess," Gabe said. That could raise more questions that he didn't want to discuss. His dealings with Alvarez Armory had always been on the quiet, except for family.

"Understood," Kathleen said.

"Tim?" Gabe asked.

"I agree with Kathleen," Tim said. He got up and poured himself a cup of coffee, then refilled their cups. "You went above and beyond in caring for Rachel. And from the mess we cleaned up after you two were medevacked…what you experienced was horrific. Going through the G9 and losing Rachel is part of your story. Part of Moondance's story. You need to tell it."

"Thanks," Gabe said.

OCTOBER, 2058

GABE'S NEXT STEP, NOW THAT HE WASN'T LOCKED DOWN BY PHILIP'S MIND control, was to consolidate the references he had used for his testimony almost thirty years ago. It was with other data that he had kept in an archive but been unable to touch since Philip had restricted him. That included pictures that Justine had taken of his scars, right after Philip had beaten him. He updated references, documentation, *everything* that he could think of, including data he'd kept from his work with Alvarez Armory and what little he could remember of what Mariah had done to him.

It would be a crucial reference when Gabe came forward to challenge Philip as the Martiniere. Or Brandon, if things went really bad and something happened to Gabe.

But if he ever got a chance to explain things to Ruby…it might help as well. It certainly would be important background for Brandon.

He titled the folder *GMR — whatthehell.*

And he left accesses open for Ruby, Brandon, and Serg. After considering things further, Gabe added Justine to the list.

In spite of the rumors he had heard about her now being Philip's enforcer. If it were anyone else, he'd think that Philip had control of her.

Knowing his cousin, he suspected that Justine had her own plans.

NOVEMBER, 2058

. . .

Brandon made a beautiful introductory video for Gabe and Moondance that played on the first episode featuring the AgSuperhero finalists. The story of Gabe and Rachel was front and center, but there were small bits about Gabe being a previous Superstar winner, and a little bit about his life with Ruby.

Bran had gotten his hands on footage of that fantastic ride Gabe had made on Skydancer at the Sweets Rodeo. Gabe half-grinned as he watched his younger self bow to Skydancer while the big stud reared, then throw his fists in the air when he spotted his winning score.

The camera briefly caught him talking to Ruby. God, they had been so young in those days.

Ruby's segment was similarly evocative. While it briefly touched on their divorce, there were clips of Ruby as rodeo queen, including a couple of run-ins at the Pendleton Round-Up, one where Sunshine blew up in a fit of bucking. But much of it was about Ruby as a single woman rancher and scientist, and what she'd done with the Double R labs.

Gabe was impressed. He hadn't realized how much Ruby *had* done during their years apart. It didn't necessarily show up in the financial reports. She'd used her AgI funding effectively. No wonder the ranch finances looked like they did—Ruby had poured everything into making those labs work, where he'd had to divert finances into dealing with his heart attack and then Rachel's cancer.

She was well on her way to accomplishing what he had thought she might be capable of doing all those years ago. A brief frisson of regret passed through him because he hadn't been a part of her later success.

The other finalist contenders were Mariah Meyers—Gabe winced at that—Temira Cho, operating a closed-system hog farm; and Jeff Swait, a dryland rice farmer. Gabe frowned as he watched Swait's segment. Then he pulled up his files, choosing not to watch the segment about Mariah. There was a risk that they'd use footage from the divorce, and he didn't think he could stomach it. Much better to check his files.

Yes. Swait had been involved in one of the last Alvarez Armory actions that Gabe had participated in. He'd met the man. Four kids, if he remembered correctly. And while the AgI segment didn't say anything about the Alvarez Armory action, Gabe knew that the Swaits were heavily involved in the indentured freedom underground. The segment cited the Swait descent from slaves who'd escaped bondage via the Underground Railroad. As a result, they refused to use indentured labor on the small cooperative of family farms owned by the Swaits and their relatives.

Gabe wouldn't regret losing to Jeff Swait.

But his financials told him that he damned well better focus on winning, or be prepared to sell Moondance as-is.

All in, he thought grimly to himself. Not just for the AgSuperhero, but for his battle against Philip. Gabe's research revealed that Philip had invested in the AgI.

Perfect for a showdown.

FEBRUARY, 2059

GABE GOT TO THE GREEN ROOM EARLY, CITING HIS PERIODIC POST-G9 syndrome vertigo as a reason for special access. His condition really wasn't *that* bad, but it gave him the excuse to watch other competitors and the investors wanting to mingle with them as they entered. Brandon settled him in a stuffed chair parked in a corner, then moved another chair close to it, grouping three more further away.

"When Mom comes, I'll sit her there," Bran said, pointing at the other comfortable chair.

Gabe laughed. "You're gonna put her off her game if you do that." He was almost giddy in anticipation of Ruby's arrival.

"Ma? No. It'll piss her off, which will make her sparky and more brilliant on stage," Brandon said, lowering his voice. "I watched her old videos. The harder she's challenged, the sharper she gets. *Technically,* I can't help you two. But if I can make Mom feisty, that's going to help her. And you."

"Ain't that the truth." He still remembered how Ruby had lost Miss Rodeo America. The advisor who had replaced Vickie for the national competition had insisted that Ruby moderate her sharp tongue. Become more like—Rachel, he realized. Not Ruby's natural behavior. If he had been there, he would have objected to *that* advice. But he had needed to stay at home with Ron.

"Then you need to work your silver-tongued charm to convince her to reunite."

"I'm not *that* good." But Gabe grinned at his son, met with a matching smirk.

"Seriously, if you two can play at a reunion, it'll bump your combined scores pretty high," Brandon said in a quieter voice. "And—I'd really appreciate it if you'd give that a try."

"Oh? Why?"

Bran started up. "Gotta go, Dad."

Gabe frowned after him. Now what was *that* all about? His son usually wasn't this evasive now that he was an adult. But he had clearly dodged that question.

Takes a skilled liar to recognize another.

And Bran wasn't as good at it as he was.

No time to think about that further. Gabe watched the door hungrily as the other competitors came in, looking for Ruby's arrival. Philip and Mariah as well, but those weren't going to be pleasant encounters.

At last Ruby entered the Green Room. The simple sight of her was enough to make Gabe catch his breath—it had been eight years since he'd seen her in person. An ineffable quality hung about her that just didn't carry over to video, an extra spark to that smile and the look in those blue eyes. She wore one of her old Pendleton Round-Up Princess outfits, complete with the crown on her hat. Long red hair streamed down her back just like it had then, and from a distance—oh God, she was still that brilliant, beautiful, redheaded rodeo queen that he had fallen in love with so many years ago. In spite of everything she'd gone through, she'd aged well.

Gabe gulped, a mountain of resolutions about being casual and indifferent and nonreactive when initially talking to his ex-wife evaporating as he watched Ruby chat with other competitors. Brandon smoothly intercepted her, and Gabe inhaled sharply again at the sight of the two of them together. Bran looked a lot like him, he knew that. But the degree to which some of Bran's movements and mannerisms echoed Ruby....

Regret filled Gabe. In spite of the joy he'd experienced with Rachel, he'd have given up those years in a heartbeat to have remained married to Ruby, to be at her side watching Brandon grow up. Not apart.

I fucked that up.

Not Philip—*him.*

He should have revealed his true identity to her from the beginning. Ruby would have made a *superb* Martiniere wife. He'd wager that Donna-gran would have admired her, and Ruby would have charmed the European Martinieres, especially with her equestrian ability. But together—oh, they would have been a formidable challenge to Philip.

And he'd been too damn stupid and protective to realize it then.

Ruby's gaze softened momentarily when she spotted him. Then it hardened. But there had been that soft moment first. Maybe he still had a chance. She hadn't gone looking for another relationship after their divorce. Did that mean she still had feelings for him—or had he hurt her so bad that she never wanted to try relationships ever again?

He rose to take her hand. She hesitated. Then accepted.

Something surprised Ruby as their hands touched, her eyes widening briefly. Up close, he could tell she was wearing heavy makeup that obscured a lot of the lines on her face and gave her a glamor of youth. Silver streaked through her glorious red hair. But age didn't matter. She was Ruby. Still Ruby.

Not *his* Ruby anymore, alas.

Gabe's legs betrayed him and he had to sit back down. Some of it was the G9 and some of it was just being overwhelmed by her presence again. Brandon asked for a picture of the two of them and he gladly agreed. Ruby was hesitant, but their son persuaded her.

With a pitch for them to get back together, of course.

Gabe deliberately kept her hand in his after the picture poses while they talked about the G9 and Rachel.

Then he spotted Philip. His uncle had entered the Green Room while Brandon was taking pictures, and Gabe hadn't noticed Philip until now. Philip walked toward them. Gabe tensed. Their first face-to-face encounter since that damn day when he wasn't certain he would walk away alive.

Thankfully, Mariah intercepted Philip. Not that he was any happier to see her, either. But seeing her bothered him enough that he and Ruby briefly argued about their last day together—and then Mariah joined them, slinking over, smirking at Gabe. And setting Ruby off.

The rest of the night was a blur until the afterparty. Gabe fought off G9-induced exhaustion starting midway through the taping, due to being on his feet for too long. He didn't get a chance to talk to Ruby at the party. When he realized that she was gone, Gabe hobbled toward the exit, done for the evening.

Mariah stopped him. "Got a moment, Gabe?" she purred.

"Not really." He had overdone today, and wanted nothing more than to go back to his hotel room and take his meds. He'd underestimated the dose he needed.

At least Philip hadn't come to the party.

"I think you'd better take the time," she said, a malign tone underneath the silky seductiveness.

"All right," he sighed. He followed her to an office—expensively but garishly overdone in faux mahogany veneer. Not a Philip office, but a style common for Martiniere subordinates.

"Drink?" Mariah raised a bottle of Scotch.

He shook his head. "Not the way I'm feeling right now." Time to return to paranoid Martiniere food protocols, for one, and for another, he was just too damn tired.

"You didn't used to turn drinks down." That seductive purr was back in her voice. She poured herself a drink and minced toward him. Gabe rested his cane across his lap to discourage her sitting there. Mariah pouted and went back behind that huge abomination of a showplace desk, slouching in the black faux leather chair, throwing one leg over the chair's arm and angling her crotch toward him to show that she wasn't wearing panties.

He deliberately ignored her. Blondes had never really been his type, anyway, especially artificial platinum blondes like Mariah. Brunettes, especially dark-skinned like Rachel—or redheads, like Ruby. With long legs and long hair. Not short-legged and with angled, sculpted hairstyles like Mariah favored.

Besides, nothing good had ever come to him from a blonde.

"A lot of things disappeared with the G9," he said. "Including sex."

"And here I thought there would be possibilities for us to play," she sulked.

"Even if I had the ability, I wouldn't be interested in *you*, bitch," he snapped. "Now. What the hell did you want from me? I'm tired and still dealing with the G9."

Mariah straightened up. She snapped on a camera.

Interesting.

"So, Gabe. Here's the deal. You own a ten percent share of the Double R Ranch, right?"

"Right," he confirmed. *What the hell is her game here?* He narrowed his eyes to glare at her, suspicion rising.

"And I know your financial situation is pretty damn tight. So. After the competition is over, win or lose. Would you be interested in selling your ten percent share in the Double R to me for—say—seven hundred and fifty thousand dollars?"

"*What*?" He hadn't expected *this*.

Mariah twiddled her drink in her fingers. "You heard me. Seven hundred and fifty thousand dollars for your interest in the Double R. If you sign the contract tonight."

Gabe burst out laughing. "That's bullshit, Mariah. What the hell do you expect to gain?" His share was worth more than *that*, and he wasn't going to handicap Ruby by hanging Mariah around her neck. No matter how desperate his finances were.

Her face hardened. "None of your business. Unless you'd like to renew some past connections?"

"I have absolutely no interest in doing any business with you, and that includes anything personal," he said flatly, and got up.

"The offer goes down every time I make it," she said to his back as he headed for the door.

Gabe turned to face her. "I'm not that fucking hard up, and even if I were, I wouldn't sell it to you, you damned bitch."

"You'll regret this, *broken angel*," she sneered.

He tensed a little, then laughed at her again when the only result was a brief moment when he couldn't move.

Her expression was priceless.

But he'd have to be even more careful, because Philip would now know that the old programming had been mostly deleted.

No chance to talk to Ruby at the contestant breakfast the next morning. She sat between Jeff Swait and Temira Cho, ignoring him, then darted out early. Gabe spent his time snubbing Mariah's overtures, until Ruby left, then pointedly got up and sat in Ruby's seat to talk to Cho and Swait. Mariah sulked after he moved. She joined Philip and Georgy Batineau at a nearby table.

Interestingly, he discovered that Mariah had made purchase offers to Cho and Swait for their properties and technology.

What's her game?

He began to suspect that this was a scripted performance...all except Mariah's attempt to seduce him at the beginning of their meeting. And that might well have recorded on a separate set of videos.

The flight back to Portland was a white-knuckle express, with a lot of turbulence. Gabe had never resigned himself to flying, even back and forth to Seattle during his marriage to Rachel. And now rough flights like this played games with the post-G9 vertigo effect, making things worse. He was grateful once he was back in his truck, driving out I-84, and had passed The Dalles, where he could switch on the autodrive. Still couldn't sit back and nap, but it was a break from constant vigilance.

At least these days he didn't have to think about raiders along the freeway.

He stopped to charge the truck and use the restroom at the plateau charging station after the freeway left the Columbia River. A dense, damp fog had settled in after dark, making his joints ache and his fingers clumsy. He struggled with unplugging the charger as another farm truck pulled up next to his.

Gabe straightened up, taking a deep breath, then bent down to try again. He couldn't get the damn thing to unplug. Sticking. Maybe he could ask whoever this was to help—*Ruby!* Yes, her familiar shape, and the same profane mutters he remembered from oh-so-many years ago as she wrestled with her connection.

"Ruby? Is that you? Damn chargers."

She joined him. "Let me get this."

He grabbed his cane as she struggled with the charger. It was tough for her, too. Made him not feel so bad about having problems.

"Thanks."

"There!" she said triumphantly, reeling the cord back into the holder for him as well.

"Thank you," he repeated, flexing his hands. "These fogs sink into my bones so my hands don't work right. Doesn't matter if it's here or on the West Side. If it's foggy, they hurt and I can't get a good grip. It was a real fight just to get plugged in." He sighed. *Gabriel, damn it, you're rambling.* Ruby had that effect on him. "If I can get the Superhero, that might just be enough cash for me to get things in good enough shape that I can afford to sell out and relocate."

There was enough light for him to see the sudden surprised expression on Ruby's face.

"Mariah hasn't made you an offer yet?"

He snorted. *Not anything I'm going to take her up on.*

"The only offer she's made me is for my share of the Double R." He coughed—damn fog. "Unlike the rest of the Superhero finalists, or so I've heard."

Another surprised expression, followed by worry and then a tight blankness.

"I'll match or beat any price she gives you. No questions asked."

He couldn't help laughing, because he knew they were in similar financial straits. "With what? I see your quarterlies, Ruby."

Damn it, that was a stupid thing to say.

"I'll find a way." Oh, that was a familiar set of her jaw. Not just her but Brandon.

Gabe sighed. "You're getting old, too. Maybe you need to be thinking about retirement."

With me, maybe?

Ruby pressed her lips together, if anything looking even more stubborn. "If I recall the prenuptial agreement and our divorce settlement properly, you have to give me first purchase option. I want to do it, and I'll do whatever it takes, Gabe."

Aw fuck. I've pissed her off and she took it the wrong way.

"Ruby, Ruby, Ruby," he sighed, doing his best to defuse her reaction. "We need to talk." This was *not* the best location.

"Yes. But not here." She bit off each word, still angry.

"I'll be in touch." Gabe leaned against his truck, sagging his shoulders and doing his best to convey to Ruby how exhausted he was. "Right now, I just want to get off of the road. Let me know if things are too bad on the pass over the Blues…I'd be happy to let you stay at my place."

"I'll be all right." Still defensive, but softer.

"It's an option." He hobbled over to the door and wrestled himself into the cab, running the window down so he could keep talking. "Thanks for your help. And keep the offer in mind. Please."

"Talk to me before you sell to Mariah."

"All right," he said.

She looked really worried, now, and he didn't blame her one bit.

Gabe drove off, berating himself. He should have been smoother. Damn it, he'd been able to sweet-talk Ruby when he was younger. Why not now?

Because Rachel lacked Ruby's hard edge, and you got out of the habit of banter.

Rachel had been yielding, but at the same time quietly guiding and firm when she dealt with him. She had been the smooth talker. The water wearing away stone, grain by grain, eventually achieving her goals.

Ruby was more like the stone. Unyielding except by small grains at a time.

He needed to become more like Rachel, and be the water working on the stone, instead of stone pounding on stone.

———

GABE SLEPT LATE THE NEXT MORNING, THEN WAS BUSY DEALING WITH paperwork and lab work until late, ignoring all calls so he could focus. His brain was still fuzzy from doing too much at the AgI. It wasn't until after dinner that he felt up to dealing with the messages that had accumulated—one of the drawbacks of participating in the AgI.

Midway through his messages was one that sent his heart into his throat.

> Someone took a shot at Mom on the ranch today. Please be careful, Dad. BR.

He called but only got Bran's recorder. Gabe flipped through his other messages. Nothing. He flipped over to the AgI feed. There was a video of Ruby talking with the neighbors. Celebration of her AgSuperhero nomination, and then a short talk about the shooting, abruptly cut off when they moved to a new topic. Apparently fences had been cut too—what the *hell?*

He knew those sensors. Unless Ruby had upgraded, they were the ones he'd installed years ago, before leaving the ranch. There should have been a warning. What had happened?

But there was a scratch on Ruby's face, just under her eye. He stopped the play to zoom in as best as he could. It didn't look too bad.

What the hell happened? Had Philip gotten pissed off because Gabe rejected Mariah, and sent his people after her?

Damnit, I wish Rafe was still here. Maybe he needed to invoke that emergency call to Serg—but he'd been holding off on that because he wasn't ready. When he talked to Serg again, it would be as *Gabriel Martiniere*, not *Gabe Ramirez.*

Needed to be that.

Gabe shuddered. He rose. Between traveling and overdoing at the Ag Superhero, he hurt all over. Time for a drink.

As he poured the drink and sipped a little, he decided to call Ruby. They did need to talk, after all. He glanced at the clock. If he was going to call her, he'd better do it soon. Not long before she'd be in bed, if her routines hadn't changed. He downed about half the whisky, then topped it off.

He settled in his office rocking chair, and called Ruby.

It took a little persuasion, but he talked her into dinner tomorrow. At the Happy Flower in Grande City—not one of his favorite places, but it *was* one of the better restaurants in Grande City.

———

AND…DINNER TURNED OUT TO BE A BUST, AND IT WASN'T JUST THE END-of-storage season food. Ruby blindsided him with the revelation about rogue killbots discovered on both hers and her neighbors' fields. The killbot programming was based on *his own damned fucking work*, and he couldn't persuade her that he didn't have anything to do with it. She came into dinner angry, and left even more so, convinced that he and Mariah were scheming against her.

Damn, that woman's good at holding a grudge.

Gabe was pissed, too. He left an angry message with Bran.

But he was worried as well. Killbots were designed to have a specific function. Dump them into a field with preprogrammed targets to clear it of other bots. Sometimes pests or unwanted microbials. Once that function was done, they died and biodegraded.

They weren't *supposed* to move beyond field parameters. They weren't *supposed* to keep going past a shutoff period. Gabe brooded about that on his way home. He'd need to do a hard-core security sweep of his archives. Where the hell had a saboteur gotten hold of his programming—and who the hell had done it?

Bran returned his call before he reached Moondance.

"Dad." Bran was wild-eyed and tense. "What the hell was all that about?"

"Your damned mother thinks that I'm trying to sabotage her and she isn't fucking listening to me!" Gabe snapped, still fretting about this damned new situation. "And now I *need to fucking figure out what happened!*"

Bran sighed. "Dad. Can you just calm down?"

"No. I know what I did and didn't do. I've got a monster problem because if your mother keeps blaming me, it won't just be your mother on my back but her neighbors. It's my damned reputation on the line,

Bran! Shit! And for her to imply that I'm collaborating with *that fucking bitch Mariah* is just over the goddamned top!"

"Dad—"

"Why the *hell* didn't you warn me about those damned killbots?" Gabe rubbed his face. "I'm sure you knew. Look. I'm going to deal with this tomorrow. Right now I'm getting close to my exit and I have to go on manual. Will you *please* talk to your mother and tell her to knock that damned chip off of her shoulder?"

He signed off and shut down his comm for the night.

God damn it, he should never have signed up for this fucking program in that stupid longshot hope that he could reunite with Ruby.

God damn it.

Another night of drinking heavily sounded awfully damned good.

16 / COMPLICATING FACTORS

FEBRUARY, 2059

BRAN CALLED THE NEXT EVENING. "DAD. I NEED TO TALK. FACE-TO-FACE."
He looked subdued and shame-faced. He was supposed to have spent
the day at the Double R installing cams. Ruby must have ripped into
him pretty hard about something.

"All right," Gabe said. "How soon?"

"I'm turning off of 84 right now."

So, in half an hour. Gabe checked the time. "Dinner?"

Bran shook his head, then turned off the comm.

What the fuck is wrong now?

He waited for Bran's arrival upstairs. Met him at the door, uncom-
fortably remembering that time that Charlie and Martin had dragged
Bran to Moondance. His son's expression wasn't defiant but—if
anything, he looked worse than he had when he called.

Bran took a deep breath. "I'll officially be back tomorrow to install
cams and mikes for the Superhero. But I've got to tell you this before
then."

"High security?"

Bran nodded.

"Let's take it to the office." Gabe limped down the stairs and
plopped into the big chair behind his desk. Once Bran sat, Gabe
switched on his security screen to the highest level. "All right. Spill it.
How pissed is your mother?"

Bran stared at his hands. Rubbed his face. Then he looked up. "She's past that, Dad. That's not the problem. It's me."

"What?" Gabe startled. Bran didn't usually do stupid stuff.

Bran took another deep breath. "I've really fucked things up, Dad. I'm gambling big on the reunion storyline with you and Mom, because —" Exhale. Inhale. "If the Superhero doesn't earn a certain number of clicks, then I go into full indenture at AgI."

No. Fuck no.

Gabe stared at his son, horror-struck. "How?" he managed to croak.

Bran shook his head. "Student loans. Gambling debts to offset payments."

"How much?"

"Three point five million."

"*Three point five million?*" Gabe's jaw dropped. "How on earth?"

Bran rubbed his face. "Creditors came after me for your debts as well," he sighed. "When Hernan pulled Rachel's financial support, well—"

"Brandon, you shouldn't have done that."

"I *had to do it,* Dad!" Brandon flared up, his eyes widening as his voice grew louder. "I wasn't fucking going to let them boot you out of the hospital before you recovered, and I wanted you to have the best damn treatment possible, all right?" He gulped. "Losing Rachel was bad enough. But you—you would have died or been more crippled than you are now without that damn treatment!"

Gabe sank back in his chair, rubbing the bridge of his nose, suddenly sick to his stomach.

Fuck. And how much of this mess is Philip's doing?

At last he dropped his hand. "How does the Superhero play into all of this?"

"AgI has been losing money on the Superstar for years," Bran said. "The Innovator and the Star Innovator are doing just fine. But the Superstar—between the difficulty to complete it and assorted scandals that AgI has kept hushed up, we've had fewer and fewer applicants. People want to do the Innovator and the Star because they're more of a sure thing."

Gabe nodded. "That was my feeling as well, after what happened with your mother and me."

"Yeah. And you're not the only one." Bran sighed. "The Superstar has had a lot of issues. But the key is that there are fewer applicants, especially the sort of cutting-edge hopefuls the Superstar was created to fund—and less interest from viewers and from advertisers." He looked down at his hands again, clearly organizing his thoughts.

Gabe waited.

No wonder he looked like he'd been whipped when he called.

Ruby would have ripped into Bran *hard* after she heard this news. And he didn't blame her one damned bit. The only thing that kept *him* from yelling was the knowledge that Ruby had already done it for him. The kid didn't need to be torn apart by both of them. It didn't solve anything, and Bran already realized the consequences.

Bran sighed again. "The Superhero is my baby. My creation. I went to Georgy Batineau with the idea, to try to bring back some of the old participants, see where you are now, mixed with new ones. Georgy's idea was to run Mariah as a dummy contestant with a script."

"Those offers of hers are bogus?"

"Oh, they're real enough," Bran snorted. "But the ownership goes to AgI, not Mariah. I have no idea what her obligation is and I don't care. Beyond the fact that she kept the bounty hawks from grabbing me at work. She talked Georgy into buying out my indenture obligation from the Martiniere Group."

Gabe hadn't thought he could have been more aghast at this situation until that moment. Mariah and the Martiniere Group were combined in this sorry mess. *Fuck.*

"And then," Bran continued. "I cut a deal with Georgy. If the Superhero gains enough clicks, then my entire indenture obligation is wiped out. Period."

"And are you close?"

Brandon shook his head. "Not enough, even if current trends continue. Not without you and Mom juicing up the reunion storyline."

Gabe groaned. He smacked his head against the back of his chair.

"What about your interests in the Double R and Moondance?"

"Already borrowed against."

"Fuck."

Brandon winced. "Yeah, Mom already yelled at me about that, too, because both ranches are at risk."

Gabe shook his head. He rested an elbow on the arm of his chair and covered his eyes while he thought, not wanting to be distracted by Bran's worried looks.

This was a disaster. This was a *fucking* disaster. He and Ruby would be fortunate if *they* managed to escape indenture, along with Bran.

Goddamn Philip. Goddamn kid.

Bran should have just let him die. Then Ruby could have filed a claim against the Family Trust and—

But it was done, and no amount of recrimination would change things.

How the hell could the three of them get out of this mess? He and Ruby had to work together now. Should he suck it up and go public with who he really was, and hope that he could brazen it out enough to free Brandon, coerce the Family into forcing Philip to do the right thing?

Good luck with that.

If the Family hadn't reined Philip in before, why would they do it to benefit Gabe's son—a Martiniere scion they didn't know?

They wouldn't. Except for Serg and Piotr, they'd not lifted a finger to help *him*. Gabriel, the son of the former Martiniere. And Philip had already stopped Cousin Artie's move to take over the Family—from what Serg had said several years ago. No. That wasn't a viable strategy.

He raised his head. "Is there any way—*any way at all*—that the Superhero can be salvaged to save you from indenture?"

"Clicks have been really good when I've pushed the reunion story-line," Brandon said.

God. He didn't want reunion with Ruby to be forced like this. Not on these terms. But they had no choice. Absolutely no choice at all.

"What does your mother say?"

"She wants to talk to you. At the ranch, where it's safe. She's on board, but says you two have things to work out. Away from cams."

Oh boy, do we ever have things to work out.

"It's going to take a few days." Gabe was seeing some distressing data from his microbial seeding results that he and Tim needed to figure out if he was going to be competitive in the Superhero.

"As long as you can get something happening before the next taping session. We've got a break because—" Bran sighed. "The drama with Mom getting shot at has helped a little bit."

Gabe exhaled. "I'll give her a call in the next couple of days and get a meeting set up for the middle of next week. We'll script things out."

The relief on Brandon's face was unmistakable.

AND THE HITS JUST KEPT COMING.

By late afternoon the next day, Gabe knew he was in big trouble. Tim had brought back samples from the fields—and there were rogue killbots targeting his microbials. Killing them. The programming matched the sample that Ruby had shown him during that abortive dinner meeting.

Before he could go very far with his analysis, Mariah yanked him away from his work. Gabe bellowed at her, not giving a shit about what it looked like, because if he didn't get this damn problem *fixed*, it wouldn't matter what he and Ruby did. He'd be out of the Superhero.

Gabe did watch that night's Innovator episode, tense because he figured the clip of him and Mariah would play, and that would really screw him up with social media. He should have thought about the optics before he did it.

Damn it, his mistakes were *all* piling up on him now.

The clips of Mariah pitching to Cho and Swait led the episode. But then Georgy Batineau himself came on.

"You think those were good?" Batineau said to the studio audience. Loud cheers. "Then let's see what our rodeo queen Ruby Barkley did— how many of you want to see Ruby and Gabe back together?"

Gabe straightened up as the crowd whooped and hollered.

"How many of you were sad about their fight?"

Groans and boos.

"Well, there's hope. Watch this clip and see what you think."

The first thing Gabe noticed was that Ruby wore the blue topaz lavaliere earrings he'd given her when they won the Superstar. She had that sparkly, sharp edge of hers when sparring with Mariah, that sly little grin popping up in the corner of her mouth when Mariah reacted to her.

But one thing she said gave him hope.

Who says that the Ruby and Gabe reconciliation story isn't going to fly? After all, that is a known quantity of our past relationship. We fought. Dramatically. And the makeups were—ooh, they never got shown, but they were equally dramatic. Don't you think the fight the other day added to the dramatic tension? We are good at that, as you should know. Just imagine what the makeup session after that fight is going to be.

It was almost as if she were speaking directly to him.

Without hesitation, he called her.

As the call began to connect, he heard Ruby say that she would go to Philip Martiniere first.

No. God no, Ruby.

He was quick to warn her off of Philip, then told her about *his* rogue killbots. She was further along in developing a solution, and offered it to him.

They set a date for Wednesday. Riding out—and she would have his counterbots ready by then.

Six days away. Gabe reined in his impatience.

Tim followed Gabe over to the Double R in a separate truck on Wednesday. After loading up the counterbots so that Tim could get them started sooner rather than later, Gabe and Ruby went to the horse pasture to catch their rides. They'd watch the RubyBot releases—as filmed by AgI, then be filmed riding off together. That was the plan.

Gabe gasped at the sight of the ancient palomino mare who led the herd as the horses galloped toward them. Even at thirty-five years old, with the prominent spine and sagging belly of an elderly horse, Sunshine still dominated the herd, snapping at the others to keep them back until she had gotten a treat from Ruby and a scratch from Gabe.

Ruby pointed out Sunshine's descendants—a chestnut mare, a chestnut colt, and a younger palomino mare that could have almost been a copy of Sunshine, except that her blaze was smaller.

"Isn't she the one you were riding when you were shot at?" All the reports said that Ruby had been riding a palomino—and the only other one in the field was Sunshine. He didn't think Ruby would still be riding the old mare.

Ruby nodded. "That's Legacy."

She haltered a sorrel gelding—Red, of course—and a black gelding for her—Pard.

Gabe was slower about grooming and tacking than he liked. His fingers fumbled with the brushes. But it felt good to brush a horse again, run his fingers under the long mane to let them warm, chuckle as the big sorrel stretched out his head and neck to wiggle his upper lip blissfully when Gabe hit an itchy spot.

Ahhh, he missed being around horses. It had been too many years, especially since Rachel hadn't been a rider.

Too many years for a lot of things.

THEIR TALK BY A SMALL SPRING DEEP IN A DRAW WHERE CONNECTIVITY WAS nonexistent went well. Things about AgI this time around had put Ruby on alert, even before Brandon's revelations. She had noticed things Gabe hadn't. And she yelled about Gabe's gambling, but forgave him.

He apologized. Repeatedly.

I fucked up, Ruby. I fucked up.

Everything except telling her who he really was. He didn't want *Gabriel Martiniere* interfering with what Gabe Ramirez had to do—and reunion had to happen with Gabe Ramirez before *Gabriel Martiniere* came on the scene.

Then it was time for the hard question.

"Are we doing this for Bran's sake only?" he asked.

"I have enjoyed being friends again." Her voice was soft and she looked away. "Until the last few days, I didn't realize how much I missed being able to talk to you."

"Friends, then." He could live with that. It was a start. Better than nothing. Better than loneliness.

"Friends. Colleagues. Allies." They shook hands on it.

Then he spotted a ladyslipper orchid, and pointed it out to Ruby.

"I haven't seen one for years. Not since—we broke up," she said, her voice raw.

An omen?

GABE FELT WATCHED AS THEY RODE OUT OF THE DRAW. NOTHING HE COULD pinpoint, except that it was the same *eyes on me* sensation he'd experienced in Tucson, during the early days of the witness protection program. They rode by the Homestead field, Gabe wincing as he remembered fighting that damn irrigation system.

Red staggered slightly under him. Crack of gunfire. Hard blow in his left shoulder almost like his heart attack. More shots.

I've been hit, he realized distantly as Red leapt into a huge buck and pain throbbed through his shoulder. He fought the instinct to grab at the pain because he had to focus on the damn horse bucking. Big, huge, leaps, hard bucks. He gripped the saddle horn and slid his hand down to the pommel instead for more security.

Then Red started running. That was worse because Gabe slipped in the saddle once Red picked up a gallop. Something was wrong with the sorrel gelding because the rhythm was erratic, throwing Gabe from side-to-side unevenly and not smooth like it should be. The buck was easier to sit.

Hit in the hindquarters?

Ruby galloped her horse alongside, extending her left arm as she brought Pard close.

"Got you!" She'd done some pickup rider work during their rodeo days, thank God.

He slipped his right arm around her waist, trusting that Ruby was steady in her saddle and that her horse wouldn't buck him off. She grabbed Gabe around his torso and pulled him off, doing her best to haul him up behind her instead of drop him to the ground. He managed to swing his leg over Pard's back as more shots rang out.

"I'm on I'm on I'm on!" he gasped to her, clinging to Ruby's waist as tight as he could with his left arm. "Let's get the fuck out of here!"

Gabe panted—pain and post-G9 making his breath come short and fast as the gelding extended into a hard gallop, things turning fuzzy around him. Ruby eased Pard back once they dropped below the ridgeline. Gabe crashed into her as the horse stopped hard.

"You okay?" she asked.

"My shoulder hurts like a son-of-a-bitch, but I think it's superficial." It was easing a little bit. But he was starting to shake, and that wasn't good.

Need more meds.

He told Ruby where they were when he couldn't reach them without risking dropping the bottle. Ruby managed to fish the pill bottle out of his coat pocket and shake two of the small tablets out. Gabe dry-swallowed them. Then he focused on just staying on and not messing with her balance as the black gelding first trotted, then moved into a slow lope.

Charlie and Martin met them halfway to the main ranch, driving the big crawler. Gabe rode back to the house with them.

WELL. *THAT* EXPERIENCE WAS A GAME CHANGER, ALL RIGHT.

Ruby spent part of the night in a rocking chair by his bed after Sheriff Wilhite finished talking to them. He rode to the airport with her for the AgI show because he couldn't drive with his shoulder messed up like this. They stayed in his hotel room—with a recliner for him to sleep in. They kissed publicly, in big and dramatic ways, both of them playing with it and having fun.

Mariah was clearly pissed by their reconciliation.

The clicks shot up, and Ruby was becoming more affectionate in private. Not just playing the AgI reunion game but—whispers of true feeling from her.

Maybe there was hope.

———

Wᴉʟʜɪᴛᴇ ᴄᴀʟʟᴇᴅ ᴛʜᴇᴍ ᴏɴ ᴛʜᴇ ᴡᴀʏ ʙᴀᴄᴋ ғʀᴏᴍ Pᴏʀᴛʟᴀɴᴅ. Nᴏ ʟᴇᴀᴅs ʏᴇᴛ, but she mentioned the likelihood of a professional assassin. Female.

Ruby wanted to talk after Wilhite's call, but Gabe avoided the conversation, thinking hard about who, if anyone, he could contact from the Alvarez Armory days to track down that assassin. He agreed to meet the next day with Ruby and Vickie Chandler, to choreograph their reunion performance. He had a water resources meeting with the Confederated Tribes in the morning, but he could join them in the afternoon. Tim would drive him over, then bring him back.

Easy. Things were clicking right along.

———

"I'ʟʟ ᴅᴜᴄᴋ ɪɴᴛᴏ ᴛʜᴇ ʀᴇsᴛʀᴏᴏᴍ, ᴀɴᴅ ᴛʜᴇɴ I'ʟʟ ʙᴇ ʀᴇᴀᴅʏ ᴛᴏ ɢᴏ ᴛᴏ Thunder County," Gabe said to Tim once the water resources meeting was winding down. This had been a long but productive gathering.

As he was washing his hands, several persons pushed into the restroom. Gabe spotted them in the mirror. Full body suits with masks, two fanning out to flank him as two other people took care of the security cams. *Trouble.* He whirled and raised his cane.

"Get back," he growled.

"*Broken Angel,*" one snarled—was that Anne Wright, from the old days with the Feds? *What the hell?* Gabe lunged at them, swinging the cane, not even perceiving a quick lockdown from the code words this time.

He fought back, yelling, hoping that *someone* would hear him and call Security. They swarmed Gabe. One person against four. A shot jabbed into his right forearm.

Shit. Here we go again.

THIS TIME THE SEDATIVE WAS SHORT-ACTING. HE SLOWLY BECAME AWARE that he was lying on his side in a van of some sort, hands and feet bound. Moving but on a paved road, not much jouncing around or cornering. Probably I-84, then.

Gabe kept his eyes closed and carefully explored the wrist bindings. Zip-cuffs, of course. He could find a means of getting loose if they hadn't relieved him of his Kevlar cord…damn, they had.

Lie still and listen.

He still could get loose but it'd take more time. Best to take the time to rest while he could, figure out the situation.

"He's awake." That voice that sounded like Anne Wright.

"I'll help him wake up if he's not." Damn it, that was Gerry Rothman. Talk about ghosts from his past. He hadn't considered that his betrayers from the witness protection days would come back to haunt him.

Rothman kicked him in the gut. Gabe doubled over and groaned. He opened his eyes, doing his best to exaggerate the pain. Quick assessment. Solid divider between back and front, so he couldn't take control even if he had the strength and ability to fight off all four of his kidnappers. If that was all.

Two in back with him. Wright and Rothman.

Assume they have more training than before.

He might have a chance to improve his odds, nonetheless.

Rothman, the fool, was standing just in the right spot. He shifted his weight slightly, like he was going to kick Gabe again.

Gabe moved first, contorting himself to nail Rothman's weight-bearing leg on the ankle. He kept kicking as best as he could, and scored a direct hit on the inside of Rothman's left knee with both feet, hard. Rothman staggered against the wall of the van.

Training but not very good.

Wright got into it. Gabe kept fighting.

Another injection. He battled the fuzziness descending on him, trying to hurt Wright.

And then things went black once more.

"You idiots, he's Vygotsky Security-trained." Male voice, not one he recognized, coming from behind the van, the back doors now open. *"You fucked up the assassination years ago and now this."*

Gabe woke to those words. He still lay on the floor. The vehicle wasn't moving anymore and he *hurt*. The damp, cool draft from the open doors didn't help, either.

Nonetheless, it was a damn fucking pleasure to overhear Rothman and Wright get chewed out by one of his other attackers. He could only catch bits and pieces of it, though, and *damn*, from the cadence, it was an epic rant. Gabe chuckled to himself, finding one piece of morbid humor in this fucking mess. He couldn't think of better targets for a good dressing-down by a pro.

Rothman said something Gabe couldn't hear.

"All you had to do was keep him quiet. Not try to kick the shit out of him." A different male voice.

"But he has post-G9 syndrome! He shouldn't be able to fight back!" That was Wright.

Something from the first voice.

Defensive response from Rothman.

"What the hell were you thinking? Fucking amateurs." First voice again, as he climbed into the van. Click of a pistol slide being cocked.

"I'm right behind you," the first voice said. "If you move at all, Martiniere, I'll blow your fucking head off."

"Understood." *All right, so he knows who I really am.* Not surprising since he knew about Gabe's training. "You gonna keep those two from whacking on me further?"

"That wasn't supposed to happen." Gun muzzle behind his ear. "You're going to sit up, real slow now. No resistance."

"Not sure how easy it's gonna be," Gabe admitted. "They beat on me pretty good."

The man hauled Gabe upright, gun muzzle not moving from behind his ear. "Number Two, gonna need help to get him on his feet."

Another man climbed in the van. He cut the cuffs around Gabe's ankles, and the two men hoisted Gabe to his feet.

"So you know that I'm Gabriel Martiniere."

"Shut the fuck up," the first man said, as the second blindfolded him.

But Gabe had learned what he needed to know. Whatever they'd injected him with, it hadn't reinstated his programming.

Mix of nanos and vocals is what Philip did in the first place.

So not likely something to be handed over to someone who wasn't high-level Family. That was good to know.

On the other hand, that said scary things about Mariah's level of involvement with the Family, since she'd been able to program him all those years ago.

His captors shoved Gabe along an extended, blindfolded walk over rough ground. At one point he heard the zing and pop of high-tension fence wire being cut.

Shit. This is so not good.

Odds were that he wasn't going to make it out alive this time. They were taking him somewhere isolated. That didn't bode well.

Goddamn it, I should have told Ruby and Bran about the envelope, now that I can talk about the Family.

He'd gotten too accustomed to being silenced.

When they stopped and yanked off his blindfold, Gabe recognized where they were. The spring where he and Ruby had talked just a few days ago.

Only the two pros with him. A cam hovered in front of Gabe as they forced him to his knees. Gabe tensed, anticipating the gunshot before the final darkness. Or would these assholes try to hack his head off?

Think, Gabriel, think.

If he could manage to get away, it wasn't *that* far to Ruby's. Or to Jim Reed's place.

Then he was shoved flat as they bound his feet again.

One of the men growled a statement to the cam. The other stood next to him, out of Gabe's reach, damn it. They faced him. One circled around and yanked him up by his hair. He spat at the man. The man backhanded him.

"Beg for your life from nature abuser Ruby Barkley!"

Recording this for Ruby… was this an opportunity?

"Never! *Ladyslipper,* Ruby!"

That earned him more blows. And this time he couldn't fight back because these men knew what they were doing, unlike Rothman and Wright. Gabe curled up after this beating, gasping as his assailants fitted a blindfold over his eyes once more.

And then he was alone. Gabe drew long, painful breaths. His injured shoulder throbbed. He rolled to his belly and managed to sit up, even though his knees were screaming as he sank back on his heels, breathing hard. For whatever reason, they'd left him alive.

Counting on exposure to finish me off. Why?

A slow death instead of the quick, sure thing. Or were they just watching and waiting to strike at him, enjoying watching him suffer? Were they herding one of the big local predators—bear, wolf, cougar— toward him? That was the most probable likelihood. He'd seen enough of that sort of thing happening during the Alvarez Armory days.

He needed to get the damned bindings on his wrists off to start with, because he *would* die otherwise. Doable, but it was going to hurt like a son-of-a-bitch.

Gabe bit his lower lip and got to work.

***

GETTING THE CUFFS OFF RIPPED OPEN THE STITCHES ON HIS GUNSHOT injury. Gabe passed out twice from the pain. But finally his hands were free, and he could pull off the blindfold.

Pitch-dark. Of course. And he could only use his right hand to crawl. Dare he try to get those damn cuffs off of his ankles? Or would that just take too much out of him?

Gabe froze as he heard voices and saw lights.

And then he recognized Sheriff Wilhite's voice. "Gabe? Gabe?"

"Here!" he called. "Over here!"

Familiar faces from the old Thunder County days. Familiar voices. Thank God.

He'd managed to dodge the Grim Reaper yet again.

Someday his number would come up. But fortunately, today wasn't that day.

"WE'VE CONTACTED BOTH TIM VANHORN AND RUBY BARKLEY TO LET them know you're safe," Wilhite said once Dr. Sheri had fussed over him, back at the road, and Wilhite had taken his statement. She sighed. "Taking you to the Double R. You'd better call Vanhorn. I'm afraid there's bad news. Your house and lab are on fire."

"What the—hook me up! Please."

Tim looked grim when he answered the call, and Gabe saw flames, smoke and fire engines behind him.

"The fire started at the same time you were kidnapped, Gabe," Tim said. "It's clearly arson. We've got investigators on site, and Kathleen and I are staying in Craig's old place."

"Damn, is the old house at all habitable?" At least Kathleen had made it out safely.

"For tonight. Getting a trailer in tomorrow, after the investigators finish in the morning."

"All right." Gabe sighed. "I'll check in with you then. I'm just whipped."

"Glad to see you alive, though," Tim said.

"Yeah," Gabe said tiredly. "And glad that Kathleen got out safely. That's more important."

GABE HAD ENOUGH TIME TO THINK ABOUT JUST HOW SCREWED HE WAS AS they drove him to Ruby's.

He was out of the Superhero for certain. Did he have a pathway out of this mess?

Other than walking into Philip's office and trying to negotiate his life for Bran's, Gabe couldn't see a means to keep his son free from indenture.

It would have been better if he had died in that draw. Whatever Philip would do to him would be long, slow, and quite painful. Gabe was certain of that.

But at least he'd be able to see Ruby first. If he could just get one more kiss from her before he died, he'd be happy.

And then he'd sacrifice himself for their son.

———

GOING UP THE STEPS TO THE FRONT PORCH FELT ALIEN, AFTER YEARS OF going in and out through the kitchen. His focus was fading a little, between drugs and pain and just dealing with everything. The warmth of the ranch house's living room crashed over him, and Gabe realized how cold he was.

Then he saw Ruby, hands at her mouth, bright blue eyes wide, puffy from tears.

"Rubes. They say you knew where I was."

A choke in her voice as she spoke. "You said the right thing. *Ladyslipper.*"

He wobbled, ready to collapse. Ruby opened her arms. Gabe staggered across the room, slumping against Ruby and burying his nose in that junction of neck and shoulder. Lavender and mint. Ruby. *Ruby.* His redheaded rodeo queen. One last treat before dying. He wrapped his good arm around her, holding on tight, trembling with the effort to stay upright.

Ruby. Mint and lavender. Ruby.

She braced herself and held him firmly, quivering along with him.

"You hungry?" she asked.

He reluctantly raised his head and shook it. "Tired. They drugged me, and I've had painkillers. I want a shower and a recliner, if I can get it."

Gabe zoned out as Ruby talked to the others, closing his eyes, utterly drained, nose back in that junction of shoulder and neck.

Mint and lavender. Ruby. At least I get this one more time before the end.

"Hey." Ruby shook him awake. "Can you walk upstairs, or do I need help?"

"You should be plenty. Just you, Rubes, if you can swing it. Please. I've had enough of people right now."

Just him and Ruby. That was what he wanted. One last night to savor.

"Okay. Let's see if we can make it without help," she said. She got them moving slowly. The aches from movement woke him a little bit.

They talked on that long, laborious trek upstairs, but whatever it was they said didn't stick in his brain. Gabe struggled to stay alert. He needed to tell Ruby who he was, *tonight.*

No more delays.

———

THE SHOWER ROUSED HIM. GABE GRATEFULLY SLIPPED INTO SOME OLD sweats that had belonged to Brandon, then slid the recliner so it was right next to the bed. Once Ruby settled in, he took her hand, raising it to his lips and kissing it several times.

This night was a gift. If only he could make love to her one last time.

Telling Ruby who he was turned out to be easier than he thought.

"I lied to you about not having any family years ago. My name wasn't really Ramirez. Well, it was my mother's name, not my father's. My family name is Martiniere. I used to prefer the Spanish naming. I am Gabriel Marcus Martiniere Ramirez, not just Gabe Ramirez."

His full, real name felt strange on his lips again.

Ruby's eyes widened. "Wait. Philip Martiniere is one of Georgy Batineau's backers—you're from *that* family? The Martiniere Group? You don't look like any of them."

"Philip is my uncle."

"Uncle? Oh shit."

They talked further, and he gave her a copy of his *whatthehell* file.

And then it was time for the really hard discussion.

"If I have to, I'll sell myself to my uncle to save you two." Gabe swallowed hard. "I'm—Ruby, I don't see any option. Trade myself for Bran."

"Indenture will kill you." Ruby's brows furrowed.

"I'm a dead man walking right now anyway. Maybe I can save Bran." He tightened his hand on hers. "Philip won't rest until I'm dead. It's personal. But if he kills me, then that gives you and Bran leverage."

"What do you mean?" Her brows cinched down harder.

"Remy Trask has an envelope I gave her years ago, just before we married. It has everything in it you need to make a claim on the Martiniere Family Trust in my name. Certificates. Contacts." Gabe drew a deep breath, wincing as another pain made itself known. "By rights, Bran is a high-level Martiniere heir. And even though I married you under a different name, then we divorced, you would still be my widow. I didn't change things after I married Rachel. I wanted you and Bran to have something."

"*Gabe*." Anguish in Ruby's voice.

"You'd be entitled to a share of my estate, whatever it's worth now." Gabe chuckled bitterly. "Serg Vygotsky is the contact you want to establish. He and his father Piotr will protect you."

"Gabe. Philip wouldn't—would he?"

"Rubes. He would. My death would be long, slow, and painful." Gabe swallowed hard. "But it would be worth it to save Bran."

"Gabe. No." She shook her head and closed her eyes tight for a moment. "I'd sell the Double R if I thought that would save Bran. And you. No, Gabe. You're not going to do this."

And then she told him about *her* wild idea. About that clause in the Superhero contract that allowed three contestants to combine their operations and their scores so that all three could win. Between her and Jeff Swait, they had enough points to pull it off—even with him pulling them down.

It was just unusual enough that it might work.

Gabe woke to the muffled sounds of sobs and gagging from the bathroom. For a moment he was disoriented—Rachel having a hard chemo night? No, this was the Double R—Ruby pregnant—no. Memory slammed back into place. And when he glanced over at the bed, the shimmer of Ruby's comp screen showed a scene from his *whatthehell* file.

His back, covered with fresh, open weals.

Oh shit.

Gabe shuddered and got up, remembering her reaction when she saw his scars their first night together. After first showing him hers, when he'd warned her. That gulp, followed by soft kisses. He switched off the comp.

The bathroom was dark and he didn't remember his way around it anymore. Gabe fumbled and finally switched on the light. Ruby didn't look up from the toilet, weeping and not puking. He found a washrag and dampened it, then knelt beside Ruby, pulling her away from the toilet and wiping her face.

She sagged into him, still crying and shaking. He rocked her back and forth, holding on to her with his good arm.

"Rubes," he said shakily. "I turned it off."

Ruby raised her head. "How the fucking hell did you keep from killing him?"

This was going to be long, and he didn't have it in him to get up just yet. Gabe slid them across the bathroom until his back was against the cabinet door. Ruby didn't resist as he pulled her into his lap. He leaned his head against hers, focusing on the tub across from them.

"I had no power, Rubes. If I dared raise my hand back to him, he would have killed my cousin Justine in one of his rages. *His own fucking daughter.*" Gabe swallowed hard. "When she married Donald Atwood and got out from under his control, that was one of the best days of my life."

"Oh, Gabe." She reached up and stroked his forehead. He closed his eyes, savoring her touch. "You were just a kid! Why didn't you report him?"

"Money and power, Rubes, money and power. I tried—once. Twice, if you count *US v. Martiniere Group.*"

"The motherfucker. The god damned motherfucker," she whispered. "But why couldn't you tell me until now? Not all of it had to be for my protection."

"Martiniere mind control, Rubes. It's real." Gabe shivered. "Between what he did to me the last time we saw each other—and what Mariah did—I couldn't even say my own fucking name. Couldn't write it or type it."

"What—how?"

He shuddered again. "Remember that day I had to stay with Craig because I got beat up?"

"Yeah. What was that about?"

"Philip demanded I meet him out in the middle of nowhere. I was certain I was going to my death that day. But I couldn't because—" oh God, it was all going to come out now. He drew a deep breath. "It started before then. Mariah dosed me that night I had to stay in Pendleton because of weather. I don't remember details. I know there were pictures. And afterward I couldn't say my real name or anything connected to the Family name. Philip was set to kill me. But he didn't. I told him about the envelope. That's when he ordered me to divorce you. Or else. You and Branny got sick. And then...." His voice trailed off and he shook his head.

"Sacrificing yourself isn't going to work," she said softly. "Not since he knows about that package."

"He wants me to suffer, Rubes."

"That motherfucker. That goddamned, sonofabitching motherfucker." Ruby continued swearing. She stroked the back of his head as he buried his face in her shoulder. "God damn it, I'm not going to let him win, Gabe. I won't let him kill you." She gently eased his head off of her shoulder, taking it in both hands.

She leaned in. Her lips trembled against his for a moment. Then they steadied and they kissed, hard and desperate, until something stabbed and Gabe flinched.

Ruby pulled back and slid off his lap. "Come on. Let's get back to something more comfortable." She helped Gabe to his feet. "I should say I'm sorry I woke you. But—" her voice wavered a little bit. "I understand things a bit better because I did wake you. And I am *pissed*.

Not just at him and that bitch." She delicately tapped his chest with a forefinger. "You are *not* going to march off tilting at windmills by yourself, *Gabriel Martiniere*. We are in this together. And together is how we're going to fix it."

Gabe sighed. He swayed a little and Ruby slid in close. She helped him back to the recliner, then kissed him again. Once he was settled, she climbed back into bed and took his hand.

I am one hell of a lucky man, he thought, before he fell asleep.

17 / REDHEADED RODEO
QUEEN'S HEART

FEBRUARY, 2059

GABE WOULD BE LYING IF HE SAID HE DIDN'T HAVE ANY DOUBTS ABOUT Ruby's scheme. But he was still a damned good liar, even to himself. He stomped his worries down hard in the remaining days before the next AgI appearance.

Ruby's lab manager and her staff were absolutely amazing. They managed to salvage more from the wreckage of his labs than Tim thought possible. Kathleen recovered what she could from the ruins of the big house, but it wasn't much. Some of his clothes and other personal items. One picture of Rachel, on their wedding day. In the same frame that he'd kept a picture of Ruby. It now sat on his old desk at Ruby's house.

A reminder that he had fucked up big time before, and could easily do it again.

HE CALLED SERG.

"It's showtime, cuz," he said.

"You're going for the Martiniere?" A hopeful expression lightened Serg's morose face.

He's getting to look like Piotr. A reminder that they were all aging.

"No, no, no. Not that far, yet. Getting there." Gabe sighed. "But

Ruby knows. And—I'm thinking hard about announcing who I am at the next AgSuperhero."

He was not going to tell Serg the details of Ruby's strategy just yet.

"So I can start telling the Family that you're in play to replace Philip now?"

"No. No, damn it, Serg, no. I do *not* want the rest of the Family to know a damn thing about what I'm doing, at least not until I figure out what happens after the Superhero! I just told Ruby who I really am. Brandon doesn't know he's a Martiniere yet. Hell, *I* don't know if I'm even going public with my connections to the Family unless I'm forced to. I want some peace in my life. Not lead a charge to reform the Martinieres."

"So what do you want me to do?" Serg clearly sounded frustrated.

"My health sucks and I've just been through hell. If you can send your own folks over to Moondance and figure out the arson there, that would help. I'll let Tim Vanhorn know."

"I can do that."

"Also find out who those two men were who kidnapped me. I know who two of them are, but those slimeballs have disappeared. The others—they got bailed out by a Martiniere Group indentured division. I can forward you that information."

"Got it."

"And finally." He glanced sideways. Ruby stood in the doorway, that expectant look that told him she had something to share. "Look, just get us a safe place with catering for a private meeting before the AgInnovator, Serg. Doesn't have to be tied to the Family. All right? Gotta go."

"I'll get it set up and forward you the information."

"Thanks." Gabe switched off the comm and stood. Then he turned his full attention to Ruby.

GABE WENT TO THIS FINAL AGINNOVATOR TAPING LOADED FOR BEAR. No matter what Ruby thought, if Jeff Swait didn't agree to the three-way agreement, then Brandon was screwed. At that point Gabe *would* give himself up to Philip. But he'd do his best to take the son-of-a-bitch with him. His favorite, protected pistol undetectable to regular airport scans was tucked into a holster hidden by his sling. Another set of weapons strapped to his calves.

Justine met them at the house that Serg had reserved. Thinner than she had been the last time he had seen her in person, outside of Lora Smith's stable in Corvallis all those years ago. She looked stressed and strained. As she chatted before leaving, she flashed handsign at him before going outside.

Need to talk. Now.

Somehow Ruby picked up on that cue and decided to talk to Justine. Gabe pulled Ruby where Justine could see her through the window and kissed her hard, sending a warning to his cousin with another glower when he was done.

This woman is dear to me and I'll kill you if you hurt her.

At least he hoped Tine got that message.

And then he waited.

"Let's talk Alvarez Armory," Swait said while Ruby spoke to Justine. "You were a part of that group that helped Swait Farms, weren't you?"

"Yes," Gabe said. "It's a complicated story, tied to Martiniere mind control."

"Believe me, I've heard enough stories about it." Swait winced. "And you're the Gabriel Martiniere who testified about Martiniere mistreatment of indentured workers thirty-some years ago?"

"Yes."

Swait nodded. "Then let's take a look at this collaboration contract. You're damn right I want to work with you further."

As Gabe and Swait reviewed provisions of the contract, Ruby returned, an odd expression on her face.

"Gabe, gotta talk. Private."

His gut clenched. "What's up?"

"I've got something for you."

Interesting.

"Let's go on the balcony." Once outside, he turned to her. "What did Justine give you?" *Could be any number of things.*

Ruby dropped two chips in his hand. "She says one chip is the record of what happened to your family. The other—it's the accesses to your trust fund. She said her ex-husband hid it in her accounts."

That cast a different light on things. He had thought he would have to go through more of a dance to get his funds back. If it was that easy to access his money....

Gabe poked at the first chip, and winced as his sister Louisa's face popped up. He closed that chip, to look at it later. But that second one...

It opened with access codes. Gabe pulled up a secondary skin and started entering data. He also toggled the account as *active.*

But still. Even on *inactive,* it was a greater amount than he expected. Donald must have been quietly shunting the regular quarterly heir payout to an account that normally would have been suspended.

Twenty million dollars. More, now that the account was officially active, because now Gabe was earning his percentage on sales of devices he'd created while still working for the Family. Backdated, so quite possibly he would be worth a lot more once everything was tallied.

Gabe whistled. He could *buy* Bran's contract, easily. He started that process.

"Did Justine give you any idea of what the trust fund was worth?" he asked Ruby.

God. Once this was over, he could rebuild Moondance. Fund the RubyBot. A lot of things—if he survived.

"Twenty million, give or take a few hundred thousand, is what she said." Still that odd expression on Ruby's face. Surprise? Intimidation? Shock that he was actually worth that much money, and that she would have gotten that much on his death?

Oh, honey. Welcome to the world of the Martinieres.

"Yeah. That matches."

"She says to expect that we will hear from the family immediately after the recording. That Philip and Joseph are in town. That you can't sit on the sidelines anymore, and that her side is going to be in touch real soon now. Gabe—does that mean what I think it does?"

He shut down his comp and put everything in his pocket. "If

you're thinking I'm going to be approached about leading the Martiniere Group—yes."

"Do you know what you're going to do?" she asked, her voice small, eyes wide.

Fear. Of what? What did Justine say to her?

He so rarely saw Ruby afraid.

"God, Ruby, I don't know yet. I've been thinking about it. You're still game to follow through? I wouldn't blame you if you just took the Superhero and went back to the Double R."

"And what about you and Brandon? I'm supposed to walk away from you two? Gabe, I'm not stupid. The Group will try to suck both of you in. You're both going to need me to watch your backs…and keep you on the straight and narrow."

That's my Ruby-girl.

Gabe patted his pocket. "This means that Brandon is safe. But I'll have to become—have started the process—Gabriel Martiniere again. And where that road leads—are you sure you want to be a part of this?"

"For you and Bran, yes. And because I personally want to make Philip Martiniere pay."

He kissed her.

And then she told him something he had suspected over the years. She had killed her father, knowingly and deliberately, at the age of six. Tony Barkley had turned on Ruby with a tire iron, after he had beaten her mother to death in front of Ruby. She had waited until she couldn't miss, then shot him. Emptied a pistol into his head.

At the end of her confession, Ruby swallowed hard. "I won't hesitate to shoot if I have to, Gabe."

He hugged her again, holding her close.

I should have trusted you from the beginning.

Something else he needed to atone for. Once the Superhero was over, he was going to spend a *lot* of time apologizing and paying Ruby back for not sufficiently trusting her.

He had to.

THE EVENTS AT THE SUPERHERO WERE ANTICLIMACTIC IN COMPARISON TO what happened before and after. Announcing who he really was to the studio audience was easy. Telling Bran they needed to leave, *now*, and that he was free of his obligation to AgI was more difficult. Encountering the roadblock of Bran's romantic involvement with an AgI indentured, Kris Markey.

And then Joey intercepted them. Fortunately, at that point, Justine intervened.

They got away from Philip, thanks to Justine. But one of the sweetest sights Gabe ever viewed was Ruby slapping Philip, then pulling a weapon on him.

Maybe his uncle would have second thoughts about challenging his redheaded rodeo queen.

WHEN THINGS CHANGED, THEY CHANGED QUICKLY.

"You're staying at the Double R, at least until you get Moondance rebuilt," Ruby said firmly over early morning coffee at the kitchen table, the first day back from the AgSuperhero. A rare moment with just them, no one else in the house stirring yet. Just Gabe and Ruby, rising early, as had always been their habit. "That old house of Craig's is unlivable, and after telling Philip to go to hell yesterday and revealing who you are publicly, I don't think that sharing a trailer with Tim and Kathleen is the safest thing for you to do. I may not know a lot about the internal politics of the Martinieres but I do know that much. That motherfucking uncle of yours meant to kill us yesterday. If it hadn't been for your cousin Justine—"

"Wanna get married again?" Gabe meant it as a distraction from this discussion because he didn't think Ruby was quite ready to remarry, and it was too damn early in the morning to think about yesterday's events. He needed some time alone to organize his thoughts. And whatever it was that Justine and Serg had to tell him about the situation within the Family.

The proposal was worth a try. She *could* surprise him.

Ruby froze, eyes widening. Then shook her head no. "I—Gabe—I—"

It was so rare to catch her speechless like that.

"Hey. It's all right," he said softly. "I know I have a lot to make up for. I just thought—"

"There's a lot I have to work through." Her voice was equally quiet, her eyes downcast. "And we have a lot to do yet." She exhaled. "With a houseful of people. I'm not complaining, but...." Ruby looked up at Gabe. "Branny and Kris. Rick and Beck. Justine and Serg dropping in. I have to get used to this life, Gabe. To who you really are. I wish you'd told me who you were back then."

He sighed, resting his hand on the table. "I still kick myself in the ass about that, Rubes. It was stupid. Yeah, some of it was the mind control working on my own substantial paranoia. But before the Superstar, I could have told you. Your grandfather guessed it. We talked the night he died. I was just—"

"Wait. Gramps knew?"

Gabe swallowed hard. "He suspected for a while, and I slipped when I showed Bran to Ron after Bran was born. Almost said Martiniere instead of Ramirez. He had questions ever since that first Christmas I came here, and he put the pieces together."

"But he didn't tell me." Ruby scowled.

"He didn't figure it out until Bran was born. I—honestly thought maybe he'd forgotten due to his stroke." Gabe sighed. "If he'd have lived, though, he probably would have nagged me into talking. It's just —every time I thought about telling you, I remembered that funeral Mass. Staring at those three coffins that were all that remained of my family. Mother. Dad. Louisa. Hurting because Philip had started the mind control conditioning, and his methods included beating the crap out of me."

"Oh, Gabe." Her hand covered his.

He shook his head. "That memory stopped me every damn time, Ruby, until it was too fucking late and I *couldn't* say my name. Even though it had been nearly twenty years by the time we married, I just —" his throat tightened, not from programming but from memory. He gulped, blinking hard. "And when—I swear, Ruby. That day I left. I saw you and Branny dead. To this day, it's so vivid that I think it was real. It still—it grabs me. Hard. And the other clear thing I remember from that day is waking from a nightmare about seeing Branny's body in a little white coffin." He left out the part about being in bed with Mariah.

Her lips pressed together. "Twenty years. What year did your family die?"

"2014."

"Aw, fuck. The same year my parents—" Now it was her turn to choke.

He took her hand in both of his as she stared down at the table. Rested his forehead on their joined hands, breathing hard.

A half-laugh, half-cry from Ruby. "We really are a mess, aren't we, Gabriel Martiniere?"

God, that name sounded strange coming from her. He raised his head.

"Yes, we are, Ruby Barkley."

A faint smile flitted across her face and she drew a deep breath. "I have to get used to that Martiniere name in my life. Have to get used to —a lot of things." She released his hand and got up.

***

MORE ISSUES TO DEAL WITH. WHAT JUSTINE AND SERG HAD TO TELL HIM was horrific, but not unexpected, after what Gabe had seen because of his work with Rafe. Philip had expanded his religious cult program, the Electric Born, to cover his most egregious abuses. Had overt political plans.

Now Gabe's focus needed to be on deposing Philip as head of the Martiniere Group, hopefully with Ruby's help. He broached that notion to Ruby on an excursion to the horse pasture.

"I can't back out now, Gabe. It's not just you. It's Bran."

"Then, even if you won't marry me, you'll be at my side?" God, he hoped so.

She hesitated. "Yes."

Ruby took his arm as they walked back from the pasture, and he leaned on her instead of using his cane.

Partners. Maybe, someday, more than that.

Barkley-Martiniere-Swait Associates was not the only structure they had to negotiate. They created an entity that combined their ranches—Barkley-Martiniere Associates. Gabe filed a holding company, GMR Group, devised with the explicit purpose of managing the corporate maneuvers necessary when it was time for Gabe to make that final move for control of the Martiniere Group.

It wasn't a marriage, but he'd take business partnerships. And—other things.

Sleeping in a recliner next to Ruby's bed wasn't quite the solution he really wanted, but given that the G9 left Gabe unable to rest comfortably in anything else, and sex was off the table due to his impotence, he'd take that small intimacy. Otherwise, he slipped back into life at the Double R easily, as if those twenty-one years away hadn't happened. He wasn't able to be as active as he had been when younger, but at least he was able to work in Ruby's state-of-the-art labs and help with ranch chores to some degree.

And one afternoon he had Remy Trask bring that envelope out to the ranch. Opened it up, went through everything with both Trask and Ruby, and modifying documents to reflect the fact that he was now actively collecting his payouts. Estate planning. Wills. Trusts. A real bitch, but necessary. Covering everything so that if something did happen to Gabe, then Ruby and Brandon inherited everything they were entitled to get from his now-expanded estate.

"That's a lot of cash," Trask said when they were through. "I'm surprised you stayed away from the Martiniere money this long."

Gabe sighed. "It was pretty much irrelevant once Philip locked me down so that I couldn't say or write my name. He controlled any access I had to making a claim. I tried to break those strictures during that kerfuffle with Bran. Piotr did his best to lift them, but there are only two people who could modify those mind control constraints.

Philip—and my grandmother Donna, who is in her nineties and lives in Quebec."

Trask arched a brow at him. "So how did you get free from that mind control? From what I remember of your testimony, the algorithms are pretty tight."

"Near as I can figure, the G9 or else the G9 treatment did it. Mariah tried to use my code words on me at the Superhero, like she had before. Nothing. Wright and Rothman tried them again when they were part of that group that kidnapped me." Gabe shrugged. "Still nothing—thankfully. I'd be dead otherwise."

Trask's lip curled. "Wright. Rothman. Both fucking pieces of work. They cost us that case. Yeah, you were the star witness. But we *should* have had solid supporting evidence. I know we did. It disappeared before trial. I suspected them then, but could never prove it." She paused. "And no news about them since the kidnapping?"

"Not a fucking word," Gabe said grimly. Vygotsky Security had taken that task on, in collaboration with the Thunder County Sheriff's Office. Sharon Wilhite had finally connected the shootings—both the attempt on Ruby, and then the one where he'd been injured—with Wright and Rothman. "I suspect that they're dead. They screwed up bad, multiple times."

MARCH, 2059

BEING BACK TOGETHER WITH RUBY ALSO MEANT *HORSES* AGAIN. GABE struck up a friendship with Red, the horse he'd been riding when they got shot. But it also meant sorrow, since he was the one to find old Sunshine's body in the field one stormy March afternoon.

Ruby cried in his arms over that, while Charlie used the backhoe to bury Sunshine. Gabe shed a few tears as well. He managed to clip some hair from Sunshine's mane and tail, planning to ask one of his friends to braid Ruby a bracelet from them.

"She brought us together," he said. Hesitated. "And maybe—again?"

"I don't know, Gabe." Ruby gulped and buried her head in his chest.

Well. He'd keep trying.

MAY, 2059

APRIL BROUGHT COMPLETED AIRSTRIPS AT BOTH THE DOUBLE R AND Moondance. Donald Atwood flew in with Justine to inaugurate the one at the Double R in early April. He put the final tweaks on Gabe's financial organization in the course of two days. Gabe watched his cousin and her ex-husband carefully while Donald was at the house—he still couldn't quite figure out how they made their not-a-relationship function—and yet there *was* something there. Maybe he could learn something from Donald and Justine that would work for him and Ruby.

The appearance of airstrips also ushered in furtive visits from other Martinieres. Younger Family members seeking alliances with Gabe and Brandon and pleas for help, both financial and political. None of them the high-level supporters Gabe needed to challenge Philip.

But it was a foundation. And with each visit, Gabe gained a greater picture of the mess that his uncle had made of the Martiniere Group over the past few years.

"It's falling apart," he said to Ruby and Justine in his office after one of those meetings, the most heart-wrenching so far. Even worse, it happened on the second anniversary of Rachel's death.

Alice, the widow of a distant cousin, Jerome, one of the American Martinieres, had brought Gabe files documenting Philip's takeover of the water supplies of several small Southwestern towns. In return, she needed financial assistance, because Philip had cut her off from the Family Trust. Not that Jerome's share would have brought Alice and her daughter much, but it would have been something. More than they had at the moment.

Gabe had given her money and sent her to Remy Trask for possible legal help.

"I've half a mind to revive Alvarez Armory and kick Philip out of those places," he continued, grimacing as he remembered those days working with Rafe. All gone, the little towns and co-ops that he and Rafe had secured, serving only as targets for Philip's acquisitions.

"And exactly how does that advance your goals *right now*?" Ruby asked.

Gabe sighed and rubbed his face. "You're right. It's a distraction. But damn it, Philip just squished Jerome like he was a troublesome fly. Killed him, and for what? And those poor damned people. They have no choice but to be forced into indenture. Swait's organization can't take care of all of them."

"Gabie. You can't fix it all. Yet." Justine scowled at him. "You've got to focus. Getting rid of Daddy-poo stops that predatory behavior. That's what you can do."

"I know, I know," Gabe sighed again. "But I've *been* in those places. I *know* what's going on. It's not right. Oh, Tine, this is going to be a horrific mess to clean up once I finally make my move. I want to act sooner, but—putting all the pieces together so it will *work*—" He threw his hands up in frustration.

"You're doing the right thing by building low-level allies," Ruby said firmly. "They're the people you'll need on your side to fix the problems, once you're the Martiniere."

"It's just taking so damn long," he groaned. "And people are hurting." Gabe shook his head. "Damn it. Damn it, damn it, damn it."

"Patience, Gabie," Justine said. A chime rang. She pulled up a screen, frowning. "And it's time for me to go. I'll be back in a couple of days."

Gabe exhaled. Ruby gazed at him from across the desk.

He stared back, despairing. Was he *ever* going to be able to strike back at Philip?

Ruby sighed. She got up and leaned against the desk, next to his chair. "Gabe. Don't let this eat you up."

"All that work Rafe and I did, just gone. Those people. I *knew* those people, Rubes. They trusted us to keep them safe, damn it. And my fucking uncle—" He buried his head in his hands.

Ruby eased them away from his face. "Look. It's going to happen."

He pulled her into his lap and held her tight. "But how many more widows, Rubes? How many? I could give away my entire fortune and it wouldn't make things right." He gulped. "I just—" He buried his head in the junction of her neck and shoulder. She wrapped her arms tight around him.

"Shh. Shh," she soothed him.

He held onto his Ruby, more precious than ever. At least he'd done his best to protect her from Philip. The assorted trusts locked up his funds so that Philip couldn't touch them if something happened to him —but they were safe for Ruby and Brandon. He'd done almost every-thing to ensure his ex-wife and son would not be in need, except the one thing that required her approval.

"Marry me, Ruby?"

"Not yet," she said, a sad note in her voice. "But will you wait for me to be ready?"

"Why wouldn't I?"

A pause. She raised her head. "You didn't before," she said, voice trembling.

Rachel. He remembered what he had said to Ruby back then.

He gulped. "I'm not the man I was, Rubes. And I'm with you here. Now. I can't do this without you. Whether you're my wife or not." His grip tightened on her. "It's not the same situation anymore. We're in this together."

JUNE, 2059

FLYING BY HIMSELF TO SEATTLE TO TAKE CARE OF ONE LITTLE DETAIL OF Rachel's estate was as nerve-wracking as ever. Ruby offered to come with him, but a crisis came up with the bots, and she had to stay behind.

Gabe had another errand that he didn't want to let Ruby know about just yet. After signing off on the last balloon payment from the purchasers of Rachel's condo, he went to the Seattle attorney who had kept the Martiniere emeralds and his mother's formal dress safe for him all these years. Once he was safe in his hotel room, he checked the dress in its garment bag, then the emeralds in their carved ebony box.

All just as they had been the last time his parents had put them away.

Soon it would be time to give them to Ruby.

August, 2059

His goal was getting close. So close. Near enough that the same prickliness he'd had just before their separation swarmed over him again. Gabe did his best to dampen his impatience and irritability, but it bled through. He and Ruby argued. Nothing like they had before the divorce, but he was getting snappish. Way too snappish.

It came to a head when Ruby decided that she not only needed to go to Chicago to attend the Biobot Producers Alliance organizational conference to help Brandon. Justine had also invited Ruby to go to the Real Truthers convention's final banquet with her, where Philip was slated to receive that party's nomination for the 2060 Presidential election.

That put the fear in Gabe like never before.

Worse, Ruby insisted on going alone, without him. That scared the fuck out of Gabe. He wanted to *be there* just in case. Where was her common sense? She *wasn't thinking*.

Unlike their previous arguments this time around, they came to blows. It was the worst fight they'd had in *years*.

And she finally admitted that she had to prove herself worthy of being the Martiniere's wife. That she was going to this banquet to show everyone else—most of all herself—that she was the accomplished, sophisticated woman he *knew* she was.

That was the obstacle to their remarrying he had to overcome. Why hadn't he seen it before now?

Well. He'd fucked up again. There wasn't much Gabe could do but quiz down Justine—who had tucked herself in the corner to observe—to reassure himself about Ruby's security at the Reals' banquet.

His cousin pitched in with a few choice words about him being a typical Martiniere sexist male, and chewed him out further. By the time both Ruby and Justine finished with him, Gabe was thoroughly whipped.

It didn't help that they were absolutely correct. And that the fifteen years he'd spent with Rachel, who *wouldn't* have done something against his will like this, who would have required and expected this degree of protection from Gabe, had influenced his response.

The one thing he held out for was his input into what Ruby was going to wear to the banquet. If she was going to represent him, then by God, he wanted her to dazzle Philip and Joey. And he had just the thing. Gabe gathered up his mother's dress and the Martiniere emeralds.

He sighed and went upstairs. Besides checking to ensure that the dress came close to fitting Ruby—there was a ceremony that went with the emeralds. While Bran could do it in his name, Gabe wanted to be the first to perform it.

His Ruby. *His* beloved. It was only right.

THE DRESS WAS NEARLY A PERFECT FIT. JUSTINE GASPED AS GABE WENT through the Martiniere's ceremony of putting the emeralds on Ruby. Years ago, he'd joked with Ruby that he would put emeralds on his Ruby. He could tell, as she looked at herself in the mirror, that she remembered that drunken conversation.

Once the dress and the emeralds were secured, Gabe held Ruby. He promised not to propose to her again, not until she was ready to say yes. The power was in her hands.

Then he walked with her down to the airstrip where Justine's private jet waited. Buried his nose in that junction of neck and shoulder again.

Mint and lavender. Ruby.

"Come safely back to me," he whispered, before that final kiss.

RUBY RETURNED TRIUMPHANT, HAVING NOT ONLY FACED DOWN JOEY AND Philip, but having earned the blessing of Donna-gran. Gabe hadn't expected his grandmother to be at the banquet. He suspected that either Justine or Serg had let Donna-gran know that he was back in play, and that his beloved would be wearing the emeralds.

Not only that, Donna-gran had revealed to Ruby, with Gabe listening in via the restored com links in the brooch, that Philip was Gabe's father, and not his uncle. Thinking about the rationale and the timing and—just everything—put a different perspective on things. Perhaps even why Philip had hated him so much.

He truly *was* the Martiniere-in-waiting.

Why did Philip care so much about Joey and not me?

Was it because Joey was the son of his own wife? But Philip had never shown much affection for Renate in the past. Or was it that Philip owned Joey in a way that he could never own his own biological son? Ownership was important to Philip.

But that was irrelevant. He was legitimately the Martiniere-in-waiting. And the most gorgeous woman in the world was his love.

Ruby glowed with that glimmering sharp edge of hers as she stepped off of Justine's private jet after the banquet, still wearing the emeralds and the dress. And she went gracefully into his arms once they were alone.

"I'm ready to answer that question now," she said. "And the answer is yes."

Even though Gabe's body was unresponsive, he made love to Ruby that night for the first time in twenty-one years. And afterwards, she joined him in the recliner, sleeping in his arms.

He felt complete once more.

THEY HAD TWO CEREMONIES. ONE, RIGHT AWAY, IN THE THUNDER COUNTY Courthouse.

The second at the newly rebuilt Moondance, with invitations to the Family. To Gabe's great joy, Donna-gran attended, ready to supervise the Martiniere Ritual that would cement Ruby's place in the Family.

Philip attended their wedding as well. He sat in the front row between Donna-gran and Mariah, his arms crossed, glowering at Gabe.

Gabe did his best to ignore Philip as Serg and Brandon's beloved Kris, then Justine and Brandon, walked down the aisle toward Gabe and the priest. On the one hand, Philip's presence worried him.

On the other, having him present at *this wedding* was sweet, sweet revenge. Especially since Gabe now knew Philip was his father.

Guess what, father of mine? You didn't manage to ruin me, hard as you tried.

And if Philip tried anything…between Serg, Piotr, Justine, Donna-gran, and Brandon, he'd pay for it. Not to speak of Remy Trask, Vickie Chandler, and their other rodeo friends in the audience. Philip was outgunned and outnumbered here.

He finally forgot all about Philip as the music swelled and Ruby stood at the end of the aisle, resplendent in a gorgeous sea-green dress that Gabe knew damned good and well hadn't come from any shop in Pendleton or even Portland or Seattle. No. That was a Parisian creation. How on earth had Justine—*sister*, not cousin—managed to find it so quickly? For that matter, how had his sister managed to locate a version of his favorite formal black suit, with the gold brocaded waistcoat, that had been lost so long ago? Then he dismissed that wonder to focus on a greater one as his Ruby, glimmering as bright as the Martiniere emeralds around her neck and in her ears, regally processed down the aisle on Charlie and Martin's arms.

They stopped. Charlie, then Martin, kissed Ruby's cheek.

Gabe glided toward Ruby, dazzled. He dropped to his knees in front of her, taking her hands in his. She half-frowned, surprised because they hadn't rehearsed this.

"My love," he said, voice half-choked. "My dearest beloved. I am so honored to marry you in front of our friends and family, as who I really am. Before this ceremony, I give my heart into your keeping. Now and forever."

"Oh Gabe," she said. "And my heart is yours."

She helped him back to his feet so they could say their vows.

His fingers trembled as he took the emerald ring from Brandon. Quivered as he lifted the veil and kissed her after saying their vows.

"It's real," he whispered. "It's really happened. I love you, Ruby, more than I can ever say."

"I love you too. And don't you dare decide to leave me again."

"I know better. And my sister and grandmother will be first in line to kick my ass if I do."

He kissed her again, and as he raised his head, he met the angry glare of Philip—*his father*, damn it—with a smirk, and the Martiniere battle glower that he'd perfected over the years.

No matter what happens from here on out, no matter if I become the Martiniere or not, I've won. You may not realize it, but I've won.

I've won. Deep inside, he knew that to be the truth.

He had Ruby at his side again, and with her, he could do anything.

Philip didn't have a chance against them.

THE END

Like this story and want to know what's coming out next, or what deals Joyce is offering on her book?

Check out Joyce's monthly newsletter at

https://joycespublishingnewsfromwideopenspaces.kit.com/a65eaa89cd

And get a free download snippet from the Martiniere Multiverse!

The Martiniere Multiverse
A Different Life: What If?
A Different Life: Now. Always. Forever.
A Very Multiversal Christmas Miracle

Goddess's Honor titles currently available (chronological order):
The Goddess's Choice: A Goddess's Honor Short Story
Beyond Honor and Other Stories: Goddess's Honor Book One
Exile's Honor: A Goddess's Honor Novelette
Birth of Sorrow: A Goddess's Honor Short Story
Pledges of Honor: Goddess's Honor Book Two
Return to Wickmasa: A Goddess's Honor Short Story
Crown Anniversary: A Goddess's Honor Short Story
Challenges of Honor: Goddess's Honor Book Three
Cleaning House: A Goddess's Honor Outtake Story
Unexpected Alliances: A Goddess's Honor Rough Draft Outtake Story
Choices of Honor: Goddess's Honor Book Four
Judgment of Honor: Goddess's Honor Book Five

Netwalk Sequence Author Preferred 2022 Editions
Life in the Shadows: Book One
Netwalk: Book Two
Netwalker Uprising: Book Three
Netwalk's Children: Book Four
Learning in Space: Book Five
Netwalking Space: Book Six

Bright Star Fair Witches
Becoming Solo: A Bright Star Fair Witches Novella

Non-Series Titles currently available:
Alien Savvy: A Western SF Novella
Klone's Stronghold
Beating the Apocalypse
Bearing Witness
Fabulist and Fantastical Worlds: A Short Story Collection

Federation Cowboy
Vision of Alliance

Vella Titles:

Falcon of the Martinieres (part of *Justine Fixes Everything*)
Bearing Witness
Beating the Apocalypse
A Different Life—What If? An Alternative Martiniere Legacy Novel
Becoming Solo
A Different Life—Linda's Story: An Alternative Martiniere Legacy Novel
Federation Cowboy

Audiobooks Available:

Alien Savvy: A Western SF Novella

Released from other publishers:

"Queen of the Snows," in *Once Upon A Winter: A Folk and Fairy Tale Anthology*, edited by H. L. Macfarlane

"My Man Left Me, My Dog Hates Me, and There Goes My Truck," in *Black-Eyed Peas on New Year's Day: An Anthology of Hope*, edited by Shannon Page

"Lost Loves," in *All Worlds Wayfarer*

"The Wisdom of Robins," in *Whimsical Beasts: A Campcon Anthology*, edited by Joyce Reynolds-Ward

"The Cow at the End of the World," in *Well...It's Your Cow*, edited by Frog Jones

"To Plant or Pull Up Stakes," in *Pulling Up Stakes: A Campcon Anthology*, edited by Joyce Reynolds-Ward

"The Notice," in *Children of a Different Sky*, edited by Alma Alexander

ABOUT THE AUTHOR

The work of Joyce Reynolds-Ward includes themes of high-stakes family and political conflict, digital sentience, personal agency and control, realistic strong women, and (whenever possible) horses. She is the author of *The Netwalk Sequence* series, the *Goddess's Honor* series, *The Martiniere Legacy* series, *The People of the Martiniere Legacy* series, and the recently published *The Cost of Power* trilogy as well as standalones *Klone's Stronghold, Alien Savvy, Beating the Apocalypse,* and *Federation Cowboy*. Joyce is a Self-Published Fantasy BlogOff Semifinalist, a Writers of the Future SemiFinalist, and an Anthology Builder Finalist. She is a member of the Science Fiction and Fantasy Writers Association and a member of Soroptimists International.

www.ingramcontent.com/pod-product-compliance
Lightning Source LLC
Chambersburg PA
CBHW031934110726
47902CB00001B/171